SISTERHOOD

Also by V. B. Grey

Tell Me How It Ends

AS ISABELLE GREY

Out of Sight
The Bad Mother
Good Girls Don't Die
Shot Through the Heart
The Special Girls
Wrong Way Home

SISTERHOOD

V. B. Grey

Quercus

First published in Great Britain in 2021 by

Quercus Editions Ltd
Carmelite House
50 Victoria Embankment
London EC4Y 0DZ

An Hachette UK company

A CIP catalogue record for this book is available
from the British Library

HB ISBN 978 1 52940 575 0
TPB ISBN 978 1 52940 574 3

10 9 8 7 6 5 4 3 2 1

Typeset by Jouve (UK), Milton Keynes
Printed and bound in Great Britain by Clays Ltd, Elcograf S.p.A.

MIX
Paper from
responsible sources
FSC® C104740

Papers used by Quercus are from well-managed forests and
other responsible sources.

In memoriam
M. C. M.
(1920–1998)

What will survive of us is love.
Philip Larkin

PROLOGUE

Freya
London, 9 November 1989

I'm still able to follow my own train of thought, but listening to other people makes me tired so I keep the sound turned off on the television. Like a child watching a cartoon, I can usually follow the action by looking at people's expressions, but on this extended news programme I'm struggling to read the earnest young faces.

The Benetton colours of their jackets are bright under the searchlights trained on them from the eastern sector. On this side, the west, the Berlin Wall is covered with graffiti. Someone has found a ladder and those already on top of the Wall are pulling others up. It's been dark for hours and they wear scarves, keeping their hands in their pockets and their shoulders hunched against the November cold.

The TV coverage cuts to another section of the Wall where young men are hammering and chiselling at a concrete surface that barely yields. The force of their misty breath and focused energy conveys hope and joy: not merely knocking down but breaking through.

Even if I could easily follow the newscaster's commentary, what would I learn? Is change of this magnitude really about to happen or will the tanks arrive in the morning to shore up the old regime once again? The anxiety on these young faces asks the same question.

I think of the Narnia books I used to read to the children when they were little, and how the snow of endless winter – always winter but never Christmas – began to thaw. But thaw can be painful, and regeneration cruel. Can I face it?

If these serious, eager people succeed in demolishing what has for so long seemed unalterable, and actually tear a hole in the Iron Curtain, then how many decades of secrets will come tumbling through?

Oh, yes, I understand all too well why sometimes it is far less complicated to keep a wall in place.

1

My mother is not an easy patient. To her, patients are submissive, impotent creatures, and she – Dr Freya Grant – has no intention of becoming one. Not that she's in denial about her condition. She knows she's dying from an inoperable brain tumour and, if she could speak, would explain it better than I can. Her doctors say that, while her mind is as sharp as ever, a rapidly spreading glioma in the left frontal lobe has left her with expressive aphasia – the inability to speak, read or write. She can still understand language and can occasionally form sounds, but they are often meaningless, which annoys her so much she'd rather remain silent.

It started with fatigue – noticeable in a woman with as much vitality as Freya – followed by headaches and an increasing inability to find the right word. Luckily my brother Archie was with her when she had her first seizure four months ago – or the first she admitted to, anyway – and he took her straight off to see a specialist. He and my mother are both doctors, and, even under Maggie Thatcher, the NHS still takes care of its own.

The consultant put her on various medications, but she's not been able to communicate with us verbally for weeks now.

We don't need a brain surgeon to tell us that her intellect is unimpaired. I don't mean to be sarcastic. I truly admire her courage and stoicism in the face of this prognosis. She's an admirable woman, always has been, much loved by patients and colleagues alike, and I can't imagine life without her. But I still go on wishing that she might have been different, that, once in a while, Freya could have allowed her professional role to take second place and simply been my mum. Now she can no longer voice her opinions, I miss more than ever the mother she might have been.

Understandably, Freya refuses to leave her home of over twenty years. But Dulwich is all the way across London from where Martin and I live in Kentish Town, and with two teenage sons at school and my job teaching women's studies at a north London polytechnic, it's a stretch. Sometimes I have to remind myself it's not her fault that I'm thirty-six and run ragged. All the same, if the traffic is bad, it can take more than an hour to get to her and, as Archie lives out in Essex, it invariably falls to me to make sure that she's safe and comfortable.

Such are my thoughts as we sit together watching the evening news after a silent supper of M&S lasagne. I used to natter away, telling her what the boys were up to, or repeating some of the gossip from work, but she finds listening an effort, especially when she can't respond beyond the odd hand signal, nod or shake of her head. So I'm glad to see her engrossed in the extraordinary news from Germany, and only wish I could hear the silent commentary unspooling in her mind.

Last week a bulldozer smashed its way through a section of

the Berlin Wall, allowing thousands of East Berliners to flood through. The watchtowers, searchlights and snipers' nests have been abandoned and, night after night, people are filmed dancing and embracing on top of the Wall. Emboldened by events in Berlin, today's news shows hundreds of thousands of protesters gathering in Prague in defiance of the riot police who, only a couple of days ago, brutally laid into them. In London, everyone has been smiling and happy, full of hope. The speed with which the Soviet empire is unravelling is astonishing, as if history is suddenly on fast forward and making up for lost time.

I am not well travelled. I've certainly never been to an Eastern Bloc country. School holidays when we were little were spent with grandparents in Scotland or Hampshire. After the divorce, Archie and I went a couple of times to stay with our father, Nick, in Los Angeles, and he took us to the Grand Canyon and to see the Californian Redwoods. Archie enjoyed the trips and went several times more, but by then I was a moody teenager and refused to go. It never occurred to me that Dad would have a massive coronary and die when I was still at university. Since then, apart from a couple of academic conferences, it's been France or Italy plus our three big family holidays in Australia, visiting Martin's parents.

I try to imagine what it's like to be literally walled in and shot on sight merely because you fancy a wander out to see what lies beyond. There have been a lot of jokes this week about East Berliners celebrating their freedom by heading straight for McDonald's or the KaDeWe department store, but I don't blame them. It's human nature. I bet people were equally excited about the latest shade in glass beads when Stonehenge was new.

But I'd love to hear what Freya has to say about it all, and ache that I never will, even though she sits right beside me in her usual chair, frowning at the TV screen.

I lean over and touch her hand. She turns to me and I smile. She pats my hand and looks back to the screen just as the doorbell rings.

It's after nine o'clock and, from the shake of her head, she's not expecting anyone, either.

It's a man I don't recognize. He stands back unthreateningly but there's something a bit off-key about his clothes and the way his hair is cut that makes him appear foreign or even institutionalized.

'Excuse me,' he says politely. 'My name is Tomasz, Tomasz Dolniak. I am from Poland.'

I give a tight-lipped smile and grip the door. 'I'm sorry,' I say, 'but if you're selling something—'

'Oh, no.' He appears stricken. 'No. I am looking for someone. The sister of Dr Freya Grant. Is this her house?'

I hesitate, not wanting to admit too much, but also mildly intrigued. He's a little older than me and seems pleasant enough – rather good-looking, in fact.

'This is Dr Grant's house,' I say, 'but I'm afraid her sister died many years ago.'

His face falls. He digs into the pocket of his patchwork leather jacket and brings out an envelope. From it he takes a small, creased black-and-white photograph and holds it out to me. The porch light isn't very bright, but I make out two young women leaning against the half-demolished wall of a bombed-out house. They wear dusty boots, trousers and shirts with rolled-up sleeves, each with some kind of identifying armband. They're smiling into the sun, but appear thin and tired, with no make-up, and one has her hair bundled up under a military-style cloth field cap.

Tomasz points to the one wearing a cap. 'This was my mother, Malgorzata Dolniak. This other lady, I was told she might be the sister of Dr Grant.'

The woman he indicates resembles all the photographs I've ever seen of my mother from before I was born. And also all the photographs I've ever seen of Mum's identical twin sister, Shona.

'You'd better come in,' I say.

I try not to have conversations behind Freya's back – it's cruel enough that she can't ask what's going on – and she'll have heard me bring in this visitor, so I lead him straight into the living room without explaining her predicament to him.

She has already turned off the television and is standing ready to greet him, as her good manners demand. She's alert and curious, as if an unexpected visitor might be a nice break from routine. I turn to the man and catch him looking from the photograph to Freya and back again. She's a striking woman and, despite her grey hair, she has retained the same deep-set dark eyes, perfect cheekbones and strong nose she had when young. It's obvious what he must be thinking – that Freya was the young woman standing beside his mother.

'I'm Kirsty,' I say. 'And this is my mother, Dr Freya Grant. She and her sister Shona were twins.' I check that he has understood, then turn back to her. 'Mum, this is Tomasz . . . Dolniak, did you say?'

He nods.

She shows no reaction to the name, but then names don't mean much to her, these days.

He offers his hand, which she takes, while I explain to him that she can't speak because she's ill, but can understand if he doesn't speak too fast. It's a lot for him to take in, but he nods as if it makes sense.

'He has a photograph of Shona with his mother,' I say, trying to anticipate the questions that Freya would want to ask. 'Can you show it to her?' I ask him.

Freya holds out her hand eagerly and stares at the small rectangular image. Her face creases in sadness as she strokes the picture gently with her forefinger, and I think for the thousandth time in my life how strange it must be to look at a picture of your dead sister and see yourself. Then she looks up at Tomasz Dolniak, examining his face. Whatever she sees, she returns to her chair as if suddenly tired. She seems reluctant to hand back the photo and he lets her keep hold of it.

'Do sit down,' I say, after Tomasz has refused my offer of tea or coffee. 'Maybe you can tell my mother more about the photograph. Where and when it was taken, for instance.'

Mum keeps her eyes on Tomasz. He returns her gaze as he speaks.

'In Warsaw,' he says. 'In August nineteen forty-four.'

I'm taken aback. I'd assumed the picture was taken here and that the two women were wearing civil-defence armbands, helping out after an air raid or something. Shona died before I was born but I can't recall it ever being mentioned that she'd gone to Poland, especially not during the war. I glance at Freya, who doesn't seem in the least surprised, which increases my astonishment.

'And your mother?' I prompt him.

'Your aunt would have known her as Gosia. It's short for Malgorzata but Gosia was also her codename as a member of the AK, the Armia Krajowa. She fought with the underground army during the Uprising.'

I realize I know almost nothing about Polish history. The Uprising: was that to do with the Jewish ghetto?

'Your relative,' Tomasz continues, 'was known in Warsaw only by her codename, Olenka.'

'Her codename?' I echo.

'She came by parachute, to help the Uprising.'

Tomasz looks at Freya, whose nod seems to say that she understands what he's talking about. She's breathing quite fast, but I can't believe how unfazed she seems by these revelations. There were aspects of her sister's life that Mum has always preferred not to talk about, but I'm absolutely certain I'd remember if she'd ever mentioned Shona parachuting into enemy territory.

I remind myself I must put my own mystification aside and ask the questions she'd want to ask.

'So how did you find us?'

'I have been around the Polish organizations here,' he says. 'At the Hearth Club, someone recognized Olenka as Shona Grant and then remembered she had a sister who was a doctor. Someone else told me that any public library would have a book that lists all the doctors. It gave this address.'

The Medical Directory, I think. 'And why is it so important to find her?' I ask.

He's embarrassed, which briefly makes him seem much younger. 'I never knew either of my parents. My mother died in a Soviet gulag when I was thirteen. That photograph is all I have.'

Freya leans forward and hands the picture back to Tomasz.

I try to recall what I *do* know about Shona. She had a degree in modern languages – not that common for a woman in those days – and had been in uniform, based in London, during the war. It's anyone's guess what she was actually doing at a time when secrecy was taken seriously. Maybe even Freya never knew the full story.

'You must have been hoping to find my aunt,' I say. 'So she could tell you more about your mother.'

He stands up abruptly. 'Yes. My apologies. I shouldn't have come here. Your mother is not well. I must go.'

'No, please,' I say. 'Stay. Tell us more.'

He sits down again on the edge of his chair.

'Do you know what my aunt was doing in Warsaw?' I ask.

He shakes his head. 'The man at the Hearth Club who recognized her said she must have gone there with one of the Cichociemni.'

'What does that mean?'

'They were Polish special agents trained here to go back and fight for their country. "Cichociemni" is difficult to translate. It means silent, unseen. That's all I know. Everything they did was secret. What happened in Warsaw during the war is hardly talked about in Poland but here they told me my mother was a heroine of the Uprising. That is why they helped me to find Olenka.'

'I'm sorry *we* can't help you,' I say. 'But you know more than I do.'

'Olenka, your aunt, also knew my father. I want to find him.'

I glance at my mother. She leans back with an elbow on the arm of her chair, a hand over her eyes. I long to question Tomasz further, but she tires easily and can only take in so much at a time.

'I'm happy to do what I can,' I tell him. 'But it's getting late.'

'Of course,' he says, standing up immediately. 'Thank you. You've been very kind.'

'Are you here for long?'

His face lights up. 'We have open borders. No more impossible bureaucracy or being denied a passport. I can go back whenever I want.'

'Then can we meet another time? I'll give you my home and work numbers.' I scribble them down as he glances at Freya but she doesn't seem to notice that he's leaving.

'It's extraordinary, what's happened in Berlin,' I say, as I walk him to the door. 'The fall of the Wall.'

'I can't believe it,' he replies.

As we shake hands rather formally I take in his strong, broad shoulders, light brown hair and very blue eyes. And then he leaves. I ought to have done more, at least offered him a lift to the station on my way home, but first I must settle Mum for the night.

When I return to the living room she is still sitting with her head resting in her hand, exhausted. We have seldom been physically demonstrative with one another, but I want to offer comfort, although I'm not precisely sure for what. The loss of her sister? Secrets she's no longer able to share? The lifetime of distance between us?

I touch her shoulder and she looks up. There are tears in her eyes. In reaction to my surprise she raises a hand and waves her palm at me, turning her face aside. *Ask me no questions*, the gesture says, as clearly as if she could speak.

2

When I get home Martin is hunched in front of his computer. His study used to be the dining room but, since we only ever eat in the basement kitchen that opens into the back garden, he has successfully colonized it and declared it a disturbance-free zone. My own desk is in a corner of the attic spare room; the boys just yell up the stairs whenever they want me. He sits in the pool of light from an Anglepoise lamp, although his skin reflects the monster green glow of the computer monitor. He offers a welcoming smile as I lean down to kiss him, then resumes typing. In a way I'm relieved. I want time to digest tonight's revelations.

Too tired to deal with whatever mess might have been left in the kitchen, I go straight upstairs, taking pleasure as I always do in the smooth touch of the wooden banister under my hand. After the war, my parents wanted everything to be new and modern, so of course I fell in love with the unpainted shutters and creaking floorboards of the early Victorian villa Martin and I moved into when I was heavily pregnant with Chris. I open his door first – noiselessly after years of practice – and peer into the dark, a habit I am loath to break even though, now he is fifteen, I should respect his privacy. Despite the cast-off clothes on the floor, the slightly rank smell of teenage boy, my heart swells with love. Chris is fast sleep, as is his younger brother Eric in the room next door.

The heating has gone off, so I undress quickly, put on my comfy old winter pyjamas and go into the bathroom. I examine myself in the mirror and think about Shona, the Olenka of Tomasz's photograph. Could I ever have done what she apparently did? And what drove her to such a feat of courage? How did she ever get involved in such an enterprise? I know she was good at languages, but did she also speak Polish? If so, how did she learn it? From friends at the Polish Hearth Club?

I review the little I know about her. So long as my maternal grandparents were alive, we were told only that Shona had been ill for some time before her death in 1947, and not to talk about her in front of them as it only upset them. There'd been one cousin the same age who died of TB and another with a weak heart, so I'd always accepted that, in those days, even young people got ill and died. It was only once my grandparents were gone that Mum admitted Shona had been in a mental hospital when she died, but immediately changed the subject before I could ask any questions.

As a teenager, I'd entertained the occasional fantasy that, like some benign doppelgänger, Shona would have understood and cherished me as my mother never could. I only became genuinely curious about her at university when I began to read the newly published feminist histories about women and madness. They argued that women who rebelled or otherwise failed to conform to suitable stereotypes were labelled 'mad' not only by a patriarchal medical establishment but also by their families. I briefly convinced myself that Shona must have been the tragic victim of repressive social norms.

It was a compelling argument in some respects, but, as I came reluctantly to realize, failed to account for conditions such as mania, delusion, psychosis or schizophrenia. I'd seldom pushed my mother to talk about the nature of Shona's illness when she made it plain she'd rather not, but studies suggested schizophrenia was more common in identical twins, and she'd encouraged me to assume that that had been my aunt's diagnosis. But what if Shona's illness was somehow linked to whatever she'd been doing in Warsaw?

As I brush my teeth, images come to mind from old black-and-white films watched on television on wet Sunday afternoons in which Anna Neagle or Virginia McKenna starred as courageous British agents risking torture and death in Occupied France. I remember how one of the hardest things was their having to lie to their families about what they were doing, even when they knew they might not return. Had Shona been able to lie convincingly enough to dupe her twin? Freya's reaction to the photograph tonight suggested she already knew, in which case not even Shona's death had freed her to speak of it. Evidently there was far more to Shona's brief life than I'd ever imagined.

I climb into bed trying to arrange the fragments I know about a young woman I never met. Freya always described her as the clever, sensitive twin, while she was the sensible, sporty duffer. Shona, who wrote poetry, edited the school magazine and acted in university revues, had wit and flair and spoke fluent French and German, while Freya became captain of hockey and was able to recite the names of all twenty-six bones in the foot.

I never believed it. My mother is ferociously clever, so I've always taken the story of her being in her twin sister's shade as a eulogy to the dead.

Shona graduated and left Aberdeen two years ahead of Freya, whose medical degree took longer. She was in uniform, I assume the ATS, the Auxiliary Territorial Service, and, according to Freya, was already part of a cosmopolitan group of friends, many of them slightly older, when Freya joined her in London. Freya often spoke of how kind Shona and her friends were when she was finding her feet as a junior doctor away from home for the first time.

And, I realize, that's it. That's all I know.

What was her mission? Did she volunteer? What kind of training did she receive? How did she get back?

It's not that, growing up, I wasn't curious about my dead aunt, especially given the strangeness of being unable to pick out who was who in their childhood photos – a game that bore a frisson of fear. What might happen if, in real life, I failed to recognize my own mummy? Yet I suppose I was as guilty as anyone of conflating them into two halves of one entity – the twins.

I remember Mum saying more than once how she had envied a school friend for being an only child, and how she felt she was only ever given half of everything, from Christmas presents and birthday treats to love and attention. I can't decide whether it's her ambivalence – love and admiration mixed with resentment and a desire to break free – or some stronger sense that she never truly felt like a separate person that made her accounts of Shona so insubstantial.

And now a whole new mystery has been thrown into the mix.

I try to stay awake until Martin comes up, but fall asleep picturing those two young women, Gosia and Olenka, in their dusty boots and rolled-up shirtsleeves leaning against a wall and smiling into the sun.

Martin enjoys the story when I tell it to him in the morning. Neither of us needs to be in too early today, and the boys catch a bus to school, so he's having a second cup of coffee while I wash up after breakfast.

Predictably, Martin, who teaches history and economics, knows more than I do about the Warsaw Uprising. He explains that it isn't the same as the earlier uprising in the Warsaw Ghetto, when thousands of Jews attempted to fight back against deportation to Treblinka. The Uprising of 1944 began in August when the Home Army, the Armia Krajowa of which Tomasz said his mother was a member, believed that Stalin's Red Army was poised to drive out the Germans from the East and claim Poland for the Soviet Union. Both events involved tremendous courage, endurance and sacrifice and both ended in brutal suppression by the Nazis, who were under orders from Hitler to destroy the city and all its inhabitants. My admiration for Shona creeps up yet another notch.

Martin thinks it's a shame that Freya should be troubled by her sister's past when she has enough to contend with, but I disagree.

'If you'd seen her last night,' I say, emptying dregs from the coffee pot into the bin. 'Until she got tired, she was so focused – more like her old self than I've seen her in ages.'

But he's not really listening. My heart sinks. He's been

distracted for weeks now. There's been a young-sounding TV researcher recently who calls him a bit more often than seems necessary to me, and I'm terrified he's having an affair. Martin and I met when I was in my last year at Sussex and he was a graduate student. I'm not sure we would ever have considered marriage if I hadn't got pregnant. But he had no family in the UK, and I'd just lost my dad, and it seemed like a good idea at the time. The trouble with twenty is you think you're all grown-up.

He's a good man and, as a rising star at the LSE, increasingly asked to share his opinions on *Newsnight* or the *Today* programme. He is still rangy and handsome in his jeans, black Armani T-shirt and well-cut jackets. I can see why a younger woman might go for him. What frightens me most is not that he's ripe for an affair but that, confronted with his infidelity, I might not care enough to fight for our marriage.

I return to the washing-up bowl, preferring to think about Shona's secrets: the fall-out from delving too deeply into my husband's might be more than I can face right now.

Martin licks his lips nervously. 'I need to talk to you about something.'

No, I think. *No, no, please no. Don't say it. Just don't, please.*

'Can't it wait?' I ask. Now the moment has arrived, I'm desperate not to hear him tell me he's in love with someone else, that it's all been a mistake and he's only stayed married for the boys' sake, even if some of that is exactly what I've occasionally thought in reverse. I stare at the tiles around the sink and consider trying to insist that I honestly don't need to know, that I'm prepared to turn a blind eye and leave him to do whatever he likes so long as he doesn't utter any words that could bring our little universe crashing down around our ears.

'I've been offered a job,' he says.

For a moment, I think I've misheard. 'A job?'

'A full professorship.' There's pride in his voice, yet, when I turn around, his eyes still won't quite meet mine.

'But that's wonderful,' I say, relief washing over me so strongly that I have to grip the back of a chair. 'Congratulations. Where is it? Still at the LSE?'

He licks his lips again. 'No. It's back home.'

I'm confused. We are home. This is home.

'At the University of Sydney,' he explains.

'Australia?'

'Yes. They're creating a new chair. I'll have my own department. They approached me. I was their first choice, apparently.'

I'm proud of him, too. And unexpectedly overjoyed that it's only a job, not another woman. But I feel my familiar planet tilt slightly on its axis. 'How long have you known about this?'

'I've been talking to them for two or three months. I didn't want to bother you with it in case it never panned out. You've had more than enough to deal with recently.'

I pull off my washing-up gloves and sit down at the table. He drains his coffee mug, although any remnants must be pretty cold by now.

'But now it's a definite offer?'

'It came yesterday.' He beams with pride but then looks at me anxiously. 'What d'you think?'

I swallow on nothing. 'When do you have to decide?'

'It's a big move,' he says. 'I guess it's reasonable to take a couple of weeks or so.'

A couple of weeks to upend my entire life? I stare at him, not really taking it in. 'Don't they have to interview you or anything?'

He shifts about in his chair. 'I had a sit-down with a couple of people when they were over for that conference in October.'

And didn't breathe a word. 'OK.'

'It wasn't that I didn't want to tell you,' he says. 'I could really have done with your input.'

'It sounds as if you've already made up your mind,' I say.

'Not really. I mean, of course not. It's a huge decision, for all of us. I see that. But will you think about it, Kirsty? Sydney is a beautiful campus. We could have a very nice life there. If you want to give it a go, we can talk to Chris and Eric.'

He's still looking at me anxiously, but I can tell he's willing me to smile and be happy for him, for all of us. I have no idea what I'm feeling.

'The academic year starts in February,' he goes on, 'but I told them, with the boys in school, and your mother, that the very earliest I could manage would be the second semester, which is July.'

He's expecting Freya to be dead by then. She probably will be, but that's not the point.

'How long would it be for?' I ask.

He looks confused, and I think of what he said, that the job is back *home*. Sydney is the university where he took his undergraduate degree, the city where his family still live. He didn't come to England for me, but now I wonder if he's only stayed because of me, that I've prevented him from going back. If he's felt exiled, he's never said.

'My parents aren't getting any younger,' he says, avoiding my question. 'They've missed out on so much. It would be great for them and the boys to have some real time together at last.'

Perched in a corner of my mind is a suspicious little goblin, angry that my husband didn't immediately involve me in his decision – maybe didn't *want* to – and anxious that it's because he plans to go anyway, without me, perhaps even without his sons, exactly as my dad did when he left for California.

Yet part of me is also thinking, *Yes*, escape, a new beginning, my own personal Berlin Wall falling down in front of me.

3

Freya, 1944

Freya glanced down at the growing pile of glass at her feet as a porter wheeled away one patient and a nurse helped the next into place in front of her. Her rubber gloves were wet and sticky with blood, making it difficult to grip the fine surgical tweezers needed to remove the tinier shards. Many of the men and women she was treating had suffered facial wounds that would leave disfiguring scars, but she couldn't afford to spend too long on any one patient. The more serious lacerations had to be closed quickly before they led to serious blood loss. No one complained, although she could hear almost constant moaning and crying all around her. Most of the poor devils were pale with shock, matching the thick white dust on their hair and clothes. Best to focus on the job in hand and not let her imagination roam too widely.

It was strange not knowing any of the other staff around her. Freya had only just found her way to the residents' mess in the former Poor Law infirmary in London's East End when a porter had knocked on the door to announce the imminent arrival of mass casualties from a flying bomb in Mile End. Following the man downstairs, she had found her chief, Dr Chiltern, waiting to introduce himself. Not bothering with formalities, he'd quickly explained that the doodlebug's engine had cut out beside a factory and the blast had blown out all the windows, showering the workers inside, and directed her to take care of the long line of walking wounded with glass injuries.

She took a deep breath and tried to steady her hands, managing not to stare at the bloodied stretchers still being carried in from the ambulances outside. The theatres were already full and one of the surgeons had no choice but to operate on a man's shattered leg on a trolley in a corner of Casualty.

Freya was twenty-three, had been medically qualified for two weeks, and had never witnessed such carnage before. Aberdeen had got off lightly during the Blitz, with only the harbour and industrial areas seriously affected, and the past year had been uneventful. Hours earlier, on her short walk from the Underground station, her heavy suitcase bumping against her bare legs, she'd seen the evidence of recent bomb damage – the splintered remains of a venerable London plane tree, the windowpanes of one wing of the infirmary patched with brown paper, the end house of an adjacent terrace reduced to a pile of rubble. What if another flying bomb got through and fell on top of them all?

She caught the eye of the nurse assisting her. Was it her imagination or did the older woman's scathing glance suggest she'd guessed how afraid she was? All Dr Chiltern had said by way of introduction was that he always asked Nurse Jolyon to show his inexperienced house physicians the ropes because she had spent time in a surgical field hospital in France before Dunkirk. Nurse Jolyon's welcome had been brusque, but she was certainly unflappable, ready with sutures or scissors before Freya had to ask. She hoped it wouldn't take too many emergencies before she managed to acquire that kind of courage and aplomb.

Meanwhile she saw how the confident eagerness to do her bit with which she'd stepped out of the crowded train at King's Cross that morning, had been arrogantly naïve. But she was damned if she'd give her new colleagues any reason to doubt the capabilities of their first female doctor. It was only thanks to the war that a major London teaching hospital other than the Royal Free would employ her, and she enjoyed the idea of being a pioneer. Determined to succeed, she wiped her bloody gloves against her white coat and gripped the tweezers more firmly.

Two hours later Freya could hardly believe how high the pile of extracted glass on the floor by her feet had become. She looked around and saw with relief that no more patients were waiting for her attention.

'Nice work, Dr Grant,' said Nurse Jolyon. She consulted her fob watch. 'If you hurry, you might still be in time for some dinner.'

Freya pulled off her gloves. Her arms were aching, the front of her coat now more red than white.

'Leave all that here,' said the nurse, with what Freya hoped was the glimmer of a smile. 'Not your job to clear up.'

The aroma of sausages at the door of the residents' mess reminded her she'd had little more than tea and a couple of biscuits all day. One of the four young men seated around the long table stood up politely as she entered. 'You must be Dr Grant.

Take a pew,' he said, pulling out the chair beside him. 'We were told to expect you. I'm Jack Turner, Dr Chiltern's junior registrar. We'll be on the same firm.'

He had floppy fair hair, blue eyes and a clipped public-school accent, but his smile was sincere and he shook her hand heartily before introducing his fellow junior doctors. Each nodded to her as she sat down. The quick-eyed one with dark curly hair looked at her curiously, the large one with the thick shoulders of a rugby player seemed incongruously shy and apprehensive, and the thin, sandy-haired man at the end of the table grimaced in open resentment at her invasion. The rugby player passed her the covered dishes of sausages and lumpy mashed potato, Jack Turner asked about her journey from Scotland, and then they all reverted to a conversation about cricket that her entrance must have interrupted.

She was happy to have a chance to inspect her surroundings as she ate. Apart from the dining table and its mismatched chairs, the large room had frayed rugs, half a dozen shabby leather armchairs, a wireless set and a bookcase full of well-thumbed paperbacks. A large oar bearing a university crest and gold-painted names had been mounted over the fireplace. This, and the narrow bedroom allocated to her along the corridor, was to be her home for at least the next six months – longer if she did well.

She assumed that the young men around the table would have trained together at the London Hospital and so be far more familiar than she with their consultants and the area from which their patients came. They must also have witnessed far worse incidents even than today's flying bomb. As the maid came in with a trolley to clear their plates and leave a rice pudding and some tinned fruit, Freya speculated on when any woman other than a maid had last set foot in the room. Two of her five aunts had worked as maids before they married. At the family tea party after her graduation, both had been tickled pink to address her as Dr Grant. She took a covert look at the oar above the narrow mantelpiece and counted Jack's name among the rest. Different worlds as well as different sexes.

The meal finished, the men rose from the table and made themselves comfortable in the armchairs. Freya was able to excuse herself, saying she wanted to unpack. She stood behind the closed door to the mess for a moment, glad to be on her own. Her little room contained a bed with thin grey blankets, a single wardrobe, and a metal-frame chair beside a grimy window that looked out over Nissen huts that she assumed housed additional hospital services. At least there was a telephone on the bedside cabinet. Its primary purpose was to wake her when she was on call at night but the porter who showed her up had said it was also for personal use. She felt a pang of longing for Shona, and a kick of excitement that she would very soon see her again. Yet a kind of shyness made her hesitate to dial the number she'd written carefully in the back of her pocket diary.

Her hand resting on the receiver, she tried to imagine her sister, now in uniform, in a room somewhere across this unfamiliar city. Although Shona had pretended that the haste with which she'd left Scotland was due only to conscription, introduced for unmarried women during the final year of her degree, she'd never come home on leave and her infrequent letters and even rarer trunk calls had done little to fill in the gaps.

Although Freya was older by twenty minutes, it had always been her sister who had the last word. To begin with, Freya had been horribly disoriented by Shona's absence and had wondered jealously if she felt the same or maybe didn't miss her at all.

'I'm not going to tell anyone I have a twin,' Shona had announced before she left. 'From now on, I have a sister, that's all.'

'Until they see us together,' Freya had pointed out, hiding how hurt she was.

Yet, slowly, Shona's declaration proved to be liberating. At home Freya now had a bedroom to herself: her sister's absence literally gave her more space. As time passed, and she saw how her ignorance of Shona's life in London also offered her the freedom to make her own decisions and to choose her own clothes, hairstyle, books, films and even friends, she grew to embrace the separation. And yet, even today, when she'd been catapulted straight into the thick of it on her first day and had surely proved herself capable and independent, she could never quite shake off the sense of not being enough to make up a whole person, and despised herself for it. She was willing to bet that Shona never felt like that.

The telephone rang, making her jump. More bomb injuries? She lifted the receiver and spoke her name. 'Dr Grant.'

'Doctor indeed! You can't fool me.'

'Shona!'

'You're here at last! I can't believe it. I can't wait to see you. When are you free?'

'I'm not sure. I haven't had a chance to check my rota yet.' Freya felt tears of joy welling up and all her anxiety melted away. 'How are you? It's so good to hear your voice!'

'Go and find out and ring me back,' Shona commanded. 'And if you're not free for ages, maybe I'll come to the hospital and you can pretend to bandage my arm or something. I have to see you!'

'The rota will be in the mess. I won't be long.'

The young men looked up from their card game in surprise as Freya ran in, her face shining with happiness. She asked where the rota was kept and Eli, the curly-haired man, pointed to a noticeboard on the wall behind her.

'Fixing up a date already?' Jack teased. 'You're a fast worker!'

'My sister,' she said, laughing. 'It'll be the first time I've seen her in nearly two years.'

She memorized her days off and rushed back to her room.

'Next Tuesday is my first free evening,' she told Shona, breathlessly.

'Good. We'll go to the club. There's someone I want you to meet.' The slight tremor in Shona's voice signalled a familiar mischief. 'And I want us to play the trick.'

4

Freya waited where Shona had suggested, by the path that ran down the eastern side of Green Park, a name that, like Berkeley Square or Piccadilly, known only from songs or novels, still seemed slightly unreal to her. The high trees cast early-evening shadows across the grass where couples strolled arm in arm. She admired their apparent composure. She had set off in good time to walk some of the way through the West End, excited to see a few famous sights. Instead she'd felt cowed by the evidence of war – propped-up soot-blackened buildings, sandbags and 'Danger' signs – that Londoners seemed happy to ignore.

She spotted Shona as soon as she came through the entrance to the park but, wanting to enjoy the moment when Shona picked her out, did not move. As Shona's face lit up, Freya felt a burst of relief and happiness, as if some chronic underlying unease had suddenly been resolved.

They didn't hug – they were seldom physically demonstrative – or even speak, but stood smiling at one another, searching out any minute changes that only they would notice.

Shona, always poised and apparently self-contained, had acquired a fresh and sophisticated gloss. Maybe it was because she'd styled her hair differently, but she also seemed somehow lighter and more carefree. Freya assumed that had something to do with the friend her sister was so eager for her to meet. She tried to guess what differences Shona was finding in her. She had obeyed the instruction to wear something smart, but now saw that her dress, a green flower print in Utility rayon, was girlish and provincial against Shona's sleekly cut midnight blue gown.

'So here we are again,' Shona said, with a grin of delight.

'Here we are,' she agreed.

'Are you ready?'

'For the trick?'

'Yes. The club's just across the road.'

'Does he know you have a twin?'

'No. That's what makes it such fun.' Shona drew a photograph out of her evening bag and showed it to Freya. 'This is Leo, so you can recognize him.'

The wallet-sized photograph showed a serious-looking young man in an open-necked shirt and jacket. He had a nice face, with a well-shaped mouth and strong, straight nose.

'His name's Leo Tarnowski,' said Shona. 'He'll be in civvies and is about four inches taller than us, fairly slight, with gorgeous blue eyes.'

The shine in Shona's own eyes and the softness of her voice told Freya immediately that her sister was in love with this man. At university in Aberdeen, Shona had attracted the poetic type, young men who wrote her ardent love letters, although she'd never been seriously interested in any of them. Freya had run around with a happy-go-lucky band of fellow medics with whom she played tennis, danced and occasionally kissed. She'd often wished for more, but so far it hadn't happened. Her glimpse of Shona's feelings made her both envious and nervous: something was at stake here that she couldn't fully understand, something that made her suddenly reluctant to play their old game. They'd swapped places many times to fool friends, teachers – even, when they were younger, their parents – but never with anyone who didn't know they were twins.

'Are you sure about this?' she asked.

'Give me your coat,' Shona said. 'He'll know I haven't the coupons for a new one.'

Knowing how useless it was to argue with her sister, Freya handed it over. Shona looked her over appraisingly, then shook her head. She took the tortoiseshell combs from her own glossy brown hair and used them to rearrange Freya's.

'Give me your necklace,' she commanded, undoing the clasp of her own dark amber beads.

'That's cheating,' Freya protested.

'No, it's not. And you only have to keep it up for five minutes.'

'If he's fooled at all.'

'Your lipstick's lighter than mine, but I daresay he won't notice that. Right, are you ready? He usually waits at the bar. He'll be watching out for you.'

Shona led her across the road. The Milroy Club in Stratton Street, as Shona had explained on the phone, was popular with Polish and other servicemen. At the bottom of the wide stairs down from the street, Shona tucked herself out of sight against the wall and gave Freya a little push forwards into the large basement room. It was already crowded, and noisy, with very few empty seats left at the little round tables and dimly lit banquettes around the walls. A few couples slow-danced to the music of a six-piece band on a small dais. Many of the men were in uniform, representing different services and countries. Freya would have loved to stop and take a proper look around – she had never been in such a glamorous place before – but had to play her part. Thinking that Shona certainly hadn't described any of this in her letters home, she walked slowly along the wide space that led between the tables towards the bar, searching for the face in Shona's photograph.

'There you are!'

A man detached himself from a group standing near the bar and moved swiftly to greet her, cupping her face with his hands and pressing his lips to hers. He drew back, smiling at her fondly. She shivered – Shona had been right about his blue eyes – and waited for his expression to change as he registered some indefinable discrepancy. But he linked his arm through hers and drew her onwards.

'What would you like to drink? The usual?'

'Yes, thanks.'

Leo Tarnowski turned away to attract the bartender's attention, offering Freya a chance to study him. He had a lean athlete's build, with dark hair and features that were characterful rather than conventionally handsome, and seemed slightly older, or perhaps more careworn, than his photograph. Aware of her scrutiny, he glanced back at her and smiled.

When the drinks had been served, he took her once more by the arm. 'Jozef and Adam are keeping some seats for us.'

She slipped off Shona's coat before taking her place on the

banquette. Jozef and Adam bowed courteously and seemed happy to see her but clearly felt no need to introduce themselves, leaving her in ignorance of who was who. She managed to return their familiar greetings as naturally as she could. Neither wore uniform although, from their accents, she guessed that they, too, were Poles. She noticed Leo glance a little quizzically at her dress, then take in Shona's amber beads around her neck. She tried to relax into him as he drew her close, hoping that Shona wouldn't wait too long before joining them.

'New perfume?' he asked.

'I borrowed it from a friend,' she said. 'What do you think?'

'Pleasant, but not really you.'

'What is me?' she asked, unable to resist teasing him.

He kissed her neck, whispering his reply, 'I'll tell you later.'

Grateful for the low lighting in the club, Freya blushed and looked towards the stairs: such attention was lovely but where was Shona?

One of Leo's friends leant forwards across the table. 'What's the latest?' he asked, in a hushed, urgent tone. 'Anything you can tell us?'

She shook her head. 'I'm afraid not.'

He looked disappointed, far more so than she would have expected. All she knew of Shona's work was that she had a clerical job in an office in Baker Street.

'The Russians are closing on Lublin,' said the man who had just spoken. 'The Germans are pulling back and risk being cut off.'

Leo's other companion gave Freya a beseeching look. 'You've heard nothing?'

'You've found a new friend, I see.'

Freya watched the three men react to Shona's arrival beside their table. They gawped from one woman to the other, then Jozef and Adam burst out laughing.

'I don't believe it!'

'My God, Shona, there are two of you!'

But Leo didn't laugh. He removed his arm, allowing Freya to shift away from him. He turned pale as he, too, looked from one to the other, although whether from shock or anger she couldn't be sure.

'Say hello to my sister, Freya.' Shona held out her hand to draw Freya up to stand beside her.

'What's in this drink? I'm seeing double,' said one of the Poles, not noticing Leo's reaction. Even the people at the next table stared openly at the two identical faces.

Freya wanted to apologize, except it would feel disloyal to Shona. Yet, for the very first time, she glimpsed the possibility of a relationship in which their being twins could have no relevance. All that mattered here was the new and delicate bond between Leo and Shona. They were in love and, rightly, it was Freya who ought to be excluded. However, by asking Freya to play their childish trick, Shona had breached the charmed circle that she and her lover had created and so excluded *him*.

Leo stood up and bowed his head formally to her. 'Forgive me for being over-familiar, but I had not the advantage of being introduced.'

'How do you do?' Freya responded stiffly, not sure what else to say. She was sorry they'd got off to such a bad start, but there was little she could do about it now. She stood aside, waiting for Shona to see her mistake, to apologize and smooth things over.

Shona, still laughing with Leo's friends, went to kiss him. It was only when he turned away that she seemed finally to grasp the depth of his silent fury. Freya, seeing Shona's stricken face, recognized the full extent of her sister's strange new defencelessness.

Kirsty, 1989

Do I want to pack up and go with Martin to Australia? How do I begin to decide? What kind of decision is it? I have no idea how to reduce his announcement this morning to a simple choice when, either way, I'd be giving up so much.

It's no good trying to imagine what my mother would say because I already know. All my life, whenever I've asked her opinion, from choosing a party dress to deciding whether to marry Martin, she's responded with two suggestions. The first was, *Take a history and make a diagnosis.* No doctor can tell what's wrong, she'd say, if the patient won't offer a helpful account of her symptoms. And usually, if I went to her in tears and was gently guided to give sensible answers to her questions, the effort of ordering my own thoughts was enough to calm me down.

But my mind can't seem to settle and keeps jumping back to the revelations about Shona. Somehow they feel more urgent than Martin's bombshell.

I try to focus. Freya's second suggestion would be, *Sing to your own tune.* Often I'd be angry that she refused to say what she thought. Why couldn't she simply tell me what to do? Wasn't that what parents were for?

If I'd been as decisive as her, I suppose her words would've been helpful, but I've never known my own mind with the same kind of certainty. Perhaps if she *had* voiced her own strong opinions, I'd have had something to push against. By rebelling I might have figured out what I wanted and why. My brother Archie never had a problem, but then he never had to measure himself against her, never felt overshadowed by being the daughter of one of very few full-time professional mothers among our friends' parents.

My father wasn't big on parental wisdom and anyway had left by the time I was eleven. And Patty Drexeler, the only other significant adult in my childhood, didn't do ordinary things like give advice. A fabulously wealthy American heiress, her chosen role was to be the fairy-godmother provider of legendary treats – a first-night box at the ballet to see Margot Fonteyn, extravagant picnics and once a helicopter flight. I know from occasional newspaper snippets that she now lives in Manhattan where, in her late seventies, she remains an important patron of the arts – there are wings at a couple of museums named after her. But I haven't seen or spoken to her in years.

Which is why I've done something I almost never do and cancelled the seminar I'm supposed to teach. I finish early on Fridays anyway, and can easily catch up with the students next week. Then I called Archie to see if he could make time for a late lunch or at least a cup of tea. It's only half an hour on the train to Billericay, and I have to talk to someone.

As it travels through east London, I gaze out of the carriage window at the post-war high-rises below a grey November sky that threatens rain, and I try to recapture my brief moment of elation at the idea of a new beginning in Sydney. Martin's right, it would be a good place to live and exciting to make a change, but is it what I want?

Of course, I'm relieved that he isn't having an affair, but he hasn't been entirely truthful, either. He deliberately chose not to tell me that he'd been approached for the job and was seriously considering it. Maybe he doesn't want me to come. And what about the boys? Is he going to try to take them away from me?

I know I'm overreacting but secrets and silences are incredibly isolating. As the train draws into Billericay, I try to imagine what it must have been like for Freya to stay silent all these years about Shona's wartime mission. Perhaps it was so top-secret that she had no choice. On the other hand, perhaps people who are already psychologically isolated are better at keeping secrets. Maybe they like it. It's tragic that she can no longer speak, but the truth is, she's always withheld her deepest thoughts and feelings.

And now my husband is doing the same.

I follow the directions Archie gave me on the phone and walk the short distance along a rather scruffy main road to the hospital where he's a newly appointed consultant. He's a burns specialist – following in the footsteps of our father's mentor, Sir Archibald McIndoe, for whom Archie was named. McIndoe, the reconstructive surgeon who helped so many badly burnt pilots during the war, worked in East Grinstead, and, although it certainly doesn't look it, the shabby red-brick Victorian building

I'm now entering is an equally prestigious regional centre for burns and plastic surgery.

A man at the information desk bleeps Archie for me and I take my place beside others waiting in a row of plastic chairs. Glad of the distraction, I glance discreetly at the more interestingly damaged hands and faces, and imagine Dad's enthusiastic proposals for repairing them. However much I need a strong dose of my brother's benign pragmatism, I'm as thankful as ever that I was never tempted to go into medicine, like the rest of my family. Too much flesh, too many imploring faces.

After a while Archie appears from around a corner. He wears suit trousers with a blue shirt, the sleeves rolled up and his tie tucked in between the middle buttons. He walks towards me with a new-found confidence that reminds me strongly of our father, even though he has Mum's dark hair and strong features. I'm the one who inherited Dad's fine reddish-blond hair, freckles and greenish-grey eyes.

'Hello, Kirsty,' he says, giving me a hug. 'I don't have long, I'm afraid, but it's good to see you. Is everything all right?'

I feel bad for making him anxious. 'Yes, everything's fine really. I just wanted to talk to you about a couple of things.'

He smiles in relief as he guides me towards the stairs.

'How are you?' I ask. 'Have you got used to being called "sir" yet?'

He laughs. 'Things are a bit more democratic, these days, although I admit it's rather nice to have made it to the top of the tree at last!'

I'm pleased for him. We don't really have much in common now but I'll always adore my kid brother.

'How's Mum?' he asks.

'Much the same. But something happened last night, which is one of the things I want to tell you about.'

As we climb a second flight of stairs, I try to order my thoughts. *Take a history and make a diagnosis.* I decide it might be easier to begin by telling my brother about Tomasz Dolniak before gauging his reaction to the Australia plan.

He takes me to his office where he hangs my coat on a hook behind the door and plugs in a small kettle to make us some instant coffee. It's a high, narrow room with a tall rain-streaked window overlooking a jumble of neighbouring buildings. There's a framed photograph of his wife, Jo, on his desk and a pot plant that must have been a moving-in gift. It's not something he would ever have bought for himself.

'So what's up?'

'Mum had a visitor last night. Someone from Poland.' I have a sudden awful premonition that Archie's going to say he already knows all about Shona, that it's only me who doesn't, but he frowns.

'She taking in refugees now?'

'No. The man's mother knew our aunt Shona. His name's Tomasz Dolniak, and he showed us a photograph of them together. He said it was taken in Warsaw during the Uprising in nineteen forty-four.'

'Warsaw?' he asks, as the kettle boils. 'There's no milk, I'm afraid.'

'Yes. Apparently Shona was parachuted into Nazi-occupied Poland to help the underground army in some way.'

'No!'

'It's crazy, isn't it?'

'Wow. You mean Shona was some kind of spy?' He hands me a mug of coffee. It looks pretty undrinkable.

'Yes. She even had a codename, Olenka. Tomasz's mother's codename was Gosia.'

'What does Mum say?' He corrects himself. 'How did she react?'

'I watched her look at the photograph,' I say. 'I think she was shocked to see it but I don't believe it surprised her in the least.'

He grins. 'Amazing! You should research it and find out what on earth Shona was doing there. It could be one of your feminist histories. But how did this guy manage to track her down?'

I explain what Tomasz had told us, and add that he was searching for information about his parents.

'And that's all he wants?'

'Yes, I think so.'

'How old is he?'

'Late forties, I reckon. I didn't ask.'

'But you think he's genuine?'

'He has the photograph. It's definitely Shona.'

'Fair enough.'

'It's made me realize I know hardly anything about her,' I say. 'Do you?'

'Not really. In fact, Jo was asking the other day what she actually died of. I always thought it was TB. She was only in her twenties, wasn't she?'

'Twenty-five.'

'And it was when she was in a psychiatric hospital, after the war? Before streptomycin?'

'Yes. Mum might have the death certificate. That would show the cause of death, wouldn't it?'

'Yes,' he says. 'Unless she was a proper spy, and the KGB bumped her off!'

'With a poisoned umbrella?'

'You never know.'

'It might not be a joke,' I say. 'If she did something important in Warsaw, they might have come after her. Tomasz said his mother died in a Soviet gulag.'

'Plenty did under Stalin.'

He drinks his coffee, and I leave him to absorb what I've told him, wondering how to broach the subject of Martin's job offer. I'd love to think I might have inherited enough of Shona's daring and courage to see me through, but that's probably wishful thinking.

'You know, now that Shona's cover's been blown,' Archie continues, 'there may be all sorts of stuff Mum's never talked about, perhaps never been allowed to, which she might quite like us to know.'

I'm not so sure about that. 'You know what she's like,' I say.

He laughs. 'Are you two still at loggerheads? Although you're always going to have the last word now!' He realizes that what he said isn't funny. 'Seriously, it might help Mum for us to find out about Shona. Just because she died, and Mum seldom talked about her, it doesn't mean that being a twin isn't still a really big part of Mum's identity. I've always wondered how alone she feels because of losing her twin. Maybe us knowing more about Shona would comfort her.'

I've always envied Archie for his uncomplicated feelings

towards our mother. He's always seen her as merely busy and sometimes understandably preoccupied with her patients, often reminding me that our Scots Presbyterian grandparents were equally undemonstrative. I should try to be more like him.

'I'll talk to her on Sunday and see how she responds,' I say. 'She'll have had time by then to decide how much she wants us to know.'

His bleep goes off. He reads the message and reaches for the phone on his desk. 'Sorry, I have to take this.'

He speaks to someone, then tells me he's needed elsewhere. He says I'm welcome to wait but he can't say how long he'll be. I tell him not to worry and grab my coat as I follow him out.

'What was the other thing you wanted to talk to me about?' he asks, as he walks me to the head of the stairs.

I smile. 'Another time.'

'I go this way.' He points along the corridor. 'Bye, Kirsty. Give Mum my love. Tell her I'll come and see her soon.'

He gives me a quick hug and I watch him stride away. I don't really mind that I never got to tell him my other news. I don't even care that I cancelled my students for a visit of barely twenty minutes. I still feel better for having seen him.

It makes me realize how profoundly I miss the sound of my mother's voice.

6

Martin arrives home an hour or so after I get back. He kisses me and, from long habit, asks about my day. For some reason that I don't want to unravel right now, I don't tell him about my visit to Archie, or that I've spent the last hour making calls to discover what official records I might access that would give me more information about my aunt.

I'd started with a colleague who's a historian and has written about the Second World War. He suggested that, if Shona was in uniform, she might have worked for the SOE, the Special Operations Executive, and explained that the SOE often preferred to use female agents because they were less likely to draw attention to themselves in occupied territory. But, he said, the SOE had been closed down at the end of the war and all records remain classified, and reminded me that it had taken thirty years to admit the existence of places like Bletchley Park. Even Shona's official wartime service record wouldn't be released for a few years yet.

We all eat supper together – a hastily thrown together tuna pasta – and Martin waits until Chris and Eric have disappeared upstairs to watch television before suggesting that tomorrow morning would be a good time to tell the boys about a possible move to Sydney. I can see that he's anxious about how they'll react and wants to be sure I'll back him up. I know it's pointless to stick my head in the sand and pretend it's not happening, especially when the university won't wait for ever for him to confirm his acceptance, but I'm not ready to promise anything yet. I'm relieved when the phone rings and I don't have to give him an immediate answer.

It's Tomasz Dolniak, asking if we can meet. I'm keen to talk to him before seeing Mum again on Sunday, and welcome his suggestion that we meet the next morning at a café around the corner from South Kensington tube station. I hang up, knowing Martin will be cross, but I decide to leave telling him that I've arranged to go out until the morning. Why should I let him rush me when he's had two months to let Chris and Eric get used to the idea? In any case, as I return to the kitchen, Martin is already heading upstairs to his study.

I tell Martin over breakfast, before the boys have come downstairs, that I'm going to meet Tomasz. 'We can talk later,' I say. 'I'll be home in time for lunch.'

He's not pleased but can see from the look I give him that it would be wiser not to argue. His tacit acknowledgement that he's relying on my support leaves me feeling a mixture of triumph and distaste. It's the more negative emotion that drives me quickly out of the house when he hovers in the hallway as I'm putting on my coat.

I find my hands shaking as I walk to Kentish Town tube, and can finally admit how furious I am about how Martin holds all the cards. He'll be going to a familiar place where he still has family and where he's been offered a specially created professorial chair. It's a great job, a real accolade, and he'd be mad to turn it down. I have nothing comparable to keep me here. I have no counter-argument other than that I just don't want to go. Plus I've convinced myself that he'll go anyway. Which leaves me with a lose-lose choice I never sought: do I go and give up the only life I know, or would I rather stay here without him?

As I change tube lines at Leicester Square, I make an effort to dismiss my angry thoughts, grateful to have a conveniently distracting family mystery to investigate.

I get to the café in South Kensington in good time. I've only vaguely noticed the place before. The tablecloths are plastic, as are the flowers on the tables, but it's busy and, if Tomasz hadn't got here before me, we wouldn't have found seats. I wasn't sure I'd be able to recognize him, but he's wearing the same patchwork leather jacket and, anyway, has quickly spotted me. I squeeze into the seat opposite him.

'Thank you for coming,' he says.

'Not at all. I'm glad you called me.'

'Would you like a coffee?'

I say yes, and he signals to the waitress.

'I made a copy for you,' he says, handing me a photocopied enlargement of the photograph of the two women in Warsaw. He's written on the back: *Gosia and Olenka, Warsaw, August 1944.* It's the first time I've seen his mother's name, which he pronounces as 'Go-sha', written down.

'Thank you.' I glance from the image to his face and catch him in the same appraisal as we search each other's features for traces of Gosia or Shona. We both laugh.

'I'm so pleased you found us,' I tell him. 'I'm thrilled by what I've learnt about my aunt, even though I never knew her. I hope it might help my mother, too.'

'Her illness, she cannot speak at all?'

'Not really. Sometimes the odd word.'

'It must be terrible for her.'

'She's knows she's dying,' I say. 'She's incredibly brave.'

His look of sympathy makes me want to cry. 'If only you'd come six months ago,' I tell him, 'you would have met the real Freya. And she could have answered all your questions.'

I'm not sure that's true. She's always been reluctant to talk about the past. Why should that be different now?

'Six months ago,' Tomasz says, 'leaving Poland would have been difficult. And without the right papers it might not have been possible to go back. Now it is easier.'

I knew about the Solidarity movement in Poland, and had watched on last night's news as huge numbers of Czechs in Prague continued to fill the streets to listen to speeches by Václav Havel and other leaders opposed to Soviet control. I try to imagine how much courage it took to defy the authorities after decades of fear and control.

'Tell me about your mother,' I say.

'I have no memories of her,' he says. 'I grew up with my uncle and aunt, her older brother. They never told me much, but here in London they tell me what she did, what so many did to fight for their country. And I learn that people back home were too frightened to speak of the Uprising. It was a banned subject.'

The waitress brings me strong milky coffee in a glass cup and saucer that are scratched and cloudy from repeated use.

'*Dziękuję.*' Tomasz thanks her in Polish. 'I knew only that my mother had died in the gulag. When she was first arrested they'd beaten her.' He leans forward so he can reach around to touch his lower back. 'Her kidneys. Without proper medical treatment, she never fully recovered.'

'That's terrible,' I say. 'I'm so sorry.'

He smiles ruefully. 'Stalin had died and she was about to be released.'

'Did you find out what she was doing in Warsaw?' I ask.

'She was employed by a magazine there before the war. After the Nazis invaded, she joined the AK, the Home Army, and helped to find paper and printing presses and then to organize the distribution of leaflets and news sheets. During the Uprising she worked directly with the leaders, issuing communiqués. Towards the end, she was delivering messages herself, via the sewers.'

I'd certainly be prepared to join a protest march, but to use a gun, crawl through sewers, be prepared to kill or be killed, or be tortured in prison? I can't begin to imagine it.

'Why did the Soviets imprison her?' I ask.

'The few insurgents who survived the Nazis were rounded up. Many were shot. The rest locked up. No one spoke about it again.'

'And my aunt,' I say. 'What was she doing there?'

'I know only that she came with the Cichociemni.'

'The agents who were trained here in England?'

'Yes.'

'So there must be official records we could access?'

'No. I was told that the Government-in-Exile burnt all its files for fear they'd fall into the wrong hands. And most of the Cichociemni who survived in Poland were killed by the NKVD.' He sees my incomprehension. 'The Soviet secret police.'

'What about the man at the Hearth Club who recognized Shona in your photograph?' I ask. 'He must know more.'

He shakes his head. 'He knew her in London, but not well. She was part of the crowd. He thought she had a Polish boyfriend.'

'Really? I didn't know that. It might explain how she got involved in the first place.'

'Possibly. But he's old and couldn't remember who the man was. Will you ask your mother?'

'I can try,' I say, 'but her words are usually meaningless and she can no longer write. What else did he tell you?'

'Only that he remembered hearing your mother was a doctor.' He smiles. 'At the time, apparently, he didn't think a woman should be a doctor, and that was why it stuck in his memory.'

'Lucky it did,' I say, 'or you wouldn't have found us.'

I look again at the image of the two young women. No matter how often I see pictures of Shona, I'm always slightly shocked at how indistinguishable she is from my mother. Perhaps it's why she's always seemed so insubstantial, as if she had no identity of her own. But this time it is Gosia's face I want to examine more closely.

'How old would your mother have been here?' I ask.

Tomasz doesn't stop to think about it. 'Twenty-nine.'

I try to imagine everything she went through. I study the ruined buildings behind the two women, their dirty clothes, the strain on their faces, even though they're smiling for the camera. I wonder who took the photograph, and how extraordinary it was, in the midst of such destruction, that the human impulse to smile for a picture should remain.

Gosia is slightly smaller than Shona, with delicate features, light eyes and a wide mouth. Her smile seems one of genuine humour, as if she's sharing a joke with the person behind the camera. In black-and-white, it's impossible to tell whether she had the same clear blue eyes as her son.

'I wish I had known, growing up, what I know now,' he says. 'That she was a fighter, that she saw such horrors, that she risked everything for Poland. I might have found it easier to forgive her for leaving me.'

'And your father? You said you wanted to find him.'

I hope I'm not treading on delicate ground. We're strangers, after all, tied together only by the thinnest of threads from the past. But he seems not to mind.

'I know nothing about him, not even his name. And they weren't married. He may well be dead. Whenever I used to ask my uncle and aunt, they said they'd promised my mother never to tell me anything about him, although I don't understand why, or even if that's true.'

'If they brought you up, maybe they wanted to think of you as their own.'

'Maybe,' he says. 'My uncle died two years ago, and my aunt says she no longer remembers anything from the war. I don't believe her, but she's old and I don't want to upset her.'

'What about other AK members Gosia fought with?' I ask.

'So many were killed. No one who survived talks about it.'

'So that's why you were hoping to meet Olenka?'

'Yes. Perhaps my father was also one of the Cichociemni. My

mother spent time here in England before the war. Maybe she met him then. Olenka, too. That might be why my uncle wanted me to learn to speak English. Perhaps they were all friends together.'

That seems to me unlikely. 'My aunt was a student in Aberdeen until the middle of the war.'

He looks disappointed that I've just shot down one of his theories.

'Who told you that Olenka knew your father?' I ask.

'When my mother died a friend of hers sent me this photograph. He told me that she'd asked him to tell me that Olenka was the only person she knew who might know what happened to my father.'

'And that Olenka was British?'

'Yes.'

'Can't the friend who gave you the photograph tell you more?'

He shakes his head again. 'I was thirteen when my mother died. I don't remember his name, if I ever knew.'

It seems to me that he doesn't stand a hope in hell of finding his father, even if he was British. And it's none of my business why, after so long, Tomasz still cares so much about who he was.

'Tell me more about Olenka,' he asks.

'I know very little. And apparently nearly all the official records are sealed.'

I relay to Tomasz what my historian colleague told me about the SOE, and how it was responsible for subversion and sabotage behind enemy lines, including training and equipping the Cichociemni.

I don't tell him that a few more phone calls confirmed I won't be allowed to see Shona's hospital records, either. I did, however, write off for a copy of her death certificate. Knowing I'd never have the heart to ask Freya for it, I'd put my letter into the post on my way to the tube.

'My mother may have papers relating to my aunt,' I say. 'I'm visiting her tomorrow. I'll see what I can find.'

'Will you ask her if Shona ever mentioned my father?' he asks.

'I can try,' I say, already certain of the answer. Shona's reason for being in Warsaw was secret and perilous. Why, following such momentous events, would she think to mention to her sister who fathered Gosia's child? And why, after forty-five years, should Freya remember his name, even if she could speak?

Mum is not yet seventy. I've always assumed there'd be plenty of time to ask questions. So many memories must be trapped inside her head but, without her words, her sister's story is lost. I have a sense of Shona and her short history floating like a chimera in the air around me, especially in this part of London where she must have visited the wartime Polish clubs and restaurants – even perhaps this one. It's as if I keep entering a room just as she's gone out by another door, leaving only a small movement of air behind her. I need some kind of magic spell to capture her spirit and make her visible to me.

When I glance up, Tomasz is watching me. His look is friendly, perceptive. 'You'll let me know?'

'Of course.'

He takes out a pen and scribbles a number on a paper napkin.

'This is where I'm staying. The landlady will take a message and I can call you back.'

Tomasz insists on walking me to the tube, even though it's only around the corner. He's about a head taller than me and moves with determined speed through the dawdling tourists here to visit the nearby museums. I, too, like to walk fast, and easily keep pace beside him.

'Where are you staying?' I ask.

'On Cromwell Road. Just a room. The landlady is Polish.'

I think of the six-storey terraces, not far from here, that line the busy arterial road heading west out of London. Battered by traffic noise and fumes, many have been turned into cheap hotels.

'It's nice and central,' I say.

He smiles, as if guessing my true thoughts. 'Yes.'

'How do you come to speak such good English?' I ask. 'Do they teach it in schools in Poland?'

'Now they do, but not when I was young. My uncle was a schoolmaster and he really wanted me to learn the language so he taught me. Tell me, is how I speak out of date? He hadn't visited England since the nineteen thirties, and his books on English grammar were very old.'

'Not in the least. And I don't know a word of Polish!'

'It's a beautiful language.'

'And are you married?' I ask. 'Do you have children?'

'A son, Tadek. He's worked with me since he finished his military service.' He shows me his hand, which is strong and hard-skinned. 'Cutting stone, carving letters.'

'A mason?'

'Yes. His mother and I parted some years ago.'

'I have two boys,' I say. 'My husband's from Australia and wants to move back there. I'm not sure I want to go.'

He smiles again. 'I've never left my country before, not even for a holiday.'

'Going somewhere is one thing. Leaving is another.'

'True,' he says. 'The old men here in London all talk about home, but none of them want to hear what Poland is like now. The homeland they dream of is long gone.'

'They're exiles. They wanted to go home and weren't able to. That's different again.'

I feel a pang of conscience that, in the seventeen years I've known Martin, it's never occurred to me to ask whether he wants to go home, assuming that, like certain more famous Antipodean intellectuals, he was happier here.

When Tomasz and I reach the little arcade of shops leading to the entrance to South Kensington Underground station we stop and move aside, out of the way of the parents herding children excited about seeing the dinosaurs. I think of all the times we've taken Chris and Eric to the Natural History Museum, just as my parents took me when I was a kid: another link to my past that I'd be leaving behind.

'It's very kind of you to help me,' he says. 'You must think I'm too old to run around after my lost father.'

'You're not old!'

He laughs. 'As a young man I was too angry to want to find him. Now I'm nearly fifty, old enough not to be angry any more.

If he left my mother, it must have been the war. And life is difficult enough without a war.'

'What will be different if you do find him?'

'Will it change me?' he asks. 'I don't know. I'm not missing a lost part of me. But I don't like the . . . *tajemnica.*'

I make a guess. 'The mystery?'

'Yes. It feels wrong not to know.'

'And if he's still alive, will you want to meet him?'

'Of course!'

'Even if their affair was only . . . ?' Embarrassed, I leave my question hanging.

'Even if Gosia hardly knew him?'

'Yes.'

'My uncle always said they had planned to marry, but I'm not so sure. If that was so, why did they never meet him or know his name?'

'Something to do with his family, perhaps?'

'Perhaps he was already married. Or a Jew.' He sees my reaction and shakes his head with a smile. 'If the Nazis had discovered I had Jewish blood, my life would have been in danger.'

'But surely, after the war, that would no longer matter. Why would they continue the secrecy?'

'The Jews were seen as anti-Communist. Even in the sixties many were still being forced to emigrate. In any case, he may be long dead, killed in the war. There are too many things I don't know. That's what I don't like.'

'And you've shown me how much in my family I have to learn,' I say. 'I never even suspected there *was* a mystery.'

'You come from a family of brave women.'

'Very secretive women.'

He laughs once more. 'Show me a family with no secrets.'

'That's true.'

'You must go home.'

'Yes,' I say, without much conviction. 'I'll be in touch if my mother is able to tell me anything.'

'Thank you.'

He doesn't offer to shake hands, and immediately turns and walks back the way we came. I go down the steps to the tube, fishing my return ticket from my bag and wishing I didn't have to face the difficult conversation that lies ahead with Martin and our sons.

7

Freya, 1944

Freya was looking forward to telling Shona her latest stories about hospital life. They'd barely had a chance to talk properly at the Milroy Club, not after her awkward first meeting with Leo Tarnowski, so they had agreed to meet for another drink just as soon as they could both manage a free evening.

Although Shona had soothed Leo's anger over the trick they'd played, the remainder of the evening at the Milroy had been so strained that Shona hadn't pretended to hide her relief when Freya had said she must leave early. Freya had spent the slow tube journey back to the East End worrying what more she could have done to help. The visceral link that had always existed between the sisters seemed broken, at least on Shona's side, relegating Freya to second place beside her sister's lover. Yet, as Freya had climbed into the narrow bed in her hospital room, she noted that she no longer minded how their bond had shifted or that Shona's focus lay elsewhere. In fact, it was a relief not to feel responsible and to be left free to concentrate on all the exciting new demands of her own life.

Apart from Robbie, the thin, sandy-haired man who, she'd learnt, was training to be an anaesthetist, she was getting on well with her colleagues, becoming used to being away from home for the first time, and finding the demands and challenges of her work enjoyable. Every day she had learnt something new and felt a little bit less of a fraud when introducing herself as Dr Grant.

Now, after counting off the side-streets along Baker Street, she found the small pub where Shona had suggested they meet. Shona was already seated in the smoky saloon bar. She was in uniform, so must have come straight from work, her cap and gloves – hardly needed in the hot July weather – laid neatly beside her. Freya realized that the three pips on her epaulette meant she held officer rank, although she'd never mentioned it. All Shona had told Freya or their parents about her job in her infrequent letters home was that it was exacting but dull, and that occasionally she had to work through the night if there was a flap on. Thankful that she would never be stuck in an office, Freya couldn't imagine how her sister stood it.

'I'm getting to know people,' she told Shona, once they'd let the barman have his little joke about double trouble and settled with their halves of cider. 'The chaps in the residents' mess are all friendly, except one who's as sour as anything and insists on calling me Scottie, but the others don't seem to like him much, either. And the patients are fine. Of course, we only get the acute cases. Everyone else is sent off to the Home Counties out of harm's way. I'd expected some of the patients to be difficult about being examined by a woman, but they're sweet. They keep making jokes that I don't always understand but, considering what they have to put up with, I'm amazed they can laugh at all.'

She glanced at Shona who was staring into her glass.

'You're not listening, are you?'

Only when Freya let the silence grow did Shona, as if startled, look up at her sister. 'Sorry, what did you say?'

'What's wrong? Is it Leo? Is he still cross about the other night?'

'What? No. It's . . . I can't really say. It's to do with work.'

'Well, tell me what you can,' said Freya. 'What kind of set-up is it?'

'Far too boring to bother talking about.'

'Then it *is* Leo. Is he always so sensitive?'

'No, not at all. You don't understand.' Shona checked over her shoulder. The saloon bar wasn't particularly busy and none of the other customers were paying them attention, but she moved closer and lowered her voice. 'It's to do with Poland. It's difficult to explain.'

Freya remembered the urgency with which Adam and Jozef had asked her for news when they'd assumed she was Shona. 'You mean it's secret?' she asked.

'I can't talk about it.'

'Not even to me?'

Shona studied her sister as if seeing her properly for the first time since her arrival in London, then smiled and grasped her hand, squeezing it gratefully. 'It's funny how easily you fall into a habit of mind,' she said. 'We have it so drummed into us never to let anything slip.'

'Careless talk and all that?' Freya asked.

'This happens to be serious,' Shona said sharply.

To Freya's surprise, her sister bowed her head, a hand hiding her eyes. Freya swallowed the rebuke and waited until Shona felt ready to speak.

'I know he loves me,' she said at last. 'But it's hard to compete with an entire country. Maybe it would be easier if I didn't know so much about what's happening, but I'm in the Polish Section, receiving signals. That's how we met. Sometimes I know more than he does, and it breaks my heart.'

Freya summoned up what she knew about Poland. Britain had gone to war in the country's defence when Hitler invaded. Many men from the Polish Army had escaped to France and were now fighting with British forces. The RAF boys she'd met in Aberdeen had spoken highly of the courage of the Polish pilots and crews. And hadn't she heard recently on the radio that Stalin's forces were beginning to break through German lines in the East?

'But surely now that the Russians are heading for Warsaw . . .'

'That's the problem.'

'They're our allies.'

'No. Stalin wants Poland as part of the Soviet Union.'

Freya saw the misery in Shona's eyes; saw, too, how desperate she was to unburden herself.

'What is it that you can't tell Leo?' she asked.

Shona gave a bitter laugh. 'I can't tell you, either.'

'Really?'

Shona eyed her thoughtfully. Perhaps it was seeing the reflection of herself, a mirror image that barely counted as a separate person, or maybe it was merely her need to tell someone, but she made up her mind.

'Let's get out of here,' she said, picking up her cap and gloves. 'I know somewhere it'll be safe to talk.'

The first rush of people had left work and the side-streets that Shona led them through were quiet. Freya had no idea where they were going.

'That's where I lived when I first came to London,' Shona said, as they passed the jagged edge of a bombed mansion block.

Freya, who was still only just getting used to the raw gaps between buildings, looked up and saw fireplaces hanging in mid-air, the remnants of striped or flowered wallpaper delineating the separate floors and rooms. 'You weren't there when it happened?' she asked in alarm.

'No. And luckily no one was killed,' Shona said, not slowing her pace. 'Not very nice to come out of the shelter and find everything gone, though.'

Freya looked back over her shoulder at the blocks of patterned paper. Her little room at the infirmary already felt like home, and she'd rather not imagine returning there later to find all her possessions broken and buried under rubble.

'Less of a shock when it happened the second time,' Shona added.

'You were bombed out twice? Why didn't you tell us?'

Shona made an airy gesture. 'Oh, well, at least we don't have Nazi tanks rolling down Regent Street or swastikas flying over the National Gallery.'

Freya didn't know how to answer. She couldn't believe that her sister had been as unaffected by such events as she made out.

They walked on in silence until they emerged into an area where elegant Georgian terraces enclosed what must once have been a rather grand square. The gardens had been replaced with allotments, obviously struggling beneath the thick canopy of some magnificent London plane trees. She thought perhaps they were going to sit in the square but Shona suddenly veered off and clattered down the steep metal stairs to the basement of one of the houses. Pausing beside the railings, Freya looked up and was shocked to see that the top storey was missing, the remains scorched and blackened, she assumed from an incendiary bomb.

'Is it safe?' she asked, catching up with Shona as she bent to squeeze through a gap that had been forced in the boarded-up door directly under the tiled steps that led to the once imposing entrance above.

'Safe enough.'

Shona disappeared inside, leaving Freya no choice but to follow. As soon as her eyes grew accustomed to the dim light she saw that Shona was picking her way across an abandoned kitchen. The floor was filthy with dust and chunks of ceiling plaster. It led into a low, bare room, perhaps a former servants' hall, covered with broken glass and soot that had been blown outwards from the shattered chimneys above. On the far wall, a smashed-in glazed back door led into a garden where, even though the ground was littered with broken roof tiles and lumps of brick, the bushes were abundantly overgrown and a second flowering of pink roses hung loosely from a brick wall smothered in ivy. A narrow path, presumably made by a cat, snaked through the long grass of what had been a lawn to a kind of bower in the far corner.

'This is my secret garden,' said Shona, as she made for the wooden bench tucked into the back of the arbour.

'Feels more like breaking and entering,' said Freya, dusting the wooden slats with her handkerchief before sitting down: her skirt was new and, as she'd used up all her clothing coupons, it would have to last. At her feet, the paving stones were littered with spent matches and cigarette stubs, evidence that Shona, who didn't smoke, wasn't the only one to come here.

Freya looked up at the broken windows of the remaining floors and felt uneasily that hidden eyes were watching them. 'Are you sure this is OK?'

Shona laughed without mirth. 'Don't be such a Goody Two-Shoes! We won't be shot as looters, if that's what you're worried about. It's been derelict since the Blitz.'

'I'm part of this war, too,' Freya objected, hurt by her sister's scorn. 'I've been patching people up all week.'

'Sorry.' Shona took off her cap and shook her hair loose. 'I suppose I've grown rather spiky and bitter lately.'

'Then tell me what's wrong!'

Shona nudged around some of the cigarette butts with the toe of her brown lace-up. Freya waited for her to speak.

'It's top, top secret,' she began. 'I could be shot for telling you.'

'Then don't say anything, unless you're sure you want to,' said Freya, meaning it.

'It's only because I want you to understand Leo, to be able to feel for what he's going through. He grew up in Warsaw. It's *his* city.'

'You don't have to explain him to me,' said Freya. 'It's as plain as day how much you're in love with him.'

Shona squeezed her sister's hand and looked up at the woody honeysuckle covering the arbour. 'It's funny, but whenever I come here, all I want is to be at home, to go fishing with you and Daddy up the Feugh, to be back among the firs and birches, and smell the clean air.'

'It's all still there.'

Shona nodded and took a slow breath. 'I'll keep it simple. No names, just the basics. The Polish Government-in-Exile here in London and the Home Army in Poland are planning an uprising against the Nazis in Warsaw. If their political leader can be in control of the city when the Soviets arrive, then it would be very difficult for the Western Allies *not* to recognize a sovereign Polish government. But if the Home Army are to go ahead, they must act before the Soviet advance penetrates too far.'

'Go on,' Freya said. 'I'm following you.'

Shona took another deep breath. 'I handle all the coded messages from Warsaw. The political leader has been injured and the signs are that an infection has set in.'

'Blood poisoning?'

'I imagine so.'

'They've tried sulpha drugs?' Freya asked. 'They can be fairly effective at fighting infection.'

'They've tried everything they have,' Shona said wearily. 'Which isn't much. And if he dies, there's no other figure of his authority who is already recognized by the Allied governments, so the plans for an uprising may have to be abandoned.'

'In which case Stalin would claim Poland for himself?'

'And Leo could never go home because none of those connected to the Government-in-Exile would be safe under Soviet rule. It would break him.'

Freya looked at her sister, realizing with a shock of self-reproach that Leo's tragedy would break Shona, too. How had she failed to grasp the depth of her sister's new vulnerability? Now it was her turn to consider how seriously she intended to abide by military secrecy. Should she tell Shona what she knew? A breeze stirred the foliage above them. She looked up anxiously at the blank windows and then at Shona, only to find her twin studying her shrewdly.

'What's on your mind?' Shona asked.

'Nothing.'

'You can't fool me. Come on, spill the beans.'

'I could lose my job, be struck off, even.'

'But you do know something that could help?'

The desolation in Shona's face decided her. 'You've heard of penicillin?'

'The mould Alexander Fleming discovered growing in a Petri dish?'

'Yes,' said Freya. 'My chief took me over to one of the military wards at the London Hospital yesterday. Since D-Day we've been packed with casualties. They're using it there and he wanted me to see its effects.'

'It really works?' asked Shona.

'It's extraordinary, the most exciting thing I've ever seen. They let me examine a soldier who'd been dying of septicaemia from an infected wound. Within a single day of being given penicillin he'd turned a corner.'

'How would I get hold of it?'

'You can't. The form of the drug they're using is secret, kept under armed guard. It's only for military use because it's so difficult to make in any kind of quantity. But once they do, it's going to revolutionize medicine.'

'So you really think it might save our man in Warsaw?'

'It would certainly give him a fighting chance.'

'There must be a way to get some.'

'You're in uniform,' said Freya, trying to shake her irritation that Shona was too absorbed by her own concerns to share her excitement at the potential of this wonder drug. But, then, Shona had never taken much interest in science. 'I assume the people you work for could requisition it.'

'The RAF is on stand-by to air-drop supplies,' said Shona, her eyes shining. 'If we could get it to him within a few days, would that be too late?'

'I'm no expert, and it's not that easy to administer, so . . .'

But Shona was no longer listening. She stood up, pulling on her cap and tucking up her hair. 'I have to go. Thank you!'

'But—'

'Not a word to anyone!'

Freya hurried after her, not wanting to be left alone in the ruined house, and wishing now she'd never opened her mouth.

'Wait. Listen. Even if your department can get it, the authorities won't want to risk it falling into enemy hands.'

'We can at least try!'

'Then promise you won't say who told you,' she begged, as she followed Shona up the metal stairs from the area. 'Please don't mention me. I shouldn't have spoken.'

'Don't worry,' Shona replied, with a backward wave, as she walked away.

Freya was left hoping she hadn't done something irrevocably

stupid. She assured herself that, although she'd been indiscreet, the existence of a miracle drug, if not exactly common know-ledge, was widely known among the troops who had received it. She could hardly be accused of betraying her country by talking about it, whatever Dr Chiltern's orders. And surely her sister wouldn't carelessly land her in trouble.

It was only after Shona had turned a corner, out of sight, that she realized she'd lost her bearings between there and the pub, and had been abandoned with no idea of how to find her way back to the Underground station.

8

In trying to retrace her steps, Freya found herself hopelessly lost. Even when she spotted a road name she'd heard of – Harley Street, the most famous medical thoroughfare in the world – she still had no idea whether to turn right or left, or which direction would lead her to a tube station. A siren began to wail. She listened for the already familiar rumbling engine noise of a flying bomb but could hear nothing. With dozens hitting London every day, she'd seen enough of the damage they could do and didn't want to be caught in the street where she might be in danger of falling masonry. She looked around but had no idea where the nearest shelter would be. She stood frozen on the street corner, trying to decide the best way to go. A van drew up and the driver, a woman, leant over to push open the passenger door. 'Shona! Get in!'

She didn't hesitate and slid with relief onto the bench seat. She'd barely pulled the door shut as the vehicle shot forwards and sped straight ahead along Harley Street. Before she could explain who she was, the driver glanced sideways at her, frowned, and then took a second, closer, look. 'You're not Shona!'

'No.' Freya was astonished at how a stranger could so instantly pick up on the difference, and longed to know what made her so sure.

'Well, I don't know who you are,' the woman exclaimed, 'but you're a dead ringer for a friend of mine!' Maybe it was her drawling American accent, but she sounded relaxed, almost amused. She certainly didn't seem very anxious about the siren, which stopped soon afterwards.

'I'm her sister, Freya Grant.'

'Well, you almost had me fooled, that's for sure. I'm Patty Drexeler. How do you do?' She raised a gloved hand from the steering wheel and executed an awkward handshake. 'I'm not even sure I knew Shona had a sister, let alone an exact replica. She certainly kept you quiet. Or do you only show yourselves one at a time, like werewolves or Dracula or something? No, that doesn't make sense, but you know what I mean.'

Freya usually hated the kind of teasing that went with being an identical twin, yet somehow found this woman's directness droll and charming.

She hadn't yet heard any explosions, but she looked anxiously out of the window and up at the sky as Patty Drexeler spun the wheel in a sharp right turn. What if they couldn't hear the drone of a doodlebug and one cut out right above them?

'Are we going to a shelter?' Freya asked. 'Or you could just drop me at the nearest tube station.'

'Too late. They'll be packed by now.'

Freya tried to peer up at the sky again. 'I don't mind a bit of a crush.'

'Don't worry, honey, there's a shelter in my garden and we'll be there in two ticks. Wouldn't you rather come and have a drink and something to eat? Or maybe you have to be somewhere.'

Freya wondered if she was overreacting. Londoners, after all, had endured the full force of the Blitz while Aberdeen had remained largely unscathed. She looked at her watch. She didn't want to be left on her own during a raid in an unfamiliar part of town. Her evening with Shona had been cut short, she wasn't on call until midnight, she'd be too late for dinner in the mess, and the mention of something to eat was very tempting.

'I'd love that, thank you.'

'Good,' said Patty. 'I want to know everything about you.'

'How do you know Shona? Do you work together?'

'Columbus, no! I know everyone because I'm for ever throwing parties. That's what everyone will tell you, so I might as well say it myself before they do.'

At that moment, to Freya's relief, the all-clear sounded.

'False alarm,' declared Patty, as if that had been her opinion all along. 'They're getting really clever at shooting them down before they reach London.'

Soon afterwards she parked the van outside an elegant town-house in Mayfair and ran up the steps to ring the bell, leaving Freya to follow. The front door opened almost immediately, revealing a man in a black coat and wing collar, who formally bowed his head as his employer stepped past him into the hall.

'Hello, Leighton.' Patty pulled off her driving gloves and handed them to her butler along with her coat. 'Is anybody here?'

'No, Miss Drexeler.'

Patty turned to Freya. 'What heaven. I can have you all to myself. Come along.'

Freya allowed Leighton to help her off with her coat, pleased that she'd saved up her coupons for a new one before starting her job, and hurried after Patty.

'Have some cold supper sent up, will you?' Patty called over her shoulder.

Freya had only seen houses like this at the cinema and couldn't help but look around as she climbed the elegant staircase. She recognized a painting on the half-landing as by Modigliani, and gasped at the realization that it was an original, as was the exquisite Cézanne still-life of a bowl of apples beside the double doors to the drawing room, and, too, the Blue Period Picasso over the marble mantelpiece, below which a coal fire was burning brightly. She wondered how often Shona had been here and, the old sly boots, chosen not to share her new experiences in her infrequent letters home. Before leaving Scotland Freya had imagined her sister's life in uniform as bureaucratic and uneventful but was belatedly learning otherwise.

She tried not to stare at her hostess as Patty crossed the room to a silver drinks tray. It was hard to judge her age, although she was certainly older than Freya. She had cropped dark hair and a thin, boyish figure, accentuated by well-cut tan-coloured Oxford bags, polished brogues and a cashmere twinset in a matching tone. Judging from the art treasures on display, her triple strands of milky pearls must also be worth a queen's ransom. And yet the wide room, with its three floor-length windows, was furnished for comfort, not ostentation, and her hostess's smile, as she turned with a bottle in hand, was open and unselfconscious.

'Gin and tonic?' Patty asked.

'Yes, please.'

'I'd like to say that my people were bootleggers, but the prosaic truth is that all of this . . .' she paused to wave the gin bottle towards the Picasso '. . . is the fruit of cough syrup and baby food. People are always dying to know where the money came from, so it's best to get it over with. My granddaddy made it and I spend it.'

'Did you choose the paintings?' Freya asked.

'Yes. After my first divorce I ran off to Paris and had a lovely time. Ice?'

'Please.'

'Here you are, honey. Come and sit. Now, tell me everything!'

'*My* grandfather was a postman and left me a Bible in his will,' she said, with a smile. 'I've never been married, let alone divorced. And I'd never even been to London until a couple of weeks ago.'

'You're not in uniform?'

'No. I'm a doctor.'

'Oh, my, but that is impressive! I call that really doing your bit.' Patty's admiration seemed entirely sincere. 'How fascinating.'

'I'm still getting used to it.'

Patty didn't respond, staring instead at Freya's face. 'You're not really identical at all, are you?' she asked.

'Most people think so.'

'No,' she said. 'Shona could never be a doctor. She takes everything far too personally.'

'That's not fair.'

Patty laughed. 'I like your loyalty.'

'It's not loyalty. Maybe you just don't know her well enough. She's so much more instinctive and spontaneous than me.'

'That's true, too. So what were you doing in Harley Street? Do you work there?'

'Heavens, no! I'm newly qualified, a house physician at a little infirmary in Mile End. It's one of the satellites of the London Hospital.'

There was a discreet knock on the door and the butler appeared with a large mahogany tray. He pressed a catch that released legs, turning it into a table that he placed beside Freya. It was the perfect height, and bore two plates, linen napkins, a silver platter of assorted sandwiches and a small bowl of fruit.

'Thanks, Leighton.'

'Will that be all, Miss Drexeler?'

Patty looked at Freya. 'Anything else you'd like?'

'Oh, no, this looks perfect, thank you.'

'Tuck in,' said Patty, as the man withdrew.

Freya realized how hungry she was and reached eagerly for the triangles of soft white bread. Egg mayonnaise, ham and mustard, smoked salmon: rationing might as well not exist!

'I know the East End quite well,' said Patty, placing one small triangle on her plate, but not eating it. 'I run a mobile canteen out of Whitechapel. Hence the van for ferrying supplies. It's staffed with volunteers, and we back up the WVS whenever things get busy. It's simply the best thing. I just love feeding people, don't you? Please, keep helping yourself.'

Freya ate several more sandwiches as the two women chatted, exchanging information about their lives. Patty, taking a pearl-handled fruit knife, expertly peeled and sliced a pear. She

handed Freya the plate with a merry smile that made Freya forget about the priceless paintings, the butler and the heirloom
pearls, and decide that she had just made her first new friend in
London. Only when at last she got up to leave, and glanced back
to make sure she hadn't left anything behind, did she notice
that Patty hadn't touched a morsel of food and had barely sipped
her gin and tonic.

9

Kirsty, 1989

I get home from meeting Tomasz in South Kensington in time for lunch and find that Martin has already laid out soup bowls, bread and cheese. Even Chris and Eric notice their father's unaccustomed domestic effort and give us sideways glances as I sit down, no doubt suspecting that Mum and Dad have had a row. I'm horribly nervous. Telling the boys about Martin's job offer is going to make the possibility of packing up the house and leaving the country far too real. I don't want to be the one to raise the subject so, as Martin ladles out supermarket ham and pea soup, I fill the silence by telling them about Tomasz and Shona and wartime Poland.

When Martin takes his place, he sits for a moment, balancing his fingers on the edge of the table, waiting for me to stop. But Eric is interested and wants to know more: what kind of training would Shona have had before jumping out of a plane? Would she have carried a gun? Did she kill any Nazis?

I tell him I don't know, that this is what I'm attempting to find out, and try to close down the conversation to leave space for Martin. He begins by talking about his boyhood in Sydney, about surfing and the outback, reminding the boys of the adventures we enjoyed on the three long summer holidays we spent there. I remain silent, leaving it to him to broach the subject of a move. It doesn't go well.

Chris is horrified. 'How long would we have to stay?'

Martin glances at me before he answers. 'Well, if works out, it could be permanent.'

'What about my friends?' Chris asks.

'It's not long before you'll all be on your gap years,' says Martin. 'Then your friends can come and stay. Could be fun.'

I silently urge Martin to sympathize with our older boy: at fifteen, three weeks can go on for ever, let alone three years, but he seems oblivious.

'Can we get a dog?' Eric asks his perennial question.

'We'll see,' says Martin, with a smile.

'Do I have to go?' Chris appeals to me.

'We've got time to get used to the idea,' I say. 'I won't be able to go anywhere while Grandma needs me here, so it certainly won't be before the end of your school year.'

The thought of his dying grandmother diminishes Eric's brief excitement, and brings home to me the finality of leaving every connection to her and to my past – the familiar London street corners, the pubs where I met school friends or went to listen to bands, paths on Hampstead Heath where I pushed a pram. How can I face losing Mum, then immediately separate myself from Archie, my friends and everything that, daily, reminds me of who I am?

Yet the same kind of associations must also play a significant role in why Martin wants to go home, making me guiltily aware of how little time we've spent with his family since we married. I try to think how Archie or I would feel if one of us had to manage our mother's final illness from ten thousand miles away.

'Think how happy Granny and Grandpa Pearce will be to have you nearby,' I say. 'You know how much they've missed us all these years.'

Martin shoots me a grateful glance and I wish I could be pleased but I'm not. And I blame him for turning me into someone so begrudging.

'What if we go for the summer holidays, and then decide?' asks Eric, the family conciliator.

'It would be a bit tough on Granny and Grandpa Pearce,' says Martin, 'if you then decided you didn't want to stay.'

Eric understands immediately. Chris, too, looks as if he's beginning to see how complex this decision is going to be.

'What can we take with us?' asks Eric. 'Will we have to leave everything behind? All our furniture and stuff?'

'The university will pay for us to ship quite a lot of our things out,' says Martin, relieved to shift the discussion to practical details. 'There are some very good schools and lovely areas to live near the campus. Great beaches. It could be a lot of fun.'

'What happens if I don't want to go?' asks Chris.

'Let the idea sink in,' says Martin, 'and then we'll talk some more.'

'You mean you don't care what we want. We're going anyway,' Chris shoots back.

'I understand it's a big move, and I'm sorry there wasn't an easier way to tell you,' Martin protests. 'But we have time to think it through and come to a decision together.'

'Yeah, right.' Chris storms out of the room.

I'm on his side. Eric, who always hates conflict, slides off his chair.

'Go on,' I tell him.

Granted permission, he edges quickly out of the room.

'That went well,' Martin says grimly.

'What did you expect?'

'You could have offered a bit more support.'

'They have to make up their own minds, don't they?'

'They're kids!'

'And what am I?'

He stares angrily at me.

'You could have told us about it when they first approached you,' I say. 'You chose not to. How do you expect me to feel?'

'I'm trying to do what's best for my family,' he says. 'It's a big step up. We can have a very nice life in Sydney.'

'So why wait so long to tell us?'

He runs his hands through his hair. 'I don't know. I guess I was afraid you'd say no.'

'But you're going anyway.'

I wait for him to admit I'm right.

'I want to go home,' he says at last. 'I only realized it when they offered me the job. But I want to go home.'

And there it is. The next decision lies with me.

10

It's a slow drive to Dulwich the next morning, thanks to a burst water main near Clapham Common, but I'm relieved to escape the tension at home where we've all been avoiding further discussion of Sydney – although I hope Chris and Eric have been talking privately. I want the boys to work out how they feel without allowing my anger at Martin to influence them. Perhaps, once I calm down, I can be more even-handed, but I'm simply not there yet.

Once the traffic starts moving it doesn't take long to reach Dulwich. Mum bought her 1960s townhouse after the divorce, moving half a mile along the road from the neo-Georgian red-brick with a driveway, double garage and large back garden that Dad had chosen. Her much smaller house has lots of rectangular windows and blocks of white-painted wood, with rather box-like bedrooms in which Archie and I spent our teenage years. The furniture, too, was nearly all bought new and now seems hopelessly dated, not that Mum would ever notice or care.

I have a key and let myself in, calling to her. I still can't get used to the answering silence, but she comes to the door of the living room as I'm hanging up my coat and greets me with her customary nod and smile. She's pale, and the hand she puts to her brow is a sign that her headache is bad today. She doesn't like being fussed over, so I don't ask her how she is.

Physically she manages pretty well on her own. She's friendly with her neighbours, a couple in their sixties who downsized here a few years ago when their kids left home, and they check in on her and know to call me if they're concerned. She's had the same cleaner since before she was ill and, anyway, insists on doing at least some of her own laundry and cooking. I guess it helps to live as normally as she can. I visit twice a week, deal with any paperwork, and take her to hospital and other appointments. Archie does what he can. Although she's now on medication, we both worry about her having a seizure and falling downstairs or spilling boiling water over herself. But it's no good arguing. She won't change things until she absolutely has to.

I take the bag of food I've brought into the kitchen and start to fit the soups and ready meals into her fridge and freezer. She follows me and sits on the built-in bench beside the window. The garden beyond her is dreary, as if reflecting the bleakness of her situation.

'I met Tomasz Dolniak for a coffee yesterday,' I say. 'The man who—'

She bats away my explanation: she hasn't lost her memory.

'Had you seen that photograph before?' I ask.

She shakes her head.

'Yet you didn't seem surprised that Shona had been in Warsaw.'

She purses her lips along with the tiniest waggle of her head, which I take to be agreement of sorts.

'I'd love to know more,' I say, folding up the emptied super-market bags. 'Do you have any papers or anything here that I could look at? I know you kept her old suitcase, but is there anything else I haven't seen?'

I used to love going through Shona's things when I was little. The suitcase was kept under the bed in the spare room and, after endless pestering, Mum gave us permission to rummage through it for dressing-up clothes. It didn't contain much: a couple of embroidered blouses, a nightdress, some stylish silk scarves, several bead necklaces and a handbag. As a student, I borrowed some of the items and kept one amber necklace that I still often wear. There were also a few books, including a gold-tooled edition of Christina Rossetti's poetry, awarded as a school prize, and some foreign novels from when she was a student. I'd always understood that the case held the few belongings that were put away when Shona suffered her breakdown and was never unpacked when she went to the asylum. I feel ashamed at how carelessly we kids once rifled through her things.

Mum shakes her head decisively in answer to my question: there's nothing more for me to see.

Frustrated, I try another tack. 'It's important to Tomasz, too. He barely remembers Gosia and never knew his father, but the man who gave him the photograph, when he was a teenager, said that Shona knew his father.'

She looks at me with an expression that is not encouraging.

'I said I'd ask if you could think of anyone he might talk to.'

She pointedly turns her head to look out at the wintry garden. I keep trying.

'The man Tomasz spoke to at the Polish Hearth Club who

remembered that you were a doctor also said that Shona had a Polish boyfriend. Is that true? Did you ever meet him?'

She stands up abruptly, walks past me out of the kitchen and into the living room, slamming the door behind her.

I'm shocked by the intensity of my reaction when she does this. I'm furious. Nothing ever changes. Even if Shona's wartime mission had to be kept secret at the time, how can it hurt to talk about it now? Why can't Mum be happy that I want to understand her sister's past? But she's never let me in, never shared her feelings or admitted any frailty. She's kept me at arm's length all her life and now she's dying, and all she can do when I try to learn more about her is slam a door against me.

I slump down where she's just been sitting and put my head into my hands. I recall how one of the cancer nurses, the one I hated most for her doleful eyes and over-caring voice, had warned us that the silence imposed upon our mother by her brain tumour might sometimes provoke anger in us, and we must remember that the patient would surely speak if only she could.

But that isn't true of Freya.

And I have been angry with her for a long time.

I try to focus on what Archie said: that being a twin must still be such a big part of our mother's life, to think about what it must have been like to lose her twin sister, to be alone in a way that no singleton can comprehend. But my resentment lingers. Why have I never been enough to fill that gap?

Mum was always so matter-of-fact in telling us the little we do know about Shona, every inch the doctor dealing with bad news, never encouraging us to glimpse the grief, and maybe even a kind of survivor guilt, of the twin who was left behind. Shona's breakdown and death must have been hugely traumatic, yet, if none of us are allowed to know what caused it and who Shona really was, doesn't that double the loneliness?

Why else might she not want her sister's story told? What is there to hide? If there's any scandal, it is surely Gosia's, and what possible harm can it do now to let Tomasz learn the truth? Is it that Mum was jealous of Shona's exploits? Or is it only that twins are naturally secretive and she can't break that bond?

My resolve to find out more about my aunt's life becomes stronger than ever. Perhaps understanding her better will help me to have more sympathy for my mother. Which may be the very reason she's resisting me: she'd hate to be on the receiving end of my compassion.

When I go into the living room twenty minutes later to tell her that lunch is ready, she shrugs and smiles, which I take to be an apology. I want to tell her about Martin's job offer, but can't face her inevitable comprehension that any move to Australia would entail waiting for her to die, so instead I chat about the boys and work and how we must decide at whose house we want to do Christmas this year. It's like talking to a stranger.

She's too exhausted to pay much attention so I'm not surprised when she pushes aside her half-eaten quiche, points a finger to the ceiling, lets her head nod down while closing her eyes to signal that she's tired and is going upstairs for a lie-down. I let her go, feeling responsible because I've bullied a dying woman into recalling events she'd plainly rather forget. But I've so often hoped to find the key that would unlock my understanding of my mother and finally draw us close that Tomasz's revelations feel hugely significant and I can't let go.

I start with the desk in the living room. Four teak drawers on spindly legs, it's where Freya keeps her chequebook, bank statements and bills. I'm in charge of all that now so it isn't prying. She's so orderly and efficient that there's nothing here that's more than a few years old, apart from her passport, which I open. There's something unbearably sad about it because she will never use it again. Also, apart from the first name – Mum always kept her maiden name professionally – this could just as easily have belonged to Shona.

I remember my childhood fantasy of how Shona would have understood and nurtured me in all the ways Mum never could. When I was younger, and badgered Freya for more details about Shona, my fantasy let me interpret her rebuffs as jealousy at knowing that, had her sister lived, I might have loved her more.

And perhaps, without knowing why, I'd been right. Is that why my mother, living in the shadow of Shona's secret courage and daring, had felt so strongly about using her work to make a difference? Have I misjudged her all these years?

I move on to the sideboard in the dining room that contains all sorts of old family stuff. First there's a soft green Morocco-leather case that closes with a zip. It's crammed with my grandparents' papers, including several black-edged condolence cards for a great-uncle who died on the Somme. There are a dozen or so family snapshots of when the twins were children, dressed in matching outfits, but very few of them as adults, either together or alone. If there was anything else about Shona, it's been removed.

Then I take out a Clarks shoebox with Archie's and my old school reports, a copy of a school magazine in which I had a teenage poem, a sealed blue envelope labelled 'Kirsty's hair, 1956', which I don't open, a pair of white satin baby shoes trimmed with swansdown, and two home-made birthday cards signed by Archie in jagged, newly acquired letters.

Underneath these, at the bottom of the sideboard, is a cardboard laundry box, the kind you never see any more. I place it on the dining table and unwind the tough thread that fastens around soft buttons. I lift the lid and, on top, there's an eight-by-ten black-and-white photograph of my parents on their wedding day in 1948. They're young, smiling, good-looking, hungry for life. I hesitate. I've no wish to stumble across secrets from my parents' marriage. And suddenly I'm back in the old house, half a mile away, on the night that Archie and I sat on the stairs as our mother dialled number after number, trying to track Dad down in time for him to reach his father's unexpected deathbed.

We never knew exactly what Mum found out, but nothing was ever the same again. Dad never came back to the house, Patty Drexeler's name was never to be mentioned in front of Freya, and within a few weeks, it seemed to us at the time, although it must have been longer, we'd moved here, taking almost nothing with us from the old house. Later that year Dad moved to Los Angeles where he became one of the most sought-after cosmetic surgeons in Hollywood.

It was Patty who'd introduced our parents and who bankrolled the pioneering healthcare clinic that Mum and her friend Phyllis Levenson set up after the war, only for Freya to walk away from that, too, after the divorce. I haven't seen Patty since before the night my grandfather died but she is, I suddenly realize, one of the few people I can name who must have known Shona before she was ill.

I begin to have bad feelings about digging up the past. There's far more buried here than whatever wartime operation took Shona to Warsaw. I don't need to help Tomasz if it means uncovering stuff I don't want to know, events I don't want to have to make sense of, and I'm in no position to judge. Perhaps Freya is right and it's best to leave well alone.

I close the lid of the laundry box without looking to see what else it contains and am replacing it at the bottom of the sideboard when I hear Mum moving about upstairs. Checking that the room appears undisturbed, I go to put the kettle on for some tea. After that I'll head home and face up to the decisions that have to be made there.

When she doesn't appear, I take a mug up to her. She's standing with her back to me staring out of the bedroom window where, although it's only early afternoon, the tree-lined road outside is already murky and cold-looking. Her arms are folded as if she's hugging herself and she doesn't move when I speak to her.

'I've brought you some tea. Mum? Are you all right?'

She turns around but regards me as if she's not entirely sure who I am. I'm gripped by fear. Is this a new phase in her condition? Is this my fault for pushing her too far?

Her mouth moves and a throaty sound emerges. When I go to put an arm around her and guide her to sit on the bed she does not protest, which is also worrying. She tries once more to speak, and then, to my relief, laughs and shakes her head,

recognition back in her eyes. She shrugs as if commenting iron-
ically on her own uselessness before taking a deep breath and,
to my surprise, taking hold of my hand. She grips it tight and
seems to be concentrating very hard, her bottom lip moving
silently in and out as if preparing to form a word. I wait.

Wheel? Veil? Wheedle? Weevil? Fidel? She repeats the same
sounds, but I can't decipher what she's trying to say.

Exhausted, she gives up. I hand her the mug of tea, for which
she nods her gratitude. Soon afterwards she makes a waving
gesture as if trying to shoo me away, telling me it's time to go
home.

The traffic has eased but it's still a long drive back to Kentish
Town. Most of the high streets have already put up their Christmas lights, and the twinkling stars, trumpeting angels and
jolly Santas add welcome brightness to the late-November
gloom. Held at some traffic lights, I gaze into a shop window
full of haberdashery – rolls of fabrics and ribbons, buttons and
trimmings. The buttons remind me of one summer when Eric
and Chris were eight and ten and we rented a cottage in the
grounds of an old house in Sussex. One of Martin's friends
turned up with a metal detector and the boys were thrilled
when we dug up a few Victorian coins and some metal buttons
from an RAF uniform. Their games for the rest of the holiday
were an inventive mix of Indiana Jones, fighter pilots and Ghost-
busters. Is that all I'm doing? Trying to help a man I barely know
by childishly pretending to be on a quest to dig up lost treasure
when in reality I have no idea what I'm meddling with?

11

Freya, 1944

'Take your tie off and hide it in your pocket,' Freya instructed her sister. She'd already given her a long white medical coat to disguise her uniform, but the tie was a giveaway.

'I can't do it,' said Shona, peering through the porthole windows of the double doors to the military ward at the London Hospital. 'I can't go in there and pretend to be a doctor.'

Visiting hour was over and the ward was quiet. Early evening sunlight slanted down from high windows; three men in dressing-gowns and slippers chatted quietly beside an unlit stove; in the two long rows of neatly ordered beds, some patients slept, while others leant back against their pillows to smoke or read.

'The only way you can see it in use is to pretend to be me,' Freya insisted.

Shona had turned up unexpectedly at the infirmary at the end of the afternoon and waited for her sister to finish her rounds, then demanded that Freya show her some penicillin so she could understand how it was administered. They'd walked the mile along Whitechapel Road to the teaching hospital in silence, each lost in her own thoughts.

'You only have to go to bed six. You can just nod to any nursing staff you pass,' Freya continued. 'No junior nurse would dare question a doctor's right to go wherever she wants, and I barely spoke to either the sister or the staff nurse when Dr Chiltern brought me the other day, so they're not going to start chatting to you.'

'What if someone *does* ask what I want?'

'Tell them you're here to see how Dr Chiltern's patient is getting on.'

'What do I say to him?'

'Pretend to take his pulse and ask him how he feels.'

'What if there's an emergency? What if I'm expected to do something?'

'You won't be. And if there is, you'll just have to slip away.'

'No,' said Shona. 'I can't do it. You're a real doctor. I could never be that.'

Freya stared at her, annoyed at this waste of a precious evening off duty, but then she saw the uncertainty in Shona's eyes and her frustration melted away. 'I don't know how else I can help,' she said. 'I told you that all the penicillin is kept locked up and it's just not possible to get hold of the key. I can't think of any other way you can get to see what it looks like except in use on a patient. Although all you're going to see is a drip. I don't really understand what you're after.'

'Then you'll have to come and speak to my boss directly,' said Shona. 'If I can't explain it to him, you'll have to.'

'Why can't he just come down here officially? You're all in uniform. It shouldn't be that big a problem.'

'He's too busy. He won't come unless I convince him it's worth it. There's so much going on right now. It's no good offering him a theory. It has to be a course of action that he can see and agree to.'

Freya looked at her sister's pleading face. 'What's the latest on your man's condition?' she asked.

'Septicaemia has set in.'

'How long has he been ill?'

'He was injured two weeks ago.'

'Then you need to get a move on.'

'He'll die, won't he?'

'Probably.'

'But there's a chance?'

'If you catch the infection in time.'

'Then please, Freya, come and talk to my boss. You'll like him. He's really smart, and it won't take us long to get to Baker Street.'

Freya looked at her watch. It was gone six o'clock. 'Are you sure he won't have left already?'

'He's often there all night.'

The cooperative instinct Freya had possessed since birth kicked in. 'Come on, then. Let's go.'

The Underground station was across the road from the hospital, and the Metropolitan line took them straight to Baker Street. The carriage was too crowded for Freya to question her sister about the secret department in which she worked, so instead she told Shona about her chance meeting with Patty Drexeler.

'Oh, Patty!' Shona waved a hand dismissively.

'I liked her.'

'Everyone likes Patty.'

'Except you?'

Shona laughed. 'She's OK. Except that she collects people, all different types, like she's an entomologist and we're moths or beetles or something.'

'Maybe that's how she realized so quickly that I wasn't you.'

'Maybe.'

They reached their stop and, among the crowd, didn't speak until they emerged above ground and were walking south.

'So who's your boss?' asked Freya.

'I can't tell you his name,' said Shona. 'That has to be his decision. In fact, it's probably best if I don't tell you anything else at all.'

'Gee, thanks!'

Shone gave her a sharp dig with her elbow and they laughed, able to be squabbling kids again for a brief moment.

They reached a large and unassuming building, faced in pale stone, where a small plaque announced the entrance to the Inter-Services Research Bureau. Shona waited while the commissionaire issued Freya with a pass, keeping his eye on them until the lift doors closed in front of them. Freya followed her sister along a fourth-floor corridor, disappointed to find that a secret department could appear so bland and unremarkable. Shona led them into an office where an older woman in uniform sat behind a desk. The officer acknowledged Shona's salute, managing not to betray the least surprise as she looked from one twin to the other.

'You'd better explain, Junior Commander Grant.'

'Yes, ma'am. I've brought my sister to talk to Major P. It's important.'

'It had better be.'

The officer stood, went to tap on a glass-panelled inner door and went straight in, closing it behind her. Shona raised her hand to show Freya her tightly crossed fingers.

Moments later, the officer came out again. 'He'll see you now.'

'Thank you, ma'am.'

The man who rose from behind the cluttered desk to greet them looked nothing like Freya's idea of a secret agent, either: probably in his late thirties, he had a slight paunch and reminded her, if anything, of the family's greengrocer back home.

'No need to explain that you're sisters,' he said, with a pleasant laugh.

As he listened to what Shona had to say, smoking a cigarette and asking only a couple of astute questions, Freya could understand why her sister admired his intelligence. Shona explained that Freya was a doctor and had mentioned the miraculous effects of penicillin and, without being fully informed as to why this information was important – at this Freya kept a straight face – had agreed to come and answer any questions the major might have about the new drug.

'How extremely kind of you both,' he said drily. 'I have heard of its extraordinary power to fight infection, but I've no idea how it's administered.'

'I've only seen it once,' Freya began, 'on the military ward at the London Hospital. It's a mould and, at the moment, can only be produced by a process of surface fermentation. Once extracted, it's stored in sealed glass ampoules. Dissolved in saline or sugar water, it can be administered either intravenously or intramuscularly, depending on the type and site of infection.'

'And how many doses would be required?' he asked.

'Six a day for about five days, starting with an isotonic concentration and then reducing until the blood cultures are negative for infection.' Freya was thankful she'd paid such close attention to Dr Chiltern's instructions as he'd shown her how to set up the drip.

'How long does the extraction remain viable?'

'Ten to fourteen days. Less if not kept cool.'

'Would you be able to transport it without static equipment, like a refrigerator?'

'There must be ways,' said Freya, 'but I don't know.'

'We can find that out.' He stubbed out his cigarette. 'I don't suppose you happen to speak Polish?'

Freya glanced at Shona, whose eyes were bright with an expectation she didn't fully understand, and smiled. 'No, sir.'

'But you would be able to produce written instructions which, if translated, a Polish doctor could follow?'

'Well, I may not be the best person to do that,' she said. 'The process is inexact. Each case can be different, with the rate of absorption dependent on a lot of varying factors.'

'So someone familiar with the substance would be needed to administer it?'

'Yes, sir,' she said firmly. 'And if you want written instructions, you'd be better off finding someone with more experience of handling it than me.'

'Will there be many with that experience?'

'Not many. Not outside London, anyway.'

'But you'd be able to reproduce your experience?'

'Yes. It's not actually that difficult to handle. It's just a matter of describing a completely unfamiliar compound to someone who's never seen it.'

'I assume you don't have figures on its success rate in treating infection?'

'No, but from everything I've been told, it's a real break-through. The Americans are trying to synthesize it, apparently, so then it would be more widely available.'

'Very well. Thank you, Dr Grant. If you wouldn't mind wait-ing outside while I have a few words with your sister.'

Shona gave her an encouraging nod as she left the room.

'I've been asked to wait,' Freya told the officer at the desk. The woman nodded, still without expression, and indicated a wooden bench along one wall. Freya could hear the occasional murmur of voices behind the glass door. Her stomach rumbled. She was hungry, and wondered how long Shona might be, and whether she would be able to join her for something to eat. The thought reminded her of last night's encounter with Patty Drexeler. She must ask Shona what more she knew about her. Mainly she was relieved that the man Freya had referred to as Major P hadn't hauled her over the coals for having told her sister about a drug that officially remained a military secret. He hadn't even seemed all that put out that Shona had brought her there, although it was obvious that the officer keeping an eye on her from her desk did not approve. If only her stomach would stop rumbling.

Anyway, at least now she'd done all she could to help Shona and could go back to her own work, her own world; a world, she realized, in which she'd told no one she was a twin.

The inner door opened and Shona followed Major P into the anteroom. He held out his hand to Freya.

'Thanks again, Dr Grant, and welcome to the organization. We'll get everything in place as quickly as we can. Just leave it all to us.'

Freya, confused, looked at Shona, who offered a small, contrite smile. 'I don't understand,' she said.

'Your sister tells me you're willing to do house calls,' Major P said, with a chuckle.

Freya remained at a loss.

'Come on,' said Shona, taking her arm. 'You don't mind leaving me to fill her in, sir?'

'Not at all.' He looked at the wall clock. 'Why don't you go and get something to eat and I'll see you back here at twenty-one hundred hours.'

Shona and the major exchanged a casual salute, then Shona hurried her out of the office. In the lift, Freya demanded to know what the blazes he'd meant.

Shona shrugged apologetically. 'Look, there's no time to start looking for someone else to do the job, so I said you'd do it.'

'Do what?'

'Go to Warsaw, of course.'

12

Kirsty, 1989

As I drive up and park outside Freya's house on Thursday evening I see her at the window looking out for me. The curtains are open and the light is behind her. She's already opened the front door as I walk up the path. I'm immediately anxious – she doesn't usually greet me with such urgency – but she smiles excitedly and beckons me straight into the living room where she fetches something from the teak desk. What she hands me is the tin in which she's always kept her sewing kit – a home-made felt needle case, thimble, stray buttons, cards wrapped with darning wool (no one has darned a sock in years) and a small pair of beautifully engineered stainless-steel surgical scissors, now used only for snipping off stray threads. I almost laugh: the emergency can be nothing more serious than a dropped hem or lost button.

'What needs mending?' I ask.

She shakes her head and taps her finger on the lid of the tin.

'You want me to sew something?'

She snatches back the tin and holds it up so that the embossed picture on the lid is facing me. I've known this object all my life. It's so familiar that I no longer see it. And then, suddenly, I do.

It's a silvered metal tin, about fifteen centimetres square and fairly deep. On the lid is a slightly embossed image of the kind of quaint European townscape with church spires and a statue on a column that might illustrate a tale by Hans Christian Andersen or an Oscar Wilde children's story. More buildings, in shiny black and silver, adorn the side panels. In the top left corner of the lid, in jaunty lettering, is a stylized signature, E. Wedel.

Wheel, veil, wheedle, weevil, Fidel. Wedel.

I look up at my mother. When she sees that I have, finally, understood, she sighs in relief.

Except that I'm none the wiser. I have no idea what this tin signifies or why the name Wedel is so important.

Freya pushes the tin back into my hands, her eyes fixed on mine.

'Is this what you were trying to say to me last time I was here?' I ask. 'The name Wedel?'

She nods eagerly.

I examine the image on the tin more closely. I'd always assumed it was some little town in France or Switzerland, a souvenir of an early family holiday, but suddenly I realize: it could equally well be Warsaw.

'Did Shona give you this?' I ask.

She stares at me blankly.

'Is it from Warsaw?'

She nods.

I want to ask her what it means, but it's impossible for her to answer such an open-ended question. I try to frame the best way to help her explain herself.

'Does it mean something I ought to understand?' I ask.

She shrugs and shakes her head.

'Should I show it to Tomasz Dolniak?'

Yes.

'Will he know what it means?'

She hovers her hand: maybe.

'But it's important?'

Yes.

'Something I should find out about?'

Yes.

'Is it the tin?' I hold it up in my right hand. 'Or the name?' I raise my left hand.

She points to my empty left hand.

I have an idea. 'Did Gosia give it to Shona?'

She waves her hand dismissively: no.

'OK, I'll do my best to work it out. Tomasz gave me a number where I can leave a message so he can ring me back. Shall I telephone him now?'

She smiles.

The effort has exhausted her, so I settle her in a chair by the window and go to make the call to leave a message with Tomasz's landlady before starting to make supper. As I'm grating the cheese for Welsh rarebit, one of Mum's favourites, I think of Archie. We haven't spoken since my impromptu visit to Billericay. I ought to let him know how she is.

I peep into the living room, where Freya appears to be dozing, and take from its base station the new cordless handset we bought her. His wife, Jo, answers and chats for a few moments before putting my brother on the line.

'Hi, Kirsty. How's Mum doing?'

'Much the same, except that she's still agitated over this Warsaw business.'

I hear a slight pause before he speaks, and when he does, it's with his professional voice. 'Agitation may be symptomatic rather than meaningful.'

'That's what I assumed on Sunday, when she kept trying to say something that made no sense,' I say. 'But just now she was waiting for me to get here so she could give me something with the word on it that she was trying to say.'

'It's not good for her to become agitated.'

'It's only because she wanted to show me something. Do you remember her old sewing tin?'

'No. I don't think so.'

'Silver and black with line drawings of quaint old buildings. It's where she keeps her needles, thimble and scissors.'

'Vaguely.'

'It has the name "E. Wedel" on the lid. That's the word she's been trying to say. I asked her and she confirmed it, and that it came from Warsaw. I think Shona may have brought it back.'

'So Mum did know about Shona's secret mission,' he says. 'And does want us to find out about it.'

'Yes. She wants me to show it to Tomasz Dolniak.'

Archie goes quiet again for a moment. 'I don't think that's a good idea.'

'Why not?'

'You may be raising his hopes for nothing. We don't know

how far the language part of her brain is scrambled. Just because she's latched onto a word on this tin doesn't necessarily make it directly significant.'

'What – you're saying she might have fixated on "Heinz" instead?'

He laughs. 'She might, yes. Look, I agree she's trying to tell us something, but the word she comes up with could be completely random. Or it'll be like "Rosebud", the painted sled in *Citizen Kane*. Meant everything to him and nothing to anyone else. Or nothing that can unlock a mystery, anyway. You don't want to set this guy off on some wild-goose chase.'

'I see what you mean, but I think I should tell him all the same.' I hear Jo calling his name in the background. 'Sounds like your supper's ready?'

'Afraid so. But, look, maybe I can get down and see Mum at the weekend.'

'She'd like that. Bye.'

'Bye.'

I've barely had time to put bread in the toaster when the phone rings. It's Tomasz. I tell him about the tin and ask him if 'E. Wedel' means anything to him. I'm rather taken aback when he laughs, a warm sound that comes from deep in his chest.

'Emil Wedel,' he says, 'was Warsaw's oldest and most famous chocolate maker!'

My heart sinks. Maybe Archie is right, and, even though the tin *is* Polish, it's merely Freya's equivalent of a 'Rosebud'.

'Can you think of any reason why the name might matter so much to her?' I ask.

'Not really,' he says. 'The chocolate is pretty special. You should see the queues outside the shop!'

'Was it there during the war?'

'Yes, I think so, though the business has been state-owned for years.'

'Can you find out?' I ask.

'I can try. I'll be in touch if I find anything.'

'Thanks, Tomasz,' I say, and hang up.

I no longer care what Archie thinks. The tin definitely comes from Warsaw. Whatever it does or doesn't mean, my mother is trying to reach out to me. It's what I've longed for all my life, and I'm not about to turn away.

13

Freya, 1944

Freya was incredulous and, when she saw that Shona was in earnest, furiously angry. Trying to shush her, Shona dragged her past the commissionaire and out onto Baker Street, then around the corner and into the pub they'd visited the day before. The saloon bar was almost empty and Shona bundled her into a corner seat.

'At least consider it.'

'No, I don't want to go anywhere. I'm happy where I am. I've only just got here. And, besides, it's insane.'

'Please, Freya. You don't know how important this is.'

'I'm not in uniform. Get someone from the Medical Corps, someone who speaks Polish.'

'But you've used penicillin.'

'So could any competent doctor. Surely you can find an army medic.'

'Time's running out. You said yourself he'll die otherwise.'

'People are dying in London. I'm needed where I am. There are more flying bombs falling on London every day, in case you hadn't noticed.'

'But this isn't just the life of one man,' Shona pleaded. 'It's the future of an entire nation. At least come back and talk to Major P again. Hear what he has to say.'

'No. There's nothing to discuss.'

'I'm going to get us both drinks and see what they have to eat.'

Freya knew that Shona wouldn't give up so easily, but it would make no difference: the very idea of her going to Warsaw was nonsense.

After chatting to the publican – probably, Freya guessed, to give her time to calm down – Shona returned with two halves of cider and some freshly cut potted-meat sandwiches. She looked warily at Freya as she sat down.

'Look,' Freya said, with a weary smile, 'you can argue all you like, but I'm not doing it.'

Shona nodded as if in agreement and sipped her drink. 'Our organization uses a lot of female agents,' she said. 'That's because it's so much easier for a woman to pass unquestioned where a man of military age is always likely to be challenged. It's not just that you've had experience with penicillin, it's also that you're a woman.'

Freya bit into a sandwich and did not reply.

'It'll be very difficult to find another female doctor at such short notice,' Shona continued. 'There aren't that many of you to start with.'

Freya had to admit she had a point.

'Look,' said Shona, 'Major P might not be your idea of a secret agent, but he knows what he's doing. And, once you're in Poland, the Home Army, the AK, will take good care of you. They're the largest and most effective of all the European resistance movements.'

'I can't do it. Shona, you know it's madness.'

'Leo and his countrymen came to England to go on fighting the Nazis. But if this man dies, and Warsaw falls to the Soviets, then Stalin will claim the whole of Poland. Everything they've fought for will be wasted. They'll be permanently exiled. It would break Leo's heart.'

And yours, thought Freya. It was the one argument she couldn't reject. She remembered the stricken look on Shona's face when their twin trick had backfired at the Milroy Club. It was clear that her sister's wellbeing was now unquestionably linked with Leo Tarnowski's. Much as Freya disliked being seen as the sensible twin, she understood how easily Shona could be hurt, and had never been able to tolerate her unhappiness. But what could she do? She had a job, she had the beginnings of a life of her own, and the idea of her playing secret agent was plain daft.

'If it really matters to you, of course I'll speak to Major P again,' she said. 'But only to explain that he really has to find someone else.'

It was just before nine when they returned to the Baker Street offices. This time the very anonymity of the nondescript fourth-floor corridor seemed to Freya to take on an intimidating purpose and power. It made her fear that, having placed herself back within the confines of this clandestine organization, refusal might no longer be an option.

The major gave each woman an appraising look before inviting them to sit in the worn leather armchairs grouped around an empty fireplace. The July light was fading but the weather was warm and a welcome breeze entered through the open window, freshening the smoky air. He placed Freya between Shona and himself, and Freya liked him for refraining from making any remark on their likeness, something most people did almost compulsively, as if the twins weren't already aware of it.

'I've come back to explain that my sister was a little hasty in volunteering my services,' Freya began. 'I'm sure you must see that I'm not the right person for this job.'

'Of course,' he replied reassuringly. 'But before you come to a final decision, perhaps you'll let me explain a little of what we do here. That will mean, however, that before you leave we'll have to ask you to sign a document undertaking not to divulge a word of what you learn. Do you agree to that?'

'Yes,' said Freya, trying to pretend she wasn't feeling a little thrill of excitement.

'Very well. There will be no names outside this office. If you do undertake the operation, you will be given a field name, as will your patient. It will be better for you if you remain ignorant of his true identity.'

'I understand.'

'I'm not sure that you do,' said the major, giving her a sceptical look. 'I run Section Six of the Special Operations Executive, a secret department of the War Office that supports underground warfare behind enemy lines. Section Six coordinates aid to the Polish resistance and the AK, the Home Army. Before I tell you any more, I should make you aware of the risks involved in what we're asking you to do.'

Freya took a deep breath. She was tempted to tell him that, as an eighteen-year-old student, she'd had to conquer her fear to dissect a human cadaver and, later, to perform surgery or watch a patient die. But she remained silent, aware of Shona's eyes on her.

'Once in Poland you will be in enemy territory. We won't be able to help you. Hitler has ordered the execution of all captured parachutists, so you won't even have prisoner-of-war status.'

'Parachutists?' She was taken by surprise, and the word had burst out. She'd never even flown in an aeroplane, let alone jumped out of one. She glanced at Shona, who looked pale and apprehensive, as if the reality of what she was asking Freya to do was only now finally sinking in.

'Normally we'd give you at least two weeks' parachute training,' Major P replied calmly, 'but I'm afraid we haven't that luxury. The best we can offer is to send you on a three-day course. Besides, the jump will be the least of your concerns. Quite a few of our aircraft flying to Poland have been shot down, so you may not even get there. And I should warn you that, of the SOE agents operating elsewhere, so far around half haven't made it back. Would you like to hear more?'

'You mustn't go, Freya,' said Shona, vehemently. 'I don't know what I was thinking. You don't have to do this. Please, just forget it.'

Freya swallowed hard. She felt sick. It was madness. Terrifying. Of course she couldn't agree. 'Carry on,' she said.

Major P studied her quietly for a moment, as if making up his mind about her, then nodded to himself. 'Your patient was injured about two weeks ago. At the first sign of infection he was treated with sulpha drugs, which seemed to be working. However, as of three days ago, they're no longer having any effect and he's showing signs of blood poisoning. You will know better than I how long he may survive.'

'No more than ten to twelve days, probably.'

He did a rapid calculation. 'Which takes us, at best, to the seventh of August. The situation on the ground is complex and remains volatile. A week ago, following news of the assassination attempt on Hitler, we had reports of demoralized German troops in eastern Poland fleeing in the face of the Red Army advance, and of German civilians evacuating from Warsaw. That encouraged the Polish Government-in-Exile here in London to support the Home Army's plans for an uprising against the Germans in Warsaw.'

Freya dared to glance again at her sister, who appeared ashen-faced and distressed.

'In the last few days, however,' Major P continued, 'fresh German troops have begun arriving from the west. The AK insists that they are prepared and want to proceed, but the reality is that they cannot do so without our support. We are pushing for urgent supplies to be dropped, but with the Allied advance into Europe under way, Bomber Support has other priorities. Unfortunately the SOE has no power to make policy.'

Freya racked her brains for everything Shona had told her. 'How long before the Soviets reach Warsaw?' she asked.

'Hard to say. Apparently the sound of their guns has been heard across the Vistula River, so they're close.'

'But if the AK does decide to act, it will have to be before the Red Army reaches the city?'

'Yes. And if the Uprising does not go ahead, your services will not be required.'

'So the patient will die?'

The major gave a sombre nod. 'This department cannot be responsible for individual lives except in support of underground warfare behind enemy lines. Meanwhile, if you wish to proceed, we must continue to plan your mission as if it were not in doubt. It's time for you to decide.'

Whether it was the seriousness of Major P's purpose, or the temptation of a once-in-a-lifetime adventure, Freya felt unable to refuse the mission, insane and impossible though it still was. She considered asking if she could sleep on her decision, but knew that, if she returned to her hospital room, in the morning this would all seem like a strange dream and she would never come back here.

She turned to her sister. 'Shona? What do you say?'

Shona clasped her hands tightly in her lap and shook her head, refusing to look at Freya. 'Don't ask me. I can't answer.'

Freya turned back to Major P. 'I assume you wouldn't be considering such a plan if there weren't some chance of success?'

'Correct.'

'Or if you didn't think I could do it?'

'You'll be the one at the sharp end,' he said kindly. 'You won't be alone. We'll be sending someone with you. A Polish speaker. But all that counts is that you believe in yourself.'

It wasn't that she wanted to say yes. She was petrified. The challenge was overwhelming. But she couldn't return to her former life with the knowledge that she had said no. That, somehow, felt just as impossible.

Freya told herself that it was the same as her first morning outside the anatomy department in Aberdeen. Only three months before that day, she'd been a schoolgirl, worrying about exams. If she hadn't made herself walk into that basement room, and face the rows of steel tables bearing lifeless human forms under green cotton sheets, and not think about the sickly sweet air she had to breathe, she would never have become a doctor. This, too, was about the kind of woman she wanted to be.

'What do I tell them at the infirmary?' she asked, doing her best to ignore Shona's involuntary little cry of protest. 'I can't just disappear.'

'Don't worry. We'll do the necessary. And prepare a suitable cover story for your return.'

Wondering how on earth her safe return was to be managed, but not wanting to lose her nerve, Freya decided not to ask.

'You can requisition the penicillin?'

'Yes. We'll take care of everything.'

She turned back to Shona, reaching over to place her hand on her sister's clenched fingers. Shona's hands were freezing, despite the close summer air.

'You'll help me, won't you?' Freya asked.

'Only if you're absolutely sure.'

'I am.' Freya took a deep breath and turned to face Major P. 'I'll do it.'

14

Freya's preparation began early the next morning in a bare little room in Baker Street, furnished with nothing but a small table and two chairs. The female officer who guarded Major P's door brought in a young Royal Army Medical Corps captain who walked with a limp and whose thin face was etched with the lines of chronic pain. He didn't give his name or ask for hers. Wasting little time over pleasantries, he explained that he had taken part in Howard Florey's trials of penicillin with British troops in North Africa the previous year.

'I have permission to share his report with you,' he said, handing her a file stamped 'Top Secret'. 'You must read it in my presence, and then I can answer any questions you may have.'

The unnamed army doctor stood smoking and staring out of the dusty window as she read the closely typed pages, learning that the trial had been relatively limited because the main problem with the drug had been producing reliable amounts. The results were undeniably impressive, yet she couldn't help laughing at discovering that Florey's greatest success had been not with infected wounds or gangrene but in treating a particularly nasty local strain of gonorrhoea. She tried to stifle her reaction but then she saw the captain give an amused smile that transformed his lean face.

'You have to remember,' he said, 'that venereal diseases can put just as many soldiers out of action as battle injuries.'

Finishing the report, she felt completely confident that this 'wonder drug' was the real thing and was excited at the thought of using it on a patient of her own. Nonetheless, the captain's careful answers to all her questions about how to prepare and administer the penicillin made the task ahead seem daunting.

'Our people will radio ahead to make sure that all the necessary equipment is available,' he said. 'That way you need carry only what we know they're unable to provide. We don't want to weigh you down too much.'

'No,' she agreed, trying not to think too hard about the proliferating challenges of her mission.

'I wish we could give you the stuff the Americans are producing,' he said. 'They're using a slightly different compound, and a couple of their companies have been able to supply the drug more reliably and in bigger quantities. They had excellent results during the Normandy landings last month. But they're commercial companies so are keeping a pretty close eye on their patents. They'll be worth a fortune after the war.'

'I can understand keeping such an asset out of the hands of the Germans,' Freya said, 'but maybe they won't want to risk their valuable work falling into the hands of the Soviets, either.'

'That may be true of the Yanks,' he said, 'but not us. Florey was in Moscow earlier this year sharing his knowledge with our Russian allies, so you don't need to worry about that.'

There was something about the idealism of medical science

that gave Freya heart, reminding her that they were, after all, fighting this war for more than mere physical survival.

The captain took back the secret file and assured her that he personally would oversee the preparation of the ampoules she would take with her – wherever she was going. With a warm smile, he held out his hand.

'I don't know any other details of your mission,' he said, pumping her hand, 'but good luck. The very best of luck.'

Late that afternoon, after another interview with Major P, Freya boarded a packed train at Euston bound for Manchester where she was to be given parachute training. The major had handed her a ticket and told her she'd be picked up at Wilmslow station. Sure enough, a young woman in the uniform of the First Aid Nursing Yeomanry was looking out for her. She insisted on carrying Freya's suitcase, but did not introduce herself, something Freya was getting used to. As she followed her driver to the car, she noticed that no one paid them the least attention; indeed, so studiously did no one look in their direction that she assumed local people must have accustomed themselves never to be curious about the mysterious arrivals and departures from this small Cheshire station.

Dusk was falling when, after a silent journey of barely ten minutes, the car drew up on the gravel in front of a venerable house of sandstone and red brick with large bay windows. Inside, it was obvious from the sparse furnishing and utilitarian lighting that it was no longer a private home. Glancing into a dining room that reminded her of school, Freya saw two long tables set with a couple of dozen places – more than she had expected. She must have missed dinner and regretfully assumed the tables had been prepared for breakfast.

The FANY led the way up the wide uncarpeted stairs, explaining that no other female 'specials' were in residence at the moment so Freya would have a room to herself. It was cavernous, with three single beds and a tall window shrouded by faded chintz curtains.

'Breakfast's at seven sharp,' the FANY told her. 'You'll be in the Blue Group with the other beginners. The first two days' training will be on the equipment here. If you complete that satisfactorily, you'll go to the RAF aerodrome at Ringway where you'll do a real drop from a Whitley over Tatton Park.'

'Only one?'

'If you were here for longer, you'd do more.'

The look the young woman gave her was both tactful and sympathetic. Freya guessed that she, too, was aware of the grim statistics Major P had given her, and knew just how many of the 'specials' she delivered here from the station would not enjoy long lives. Little wonder she chose to maintain a respectful distance.

After checking that Freya had everything she required, the FANY left, closing the door behind her. Freya felt grubby after her journey and was pleased to find that there was an adjoining bathroom – perhaps the reason why this room had been allocated to female agents.

She washed her hands and face and was unpacking her case in search of her comb when she heard a high, harsh cry outside the window. It came again, almost a scream, as if someone was calling desperately for help. Turning off the light, she rushed to look out from between the blackout curtains. The sound came again as her heart thudded against her ribs. Then, as her eyes adjusted to the gloaming, she made out the elongated form of a peacock perched on the back of a wooden bench in the garden below, its tail feathers reaching almost to the ground.

She laughed in relief, shaking her head at how easily she'd been unnerved. Pulling the curtains tight again, she steered her way back across the room. As she felt for the light switch beside the door she knocked her elbow painfully on the corner of a chest of drawers and, for a moment, wanted to cry. If she could be scared by a bird, and in tears thanks to a bumped elbow, all because she was tired and hungry and had no idea what she thought she was doing here, what possible use was she going to be behind enemy lines?

She longed for Shona to walk in and climb into one of the other empty beds so that they could fall asleep chatting in the darkness as they had in childhood. Together, each of them could be twice as brave.

But Shona was the one person to whom she could now betray no fear. If something bad were to happen, her sister must never be allowed to feel responsible.

Freya's resolve on her sister's behalf renewed her courage, and she finished unpacking, put on her nightdress, brushed her teeth and slipped into one of the beds. The springs sagged in the middle and the bedstead rocked when she turned over, but the sheets were cool and smelt fresh, and the pillows were just the right degree of softness. It was early – barely ten o'clock – but she lay quietly, determined to clear her mind before she slept.

*

Freya woke to the sound of footsteps clattering down the stairs. Looking at her watch on the bedside table, she saw it was almost seven o'clock. She leapt up, had a quick wash, scrambled into her clothes – she had been instructed to bring trousers – and ran downstairs.

The panelled dining room was already full of people, all of them men. The babble of voices included snatches of European languages that she couldn't even identify. She took the nearest seat at the end of a table only to be informed in heavily accented English by a slightly older man with flashing dark eyes that she had to help herself from the dishes lined up on another table at the far end of the room.

She walked between the lines of chairs, trying to ignore those who looked her up and down as she passed so openly – and approvingly – that she made a mental note to lock her door at night. Picking up the scent of real coffee, she went to investigate.

'Here, let me help you.'

She looked around. 'Leo!'

He held a finger to his lips. 'Field names only.'

'Of course. Sorry. But what on earth are you doing here?'

He grinned. 'Didn't Major P tell you? I'm to be your chaperone.'

'Do I need one?'

'Well, you may be glad of one once we reach our destination.'

'Our destination?' she repeated, and immediately felt stupid. Their destination. It was real, and coming closer.

15

Kirsty, 1989

One of the envelopes lying on the mat when I get home from work is for me and bears the logo of General Register House in Edinburgh. I pick it up gingerly and leave it unopened on the hall shelf, along with a letter addressed to Martin in his mother's handwriting. I hang up my coat and go downstairs to the kitchen. I finish teaching at three on a Friday but, on the first day of December, it's almost dark already. I turn on lights and the heating and fill the kettle. Chris and Eric, who have after-school activities, won't be home for at least half an hour and I'm glad of a little time to myself.

Chris has been angry and miserable all week. He insists he's not going to leave London. At first, convinced that I have no more desire to emigrate than he does, he expected me to champion him but then, realizing that I simply can't make up my mind, his anger turned to contempt. Neither of my children has ever looked at me like that before and it was awful. Poor Eric has been anxious, constantly making sure that everyone is OK, ready to go along with the consensus. We can't let it hang in the air much longer. Another week or so and Martin will have to give the university his answer.

I spoon some tea into the pot, wishing I could simply embrace this chance of a new beginning and use my conviction to enthuse the boys. Nothing really stands against it. Or won't, once Mum's illness reaches its inevitable conclusion.

Of course, I know what the envelope I left upstairs contains: it's the copy I'd ordered of Shona's death certificate. I hadn't expected it to arrive so soon, and I'm no longer sure I'm ready for any more revelations. The kettle boils and I fill the pot, telling myself I'll go and fetch it once I've warmed up.

I think about Mum's sewing tin. It proves that she does want me to find out what happened, but perhaps Archie is right and I shouldn't be stirring up the past, uncovering information that could upset her when she needs calm. After all, none of us is responsible for Tomasz or the mysteries in his family.

I pour some tea and sit with my hands around the warmth of the mug. As I stare at my reflection in the black glass of the windows overlooking the garden, I hear the front door bang shut and a few moments later Martin comes into the kitchen.

'Meeting was cancelled so I came home early,' he says, kissing me. He's been extra attentive all week, not only cooking supper two nights running but also washing up afterwards. He's carrying the post. 'That tea still hot?'

'Yes.' I fetch him a mug as he tries surreptitiously to pocket his mother's letter.

'What's this?' He holds out the envelope from Edinburgh.

'A copy of my aunt Shona's death certificate,' I say, avoiding his gaze as I pour his tea.

'Ah, right. How are you getting on with all that? Has your friend Tomasz found out anything new?'

'Not really.'

Martin sits down on the other side of the table and leans over to place the letter in front of me. 'Aren't you going to open it?'

I don't want to, but I also don't want to create unnecessary drama. I tear open the envelope. The handwriting on the official form inside is cramped and hard to decipher but, when I do, my reluctance is justified. 'She drowned,' I say, shocked.

Martin frowns. 'I don't remember ever hearing that.'

'No. And I certainly wouldn't forget Mum telling me that.'

'Does it give any detail?'

I peer at the old-fashioned script. 'Accidental drowning in river ... something. I can't make out the name. Date and time of death unknown.'

'Which would suggest that her body wasn't found immediately.'

'The informant is a medical superintendent, presumably of the mental hospital where Mum said she was a patient.'

'Well, they can't have taken very good care of her if she could wander off and drown in a river. Unless, of course ...'

'What?'

'It could have been suicide.'

More secrets? Is her death connected to her war work? Would Freya be able to explain if she could speak? I drop the piece of paper on the table. 'It would say if it was suicide, wouldn't it?' I ask.

Martin reaches over and picks it up. 'February in Scotland,' he observes, scanning the form, 'especially in that terrible winter of nineteen forty-seven. If the water was freezing, it would have been very quick.'

I remember Mum always mentioning the bitter cold as if it had contributed to whatever illness Shona died of. But she didn't die of a physical illness. She drowned.

'It could have been an accident,' he continues sympathetically. 'Do you know why she'd been hospitalized?'

'Some kind of breakdown.'

I hold out my hand to take back the certificate to see if I can decipher the name of the river but the old-fashioned penmanship defeats me. It reminds me of Freya's distress at trying to speak and suddenly, instead of resenting the way she's distanced herself all these years, I feel desperately sad for her. And angry with myself for being too immature to understand that there might have been good reasons for her silences.

'Hey, Kirsty,' says Martin. 'Are you all right?'

I shake my head.

He comes around the table and sits in the chair beside me. 'This stuff is getting to you, isn't it?'

'I feel like I've lived my life from the wrong end of a telescope. It's all back to front – who I am, who my mother is. What I thought mattered turns out not to be important after all.'

He puts an arm around my shoulders and draws me to him. I bury my face in his sweater. 'Maybe you should just drop it.'

I pull back. 'I can't. I'm starting to get glimpses of why Freya's always been so unreachable. I always thought it was my fault, but maybe it's about the past, before I was even born. Don't you see? I need to know more. Otherwise how can I know what I want or work out how to decide about the future?'

I can see the disappointment in his eyes. He must have assumed from my silence this week that our moving to Sydney was settled. I experience a flare of fear that he really is resigned to go anyway, with or without me. I feel the past crowding in on the present, dreading that my children might have to deal with what my father did to Archie and me. Nick couldn't wait to skip off to California and made no secret of how eager he was for a fresh start, with or without his family.

Finding out what happened to Shona, understanding why my mother has always felt so emotionally absent and whether that contributed to Dad leaving us, feels like the key to everything.

16

Freya, 1944

The frequent stops on the way back to London made the train journey seem interminable. Freya's cotton dress was thin and the coarse fabric of the seat scratched her bare legs. She was desperate to ease her shoulder where she'd wrenched it attempting to launch herself from one of the bizarre Heath Robinson contraptions designed for initial parachute training, but the carriage was so packed that there was no room to move.

The three-day course had been challenging, sometimes amusing and, finally, terrifying. It had been the first time she'd ever flown in an aircraft, but it had felt like she'd barely recovered from the sensation of take-off when their trainer, a wry and sarcastic RAF sergeant, had instructed her to jump out again. She guessed that he'd selected her to drop first because none of the men would want to be seen hanging back after a woman had made the leap. And in fact, once her immediate and visceral panic had abated and the expanse of silk blossoming above her had slowed her descent into Tatton Park, she had even experienced a few moments of intense joy before remembering to pin her legs together and bend her knees in time to hit the ground, which had suddenly come up at her very fast.

Leo had been the next to land, executing a neat roll. As soon as he'd released the parachute straps, and unzipped and shed his cumbersome jumpsuit, he'd run across the grass to where she stood, laughing with exhilaration and pride that she'd actually jumped, and survived!

'Next time we land it will be on Polish soil!' he'd said, with shining eyes.

Now he was tucked into the window seat opposite, drumming his long fingers on his thigh, fretting and impatient to get back to London to hear the latest news. Had he always been such a restless soul, or had the war made him so?

She'd been dismayed on first discovering that Leo had been appointed by Major P to accompany her, feeling she'd far rather rely on a stranger than on someone with whom she already had a tenuous yet complicated bond. However, over warm beers on their second evening, he'd explained that he hadn't undertaken the mission only to support her but also as an envoy of the Government-in-Exile in London, and that he'd have business of his own to conduct in Warsaw.

It hadn't taken her long to decide that she liked Leo. In spite of Shona's sensitivity to his feelings, he wasn't the soulful type her sister had attracted at university; he seemed far more rational and straightforwardly good-natured, and had revealed a streak of sharp wit. His only weakness, witnessed after dinner one night, was how swiftly his uncompromising devotion to his country's cause could usurp both his humour and his good sense. Misinterpreting an off-hand remark from a Yugoslav partisan about Stalin, Leo had nearly started a fight. Everyone was tired after a day's training, and a bit drunk, but it hadn't been easy to get him to see reason and back down.

She studied his face, the way he sat with his legs crossed, jiggling one foot, and tried to see the attraction Shona felt and she didn't – and then, embarrassed, withdrew her gaze as if he might be capable of sensing her speculations.

She couldn't help wondering what he saw when he looked at his lover's identical twin. Or didn't see. Were she and Shona unalike in ways she hadn't considered before? Did she, Freya, lack sex appeal?

Along with two other 'specials' she and Leo had spent the last three days helping each other do up and undo the various buckles and straps of their harnesses – something he was slow to get the hang of – and jostled and pushed each other as they practised repeated jumps from different types of rigging, landing on coconut matting that scraped the skin off their hands and knees even through gloves and jumpsuits. Without Leo's friendly but firm hand in the small of her back, Freya might have been too frozen with nerves ever to get off the little bus that had transported them to RAF Ringway for their first real drop. She was glad that they'd established such a comradely physical rapport, but was it proof that, unlike her identical twin, she was too 'jolly hockey sticks' to incite passion in a man?

Leo must have been making his own assessment of her over the past few days, ensuring she was up to the job. She was relieved that he hadn't asked why she was doing this, as she couldn't really explain. She hoped he didn't think she was a little fool who had bitten off more than she could chew.

She strongly suspected he hadn't yet broken it to Shona that he was going. She had initially been comforted to think he'd be there to console Shona if anything happened to her, but now, knowing how Shona already believed herself responsible for placing Freya in danger, she worried that, once her sister realized she risked losing Leo, too, her guilt and anxiety might overwhelm her.

Her suspicion was confirmed when they finally arrived at Euston and found Shona, in uniform, at the ticket barrier looking out for them. Almost ignoring Freya, she ran to Leo, her gloved hands on his chest.

'Why didn't you tell me?' she cried. 'Why does it have to be you?'

Leo gently removed her hands, holding them tight in his own as if to calm her. 'I couldn't let you send your sister and not offer my protection.'

'She didn't send me,' Freya objected. 'It was my decision. She told me not to go.'

'Have you got a car?' he asked.

'Yes,' said Shona. 'Major P sent me to pick you both up. That's how I found out. He assumed I knew.'

'Good,' said Leo. 'Then let's go.'

Buffeted by other passengers, he ushered them before him and kept them moving at a fast pace out through the station to where Shona had left the official car. Freya climbed quickly into the back to give them some privacy to talk.

'What's the news?' Leo asked, as Shona started the engine.

'The Soviets are on the banks of the Vistula to the south and are linking up with their forces in the north-east,' she said. 'They're bombarding the city.'

'So the AK will go ahead?'

'They no longer have any choice.' Shona pulled out and turned onto the main road. 'The AK has been supporting the Soviet advance in the East, as you know, but now we're receiving reports of AK officers being arrested, or even shot, by the NKVD.'

'So the Allies will have to show support for an uprising!'

Shona shook her head, gripping the steering wheel. 'Stalin has already threatened that, if the Allies push him too far over Poland, he'll make a separate peace with Hitler. The British can't jeopardize his cooperation at this stage. We'll continue to do everything we can covertly, but there will be no official statement of support.'

Leo turned his head to look out of the car window, his silence far more eloquent than the burst of anger Freya had witnessed in the mess the other night.

'And my patient?' she ventured after a moment, leaning forward over the front seat.

'No better,' said Shona. 'You'll be taken to Gibraltar Farm first thing tomorrow.'

'Gibraltar Farm?'

'For the flight to Brindisi.'

Freya swallowed, although her mouth felt dry. She'd always known that speed was essential, but now she felt the ground suddenly rushing up to meet her, just as it had in Tatton Park.

'It'll be an early start so you should stay with me tonight,' Shona added, turning left into Baker Street.

'But I need to go back and pack my things.'

'Doesn't matter, you won't need them. You won't be allowed to take anything of your own with you, anyway.'

Freya sat back, staring blindly ahead at the ribbed leather of the seat in front. This is how soldiers must feel, she told herself. Nothing personal counts any more. Only name, rank and serial number, except she wouldn't even have the protection of that. There could be no negotiation. She was here to do a job and not let anyone down. What happened next was no longer her responsibility. That last thought felt oddly liberating.

Shona pulled over to park outside the Inter-Services Research Bureau. As she drew up the handbrake Leo reached out and covered her hand with his. Neither of them spoke, or even looked directly at each other, yet, for a moment, the atmosphere in the car shifted, becoming dense and charged.

Not wanting to comprehend too fully – to do so would be an intrusion – Freya gave in to an impulse she didn't stop to question. 'Would you mind if I don't stay with you tonight?' she asked. 'Don't worry, I won't go back to the infirmary. I'll stay in town.'

'Where?'

'I'll ask Patty Drexeler if she can put me up for the night. I don't think she'd mind, do you?'

'Patty?'

'Yes. I needn't say why, obviously.'

'You've only met her once!'

'Patty's a good sport,' Leo said, turning to smile at Freya in the back seat. 'I bet she'd love to be asked.'

Freya was sure he guessed her reasons, for he pressed Shona's hand again. 'And she'll provide plenty of distraction,' he assured her. 'Might be no bad thing.'

Shona wavered and then, obeying Leo's look of encouragement, gave in. 'Well, just don't drink too much,' she said, aiming for a lightness of tone she clearly didn't feel. 'Patty always tops up your glass when you're not looking.'

'And don't be fooled by that Southern belle accent,' Leo added. 'I was told she went to all the best schools.'

Freya felt a bittersweet relief at their compliance. Even though, more than anything, she wanted to spend her last few hours with Shona, she knew that this precious time now belonged to Leo.

17

Other than a sign at the turning into an anonymous lane that read 'This road is closed to the Public', Gibraltar Farm looked to Freya like little more than a collection of old agricultural buildings haphazardly placed around an undistinguished flat-fronted brick house. As they drew up outside the farmhouse, however, she became aware of a hum of activity around a row of Nissen huts beyond the larger of the barns that didn't look like it had anything to do with farm work.

She was glad to climb out of the car and stretch her cramped limbs. There hadn't been much legroom in the back and, even with the windows wound down, as they'd driven north out of London and the sun had risen higher in a cloudless sky, the car had become hot and stuffy. And, although she'd rather not admit it, and in spite of Shona's warning not to drink too much, she did have just the tiniest of hangovers from the previous evening, enough anyway to feel a little queasy on the journey.

Patty Drexeler hadn't evinced the slightest surprise when Freya had telephoned from the Baker Street offices to beg a bed for the night. After Shona and Leo had dropped her off in Mayfair, waving familiarly at the butler from the car, her hostess had led her straight up to the most glamorous bedroom Freya had ever seen and made sure she had all she required, then instructed a maid to run her guest a bath before dinner.

Patty had warned Freya that she had some friends over and, when Freya emerged later from the fragrant, and very welcome, regulation five inches of hot water – even Patty, she was glad to see, stuck to the rules – she found a fresh gown thoughtfully laid out for her on the glossy eiderdown. The claret-coloured silk looked plain and simple but, once she'd slipped it over her head and fastened the buttons, she appreciated that its fabric and cut were anything but. She had only her own sensible shoes to wear with it, yet even so, the dress made her feel like the proverbial million dollars. Smiling at the Cézanne beside the drawing-room door, she'd happily entered a room full of people and accepted her first champagne cocktail of the evening from a laughing young naval officer.

In any case, Freya thought now as she took from the boot the canvas bag containing the box of thirty-six glass ampoules of penicillin, this morning's headache was a small price to pay for the tenderness she'd observed this morning between Leo and Shona. All three of them were anxious and apprehensive, yet Shona seemed to possess an underlying calm she had lacked the previous day. Freya, who had yet to sleep with a man, couldn't fully apprehend their intimacy, but the glow of Shona's quiet joy was unmistakable.

She also had to acknowledge ruefully that it marked yet another difference in experience to set them further apart. She'd thought that, with Shona five hundred miles away in London while she'd remained in Aberdeen, she'd already achieved a natural separation, but this felt different, and was nothing like her indulgent childhood fantasies of being an only child. Instead she felt left behind and bereft.

The farmhouse door opened and a thin woman in FANY uniform with cropped sandy hair and wire-framed glasses appeared on the step. Her smile was warm and open.

'Come in,' she said. 'You've made good time. We're all ready for you, but you'd probably like a cup of tea before we get started.'

A male figure was disappearing up the stairs as the FANY led the way into the dim hall and down three steps into a large kitchen at the back. Diamond-paned windows looked out onto flat fields. Freya could hear voices and footsteps from other parts of the house, confirming they were not the only ones there.

'That needs to go in the refrigerator, I believe,' the FANY said, with a nod to Freya's canvas bag. 'It's over here. I've cleared space ready for it.'

The evidence of such meticulous planning was reassuring, and Freya was relieved to slip the box out of the bag and onto the empty shelf.

'Sit yourselves down,' said the FANY. 'Kettle won't take long to boil.'

It stood ready on the blackened range, and there was a row of thick white NAAFI mugs on the wooden draining-board beside the cracked sink. Nothing was new but the room was spotless, and a jam-jar filled with hedgerow flowers sat in the middle of the bleached-pine table. Freya caught Shona's eye, knowing that the pale, delicate dog roses at the centre of the bunch would also remind her of home. Shona's face tightened with distress, but Freya held her gaze – *stay steady* – and the moment passed.

The strong tea, with sweet Digestives from a wooden biscuit barrel, was a welcome pick-me-up. Freya, Shona and Leo had little to say – or little that could be said – and the FANY, busying herself with kitchen tasks, seemed content not to fill the silence. However, once she had whisked the empty mugs into the sink, she sat down and placed a box file on the table in front of her.

'Perhaps we should begin,' she said. 'Have you your letters?'

Primed by Major P, Freya had written hers one evening in her room in the big house in Cheshire: one for her parents and one for Shona. Each had taken several attempts and, in the end, she'd kept them brief and been almost glad not to have anyone else to consider. What was there to say other than that she was thankful for their love and that she loved them? Most of all she wanted to absolve Shona of blame, but she knew, whatever she wrote, that it would make little difference in the event that Shona had to read her words.

She passed the two envelopes to the FANY without looking at her sister. As Leo handed over his, Shona gulped back a sob, rose quickly and went to the sink, standing with her back to them as she ran the tap to rinse out the mugs.

'Thank you,' said the FANY, matter-of-factly, putting them into a Manila envelope, which she placed in the box. 'They will be filed and, if not required, given back to you on your return.'

Freya marvelled at her calm, and wondered how many times she'd had to do this. And how many letters had not been given back.

The FANY twisted in her chair to speak to Shona. 'There's not much to see outside, Junior Commander Grant, but perhaps you'd like a little fresh air.'

'Yes, of course.' Shona picked up her cap and hurried out.

The FANY turned back to Freya and Leo. 'Are there any debts or obligations you want to make us aware of? Any special instructions you'd like carried out if you don't come back? If either of you would rather speak privately, we can do this later.'

'I have some bar bills,' said Leo. 'I'll write them down for you.'

'Good. I'll take each of you to the clothing store in a moment, so that leaves just one more piece of business for you, Mr Tarnowski.'

The FANY took another thick brown envelope out of the box, its contents bulky and rectangular, along with a sheet of paper that she pushed across to Leo.

'If you could please sign this to confirm receipt.'

Leo scanned the typed form. His eyebrows shot up in surprise and he looked across at the FANY, who nodded.

'They're złoty,' she confirmed. 'A substantial sum. You're to give them to the Home Army in Warsaw. The precise instructions are inside.'

Leo took a fountain pen out of his jacket pocket, signed the paper with a flourish and handed it back. 'I've never been so rich!'

The FANY smiled drily as she waved the paper to let the ink dry, then filed it before handing over the bundle of Polish banknotes.

'Thank you,' he said. 'And thanks to whoever authorized this.'

'We hope that a larger sum in gold can be dropped by parachute.' She stood up. 'Time for you to get dressed, I think.'

Shona spotted them walking across the yard to the clothing store in one of the outhouses and came to join them. She fussed over the selection of outfits and appropriate possessions for each of them, making sure that everything fitted and looked convincing. Freya was impressed by the meticulous attention to detail: nothing could be new, and every label and laundry mark, even the basic toiletries and the contents of the handbag she was given, right down to the half-used lipstick, had to be authentically Polish so that, 'on the other side', nothing could give her away. The FANY also impressed on them the importance of not sharing personal information with anyone, as it could be used against them if they were captured.

The process took far longer than she expected yet, when it was finally done, and their own clothes and possessions had been folded away, there were still several hours to wait. They were offered a meal for which they had little appetite. The pilot came to introduce himself and explain that they were still busy loading supplies into the Halifax that waited beyond the farm buildings but he planned to take off as soon as it was dark. Otherwise the time crawled by with agonizing slowness and none of them knew what to talk about.

Less than a month ago, leaving home and becoming a doctor in a new city had been the biggest challenge Freya had ever faced, but now she felt as if her life was accelerating at breakneck speed and taking her in a direction she couldn't possibly have imagined only a few days earlier. Wearing unfamiliar clothes only heightened her sense that she'd somehow wandered into someone else's life. Knowing that it was far too late to change her mind didn't stop her struggling against the urge to run to the car and escape, if only to prevent Shona having to drive back to London tonight without them.

As they tried to pass the time by playing gin rummy with cards the FANY provided, Shona kept interrupting to check and re-check every garment and item, asking repeatedly if Freya and Leo were both absolutely certain they'd not kept anything of their own that could betray them. Freya submitted patiently to her sister's anxiety, knowing it would be cruel to point out that it would hardly matter anyway since, the instant she had to respond to an order or question in Polish, for her the game would be up.

Looking at the cards in her hand, she tried not to think about the worst moment of all, which had been in the clothing store when her own belongings were being put away. She'd impetuously plucked back her favourite silk scarf and given it to Shona, who had always liked it.

'I'll want it back,' Freya had said, with an attempt at a laugh.

Shona's response had been to hug her. Their twinship had always made physical contact seem superfluous, and they seldom embraced. As Freya pulled her sister close she could feel the bones of her shoulder blades. They felt breakable, like those of a small bird, and it was Shona's fragility, not her own, that had plummeted her to new depths of fear.

18

Phyllis Levenson is Freya's oldest friend and my unofficial god-mother. We've been in fairly regular touch since Mum's diagnosis. She's been a huge help, mainly because, remarkably, Freya seldom argues with her advice. But it's years since I've been to her flat, and visiting without Mum, especially on a Saturday afternoon, takes me back to being an awkward teenager. I'm surprised by how clearly I remember these square, solid rooms on the third floor of a red-brick mansion block in Maida Vale. Although the parquet floor has all but disappeared beneath piles of books, journals and papers, and the curtains are faded ghosts of the original colourful sixties fabric, I have no doubt that Phyllis remains the same diligent and attentive woman I've always known.

She has the same soft skin and tightly curled grey hair but there are now even deeper lines at the corners of her eyes. Even after forty years in London she still speaks with a slight Manchester accent. She welcomes me warmly, offers coffee, which I decline, and shifts some files to make room for me to sit on the couch. I notice that her sagging armchair has a book wedged beneath one corner to replace a missing foot.

'How's Freya?' she asks.

'I'm afraid I've been upsetting her.'

Phyllis's mild gaze doesn't alter in any way. She retired from general practice a couple of years ago but retains her professional imperturbability. I can't imagine her being shocked or judgemental about anything.

'So what's happened?' she asks.

I fill her in as briefly as I can: Tomasz's visit, Freya showing me the chocolate tin, Archie's warning that it could be meaningless, and yesterday's shock discovery that Shona drowned in an icy Scottish river. When I first mention Warsaw she leans forward, her gaze keen, but remains silent until I reach the end of my story. She nods thoughtfully, and I ask her how much of it she already knows.

'Only that Shona drowned,' she says. 'I didn't meet your mother until the summer of nineteen forty-five. And I don't think I met Shona more than once, although I remember how excited she was about planning her wedding.'

'Her wedding?'

'Yes. That was what led to her breakdown,' says Phyllis. 'You didn't know?'

'No. Who did she marry?'

'I never met him. But they didn't marry. That was the problem. It was all called off, right at the last moment.'

'What?' I'm even more astounded. 'How? Why?'

'I'm afraid I don't know. I assume he changed his mind.'

'Was her fiancé Polish? I heard she might have had a Polish boyfriend during the war.'

'I've no idea. He may have been. It was a long time ago.'

I remind myself that there may be absolutely no connection between Shona's wartime exploits and her broken heart.

'So what did she do after her wedding was called off?'

'She went home to her parents,' Phyllis says. 'It was a terrible thing in those days to be jilted by a man, and this was virtually at the altar. She had a nervous breakdown and had to be hospitalized. But I'd be fascinated to know what on earth you think Shona was doing in Warsaw.'

'We may never find out. All the records are sealed and the only person who could tell us can't communicate.' My voice breaks and I take a deep breath.

'Secrets were deadly serious in those days,' Phyllis says, allowing me a chance to recover. 'You didn't ask and certainly didn't expect to be told. There must be so many people who still aren't allowed to talk about what they did in the war. Especially women. But what's rather interesting is that I remember one of the symptoms that Shona's psychiatrist interpreted as grandiose delusions and paranoia was her insistence that she was involved in secret war work and that it was Joseph Stalin who had put a stop to her marriage.'

I'm amazed. 'What did Freya say about that?'

Phyllis looks down at her hands. 'Shona was dead by the time I learnt that,' she continues, with uncharacteristic hesitancy. 'Freya wouldn't talk about it. And it's quite common for schizophrenics to hear famous people talking to them, often threateningly.'

I think about how easily Archie used his medical knowledge to dismiss the significance of the chocolate tin. 'Do you think she killed herself?'

'Who can say? In any case, the authorities would have bent over backwards to avoid a verdict of suicide if they possibly could. Why saddle a family with that? Attempted suicide was a crime back then, certainly against God, and the stigma around mental illness was so much worse.'

'And my mother?'

'As I say, she never wanted to talk about it, so I didn't ask. But she was absolutely devastated. She blamed herself. It must be so much harder for a twin, don't you think? She never really recovered. I think it was probably the most significant loss in her life.'

Phyllis falls silent. I watch her for a moment, dying to know what else she's thinking, then take another look around the room as if it might give me a clue to what's in her mind. She never married or had much family around her, but has always given the impression of a life well lived. She and my mother were colleagues as well as friends. Whenever they're together, their affection and mutual respect are obvious. Yet she says they never spoke about Shona's death. A little devil on my shoulder rejoices that it's not just me who has been shut out.

'What was Mum like before her sister died?' I ask.

Phyllis looks surprised by my question and considers her answer before speaking. 'No less fearless than she is now. But afterwards she lost her spark, her brightness. She became more guarded and careful. Also . . .'

'What?' I ask. It's really not like Phyllis to hold back.

'I had the idea that Freya had liked him, the man Shona was

supposed to marry. She tried to find him, to tell him Shona had died, but no one knew where he was. I had a sense she saw it as a kind of double tragedy. The terrible burden of Shona's death was made worse, I think, because she felt a real ambivalence at the heart of it all. And she felt responsible for what happened at the end.'

'How?'

'She tried to help but then believed she'd only made things worse.'

'And now I've gone barging in and reopened old wounds.'

'It's not your fault this Polish chap has turned up out of the blue with a photograph of Shona,' Phyllis says. 'How could you not be curious?'

'And the name Wedel means nothing to you? Mum never showed you the tin?'

'No, sorry.'

'If it is significant, then why? And what does she expect me to do with it?'

'It's extraordinary, isn't it,' she says, 'to begin to see the unseen strings that steer people's lives? How even historic events can become so muddled and disguised that they disappear from the record, making it impossible for the archaeologists who come afterwards to make sense of what remains.'

Except, I think, I'm not dealing with ancient and abandoned ruins. My mother is still alive.

'Of course,' Phyllis goes on, 'if Shona hadn't died, Freya would never have married your father. But she was almost mad with grief, and he offered comfort, I suppose. They got married right away and, when Nick finished his national service and they came back from Berlin, she and I set up the clinic. But you know all this.'

'I remember her talking about Berlin, and how she found a strange kind of beauty in the miles of shattered streets. I never understood what she meant.'

'It must have echoed how she was feeling.' Phyllis looks down at her hands again. 'I'm afraid it's a harsh thing to say, but I assume you've already realized that their marriage was a mistake from the start. Apart from you and Archie, of course,' she adds hurriedly.

'They were always such different people,' I agree. 'But if she was seeking shelter from the storm, then maybe their marriage does make sense.'

Phyllis frowns, hesitant once again. 'There is one other person who might know what happened.'

I stiffen. 'You mean Patty.'

'She's still alive, you know.'

'Yes. Are you in touch?'

The pioneering clinic that Phyllis and Freya set up together was entirely funded by some tiny fraction of the Drexeler fortune. After the divorce, and after Patty had returned to America, Phyllis stayed on alone to oversee the centre's transition to a self-governing trust that would administer the lump-sum gift Patty had donated before she left. I remind myself that, apart from loyalty to Freya, Phyllis has no reason to dislike the woman.

'No,' she says. 'But I see a couple of the trustees from time to time and they mention her occasionally. She lives in New York now. All I'm saying is that, if you really want to get to the bottom of this story, it might be worth talking to her.'

I can't imagine doing such a thing. Over the years Patty Drexeler has become like the bad fairy in an old folk tale, a mythic figure of capricious and dangerous power. Invoking her presence and attention would be at my own peril.

'You'll think this is strange,' Phyllis continued, 'and I certainly don't make any excuses for Patty's betrayal, but she adored your mother.'

'That didn't stop her sleeping with my father.'

'No, although that had started long before. It was Patty who encouraged Nick to marry her.'

'And you want me to talk to this woman?'

'She was anorexic, you know. Not that anyone understood back then that it was an illness, let alone such a serious one, and you'd have been too young to notice anyway. Her childhood was so dreadfully emotionally deprived. Her parents died of the Spanish flu when she was eight. She was pretty much raised by her grandparents' staff on their estate in Virginia.'

'Poor little rich girl.'

'I think she did her best. It's all any of us can do.'

'What's your advice?' I ask. 'Am I being selfish, raking up the past when Mum's in no condition to deal with the consequences?'

'Take your lead from her,' says Phyllis, pushing herself up from her chair and signalling that it's time for me to go. 'People have a right to keep secrets if they choose to, but she'll let you know soon enough if you've gone too far.'

'That's true.' I laugh and follow her out of the room.

In the hall, she helps me on with my coat and opens the flat door. 'Something one learns as a GP,' she says, 'is that piecing together incomplete fragments of a story can sometimes be far more inaccurate than knowing nothing at all.'

'I'll remember that, thank you.'

'And, Kirsty?'

I turn back.

'She does love you.'

I manage not to cry until I'm in the car.

I have the house to myself when I get home. Martin has taken the boys to a matinee of the *Back to the Future* sequel. I go straight to the drawer where I stashed Shona's death certificate. I know it's not going to tell me anything new, but it's the only tangible link I have to her. I feel like a clairvoyant trying to conjure up a lost spirit.

I've brought the road atlas in from the car and look up Aberdeenshire. The only named rivers are the Dee and the Don, and, with a magnifying glass, I've already worked out that the river in which Shona's body was found must be *something*-burn. I know the name of the hospital and find a village with the same name on the map. There's no river or stream close by, so what was Shona doing so far from the hospital on a snowy February day? Was she running away, or did she have a more specific purpose?

It's hopeless. I can't expect to shake a piece of paper and have the past fall out into my lap. Perhaps Archie will remember something I don't.

He picks up quite quickly. 'Mum OK?' he asks, when he hears my voice.

'I haven't seen her since we last spoke. But I've found out a bit more about Shona. I ordered a copy of her death certificate which arrived yesterday. Did you know she drowned?'

'What? No. How?'

'In a river in the middle of winter. It must have been some way from the hospital because I can't find any river nearby on a map.'

'Poor thing. Mind you, the treatments available for depression in those days could be pretty barbaric. I dare say hospitalization wasn't much fun.'

'Did you know she'd been due to get married?'

'No. How did you find that out?'

'I went to see Phyllis this morning. She said Shona cracked up because the wedding was called off virtually at the last minute.'

'What bastard did that to her?'

'Phyllis didn't know. She only ever met Shona once and Freya wouldn't talk about it.'

'No change there, then.'

'You can't remember anything about who she might have been engaged to?'

'No. And, frankly, he doesn't sound like someone Mum would ever want to see again. I mean, would you?'

'No,' I concede. 'Except that he may have been Polish. In which case his identity might shed some light on why she went to Warsaw.'

'I don't see how we'd ever find that out. Not now.'

'You're seeing Mum tomorrow?'

'Yes, and before you ask, I'm not going to start badgering her about how Shona died. What was the cause of death given on the certificate? Was it suicide?'

'Accidental death.'

'They never put suicide unless they have to. Anyway, time to let this drop, don't you think? Mum's not well. Don't stir up past tragedies.'

'She gave me the sewing tin. Which does come from Warsaw. Wedel's was a famous chocolate shop. I think she wants us to find out the truth.'

'Let me see how she is tomorrow.'

I decide to risk it. 'Phyllis did have one other suggestion,' I say.

'What?'

'She said Patty might know what happened.'

'Don't you dare! I mean it, Kirsty. If you do that, I'll never speak to you again.'

The speed of his anger lands like a punch, and I retaliate. 'You weren't there, Archie. You didn't see Mum. She's already upset. And you're the one who said it might comfort her to know that we've learnt more about her twin.'

'She could have told us any time in the last thirty years. She didn't. That's good enough for me.'

'Maybe we merely didn't ask,' I say. 'And now she wants us to.'

'Drop it, Kirsty. And don't even think about contacting Patty.'

'Why not? What harm can it do just to ask her a few questions?'

'After she destroyed our family? Mum would never forgive you. She almost got Mum struck off, for God's sake!'

'What are you talking about? Mum was never going to be struck off.'

'Oh, forget it. Just leave Patty out of it, OK? Promise me?'

'Shall we speak another time?'

I hear him take a deep breath.

'That's probably best,' he says. 'I'll do some shopping for Mum tomorrow and let you know how she is.'

'OK. Bye.'

'Bye.'

I have no idea what Archie means about Mum being struck off. No one has ever mentioned that before. But he was barely ten when Mum and Dad divorced and Patty disappeared from our lives. I assume he must have got the wrong end of the stick on something he overheard as a kid.

As I go to make a cup of tea, I realize that, while I've managed to fall out with my brother over the fate of an aunt neither of us had ever met, I still haven't told him about Martin's job offer and the possibility that I and my family might go and live in Australia.

19

Freya, 1944

Stiff after the long flight, Freya clambered out of the plane into blinding white light. It was still early morning yet the air felt astonishingly dry and clear. They had landed at a military airfield inland from Brindisi, which she knew was on the Adriatic coast halfway down the high-heel of the boot of Italy. She had never been abroad before, and was shocked by how completely unprepared she was for her first experience of a southern climate.

Leo helped her up into the jeep that had been sent to ferry them the short distance from the plane to the base. Holding tight to the canvas bag that contained the box of penicillin, she looked around in fascination. This airfield was far busier than the clandestine Gibraltar Farm. During the flight one of the crew had explained that two Special Duties squadrons were based here, providing men and supplies not only to Poland and Czechoslovakia, but also northern Italy, Yugoslavia, Greece and Albania. There was only one airstrip, but she could see at least a dozen other planes, each with attendant vehicles and ground staff.

It was exciting to witness the efficient bustle of war, and the sight boosted her energy. She glanced at Leo beside her, and he grinned back as if feeling the same elation. They were here. It was happening.

They were taken to a large newly constructed hut, fuggy with strong tobacco smoke, where she listened helplessly as Leo enjoyed an animated conversation in Polish with the station commander, a stocky, dark-haired man of about forty. Although Freya could sense the earnestness with which Leo was clearly asking a series of questions, and she found the sounds pleasing, she was unable to pick out individual words or gain any sense of meaning. Shona would no doubt have picked it up in no time. Perhaps she already had – Freya had never thought to ask. She wished now that she shared her sister's ear for languages. It could turn out to be a matter of life or death.

Eventually Leo translated for her. 'It's started! General Bor gave the order to begin the Uprising at five o'clock yesterday afternoon. The crews here have already made one drop of weapons and supplies into the cemeteries in the Wola district.'

'So when do we go?' Freya asked.

'Not yet confirmed. Full moon is on Friday, which is the best time to fly, but it will depend on the meteorological reports from England, which come in at ten every morning. Meanwhile they're putting us up in the local village. He's already been told you have a package that needs to be refrigerated. There's no electricity where we're staying, so he'll store it in a refrigerator here in his office where it can be guarded around the clock.'

Rather reluctantly she handed over the box and watched as the station commander placed it in the empty fridge and fastened the door with a small padlock. Then they climbed back into the jeep and were driven off the base and along narrow dusty roads through parched fields to a village of paved streets and white stucco houses, many with bizarre conical roofs of layered grey stone, like giant beehives. The sun was higher now, and Freya, who had tied back her hair to stop it blowing about in the open vehicle, could feel the heat building on the exposed skin of her neck. Every new detail and sensation was strange and wonderful.

The driver skidded to a stop outside one of the beehive houses and, speaking in Polish to Leo, opened the door and led them inside. It was blessedly cool and larger than it appeared. She looked around curiously at small arched chambers, all of the same cream-coloured stone and plaster and screened off with woven hangings. The room she was allocated was dim – she could barely work out where the light was coming from – and furnished with a single bed and a rush-seated chair. Cavities and niches in the thick walls provided storage space as well as bathroom facilities – a large pottery jug and matching bowl, both patterned in vivid splashes of green and ochre. The driver also pointed out the wooden lidded chamber pot under the bed.

Leo translated once more: 'These houses are called *trulli*. There's a woman who'll come and bring us food. She'll do any laundry we have. But with any luck we'll only be here for one night, or two at most. Anything else you need?'

Freya said no, and the driver saluted and departed.

'He said it's perfectly safe for us to walk around the village,' Leo told her. 'It's a poor area where the Fascists have treated people badly, so the Allied forces are very welcome.'

Once they'd washed and brushed up they went out. Freya was amazed by the contrast between the brilliant white buildings and the deep shade of the side-alleys, from some of which she caught pungent odours of human and animal dung mixed with the scent of carbolic soap from the washing that hung out of the occasional un-shuttered window. Posters or paintings had given her an impression of Italian village life that was brightly coloured, balmy and abundant, and she had not expected such austerity, yet she found the sparseness of the place appealing. The few people they passed were mainly old women. Dressed in black and sitting on chairs in their doorways, they smiled and nodded to the strangers. But soon it became too hot to walk and, with the sweat trickling down their backs, Freya and Leo retraced their steps to the shelter of their peculiar little house.

A woman of about thirty arrived soon afterwards with a basket, and laid out bread, olive oil, soft white cheese and figs on the small table in the main chamber. She communicated with hand gestures, nods and smiles, the beauty of her features marred by broken teeth. The simple and unfamiliar food was delicious and they ate hungrily. Then, exhausted, they retreated to their curtained-off rooms, stripped to their underwear and slept.

Freya awoke a few hours later to the sound of a tolling church bell. It took her a moment to remember where she was. It was still light and she had no idea what hour of Catholic prayers the bell was marking. She lay in the narrow wooden bed, glad of a quiet moment to file away some of the overwhelming experiences of the past twenty-four hours. It still seemed extraordinary that she could have been whisked so effortlessly to such an utterly foreign place. Flying across Europe in so short a time, even in the unheated fuselage of a Halifax, had been like travelling on a magic carpet from one of her childhood storybooks. Except this story, she remembered, as she came fully awake, was in deadly earnest.

She went to lift the heavy jug and pour some water into the bowl. The act of splashing her face and washing the rest of her body as best as she could brought back memories of staying in her grandmother's tiny cottage on the shores of Cluny Loch where she and Shona and half a dozen assorted cousins had camped for so many childhood summers. They had been hand-to-mouth gypsy holidays that, as kids, they'd adored, but really, her grandmother's existence wasn't so different from that of the peasant women she'd seen sitting in their shady doorways along the street. The idea comforted her. Despite the alien landscape and climate, she wasn't so very far from home.

Patting herself dry with the small towel provided, she dressed once more in the trousers and blouse she'd been given at Gibraltar Farm and went to see if Leo was awake.

Through an open door she'd not noticed before, she found him sitting on a low wall in a stone courtyard at the back of the house. In the otherwise motionless air, bees hummed around pots of sharp-scented herbs, only some of which she could name. The sun was lower but still bright and the light sliced the space diagonally in half. She sat on a wall on the shady side and waited for the dazzle of the whitewashed walls to fade.

'Did you sleep?' he asked.

'Dead to the world. And you?'

He nodded.

She was grateful for the way he seldom saw a need to fill a silence, and felt they'd established a balance that meant they were on parallel lines, running smoothly in the same direction, but agreeing not to come too close. It suited the circumstances: a greater intimacy might prove burdensome.

All the same, there were things she wanted to know. Some – about Shona and how they'd met – she couldn't ask, but others ...

'What can you tell me about Warsaw? Did you grow up there?'

He took a moment to reply, and she hoped she hadn't crossed their invisible line. But then he smiled. 'Yes. In a district called Żoliborz. My father was an architect and we lived in a block of flats that he designed. I used to consider Żoliborz rather tame and dull. Little did we know. It's one of the areas where the AK began the Uprising on Tuesday.'

'Are any of your family still there?'

'I don't know. I've sent so many messages over the years, but there's been no word. Almost the first thing the Nazis did was round up anybody with an education, murdering some, sending others to camps or for forced labour. Their openly declared aim was to annihilate Polish culture and turn us into slaves. A man like my father would have stood no chance. And my mother, my sister Marianna, who knows?'

'I'm sorry.'

'It's a beautiful city.' He spoke as if the words had been waiting to burst out of him. 'The parks are full of children feeding ducks on the lakes. On Sunday after church the old ladies carry packages of cake tied up with string. There's music and fountains and old trees. You can go everywhere by tram. The shops have bright-coloured awnings. I used to fritter away my time in the bookshops around the university district.'

He stopped short and hung his head. Freya had to crane forward to hear what he said next.

'I'm so afraid of what I'm going to find. I'm so afraid my city is already lost.'

The timeless sound of the bees in the hot, still air made it impossible for Freya to imagine what lay ahead. She reached out to pluck a stem from one of the nearby herbs, thinking she might keep it to remind her of what felt like an almost surreal interlude, only to recall Shona's anxiety at Gibraltar Farm – was it really only yesterday? – that she must keep nothing, however tiny, that could give her away. She breathed in the rich peppery scent, certain she'd remember this moment without the need for pressed leaves.

With the morning weather report came confirmation that they would fly that night. It would be full moon, and the weather in Warsaw was continuing hot and clear. The tension of waiting out the rest of the day was almost unbearable, although Freya found it far easier without Shona's dark, fearful eyes fixed upon them.

She knew she should try to take a siesta to prepare for the night-long journey ahead but, even in the unaccustomed heat of a Puglia afternoon, sleep remained elusive. It was a relief when, around six o'clock, the driver arrived to take them back to the airfield. The young man could hardly contain his excitement that the waiting was finally over and the squadron had been given the clearance they'd been waiting for. Fourteen planes loaded with desperately needed supplies – everything from boots to guns and ammunition – would be heading for Poland tonight.

Reaching the airfield, Freya and Leo stood for a moment to watch the jeeps and trucks coming and going to load and unload large, tightly bound packages and a number of strange cylindrical metal containers that looked just like huge bombs, each attached to its own parachute pack, while ground crew checked and re-checked every inch of the huge planes.

They went in search of the station commander who told them they'd have to wait for all the supplies to be loaded first. He unfastened the padlock on the refrigerator in his office and took out the cardboard box containing the penicillin. Freya itched to check that all the ampoules were still intact. The RAMC captain who had briefed her had stressed how dangerous it would be to use penicillin to fight an infection if she didn't have enough to complete the course of treatment, but the longer they were kept cool, the longer the penicillin would remain active. She packed the box into her canvas bag, hoping for the best. It would be strapped to her chest when she jumped – sufficient protection, she hoped, for the precious contents.

The commander seemed unexpectedly subdued, given the excitement elsewhere on the base, and, as soon as he went off to attend to other business, Freya asked Leo, who had been talking to him in Polish, if he knew what was wrong. Leo explained that this morning the Luftwaffe had begun bombing raids on civilian targets in Warsaw to discourage support for the Uprising. That was to be expected, but the Soviets, who could so easily have controlled the airspace from their present positions, or

bombed the airport at least to delay the German planes in taking off, had chosen to do nothing. Stalin clearly intended to
leave the Nazis to kill civilians and destroy the city. The AK,
fighting this battle alone, was now more dependent than ever
on the supplies that were to be dropped tonight.

This news was frightening, but, seeing how clearly it strength-
ened Leo's resolve, she strove not to let him see her alarm.
Inwardly she realized it was time to face up to the grim reality
of the fight she was about to join.

With shaking hands she pulled her jumpsuit up over her
clothes. Their other necessary belongings issued at Gibraltar
Farm, including toiletries and a change of clothes, would parachute down in a separate pack. The station commander returned
and, after advising a final visit to the bathroom, shook both
their hands and wished them good luck.

Dusk was falling as she and Leo were driven the short distance to the plane. The air was hot and dry and, as they climbed
out of the jeep, carrying their parachute packs, the first Halifax
bomber thundered down the runway, its propellers an all but
invisible whirr, and climbed heavily into the velvety sky. Freya
watched as it rose and banked to head almost due north towards
Yugoslavia. Their Halifax reared above them, the cockpit out of
sight aloft. The last rays of the setting sun glinted off the glass
of the forward gun turret and threw the undercarriage into
deep shadow. She took a last look around, placed her hands on
the ladder and hauled herself up.

Waiting above was the dispatcher, a young corporal who, in
impeccable English, said to call him Marek. Addressing her as

Olenka, he reached down to take her hand and pull her into the belly of the plane.

'We have a few cushions,' he said, 'but it's not very luxurious, I'm afraid. We're short on space so, once we take off, you won't be able to move about much.'

In the dim light Freya saw that most of the fuselage was taken up with about a dozen of the metal containers she had watched being loaded, leaving only a little floor space around the bomb bay through which she'd just climbed. Beyond the stores she could see the backs of the wireless operator and navigator, and knew that, above them in the cockpit, sat the pilot and flight engineer. Along with front and rear gunners, these young men, who all turned to wave cheerfully at her, were risking their lives to make the journey to Warsaw. Not only was there the danger of being shot down, but the return journey would take the Halifax to the absolute limit of its fuel capacity.

'Whichever of you is going out first must sit nearest the bay,' said Marek, cheerfully, just as Leo's head appeared through the hole.

'Wedel will go first,' she said, still not accustomed to using Leo's field name. They had decided that, as the Polish speaker, he should jump first and assess the situation on the ground. If he sensed any kind of trap, he was to give an agreed signal and she was to pretend to be concussed and unable to speak clearly or make sense of questions or instructions. If they had been betrayed, it wouldn't fool the Gestapo for long, but it was better than nothing.

'Then you're here, Olenka.' Marek told her, pointing to a

couple of dusty cushions on the floor in a cramped space between the internal ribs of the fuselage. 'With Wedel beside you here.'

Marek helped them strap on their parachutes and padded helmets and got them settled, fitting their radio sets and the oxygen masks and tubes, all of which were familiar from the outward flight. Leaving the radio channels free for the crew, they wouldn't be doing much talking, but they would need the oxygen once they flew above a certain height, which was also when the temperature in the unheated plane would plummet. She might be sweltering now in all her kit, but she knew she'd be glad of it later: crossing the Alps on the way here had been even colder than the very worst Aberdonian winter.

Hearing and feeling the vibration of the plane's four propellers begin to rotate, Leo turned to her and grinned. She felt queasy with trepidation but managed to smile back. The dispatcher closed the hatch and took his place opposite them. Freya heard the increasing roar of the engines as the Halifax lurched into motion, its tail swaying as it taxied onto the runway. She braced herself for the acceleration and, for the third time in her life, experienced the strange initial moment of weightlessness as they became airborne. Soon afterwards most of the lights were turned off and, in the sudden darkness, she fought a wave of claustrophobia. It would be at least a five-hour flight, the only distraction the sickly sweet smell of the chemical lavatory and the voices of the crew talking to each other in Polish on the intercom.

Perhaps it was her sense of resignation but Freya's mind leapt to the weeks before her final medical exams when she and her fellow students had tried to cram every fact they'd ever learnt about anatomy, physiology, pharmacology and the rest into their exhausted memories. Perhaps if she recited her knowledge silently to herself now – the bones of the hand, the anatomy of the heart, the different areas and functions of the brain – it would help to steady her juddering breath. She felt for the pack containing the penicillin and, as she did every day, ran through the precise instructions she'd been given for its use.

Marek leant forwards to tap her knee, offering a stick of chewing gum, which she accepted gratefully.

It grew chilly, and she pulled the sleeves of her jumpsuit as far over her hands as she could.

An hour or so later Marek offered them small cups of watery coffee, poured carefully from a Thermos flask, and some sandwiches wrapped in greaseproof paper. Made with local Italian ham and bread, they tasted like nectar.

After that she managed to doze until woken by the increasing cold. They were flying over the Tatra Mountains, Leo told her. In Poland at last! Not long to go now. It was all she could do to control her shivering and she longed to lie down and huddle into a ball, but it wasn't possible.

They'd been told that the planned drop zone lay on the edge of the Kampinos Forest to the west of Warsaw where resistance fighters from the large AK unit operating out of the deep, almost trackless woods would be waiting to pick them up and escort them into the city. Freya tried mentally to rehearse everything she'd been taught to do on the single parachute jump she'd made from the Whitley over Tatton Park. But that had been in sunshine, not in the dark and cold. She reminded herself sternly that everything else remained the same, yet she still couldn't control the bouts of violent shivering.

The chatter inside her headset turned to English as Marek assured her that he'd give them plenty of time to prepare once they were approaching the drop point.

She felt her bowels turn liquid but wasn't sure she dared risk unstrapping and undressing to use the Elsan lavatory, afraid less of the embarrassment and more that she wouldn't have the courage to buckle her parachute back on and go through with what she'd promised.

She could feel the aircraft descending, confirmed by Marek dispensing with his oxygen mask as he got busy checking the parachutes and the tautness of the steel wire that ran horizontally across the roof of the fuselage. Her ears began to pop and she remembered how she'd been advised that it might happen as the plane lost altitude; she should hold her nose and blow.

Taking back even such a tiny bit of physical control helped to steady her nerves, and she made an extra effort to concentrate on the dispatcher's preparations. It wasn't long before he beckoned Leo forwards. Leo's eyes shone with excitement as Marek clipped his static line to the wire that crossed the roof and pushed the metal safety-pin through the clip, tugging at it to make sure it was secure. Then it was her turn.

First she asked Marek to check that she'd correctly fastened the pack containing the ampoules of penicillin to her chest and then swivelled around as best she could for him to clip her parachute's static line to the wire.

Another five long minutes passed and then, receiving the go-ahead from the navigator, Marek lifted the hatch covers and folded them back. A blast of chill night air hit Freya's face and the engine noise increased. Leo craned forwards, looking down through the open hatch where a twisting river and small lakes or ponds glittered in the moonlight. He turned to her, pressing her forearm and mouthing, 'Poland,' then returning to gaze in wonder at the slowly unfolding nightscape below.

The sky was clear and the roar of the engines seemed deafening. Surely it was only a matter of time before they were spotted by some German anti-aircraft gunner on the ground below. What if they were shot down? She couldn't bear for the seven brave young air crew to be killed because of her mission, which suddenly seemed impossibly foolish.

As if sensing her alarm, Marek made a soothing gesture with his outstretched hand.

'It may be a few minutes yet,' he reassured her, over the intercom. 'We're watching for the bonfire that will mark the drop zone.'

Now she leant forwards, too, trying to spot the signal that would bring the waiting to an end.

The pilot must have sighted it before she did, for the floor tilted as the plane banked, turning and descending in a single smooth movement. Bracing herself with her hands against the floor, Freya thought she caught sight of a tiny flashing light on the ground far below, a member of the reception committee using a torch to send a message in Morse code. The plane responded with its own blinker lights and suddenly two lines of light in the form of a cross, with a single red light at its centre, appeared on the ground, a little distance from the bonfire.

'That's where you're aiming for,' said the dispatcher. 'Keep an eye on the wind direction.'

The engine noise changed again as the plane circled the drop zone. Behind her another member of the crew came forward and began preparing the metal containers and other packages ready to be dropped after them. Leo shuffled forwards until his feet were dangling terrifyingly over the edge of the hatch.

'We're making the first run-in,' said Marek. 'You can take off your headsets. Just watch the signal lights.' He pointed to two small bulbs on the roof above them.

Leo, his static line still hooked to the wire, inched further forwards, ready to jump, his eyes fixed on the unlit bulbs. Freya knew that she had to follow immediately so that they would land as close to one another as possible. How was she going to tell Marek that she couldn't do it? She was paralysed, petrified. It was hopeless. She looked at the two bulbs. She had to say something. She couldn't let Leo go on his own, send him to a possible death for no reason. Instinctively she wrapped her arms across her body and felt the pack carrying the penicillin. The miracle drug. Life-saving medicine for a dying man.

The red light came on. *Action Stations.*

Leo sat up straight. She saw his hand move across his chest and realized he was making the sign of the cross.

She was a doctor taking penicillin to a patient. She had sworn an oath when she got her degree. She had a duty to fulfil.

The red light gleamed for a few seconds and went out, replaced by the green. Leo disappeared. His line jerked taut, then flew back up, the now empty parachute bag to which it was attached blown backwards beneath the plane.

As Marek swiftly and expertly hauled in Leo's line, she swung her legs out into empty space, feeling the rush of cold air blow her jumpsuit flat against her skin. What if the line broke free and her parachute failed to open? What if her harness wasn't secure? The red light came back on. The dispatcher peered below and turned to her with a grin and a thumbs-up.

The red light went out. The green came on. She pushed herself away from the floor of the plane and dropped into darkness.

20

Kirsty, 1989

I'm on my way to meet Tomasz. He called me yesterday evening to tell me excitedly that one of his new friends at the Polish Hearth Club has tracked down an elderly Polish man in Guildford who remembers Shona and will be at the club tonight if I want to meet him. I'm immensely grateful that he's turned up a new lead as it means I can shelve any idea of trying to contact Patty Drexeler.

I'm late, thanks to a rancorous departmental meeting that ran over time – some of my colleagues seem to revel in finding smaller and smaller splinter groups to support or vehemently oppose – as well as battered from the rush-hour tube trains and cold after the foggy walk from Knightsbridge station. It's not actually raining, but the sodden air glistens beneath the streetlights. I wonder if it might even snow tonight. Tomasz is waiting as arranged on the corner of Exhibition Road opposite Hyde Park. He sees me from afar and smiles in greeting.

It's only a short walk to the Hearth Club. He insists on carrying my heavy work bag and chats about what he's been doing since we last met. He picked up a few days' work, cash in hand, through an old friend who left Poland five years ago, cutting stone for a patio for a rich man in Holland Park, and was delighted when the contractor said he'd be glad to use his skills again. It means he can afford to stay longer than he originally planned.

We leave our damp coats at Reception and enter a large, dimly lit, high-ceilinged room. Tomasz leads me over to where five elderly men sit around a big corner table at the back. They rise gallantly to greet us but, once Tomasz has made the introductions, it's clear that we're interrupting their reminiscences, so we squeeze into the circle and listen.

They're in their late seventies or early eighties and have lived here for fifty years. Still proudly regarding themselves as exiled Poles, they converse in a flowing mixture of Polish and English. Tomasz sits close to me so that he can murmur a translation into my ear whenever necessary. I don't really look at him, concentrating instead on the men's faces – lined, craggy and still striking – but I'm aware of the feather touch of his breath on my cheek.

He explains in a whisper that it's been months since these men were all together, and they have much to catch up on. They are excited about the declaration two days ago by Thatcher, Bush and Gorbachev that the Cold War is over, and question Tomasz eagerly about public opinion back home. While they don't seem to agree wholeheartedly with his support for Lech Wałęsa or Solidarity, they're jubilant about the speed of events in Eastern Europe and the ignominious retreat of the Soviet regime. One mentions Yalta, the bitterness in his voice belying the fact that the post-war agreement that handed Poland to Stalin happened more than four decades ago.

At last, as they pause long enough to order a second round of strong coffee, Tomasz is able to remind them why he and I are here. They laugh and apologize. Jan, who sits on my other side, takes my hand and kisses it as courteously as I imagine a nineteenth-century cavalry officer might have done. Despite his thin grey hair and the liver-spots on his temples, his eyes flash with the same style and charm he must have possessed when young.

I pull from my bag the two photographs I've brought of Shona and Freya as young women, along with the photocopied enlargement Tomasz gave me of his small image of Gosia and Shona in Warsaw. I hand them around the table. Daniel, the frailest of the group, is the man who first identified Shona and whose recollection that her sister was a doctor brought Tomasz to Freya's door. He repeats that he recognized Shona because – he's fairly sure – she was romantically involved with one of his friends, although he no longer remembers which friend or how serious the relationship was. Three of the other men shrug, noncommittal: there were so many pretty women. I can well believe it.

Jan, who has travelled up from Guildford and is the principal reason we are here, has pushed up his glasses to stare more closely at the picture he holds. It's of Mum and Shona beside a Highland loch, taken when they were both still at university. They're laughing and my mother's profile is slightly blurred, as if the photographer had caught them unawares. It's always been one of my favourites of the two of them together.

He taps it with a gnarled finger. 'One of them is Shona Grant,' he says. 'The girl Leo Tarnowski was in love with.' He appeals to his friends. 'You remember Tarnowski. He was in Intelligence. Had to pretend he was employed by the BBC, but he was our liaison with the Baker Street boys.'

'Do you know how he met my aunt?' I ask. 'She was in uniform, but I don't know what her role was.'

'I only knew her as Leo's girl.' He taps the photograph again. 'How did you ever tell them apart?'

'You didn't know she was a twin?'

'No.'

'What was Leo like?'

'He was supposed to be a civilian, but he must have had military rank. An intellectual, a hot-head, death is preferable to dishonour, passionate about all the things we believed in then.'

I think of Shona's breakdown, her ambiguous and desperate death. If this hot-head was her fiancé, then was jilting the woman you loved an honourable thing to do? For all their ornate courtesy and charm, I wonder which these men, Leo's former comrades, would put first: idealism or fidelity to a woman?

'Do you know if they planned to marry after the war?' I ask.

'I don't see why not,' Jan says. 'They were very involved with one another. But I don't know what became of him.'

'I don't remember seeing much of him after the war,' says one of the other men.

'I heard he went home,' says another.

'Back to Poland?' I ask.

'He was a fool if he did,' Jan says decisively. I notice that the others defer to him as their de-facto leader. 'The UB or the NKVD would've shot him on sight.'

'Is there anyone else who might know more about him?' I ask, pushing the thought of Patty to the back of my mind.

Jan looks at each of his companions around the table but they all shake their heads. 'We're about the only ones left,' he says.

'Back then, he was good friends with Adam Zeromski,' recalls one, 'but Adam died of cancer a couple of years ago.'

Tomasz pushes forward the photocopy of his picture. 'What about this woman?' he asks. 'My mother, Malgorzata Dolniak. The picture was taken in Warsaw during the first weeks of the Uprising.'

The men seem to straighten a little, as if out of respect, their expressions sombre.

'They both survived?' Daniel asks, as if surprised at such a feat.

'My mother died later in a Soviet labour camp,' answers Tomasz.

'My aunt made it home,' I say, as the image of Mum's sewing tin jumps into my head. 'She brought back a tin from Wedel's.'

The men smile at one another, perhaps sharing childhood memories of chocolate.

'Do you have any idea why it might be important? My mother thinks it might be significant.' I search for a phrase to explain Freya's predicament. 'She's not able to say why.'

'The tins were popular souvenirs,' says one.

'Emil Wedel's son kept the factory going during the war,' says another. 'They were always good employers. Although, of course, the Nazis took everything they produced.'

'Didn't he also run secret education classes?' asks another. He turns to me. 'That was a dangerous thing to do when such things were banned.'

'So he might have been sympathetic to the Home Army?' I ask. 'Was he involved in the Uprising?'

'It's possible,' the men agree.

I think how often I've handled the tin box and never dreamt it was linked to such a fateful time in history.

'"Wedel" could have been a codename,' Jan suggests. 'Maybe that's the significance of the tin.'

Tomasz points to the two women in the photocopy. 'Their codenames were Gosia and Olenka.'

'"Wedel" would more likely be for a man,' says Daniel.

'If so, do you know who "Wedel" might have been?' The eagerness in Tomasz's voice reminds me of how much this matters to him.

Jan laughs. 'Someone with a sweet tooth.'

'Could he have been one of the Cichociemni?' Tomasz presses.

'It's possible,' says Jan, 'but there weren't many of them. He's far more likely to have been a member of the AK who was already in Warsaw.'

We're both disappointed: not only another dead end but yet another layer of disguise and obfuscation. If neither my mother nor the elderly survivors of the events of 1944 around this table can tell us anything, and all official records are sealed, we may never find answers to our questions.

I begin to collect up the scattered photographs. The picture of Gosia and Olenka lies next to the other few images of my mother and my aunt. I look again at the smiling face of the woman standing beside Gosia. The room starts to spin. I recall Phyllis's warning that piecing together incomplete fragments of a story can be more inaccurate than knowing nothing at all.

I turn to Daniel. 'You recognized Olenka as my aunt Shona.'

'Yes. She was a lovely girl.'

'But you never met her sister?'

'No.'

'And never knew they were twins?'

'No.' Daniel looks confused.

I take note of his milky eyes and a slight tremor in his hands, and speak more gently. 'Yet you told Tomasz that her sister was a doctor. That's how he found me. But how did you know that?'

'I don't remember,' he says apologetically. 'Shona must have mentioned it, and it stuck in my mind because I thought it was unusual.'

The world stops spinning, the revelation fades, and I'm uncertain. OK, even though Daniel couldn't have known which twin he was looking at in Tomasz's photograph, there's absolutely no reason why 'Olenka' would be Freya. Why on earth would my mother go to Poland? It's far more likely to have been Shona. Especially if her lover, Leo Tarnowski, was with Polish Intelligence. And Freya has never protested my assumption that it's her sister standing beside Gosia.

'What is it, Kirsty?' Tomasz is frowning at me.

'Nothing.' I give him a reassuring smile as I gather together the photographs and tuck them safely out of sight in my bag.

It's cold and drizzling when we leave the Hearth Club. As I put up my umbrella Tomasz invites me to join him for an early dinner at the little place in South Kensington where we met before. I tell him I have to get back for supper with my family but I can't help finding some small pleasure in his apparent disappointment. He takes the umbrella from me, links his arm in mine and holds it over us both as we walk towards Knightsbridge, even though his way home takes him in the opposite direction.

'If Wedel *was* a codename,' he says, 'do you think your mother would know his real name?'

'Even if she does, she may never be able to voice it.'

'Did you ask her about my father?'

'Yes, I did.'

'Before she gave you the tin?'

'Yes, but . . .' I think of Archie's warning about Rosebud and *Citizen Kane.* 'You have to remember that my mum's mind could be completely scrambled. The chocolate tin might not mean anything at all.'

'Then why did your aunt bring it back from Warsaw? Why did your mother keep it?'

He has a point, but I still fear he's making too big a leap. 'The name obviously means *something* to my mother,' I say cautiously. 'But it may have nothing to do with your father. Perhaps Shona merely kept the tin as a memento, and all my mother meant to show me was its connection to Warsaw. It could date from before the war.'

'What about Leo Tarnowski? Had you heard the name before?'

'Never,' I say. 'What about you?'

He shakes his head. 'Can you ask your mother?'

'I can try.'

'We don't know anything, do we?' he says hopelessly.

We walk on in silence. I'm glad when the cheerful yellow light of a bus emerging out of the rain breaks up the darkness of Hyde Park across the road.

'You're sure you can't recall any other scrap of information from your mother or your uncle?' I ask. 'Or the friend who sent you the photograph? Nothing else about why he said Olenka would know your father's identity?'

'No.'

'Do you think Shona knew about him because you were conceived while she was in Warsaw?'

Tomasz is taken aback. 'No. I was already four years old.'

'So why would Gosia tell my aunt about your father, especially in the midst of a war zone? And why would Shona then tell Freya? Gosia was still alive when Shona died, so why would it seem important to her?'

'I don't know.'

'I'm not being negative, only trying to make some sense of it.'

'I wish I understood why it's always had to be such a mystery,' he said. 'Is it because it was dangerous to know my father's identity? Was he a Jew or a Nazi or just a married man she didn't want to make trouble for?'

'Maybe you're the heir to a chocolate company,' I say lightly.

Tomasz slows down as we approach the brightly lit shop windows of Knightsbridge, all crammed with colourful Christmas displays.

'I still can't get used to this,' he says, looking around. 'At home the shops are bare. Only ever one type of lamp or toy or pillowcase, and if you don't start queuing early, they're gone. However do you manage to choose what you want?'

I laugh. 'Capitalism is about wanting it all, and always wanting more. Department stores are shrines to unfulfilled desire. It's what I teach.'

'Is that what you want?'

He looks down at me and suddenly something changes between us. Quickly he pulls me into the doorway of a shop that has closed for the night. I realize why when the front wheel of a passing bus jolts into a pothole, sloshing dirty icy water over the pavement where we'd just been.

I laugh nervously, feeling his hand still around my waist. 'Good timing!'

He looks down at me again and I think he's going to kiss me. I haven't kissed any man except Martin since I was a student and yet, even though to do so now would be to cross some invisible line, I know I want him to.

But Tomasz lets me go and steps back to the pavement. 'Your family will be wondering where you are.'

I don't care, is what I want to say, but don't.

Maybe he sees it in my eyes anyway, for he smiles. 'You have Olenka's spirit,' he says. 'It tells me something about my mother that she and your aunt fought together, that they were friends.'

'I'm glad.'

'That's the station there, isn't it?' He points towards the red, white and blue circular sign for the Underground.

'Yes.'

'I'll call you soon,' he says, and walks away.

I cross the road and descend to the northbound platform where a train arrives not long afterwards. Too many thoughts crowd into my head as the carriage rattles along the tunnel. Did Tomasz want to kiss me or did I just imagine it? The way in which desire, the absence of his kiss, seems to cling around my mouth reveals how much I wanted it to happen. Yet I don't pause to examine my feelings because a greater unease nags at me.

I hold my bag tight on my lap and think back to the night when Tomasz turned up on Mum's doorstep and we showed her the photograph of Gosia and Olenka. All the circumstantial evidence points to it being Shona in the picture – it makes no sense for it to be Freya – but the photographs of the twins in my bag remind me that I have no proof. The world starts to spin around me once more. Did I railroad my mother with my instant assumptions? Did I miss any attempt she'd been making to direct me to the truth? What does it mean if I'm wrong?

If it *was* Freya in Tomasz's photograph, then how did I fail all my life to catch a single glimpse of the young woman who parachuted into unknown enemy territory, into a country where she couldn't even speak the language, and witnessed God knows what death and destruction, and who managed to return safely and never breathe a word of what she'd done? I'd believed easily that Shona had accomplished such feats because I'd never met her, but my own mother?

But *why* should it be Freya? She had no connection with Poland. As far as I remember, she'd only recently qualified and started work in London when that photograph was taken. What reason did she have to volunteer, or be chosen, to go to Warsaw? I think of what Archie said on the phone about Patty being responsible for Mum almost being struck off. Had Freya got into some kind of professional trouble for going? But, then, if Patty was involved, it must have been something to do with the clinic she financed. I don't want to rake up trouble again by asking Archie and, besides, I suspect he doesn't really know.

As I negotiate the stairs and passages to change to the Northern line at Leicester Square, I reflect that there's nothing mysterious about Mum keeping things to herself. To me that's normal. But now suddenly she threatens to become someone I've never known at all. No, that's not right, either. It's not as if I've ever felt I truly know her. But now I glimpse the possibility that I might have badly misjudged her.

I thought she took after her Scots Presbyterian father, that duty, hard work and self-denial took precedence over spontaneity, warmth and emotional candour, that she simply wasn't interested in a close and loving relationship with her children. I can't square that with the smiling young woman amid the ruins of Warsaw.

How much of herself has she hidden all these years? Why? Surely she could have kept certain facts secret, if that was what she had to do, and still given us sight of the courage and daring she must possess if she is the woman in Tomasz's photograph.

Phyllis said Freya lost her spark after Shona died, in which case maybe her grief was enough to eradicate the spirit that took her to Poland. It's inexpressibly sad that she never looked to us for comfort. I've always seen her reserve, her detachment, as selfish, yet if my mother *was* Olenka and never felt able to speak of it, her silence has been tragic, for all of us.

If my mother was Olenka.

21

Freya, 1944

Listening to the roar of the Halifax's engine retreating into the distance, Freya was suspended in darkness as the cold air gripped her chest. She would never forget that first heart-stopping moment before her parachute was ripped open by the pull of the line attached to the plane and its silken canopy blossomed safely above her. She forced herself to breathe as she tried to press her hands to her sides and pull her knees and feet together as she'd been taught but it was far harder than she remembered. Managing to look down, she realized she could no longer locate the signal fire and tried not to panic. Then suddenly she saw it, not far below as she expected but closer and off to one side. She felt the rush of the crosswind and, before she was ready, crunched into the ground, bruising her hip as the billowing parachute dragged her awkwardly across dry, rough grass.

Almost immediately she was surrounded by the beams of torches and by excited voices repeating the same word. As she dug in her heels and twisted the parachute cords to bring herself to a stop she remembered to shout the countersign to their password. She felt a hand on her shoulder.

'Welcome to Poland!' Close to her in the darkness Leo's face shone with happiness.

Unseen hands were pulling at her, unbuckling her parachute and dragging off her jumpsuit and padded helmet. She clutched at the canvas bag strapped to her chest, praying that none of the glass vials had broken as she hit the ground.

'Come on,' Leo said. 'We need to get out of here before the plane circles back to drop the supplies.'

He took her hand and pulled her across the uneven field. She was aware of others hurrying beside them. As they left the brightness of the bonfire, her eyes adjusted to the moonlit night. Ahead, a dark line of trees lay below a starry sky – this must be the Kampinos Forest.

As they drew near Freya could make out two horse-drawn carts and a small band of people, men and women, beckoning to them from the edge of the forest. After five hours of chemical smells inside the fuselage, the scent of fresh pine and earth was intoxicating. One man, taller than the rest, wearing a cartridge belt across his chest and a rifle over his shoulder, stepped forward. He had an open, reassuring expression as he held out his hand to Leo, who shook it vigorously. The man extended his hand to her, talking all the while in Polish. The only words she recognized were their own codenames, Wedel and Olenka. Others came forward to pat her on the back. One of the women, who had retrieved their personal belongings, embraced her with tears of joy, but Freya could only nod and smile in reply as her ears picked up the drone of the returning plane.

'We must go.' Leo pointed to a sandy track that led into the woods. 'Alek and Piotr will show us the way.' He pointed first to the man with the kind face, who had shaken her hand, and then to a youth who, despite the cumbersome weapon he carried, looked little more than a boy.

'The rest are staying to load up the supplies and put out the fire,' Leo continued. 'Are you ready? It's dangerous to hang around any longer than we need to, and we've a long walk ahead of us.'

'Just a minute.' Freya knelt down to retie the straps on the canvas bag so that she could carry it as a backpack. Standing up, she took a deep breath. 'OK.'

Their guides set off at a good pace, leaving Leo and Freya to follow.

'Where are we heading?' she asked him. 'Do you know?'

'To a village on the eastern side of the forest. From there it's not much more than ten miles into Warsaw, and there'll be others waiting to take us into the city.'

She looked at the narrow track leading off into darkness. 'Is it safe? Are we likely to be ambushed?'

He shook his head with a smile. 'Don't worry. The AK have a force of more than two thousand men hidden here.'

Astonished, Freya peered into the trees as Leo moved ahead to walk beside Alek, speaking softly to him in Polish. Piotr dropped back to accompany her, and she was relieved to discover that they each knew enough French to establish some basic communication. As the darkness increased beneath the thick leaf canopy she had to concentrate on watching her footing on the rutted trail and they marched onwards in silence.

She'd always liked hiking, and the sturdy shoes provided by Gibraltar Farm fitted surprisingly well. Had it been daylight, she might almost have been able to imagine herself back in the Highlands, walking between the rowan and birch along the banks of the Feugh. When the track dwindled to a winding path and they had to walk in single file, she enjoyed hearing the woodland sounds – leaves rustling, crickets chirping, frogs croaking on a distant pond. After a couple of hours they stopped and Piotr produced two bottles of water, some hard-boiled eggs and a loaf of dark crusty bread that he tore into chunks and handed around. Freya shelled her egg and ate the bread greedily, only now realizing how long it had been since she'd had a proper meal.

Setting off again, she was almost too tired to notice when the birds began to sing and the first grey light of dawn trickled down to the forest floor. She longed to rest her aching muscles, but Alek never dropped his pace. She had lost track of time when, an hour or two later, she looked up from the path to see sunlight glinting through the thinning foliage ahead. Alek stopped and motioned with his hand for them to sit, which she did gratefully. It was all she could do not to roll onto her side and fall asleep. Leo groaned as he lowered himself down beside her.

'I've spent far too long sitting at a desk,' he muttered.

After a brief discussion with Alek, Piotr laid aside his gun – Freya could see now that it was an ancient-looking hunting rifle – and strode confidently out into a recently mown field dotted with rounded stacks of hay. In the daylight, she saw that he couldn't be more than fifteen or sixteen, pale with fatigue and scrawny beneath his frayed and ill-fitting clothes.

'He'll go ahead to make sure there are no unwanted visitors in the village,' Leo explained, 'just in case our plane was spotted. It's not far. He shouldn't be long.'

Freya watched the boy make his way across the field, and tried not to think about what it would mean if he failed to return.

Fear kept her alert until Piotr reappeared less than twenty minutes later to report with a happy smile of relief that all was clear and the 'birds' were expected. As Leo offered a hand to pull her up, she barely noticed her stiff legs and sore hip.

Alek held out his hand again as Leo explained that he and Freya were to go on alone. Alek and Piotr would wait to give them cover so long as they were in view before returning to their unit in the forest. They were to cross the hayfield to a little wooden gate that opened into an orchard belonging to a small farmhouse from where they'd be taken into Warsaw. She shook Alek's hand and thanked him as best she could. She wanted to hug Piotr, but was afraid to offend the boy's dignity. Then Leo took her by the elbow and they walked together out into the open field.

Although the early-morning sun had begun to warm the new-mown hay, releasing a familiar and comforting fragrance, as they reached the orchard the sight of wasps burrowing remorselessly into the brown and rotting flesh of fallen apples and plums reminded Freya of the dangers that surrounded them and she looked fearfully from side to side as they wove between the lichened trees. In spite of what Leo had said about the size of the local AK units, the possibility of German soldiers in close but unseen proximity was terrifying.

The door of the whitewashed farmhouse stood open. Beyond

the low ridge of the roof Freya could see several columns of wood smoke rising lazily into the still air, evidence of a nearby village. Leo entered the stone-flagged kitchen without knocking and was met by a young woman who held a small child on her hip while, with her spare hand, she laid out plates and cups on a scrubbed wooden table. Beckoning immediately to Freya, she led her through a low door into a scullery where a sliver of soap was laid ready on top of a threadbare towel beside a deep square sink with a single tap. Nodding and gesturing, the woman went back out, closing the door behind her.

Refreshed by her wash, Freya returned to the kitchen where Leo sat alone at the table, an earthenware jug of milk, a loaf of bread and plates of cream cheese and smoked sausage in front of him.

'Where has she gone?'

'Upstairs,' he said, taking a bite of his thick sandwich. 'The less able she is to describe us, the better. Help yourself.'

She pulled out a wooden stool and reached for the bread. It was warm to the touch and released a sharp tang of rye as she cut a slice. 'Did Alek give you any news from Warsaw?' she asked, relieved to have an opportunity to speak freely. 'Anything about my patient? Has his condition worsened?'

He shook his head. 'They wouldn't be told anything about that. But the AK have already taken control of more than half the city – the suburb of Mokotow, the centre and the Old Town.' His eyes were bright, almost feverish. 'There have been heavy casualties, but morale is high.'

She understood his joy at being back on his own soil, his eagerness to strike a blow at last, but it didn't help her deep anxiety. This wasn't her country. She didn't speak the language. She had no real idea of where she was. The pure folly of her presence here felt overwhelming. Trying not to think about what would happen if she were to be challenged by a German patrol, she pushed aside her plate.

'Eat,' he admonished. 'Food will be in short supply from now on so don't waste it.'

Recalling Piotr's thin wrists poking out of his oversize man's shirt, she spread some cheese on her bread and nibbled at the edge, her mouth too dry to chew. She wished Leo would be more sympathetic and at the same time was relieved that he kept his distance. Perhaps his way did after all make it easier to cope.

He finished eating and went to take his turn in the scullery. Left alone in the quiet and orderly low-ceilinged kitchen, Freya savoured what might be her final experience of calm and safety.

Freya's sense of shelter vanished instantly when she heard the door to the outside opening softly. She gripped the edge of the table as a young woman slipped into the kitchen. Overcoming the urge to leap to her feet and be ready to run, Freya examined her potential foe. The young woman was about her age, with bright, dark eyes and brown hair in pinned-up plaits. She wore a faded dress of flowery green cotton, and did not look either surprised or threatening. She greeted Freya in Polish and, from the inflection in her voice, asked a question. Uncertain what to do, Freya tried hard not to glance towards the scullery door. If this woman was not a friend, she must not give away Leo's presence, however desperate she was for him to come and tell her what the unexpected visitor wanted.

But the young woman smiled and pointed at Freya. 'Olenka,' she said, then pointed at herself. 'Rudzik.'

Freya let out a deep breath of relief. 'Olenka,' she agreed.

'Wedel?' the young woman enquired, just as Leo emerged from the scullery.

After a terse exchange in Polish, Leo told Freya to finish eating and be ready to leave. Rudzik had bicycles prepared for them to ride the ten or so miles into Warsaw and they should waste no time.

Rudzik led them to an outhouse where they found three bikes, their baskets and panniers already laden with apples, potatoes or strings of onions. After adjusting their saddles, they set off immediately, Rudzik leading the way and Leo bringing up the rear.

They took a small country road that wound between flat fields of potatoes or corn and was quiet enough for Freya to look about her as they rode. The sky was a cloudless blue and she could hear the high trill of skylarks, making it hard to believe this was occupied territory. It had been a while since she'd ridden a bike, and, as time went on, the ten miles proved to be long, dusty and, as they finally reached the northern suburbs of the city, oppressively hot. She was thirsty and her legs ached; she worried, too, about the sun beating down on the precious cargo in her backpack.

She dared not stare too openly at the bold swastikas draping the entrance to even the smallest official buildings or the posters in aggressive Gothic script. They began to pass more, and bigger, groups of German soldiers, then a concrete machine-gun pit fortified with sandbags, and, a little further on, at the intersection of two shopping streets, a stationary Panzer tank with two helmeted soldiers standing in the turret behind the long barrel of the gun.

Freya dropped her head and pedalled up even closer beside Rudzik. Her knuckles were white where they gripped the handlebars and sweat ran down her back beneath the canvas bag. The soldiers idly followed the view of her and Rudzik's legs as they rode by but otherwise showed little interest. All around her local people kept their eyes on the ground as if, shockingly, the Nazi flags, machine-guns, tanks and soldiers had become an all but invisible backdrop to their daily lives.

Soon afterwards Rudzik turned into a side-street, coasted to the kerb and dismounted beside a greengrocer's where boxes of potatoes and cabbage were displayed on the pavement beneath a faded awning. Without glancing back at her companions, she wheeled her bike into a cobbled yard and propped it against a wall. As soon as Freya and Leo were inside she unhooked and shut the tall wooden gates behind them. Freya, exhausted, was glad to catch her breath and stretch her back, wincing at the pain from her bruised hip. She watched as Rudzik dug around beneath the apples in the basket of her bike and produced a torch. Holding it up, she bobbed her head at them to do the same. Leo laughed, and Freya looked at him in astonishment.

He put his mouth close to her ear. ' "Rudzik" means "robin". She looks like one, doesn't she?'

He was right: Rudzik did look just like a fierce, beady-eyed little bird.

Delving into her basket to find the hidden torch, Freya dislodged a couple of potatoes that went bouncing over the cobbles.

Rudzik picked them up and replaced them carefully before beckoning them to follow. A door in the low, dimly lit workshop that ran along the back wall of the yard led into a further store-room that Freya assumed must be at the back of the shop. Freya inhaled the clean earthy smell as Rudzik took them past stacks of empty wooden boxes and out again into a paved courtyard overlooked by several storeys of windows. Lines of washing fluttered above their heads as they crossed to another door that opened onto a stone-flagged passageway. At the top of a narrow flight of steps Rudzik paused long enough for them to switch on their torches before heading down.

They passed through a couple of interconnected cellars into one where the beam of Rudzik's torch illuminated a hole smashed through the far brick wall. Their guide ducked down and disappeared through it. Leo gestured for Freya to go next and they stumbled behind as Rudzik led them unerringly through the twisting turns of this strange subterranean pathway. Occasionally they surfaced to cross another courtyard before diving back down into the dark. In one, four young children, intent on a game of hopscotch, took little notice of their passing.

After nearly an hour of scrambling beneath the buildings of Warsaw they emerged onto a wide street where they were immediately challenged by a teenage sentry wearing a beret pulled back on his head and armed with a heavy handgun. Rudzik gave the password, then explained to Leo and Freya that, despite the high barricade formed by an overturned tramcar piled with paving stones and broken furniture that closed off the far end of the street, there remained a danger of German snipers on nearby rooftops. To cross to the far side they would have to run, one after another, as fast as they could. Freya was to go first. The distance was not great and, once she was out alone in the open, her backpack bumping against her shoulder blades, she forgot her exhaustion and sore muscles and sprinted as if she was in a race. Taking cover behind sandbags on the other side, she watched, heart in mouth, as the others followed.

Once they were all safely across, Rudzik led them around a corner into a side-street. Entering the courtyard of a handsome apartment building, she headed up the stone stairs to the first floor. Freya could hear the notes of a piano drifting down. Rudzik knocked on an apartment door and, answered by a woman's voice, gave the password.

The door opened and a young woman stepped aside to beckon them in. Freya entered first, then, hearing Leo exclaim in astonishment, turned to see him clasping the woman's hand in both of his.

The woman held a finger to her lips until she had bolted the door behind them, then she turned and smiled, ushering them into a heavily furnished dining room.

'Welcome,' she said in English. She didn't seem as surprised to see Leo as he evidently was to see her. She turned to Freya. 'I'm Gosia.'

She wore baggy trousers and a khaki shirt with rolled-up sleeves. Her face was more interesting than pretty, with striking violet-blue eyes and a mouth too wide for her otherwise delicate features.

Freya caught sight of her own face in a mirror over the mantelpiece and, shocked by the streaks of dirt, saw that her hair and clothes, too, were coated with dust. She hastily wiped her hand on the back of her trousers before accepting Gosia's.

'You made it through!' Leo was still staring at the young woman in amazement.

'So far,' she replied in English. 'And you, too?'

'Long story, but I have so much to ask you.' His expression changed and he seemed to search her face with dread. 'My parents?'

She shook her head. The calmness with which she spoke suggested she was prepared for his question. 'Your father's dead. Your mother was taken away soon afterwards. I'm so sorry.'

'And Marianna?'

'She and your mother were taken separately. That's all I know. You didn't get my letters?'

'No, nothing.' The way in which he seemed to crumple in on himself told Freya that Leo had never fully given up hope of finding at least some of his family alive.

'I'm sorry,' Gosia repeated, touching his shoulder in a gesture of sympathy, then tactfully turning to Freya and leaving him to his thoughts. 'I was chosen to be your guide because, among Bartek's staff, I speak the best English,' she said.

'Bartek?'

Gosia shot a warning glance at Rudzik. 'The codename for the man you have come to see.'

'Of course.' Freya knew not to discuss the reason for her mission.

'I'll take you to him in the Central Sector and Rudzik will take Wedel to meet with others in the Old Town.'

'We aren't staying together?' Freya asked in alarm.

'He'll join you again later. We should get moving, but first I have food for you.' She turned to Leo with a warm smile, indicating the bowl of lard and loaf of dark brown bread on the table. 'No more doughnuts from Blikle, I'm afraid, and the coffee is only roasted barley. I also have these for you to wear.'

Two armbands, made of equal strips of red and white fabric machine-stitched together and similar to the one Gosia herself was wearing, were laid out on the tablecloth. Printed in the middle of the white strip were the letters A and K either side of the Polish eagle. Gosia pinned one to Freya's sleeve while Rudzik helped Leo with the other.

He took a cup of coffee over to the window where he stood silently, turning to stare in each direction along the street below. Freya tried and failed to imagine returning to an Aberdeen from which her parents had disappeared.

She tasted the ersatz coffee, which smelt much like Camp coffee at home and was hot and really not too bad. Cutting a slice of the hard bread, and realizing how hungry she was, she watched Gosia join Leo at the window where they talked softly in Polish. Gosia was slighter and about half a head shorter than Freya, her slenderness accentuated by the oversize men's trousers she wore hitched up at the waist with a thick leather belt.

Something in the way Gosia stood beside Leo suggested an easy familiarity that made Freya curious about the distant pre-war world in which they'd known one another. They must have been quite old friends if she'd written to him about his family. The reassuring thought that perhaps they'd been neighbours or school friends made her slightly less anxious about being parted from him.

Rudzik began collecting the dishes. Freya picked up the

coffee pot and cups and followed her to the kitchen. Matching portraits of a man and a woman hung in the corridor. They clearly belonged to an earlier generation, grandparents, perhaps, of the current owners of the apartment. She wondered if the owners were here, keeping out of sight behind one of the closed doors she had just passed, and silently thanked them for harbouring the 'birds'.

Freya studied Rudzik as she helped to tidy up, wishing she at least knew enough Polish to thank her properly. She would never know her real name, had no idea why she had been willing to risk her life to help them, and would probably never see her again.

'We should get going.' Gosia stood in the doorway. 'It ought to be a half-hour walk, but today might take us a bit longer,' she said, with a wry smile.

In the dining room, Leo handed her the backpack. 'Gosia will take good care of you,' he said, with a comforting hand on her arm. 'She's been with the AK almost from the beginning, so she knows the ropes.'

'But you will come and find me soon, won't you?'

'Of course.'

'Promise me you won't just disappear?'

'Don't worry. Focus on what you've come to do, and I'll see you again in a few days.'

Gosia returned from the kitchen. 'Ready?' She pulled a soft fabric cap out of her trouser pocket and, bundling up her hair, pulled it down over her head. Then she turned to Leo. 'I'm glad you're back,' she said. 'Maybe we'll have a chance to talk properly another time.'

'I hope so.'

Freya felt completely panicked and disoriented. She didn't want to leave Leo. He was her only link with home, which suddenly seemed impossibly far away. She would never get back! She'd been mad to come!

But then Gosia was at her side, murmuring in her ear, 'We're all afraid. You're not alone. I know how you feel. Let's just go quickly and it won't be so bad.'

Not trusting herself to speak, Freya nodded her assent.

'Good, come along.'

Gosia placed a steadying hand on her shoulder and, with an encouraging smile, guided her into the corridor. At the front door she drew back the bolts and pulled it open. Relieved to relinquish responsibility for whatever happened next, Freya followed her out.

22

Kirsty, 1989

My students file out after a seminar that has gone better than usual. I feel energized and renewed, reminded of the passion that pushed me to complete my MA dissertation on Mary Wollstonecraft literally days before Eric was born. For I do enjoy teaching, in spite of the departmental in-fighting and Mrs Thatcher's reforms to higher education, and it's a real boost to see them discussing their ideas as I follow them along the corridor.

The possibility that my mother might be a wartime heroine has somehow changed my whole outlook, and chimes perfectly with the inspiring news footage from former Eastern Bloc countries winning their freedom. A part of my life has smashed – like a picture falling off its hook on the wall – and left a tantalizing blank space behind.

What seems to have gone is my idea of Freya as one of those briskly competent women who refuse to acknowledge any emotional hinterland. She's always been skilful at dodging personal questions, repeating only the same few stories about her life before Archie and I were born, and showing little interest in the past. The reflection of myself that I've sought in her has been equally thin and lacklustre. I know she loves me, but I've always blamed myself for my innate failure to inspire her interest or compassion. But what if her unresponsiveness has been a strategy to cover not an absence but more than can be told? A strategy that wasn't natural, but had to be unwillingly self-imposed? In which case, isn't there also a chance that my reflection, too, has been distorted and there's nothing lacking in me after all?

If Freya is Olenka. I mustn't rush to fill the blank space on the wall with an equally mistaken assumption.

Last night I used the magnifying glass to compare all the photographs I have of the twins, searching in vain for some small detail that would confirm which of them was in Warsaw. I can only conclude that their differences lay not in their features but in their gestures and movements: a smile, a raised eyebrow or a wave of the hand. I remember how those were the moments, when Chris and Eric were babies, when we exclaimed that one or other of them was the image of a particular family member. There was nothing to swing it in favour of either sister and I put down the magnifying glass with the reluctant admission that it still makes more sense for it to be Shona in Tomasz's photograph.

Yet I can't get it out of my head that, on the night Tomasz turned up on Freya's doorstep, I never offered her an opportunity to convey to us that it was her in the photograph with Gosia. I want to go back and have him show it to her again, so that I can watch her reaction more carefully. I've left a message for him, asking him to call me at work around this time, if he can.

I reach the departmental office, a poky little space granted to Women's Studies by a wag of an administrator who quipped, 'Whatever next? Budgerigar Studies?' My colleagues are elsewhere, and I try to settle down to some marking. I'm also aware that some of my new-found energy is due to the almost-kiss with Tomasz.

Although Martin and I have maintained a perfectly satisfying sex life, I can't remember when I last experienced such a sharp stab of pure lust. Enhanced, of course, by the risk of transgression. I ought to have felt guilty when I got home and found Martin in the kitchen with the boys, but I didn't. Even though nothing had happened, I felt a kind of triumph: if he can threaten to upend our family on a whim, why shouldn't I do the same? Childish and stupid, but there it is.

Tomasz is undoubtedly an attractive older man with an appealing mixture of self-possession and energy, the enticing promise of otherness, discovery, self-revelation. If I am to rethink myself – just as he wishes to do by finding out about his father – who better to share my journey?

But deep down I also know that, by building up my feelings for him, I can avoid looking at the real issue in my marriage: do Martin and I have a firm enough foundation to up sticks and change continents together? Would we ever have married if I hadn't been pregnant, or stayed together if not for the boys?

The ringing phone on the desk makes me jump. It is Tomasz, who seizes on my suggestion that we visit Freya together, especially when I explain that I may have too easily dismissed the possibility that it's Freya herself in the photograph. He asks lots of questions, excited at the possibility that there could be someone still alive who might have known his mother. He also wants to ask if she knew Leo Tarnowski.

We arrange a time for me to pick him up from West Dulwich station on Friday afternoon.

Tomasz gets into the car, greeting me with a smile that is warm and open. 'You look tired,' he says.

I glance at him in surprise. 'I am a bit.'

'Would it help to talk?'

I'm about to say no, that I'm fine, and then I think, why not use the ear of a friendly stranger? 'It's my son, Chris,' I say. 'My older boy. I think he hates me.'

Tomasz doesn't respond, but his silence indicates that he's ready to listen.

'How old is *your* son?' I ask him, suddenly reluctant to betray Chris's private feelings.

'Twenty-six. And Chris?'

'He's fifteen.'

Tomasz smiles. 'I remember that age. They think they're all grown-up.'

I feel awkward talking about Martin, too, but I desperately need to speak to someone. 'My husband's been offered a job in Australia. It's where he's from.'

'I remember you told me that before.'

'Chris refuses to go. He says he's old enough to decide for himself, and insists he'll be able to manage if he stays here on his own. I thought he'd come around to the idea, but now he won't even discuss it. I can't seem to get through to him at all.'

'What about you? Do you want to go?'

'I can't decide. That's the problem. If Chris really won't go, then I'll have to stay. And so will Eric, his younger brother.'

'And your husband? He'd go on his own?'

'Maybe. But I can't get into a situation where Chris might feel another day that he's in any way responsible for breaking up the family. I need to get a grip, but I just can't work out what's for the best.'

Tomasz nods but says nothing, leaving my thoughts to churn uselessly. These days the inside of my head feels like a washing-machine on a particularly slow cycle.

Any distraction is a relief. I feel the warmth of Tomasz's body beside me, the closeness of his thigh when I change gears. If he were to take me in his arms and beg me to run away with him, would that make my decision any easier?

As I draw up to park outside the house, I spot Freya's next-door neighbour, Lillian, looking out of my mother's living-room window. She beckons to me anxiously before reappearing at the open front door as I climb out of the car and hurry up the path.

'Oh, Kirsty! I've been leaving messages for you everywhere.'

'What happened? Is she all right?'

'I called the GP. He's with her now. She couldn't raise her arm.'

I glance back to where Tomasz is taking the bags of supermarket shopping I've done for my mother out of the back of my car before I follow Lillian inside, trying to damp down my alarm.

I've got to know Dr Sarmah well over the past few months. He's young and good-looking and Freya has always appreciated his dry humour. But I don't like the worried look he gives me as he sits beside her, inflating a blood-pressure cuff. My mother, typically, raises her eyes to the ceiling in mock exasperation.

Her smile is meant to be reassuring but she seems unaware that only the left side of her mouth is under her control.

I strive to keep my expression neutral. 'Hi, Mum. Looks like I got here just in time.'

Dr Sarmah removes the cuff and tactfully pulls down the sleeve of Freya's cardigan before she tries and fails to do it herself. She looks up as Tomasz passes the open door en route to the kitchen. Tactfully, he does not look at any of us.

'It's Tomasz Dolniak, Mum,' I remind her. 'He came with me because he wanted to talk to you again.'

Her face is blank.

'He came here before, do you remember?'

She waves her left hand impatiently, but there's still no recognition in her eyes.

'He's just going to put the shopping away for you.'

She nods. She looks as if she doesn't care.

'Blood pressure's a bit low,' says Dr Sarmah, 'but nothing too concerning. All the same, I'd like the neurologist to take a look at you. I think you should go in.'

Freya shakes her head vehemently.

'It's just to check you over, Mum.'

'They may want to modify your medication,' he said. 'I don't want to risk you having another seizure.'

She glares at him and he laughs. 'You trying to tell me how to do my job again, Dr Grant?'

I've watched them have this conversation several times, and usually Mum would also laugh and give in, but this time she turns her head away. Dr Sarmah and I exchange glances: we both know she can be stubborn, but this almost petulant gesture isn't like her at all. I try not to panic. We've been told that the pressure of the tumour inside her brain may eventually cause changes in her personality but I've never let myself believe that would happen. Mum's sense of self seems too strong, too certain, to give way.

'I can drive her to the hospital,' I say.

'I'd rather she went by ambulance,' he says gravely.

As he goes to the telephone, I move to his place beside Freya and take her hand in mine. Her fingers have always been long and elegant but now the skin is paper-thin, the knuckles bony and arthritic. I want to cry. She suddenly seems so much more vulnerable, not only because she's unwell but because I'm afraid she has had a lifetime of being alone with her past – and of being misjudged because of it.

She looks back at me, a terrifying vacancy in her dark eyes, and I want to know what secret she has felt obliged to hide for so long. Is it just the outdated wartime discipline of 'careless talk costs lives' or something deeper and more personal? I am stupefied by my sorrow that I have left it too late to ask her to share her history – herself – with me.

23

Freya, 1944

Bartek lay on a camp bed in a bank vault lit by a single overhead bulb. Freya quickly took stock of her patient's appearance. He was balding with lank grey hair, a high, domed forehead and a clipped moustache. His eyes were glassy and bright with fever, his cheeks sunken, his skin dry and scaly and his breathing laboured. Although clearly very unwell he lifted a thin hand a few inches off the mattress in greeting and, in almost inaudible English, thanked her for coming.

Gosia looked on curiously as Freya went immediately to unpack the ampoules and stack them in the empty refrigerator – placed there, she assumed, thanks to Major P's signalled instructions. The electrical wires that led from it and from the overhead light-bulb snaked off around a corner and must lead, she thought, to a generator somewhere; the building was so solidly constructed that all sound was deadened.

Sitting on her heels with the box beside her on the floor, she caught her breath when, with six vials safely stored away, the next one she unwrapped was broken, its precious contents spilt uselessly into the stained cotton wool padding. If too many were damaged, all her efforts, the whole point of her coming here, would have been in vain. Gingerly she picked up the next ampoule and breathed again only when she found it intact. The next one, too, was undamaged. Emptying the rest of the box, she was relieved to find only one more broken vial – a loss within the allowed-for margin of error. Silently she thanked whoever had packed them so carefully.

Rising to her feet, she found herself under close observation by an imposing man of about forty standing at the entrance to the vault. Rather incongruously, it seemed to her, he wore a formal dark suit and tie. He stared at her, unsmiling, then turned to say something in Polish to Gosia. Freya might not have understood the words, but the repugnance in his tone was clear. Gosia replied abruptly in Polish, then turned to Freya.

'This is Dr Henryk. He has been responsible for Bartek's care until now.'

'What did he say to you?' Freya held Gosia's gaze.

The other woman hesitated for just a second. 'He hadn't expected them to send a girl.'

Freya was grateful for her frankness. The doctor reddened, suggesting he had no trouble understanding English. 'Well, please tell Dr Henryk that I'm here now,' she responded, lifting her chin and looking directly at him. 'I'd be grateful if he could give me the patient's history.'

'He gashed his right thigh in a fall eighteen days ago, causing a ragged wound,' the doctor said, in heavily accented but perfect English. 'At the first sign of infection we administered sulpha drugs stolen from the Nazis. Ultimately they were effective only in slowing down the course of the infection and now we have nothing but iodine and salt. As you will see when you examine him, the wound is inflamed. His temperature is fluctuating and he's showing early signs of septicaemia.'

'His mouth looks dry,' she said. 'Are his salivary glands infected?'

'Not yet. We have been keeping him hydrated.'

'When did he last pass urine?'

'At ten last night.'

This meant Freya had got there just in time. 'I need to set up a drip straight away.' She turned to Gosia. 'Do we have all the supplies that were requested?'

'We do.'

Freya held up her hands. 'Where can I wash?'

'I'll take you.'

'Dr Olenka?' Henryk's peremptory tone made both women turn back. His eyes were wary. 'What are the side effects of this new drug? How am I to know that it won't do more harm than good?'

'I have seen it used and also read the secret report prepared by Professor Florey for the prime minister, Winston Churchill.' Freya did her best to speak firmly. 'It detailed Professor Florey's trial of the drug on British troops in North Africa. I'm satisfied that it's not only safe but remarkably effective.'

'Why didn't they send a military doctor?'

'There wasn't time.'

He frowned, still unconvinced, but Freya didn't stay to argue. She followed Gosia to what looked like a large store cupboard. The narrow space was impressively supplied as a makeshift

sluice room, with an autoclave, a sterile metal and glass cupboard containing syringes, different-size needles and steel
kidney trays, then, on shelves, rolls of bandages, dressings and
other essentials. Yet she watched in consternation as Gosia took
a bowl and ladled water into it from a barrel beside the door.

'Are there no bathrooms upstairs?' she asked. 'Surely the
bank staff must have had facilities.'

'There are, but the water's cut off. The Germans have control
of the pumping station, so I'm afraid we have to make do.' She
pointed to a covered chamber pot in one corner of the adjoining
lobby.

There was a slight edge to her voice and Freya hoped she
hadn't offended her or appeared snooty. 'Oh, I'm used to those
from my grandmother's cottage,' she said, with a laugh, as she
washed her hands in the bowl Gosia had filled. 'But tell me about
Dr Henryk. How come his English is so good?'

'I believe he studied in London.'

'Is he always so prickly?'

'He and Bartek are old friends.'

Freya's indignation at the man instantly melted away. Why
had she not perceived that Henryk's lack of trust stemmed from
concern?

Wearing a clean apron from one of the shelves, she returned
to the vault with Gosia, who carried a drip stand, rubber tubing
and other equipment. Henryk stood beside Bartek's bed taking
his pulse.

'I'll do the very best I can for him,' Freya told him. She had to
accept the older doctor's nod as sufficient acknowledgement
that he had decided to accept her competence.

She took an ampoule from the fridge and placed it in one of the sterile trays. Gosia handed her a bottle of saline solution and held the tray for her as she used the syringe she had assembled in the makeshift sluice room to draw up some of the solution into the body of the syringe, measuring the amount by the graduations on the glass and hoping she had remembered the concentration correctly. Then, with trepidation, she placed the syringe in the tray as she carefully broke off the sealed glass tip of the ampoule. Taking up the syringe again, she inserted the needle into the vial and drew up the contents, shaking the syringe to mix the saline and penicillin. Holding it with the needle pointing upwards, she went over to Bartek.

'I'm going to start by giving you an injection directly into the muscle,' she said, as Henryk stepped back to make room for her.

Bartek nodded, his glittering eyes fixed on hers while his body juddered from an uncontrollable shivering fit.

'If you could please uncover his leg for me, Dr Henryk.'

The unpleasant smell from the discarded dressing was not encouraging. The wound in Bartek's thigh had been cleaned and Freya could see where dead tissue had been cut away, but the site was so red, swollen and oozing with fresh pus that it was hard to make out the outline of the original cut. Around it, his mottled skin showed the acute spread of the infection. Freya realized how much pain he must be enduring – without complaint – and gave him a reassuring smile.

'I saw a case like this in London a couple of weeks ago,' she told him. 'A soldier. After treatment with penicillin, he was up and about within days.'

Behind her, Henryk cleared his throat but made no comment.

If Bartek's blood poisoning was already too far gone to respond to treatment, she had no doubt that Henryk would hold her and the unknown drug she was about to administer responsible for his friend's death.

Her lack of sleep and more than twelve hours of hard physical exercise suddenly caught up with her and Bartek's shivering made it difficult to land on the best spot to insert the needle. She steadied her hand, her thumb poised on the plunger, and, praying she got it right, pressed the needle through the lateral side of the thigh muscle above the infected area and kept pushing until she felt the greater resistance of the underlying fascial band. Aware how large a volume of fluid had to go in, she pushed the plunger slowly and steadily, calming her own breathing as she did so.

At last it was done. She drew out the needle and, placing the syringe carefully back into the dish, ready for sterilization, tried to disguise her sigh of relief.

'That must have hurt,' she said to her patient. 'I'm sorry for that, but it will deliver the first dose right where it's needed. Now I'm going to set up a drip that will feed a constant amount of penicillin into your body over the next few days. With any luck, you'll start to feel the effects within twenty-four hours.'

Bartek nodded, his eyes already closing over as he sank back into semi-consciousness. His thin chest rose and fell laboriously, his head on the pillow was skeletal, and his waxy skin was covered with a sheen of sweat.

Freya began setting up the equipment for the drip, wanting everything perfectly prepared before she removed the next ampoule from the fridge. Tiredness made her fingers feel fat and clumsy and she hoped she wasn't forgetting any small but essential step in the process. Performing under the sceptical eye of a far more experienced doctor in an inadequately lit bank vault didn't help.

Bartek began muttering and then calling a name: 'Irena, Irena!'

'His wife,' Gosia said softly.

Henryk came forwards, this time looking to Freya for permission. She moved to give him room and he took Bartek's frail hand in his, murmuring comfortingly in Polish before looking up at Freya with an anguished expression. 'She's expecting their second child,' he said. 'She hasn't even been told that he is ill.'

Steadying her own anxiety as Gosia handed her a length of narrow tubing, Freya managed to attach a needle to one end without further fumbling. She fetched a second ampoule of penicillin from the fridge, broke the glass neck and, after placing a fresh needle on the syringe, added the contents to the bottle of saline. The other end of the tubing passed through a stopper that sealed the bottle. Fixing the bottle securely to the top of the drip stand, she made sure that the tubing was free of air before inserting the needle at the other end into the vein on the inside of Bartek's elbow. She strapped it into place and checked she had done everything correctly. Now she would just have to wait and see.

Freya awoke to feel someone gently shaking her shoulder. She'd been so deeply asleep that for a moment she thought she was back in her own bed in Aberdeen. But that couldn't be right: she was fully clothed and lying on a bare mattress on a floor. The air around her felt dense and still, the shadows at the outer edges of the chamber impenetrable, and it was as silent as a tomb. Every muscle ached as she struggled to sit up and focus on the person beside her.

'I let you sleep as long as I dared,' said Gosia.

Now she recalled that Gosia had offered to take the first watch so she could snatch a few hours' rest. She must have fallen asleep the moment she lay down. There'd been another man here. Where was he? She must wake up. Oh, yes, Dr Henryk. He'd left soon after she set up the drip. It must be time for the next dose.

'Four hours already?' she asked.

'Yes.'

'What time is it?'

'A little after ten.'

'In the morning?' Freya did not hide her confusion.

Gosia laughed. 'No. We only arrived here in the afternoon, remember?'

Had it really been less than twenty-four hours since she'd jumped out of the Halifax? Time seemed to have concertinaed, increasing her sense of disorientation. But it didn't matter. All that mattered was attending to Bartek's drip.

'I must wash my hands first.'

'I've got everything ready.'

'How is he?'

'He woke for a little while and took some sips of water.'

That, at least, was a good sign. In the sluice cupboard Freya washed her hands carefully, splashing water on her face to bring herself more fully awake. She couldn't afford to make a single mistake.

'I'll change over the solution, then examine him,' she said. 'I'm so thirsty. Is this water fit to drink?'

Gosia shrugged. 'It's well water. It's all we have.'

Telling herself to stop asking stupid questions, Freya went to take another ampoule from the fridge. Counting the two that had broken, that left thirty-one. One dissolved in saline and administered every four hours meant she had enough for a further five days of treatment. That should be more than enough, yet it still seemed unbelievable that such a raging and dangerous infection could be brought under control in only five days. In spite of all she'd read in Florey's report, she sympathized with Dr Henryk's scepticism. The soldier she'd seen recover so swiftly at the London Hospital had also had the finest nursing care in a pristine ward with clean water and nourishing food.

Her patient was asleep. As Gosia helped her to switch over the bottle on the drip stand, she scanned his face for traces of improvement but could see none. His skin remained worryingly yellow and waxy, and both the lines of his face and the shadows beneath his eyes appeared almost black in the light of the single bulb. She changed his dressing. The wound, too, looked much as it had before. The RAMC captain had warned her not to expect much of a recovery in the first twenty-four hours, but she would have been overjoyed to find even the smallest indication that she had not arrived too late.

Her ministrations didn't wake Bartek – a good sign, she hoped – and there was little for her to do until she had to prepare his next dose. They were safe from German bombs down here, but she was eager to know what was happening in the streets above. Was there fighting? Were they winning? What would happen if the Uprising did not succeed?

'Why does no one else come to see him?' she asked.

'We don't want news of his condition to leak out,' said Gosia. 'We tell people he's working and must not be disturbed. I'm a credible go-between because I've been his liaison for the AK's regular news sheet.'

'He's not had a nurse?'

Gosia shook her head. 'Only Dr Henryk – who said he'd be back in the morning.'

'Is that what you do? The news sheet?'

'Yes. I worked on a political magazine before the war. Are you hungry? I can offer you some tinned meat and slightly stale bread.'

'Maybe later, thanks.' Freya *was* hungry, but felt too tired and disoriented to digest anything. She wished there was some daylight to help her judge the time correctly.

'Shall we sit on our mattresses?' Gosia asked. 'There is nowhere else.'

They sat facing one another, backs against the walls, legs stretched out before them.

'Are you in uniform at home in England?' Gosia asked.

'No. I work in a hospital.'

'Is it difficult to become a doctor there? For a woman?'

'It's easier in Scotland, where I'm from.'

'Ah, your accent! Of course.'

'How did you learn such good English?' Freya asked. 'You must have visited?'

'Yes, several times, with my family, when I was still at school. That was during the Second Republic.'

Freya was intrigued by the hint of pride in Gosia's voice. 'The Republic?'

Gosia raised her eyebrows in mock reproof. 'You've come to the aid of a country you know nothing about?'

Freya laughed but tried to defend herself. 'The decision to send me here was taken rather quickly.'

'So why were you chosen? You must have *some* connection with Poland? Do you mind my asking?'

'No, I don't mind. Although I should've remembered, we're not supposed to give away too much personal information, are we?'

'Quite right. No need to answer.'

'Although I don't see what harm it can do,' said Freya, feeling very much cheered by such ordinary, friendly chat. 'To be honest, I'm here because of my sister.'

'Do you always do what she wants?' Gosia teased. 'Your sister must be older than you.'

'No.' Freya was about to say that they were twins but she was growing to like being accepted as a singleton. 'I'm the older one, but she has a connection with Poland, if you can call it that.'

'Why do you smile?'

'Her connection is that she's in love with a Pole. But I probably really shouldn't tell you any more.'

'No, maybe not.'

'Do you want to sleep?' Freya asked. 'I'll wake you if I need you.'

'I am tired,' Gosia admitted. 'We can take each shift in turn. You must rest, too.'

'I'll call you when I change the drip,' Freya promised.

Gosia lay down, turned to face the wall and bent her knees. Freya waited until her breathing slowed and she seemed to have fallen asleep, then got up to check on Bartek. He, too, was asleep. As she stood watching over him he had a short bout of shivering that she tried hard to believe was far less extreme than before.

She went to relieve herself. As she squatted over the pot she recalled Patty Drexeler's luxurious Mayfair bathroom and had to stop herself laughing. As she stood and buttoned up her trousers she peered through the grilled metal gate in the wall beside her. Through it, in the shadows, she could make out rows of safe deposit boxes. Who might own their contents? Or had the Nazis already looted them? Jewellery, gold, deeds and share certificates, as well as passports and other vital documents. What had become of the people who'd believed that they and their precious belongings would be safe?

Freya made her way back to the lobby area where Gosia lay asleep. At the far end, wide shadowy stairs led upwards into darkness. At the top, behind closed doors, lay the main floor of the bank – the way they had come in. The thick basement walls shut off all sound from above, but as Gosia had hurried her past, she'd caught a glimpse of serious-faced men and a scattering of women in an assortment of military-style uniforms, all wearing red and white armbands. Many carried weapons. It seemed to be some kind of headquarters, yet even those carrying out administrative duties had rifles propped against their desks. She wished again that she knew what was happening, whether Stalin had changed his mind and come to their aid, and how many were dying for this cause.

She was afraid of dozing off if she returned to her mattress but couldn't just wander aimlessly about in the gloom worrying about what would happen if Bartek's condition did not improve.

After a day of such tense activity it was hard to do nothing. She remembered she had a nail file – specifically a *Polish* nail file – in her Gibraltar Farm shoulder bag, and went to fetch it, along with the only chair, which she quietly moved from beside Bartek's bed.

Any action was better than none, and the familiar movement was soothing. She thought about Shona. Had Leo been able to radio news to Major P of their safe arrival? Freya had not yet seen where her sister was living so it was hard to picture her. Instead, she brought to mind their bedroom in Aberdeen: two iron bedsteads painted the cheerful blue of a blackbird's egg, each with a cosy Paisley pattern eiderdown, and a large chest of drawers that they had shared and fought over. In winter frosts the deep dormer window bore intricate fern patterns, and in midsummer the northern light behind the curtains barely faded. Wakeful, they would lie in bed, staring at the ceiling, and talk for hours.

It was easy to conjure up a comforting sense of her sister's physical presence, but harder to imagine Shona speaking the encouraging words she needed to hear. If Shona were here, it would be Freya supplying the reassurance. Freya inspected her shortened nails and allowed herself to entertain the novel and renegade thought that perhaps, once she returned to London, she should go on thinking of herself as a singleton; perhaps she might do better on her own.

24

My mother hardly seems to take up any space in her hospital bed. She has her eyes closed. She's either asleep or exhausted by the frustration of our discussion about what's best for her imme-diate future, but at least the vacancy in her eyes has gone and she does understand who we are and where she is. The medical staff have been wonderful: she's on new medication and the physiotherapist has returned some movement to her arm. The prognosis doesn't change, but her consultant has just agreed that she's stable enough to go home if, as she's made abundantly clear, that's what she wants.

'Shall we leave her to rest?' I ask.

Martin, who took a morning off work so he could drive me to south London and back, nods. Archie leans over Freya to kiss her cheek.

'Bye, Mum.' He presses her inert hand. 'I'll come and see you again soon.'

She shows no sign of hearing him. Perhaps she *is* asleep. I take advantage of her unresponsiveness to smooth back her hair, which feels reassuringly strong and springy. As I bend to kiss her forehead I wish I could somehow suck out the lifetime of experience stored in the memory inside her skull before it is erased by the tumour growing deep inside her brain, but all I get is the scent of hospital laundry detergent.

'Love you,' I whisper. I can't remember when I last said that aloud to her – or her to me. I feel suddenly that I must have been a terrible disappointment to her and long for it not to be too late to make good.

Out in the corridor Archie heaves a sigh. He's seemed tense and jumpy since he got here and has avoided making eye contact with me. He'd been delayed by bad traffic but also, I think, he finds it hard dealing with a patient without the protective cover of a white coat and stethoscope. He waits for a porter to push a gaunt figure swaddled in blue cotton blankets past us, then turns to me.

'This is all your fault.' Now he looks at me directly, his eyes are blazing. 'Dr Sarmah told me you had that Polish chap with you when you turned up at Mum's house.'

Martin glances at me in surprise. I hadn't mentioned to him that I'd been taking Tomasz to see Freya again. I keep my gaze on Archie's reddened face.

'I thought you were going to stop all this meddling with the past,' he goes on. 'I warned you it was distressing her, and now look!'

'That's not fair!'

'What does this guy want, anyway?'

'His name is Tomasz Dolniak and Mum may be the last link he has to discovering his father's identity.'

'So what? Why do we have to care?'

'It's not about him.' The stress of the last few days – weeks – makes me lose my temper. 'If Mum *is* distressed, it's because there's something *she* wants me to understand about the photograph Tomasz showed her. If you came to see her more often, you might know that.'

'I come as often as I can. It's not easy to get away.'

'I work, too, but I manage. One of us has to.'

'Yes, but . . . Anyway, look, that's not the point. You've always had issues with Mum, Kirsty, but they're *your* problems. You can't go upsetting her like this just because you've left it too late to sort them out.'

'That's not what I'm doing!'

'No? Then what is all this about? Who cares what happened in the war?'

'I told you. Mum showed me a chocolate tin from Warsaw with the name Wedel on it.'

Archie shakes his head in exasperation. I ignore him.

'She keeps trying to say the name,' I tell him. 'It means something that matters to her, maybe to do with Shona, and I'm trying to find out.'

'Shona's been dead for over forty years,' he says, looking at me with what, shockingly, appears to be real dislike. 'Why rake all that up again? If Mum wanted to talk to us about Shona, she'd have done so before now.'

'And what if it's not Shona in that photograph?' I ask. 'What if it's Mum?'

Archie throws up his hands. 'This has to stop. You sound as deranged as she is.'

'She's not deranged!'

'You're concocting an entire fairy tale on the evidence of a chocolate tin and a poor defenceless woman with brain damage. You tell me what the right word is for that!'

'OK, OK, time out.' Martin stretches his arm between us, like a referee.

But Archie ignores him, moving forwards so he's almost spitting in my face. 'You've gone too far, Kirsty. Just grow up and leave her in peace. Face it, whatever's broken in your life, this nonsense isn't going to fix it!'

My brother's words land like a punch. It hurts. Tears sting my eyes but I'm damned if I'll cry in front of him.

Martin puts his arm around my shoulders and pulls me close. 'Kirsty isn't just doing this for herself,' he tells Archie calmly. 'Whatever it is that Freya's so desperate to say, she's the one offering an object that came from Warsaw to try to make Kirsty understand.'

'It's just a tin,' said Archie, wearily. 'The pathways of her brain are scrambled. It's not the key to some big dramatic family secret. Mum's not like that. She's too grounded. It's Kirsty who's letting her imagination run away with her.'

He closes his eyes for a moment, then holds out his arms for a hug. I go warily.

'I'm sorry,' he says. 'It's tough, watching what's happening to her. And you're right, I should do more. But you have to accept that she's dying and let her go in peace.'

I nod and step back. I agree with what he says, but my idea of her being at peace isn't the same as his.

We walk in silence to the hospital exit where two paramedics wearing Santa hats and tinsel are singing 'Do They Know It's Christmas?' and rattling plastic cans to collect for famine relief. We say our rather awkward goodbyes and promise to speak on the phone about carers, visits and all the other arrangements still to be made. It's only mid-morning, and we all have to get back to work.

At least it's dry and sunny, an unseasonably warm December no doubt connected to the famine in Africa and a useful reminder that my worries are nothing in the great scheme of things. When I was little, at my grandparents' house in Aberdeen, I'd be told I had to eat everything on my plate because there'd be a starving child in Africa who'd be glad of it. Archie's right that Mum's Scots Presbyterian upbringing grounded her. But I also remember the sorrow that never left my grandparents' eyes, their grief, as I came to understand later, for my mother's dead twin. It was why, Dad had once told me, my grandmother could sometimes be frosty and distant with Freya.

As Martin drives he reaches out and covers my hand with his. 'Archie shouldn't have spoken to you like that.'

'He can't bear to see Mum the way she is,' I say. 'He's always seen her as indomitable.'

'Well, she is!'

'True. But how much of that was a mask? She's had a lot of suffering in her life. I wish she hadn't chosen to hide it.'

He puts his hand back on the steering wheel. 'It's that generation, isn't it? The Blitz spirit, make do and mend.'

'What should I do, Martin? Do I go on trying to find out everything I can while she's still alive, or just drop it completely?'

'What else *can* you do? Sounds like you've hit a dead end.'

I take a deep breath. 'I could speak to Patty Drexeler. Phyllis knows people who are in touch with her.'

'That would be opening up a big can of worms,' he says. 'Are you ready for that? For all the stuff about her and Nick and your parents' marriage?'

'Not really. No. Definitely not. But she's the only one who knew them during the war.'

Apart from swearing at the dawdling car in front that leaves us stuck at another red light, he says nothing for a while. Do I want to be in contact with Patty? Do I want to risk pissing Archie off completely? Would Freya ever forgive such disloyalty? I need someone else to tell me that it would be the right thing to do.

'What do you think?' I ask, when he remains silent.

'How much of this is to do with Tomasz?' he asks gently. 'Because if you do speak to Patty, it has to be for Freya's sake, not his.'

I'm glad he's given me a ready-made answer. I feel guilty enough about Tomasz as it is. I've tried not to think about him, but that didn't stop me waking this morning from a delightfully lurid dream.

'I can't see how Patty could know anything about Tomasz's father,' I say. 'So, no, it's not about him.'

'And us?' he asks quietly.

For a horrible moment I think he can read my mind. I'm too flustered to answer coherently. 'Us?'

'Making a decision about the job in Sydney. Would that be easier if you felt you'd finally sorted out some of the issues with your mother?'

I sigh with a mixture of relief that he doesn't suspect

anything to do with Tomasz and acknowledgement that of course there was more than a grain of truth in what Archie said about fixing what's wrong in my life.

'Maybe.'

'Have you discussed it with Archie? What does he think?'

I feel awkward admitting the truth. 'I've not really had a chance.'

'Look, I'm sorry I sprang it on all of you the way I did. I should have told you earlier.'

'Yes, that would have helped.'

'I've let the university know that your mother's in hospital and they've agreed to give me a little more time.'

'Thanks,' I say, although I'm no nearer clarifying what I want than I was when he first told me.

'Do you think resolving this business about the photograph would help?'

'Yes, probably,' I say. 'I'm so afraid of discovering that I've never really known Freya, that I've constantly misjudged her. Let her down. I'd like to put that right.'

Martin nods, staring at the back of the bus ahead of us. 'Then maybe you *should* ring Patty,' he says. 'I ought to tell the university as soon as possible if we're not going. We really do have to make a decision one way or the other. Maybe hearing what Patty can tell you is the only way forward.'

I turn my head sharply: he's never once mentioned *not* going to Australia as a real alternative. Maybe I've been misjudging my husband, too. Martin returns my look with a smile. Suddenly I feel comforted, reassured, safe. I know then that I will call Patty in New York.

25

Freya, 1944

Barely forty-eight hours after his initial injection of penicillin, Bartek awoke from a long sleep, managed to push himself up against his meagre pillows and demand to be given the latest news. When he started ordering Gosia, who was equally impatient to return to her usual duties, to write messages to send to the sector commanders, asking them to update him on the situation in the city, Freya had a hard job persuading him to wait.

'Your temperature hasn't returned to normal,' she told him. 'And, although your thigh is less inflamed, the wound is still open. You mustn't exert yourself. You have to rest and stay where you are, attached to the drip.'

Bartek was still grumbling about her refusal to give him a pen and paper when Dr Henryk arrived. Bartek begged him to describe conditions in the city, but Henryk refused.

'You must stay calm and do exactly as Dr Olenka says,' he said. 'Even once the infection is completely gone, you'll need rest and as much high-calorie food and vitamins as we can find for you. She hasn't come all this way to see you undo her good work.'

Bartek was too weak to argue any longer and fell asleep immediately after Freya had finished changing his drip.

'Thank you,' she said to Henryk. 'Although I'm very happy he can find the energy to be stubborn.'

'Indeed. I honestly never expected to witness so rapid a reversal in such a case.'

'I admit I was worried, too,' she said. 'The spread of the infection was worse than I'd hoped.'

'This drug is going to be truly life-changing for everyone.'

'Yes,' she said, 'but he's not out of the woods yet.'

'I understand. I'll sit with him, if that's all right with you?'

'Of course.'

'Perhaps you and Gosia would like to go and catch some daylight? Then she can tell him what's going on in the streets. That might help calm him.'

Freya turned to Gosia. 'Would that be OK? Can we go out?'

'Yes, come along.'

Freya ran up the stairs after Gosia. Emerging into the main banking hall, they were spotted by a group of young people who rushed to greet Gosia. Their expressions were tense and serious as they crowded around her, clearly asking questions, as she did eagerly of them. All wore makeshift uniforms, the men lean and handsome, the women, she was surprised to see, wearing bright lipstick, their hair pinned up fashionably high. Freya heard the name 'Olenka' as Gosia presented her, and was taken aback when one of the young men took her hand and kissed it and others, their faces lighting into smiles, patted her on the back.

'They want to thank you,' Gosia explained. 'They know you're

British but not why you're here. Last night the RAF made huge drops into the cemeteries in the Wola district, not far away. Anti-tank weapons, machine-guns, grenades, everything!'

Freya smiled and nodded, returning their greetings as best she could, although she couldn't help thinking of the air crews from Brindisi who must have made the flights and hoping they'd returned safely.

As the others went back to their exchange of information, Freya was drawn towards the bright sunlight streaming between the open double doors of the main entrance. Feeling a wave of hot August air, she automatically looked up at the sky; expecting a cloudless blue, she was shocked to find it disfigured by several high columns of black smoke in the near distance. She glanced back inside, but either no one was aware or they weren't especially alarmed by it.

Ahead of her the wide avenue was littered with masonry rubble and also partly covered with sheets of paper as if a dozen filing cabinets had been emptied and their contents flung about, like confetti. Two elderly women, heavy metal pails in each hand, were making their way along the opposite pavement. A small plane suddenly screamed overhead and they ducked their heads and quickened their step, barely spilling a drop of the water they carried. Freya covered her ears as it shot past only a few feet above the distant rooftops. Moments later the ground quaked as a bomb exploded. Soon afterwards, as if in delayed reaction, a haze of dust billowed from a side-road, briefly lifting and redistributing the carpet of paper, and then, several streets away, another shroud of thick smoke belched upwards.

Shocked, and recoiling from the acrid smell, it took her a moment to feel a hand gently tugging her elbow.

'That's Wola,' Gosia said, indicating towards where bright orange flames were now roaring upwards amid the distant smoke. 'The Luftwaffe are dropping incendiaries while the SS go from house to house, murdering civilians. They want to terrify them into not supporting us.'

Freya couldn't find the right words. 'I'm sorry,' she said. 'So sorry.'

Gosia shrugged. 'We knew what to expect. I need to speak to my colleagues on the news sheet. Do you want to come with me?'

'Yes.' Freya's pulse was racing, but she knew she mustn't allow herself to run back into the safety of the bank. 'So long as I'm back in time to change the drip.'

'Of course. It's not far.' Gosia pulled her cap out of her trouser pocket and, tucking her hair up under it, settled it firmly in place. She linked her arm in Freya's. 'Right, let's go.'

Staying on the same side of the street and keeping close to the offices and boarded-up shop fronts, Gosia walked quickly to the corner where she turned right, away from Wola, just as another Stuka streaked past. Gosia did not look back as a second explosion rocked the surrounding buildings but continued along the side-road for some way, again keeping close to the wall. She stopped beside the entrance to a cobbled mews that stretched in both directions and seemed to house stables, stores and workshops. Stretching out her arm to keep Freya from walking forwards, she scanned the surrounding windows and rooftops.

'We have to cross the road,' she said. 'Be ready to run.'

Freya remembered Rudzik's warning about German snipers. 'You go first,' she said hoarsely, her mouth dry with fear.

Gosia darted to the entrance of the opposite mews, then beckoned to Freya. Taking a deep breath, Freya ran, laughing in relief when she safely reached the other side.

'Good, come on.'

Near the far end of the mews Gosia tapped on a grimy window. A face appeared, followed by the sound of bolts being drawn back on the nearby door. It opened a crack and a young boy, who couldn't have been more than twelve or thirteen, peered out, preceded by the barrel of his pistol. Gosia gave the password and the boy let them in, securing the door behind them.

The space they entered was a storeroom, with neatly stacked bales of paper and other materials. Freya couldn't immediately place the smell of something metallic and faintly sweet but, following Gosia through into the main workshop area, the sight and repetitive noise of a small printing press in operation told her that, of course, it was ink.

At the sight of visitors, the five people grouped around the machine cried out in pleasure and came forward to embrace Gosia. After an excited exchange she turned to introduce 'Olenka', who was soon forgotten again as Gosia took a copy of the latest bulletin off the press and became involved in a discussion about its contents. Freya admired Gosia's self-possession – she had yet to feel genuinely confident at work – and could tell from the respectful way her colleagues waited to hear her opinion that she was an important member of the team.

Freya didn't mind being excluded from their eager talk. She

had never seen the process by which any kind of newspaper was produced – it was Shona who had helped edit the student magazine – and was intrigued to look around. Aside from the clanking press, churning out its printed pages, and the tidy trays of metal type, there were other machines, whose purpose she didn't know, as well as filing cabinets, typewriters and, on one wall, wide shelves stacked with what looked like different types of camera next to circular metal tins that she was pretty sure contained reels of film. Graphic posters were tacked to the walls. If this was the AK's information and propaganda unit, it was certainly impressive. She pictured Gosia sitting at one of the desks, focused on the words she was typing before handing her copy to a compositor, fully committed to a vital and no doubt dangerous task.

A cheer went up, and Freya looked around in surprise. One of the group – a man in his late twenties with light curly hair, mischievous eyes and an infectious grin – was holding aloft what looked like a jar of preserved fruit.

'Cherries in brandy!' Gosia informed her. She nodded towards the young man. 'Feliks found them at the back of a cupboard!'

Feliks made a pantomime of unscrewing the tight, slightly rusty lid and, inhaling the aroma, pretending to stagger backwards as though overcome by the alcoholic fumes. His friends laughed and shook their heads, clearly used to his clowning. He held the jar out towards the eldest of the men but, just as he was about to scoop out one of the plump, almost black cherries, Feliks swung it around and, tapping his heels together and bowing his head, presented it instead to Freya.

'Take one,' said Gosia.

Feliks raised an eyebrow as Freya hesitated, expecting him to whip the jar away the moment she went to dip in her fingers. She was right: he did withdraw it, helping himself to the first. He tapped the fruit gently against the glass rim to disperse the dripping syrup and then, instead of eating it himself, held it delicately towards her, miming for her to open her mouth. Unable to resist the succulent-looking fruit, she obeyed and let him drop it into her mouth. Everyone clapped and Freya tried not to join in the laughter in case she spat out the deliciously sour fruit. Instead she bowed to them all, just as he had done, earning further applause.

Handing the jar to the older man, Feliks said something in Polish to Gosia before going over to take a camera off the far shelf.

'He wants to take a picture of us together,' she said. 'He's one of our best photographers. But I want my taste of brandy first!'

Feliks, his expression now serious, opened the back of the Leica and threaded in a new roll of film, then hung the strap around his neck and returned to where Gosia stood savouring the fruit. He placed an arm around her shoulders and whispered in her ear. Watching her smile and nudge him playfully away with her elbow, Freya wondered what history lay between them and felt a peculiar stab of envy. She didn't always have patience with such silliness, but there was something so light and vibrant about him that it was easy to imagine being seduced by him.

She blushed when Feliks caught her eye and held out his hand to lead her to an open door that led into a back courtyard, and went with him willingly.

The outdoor heat was like a wall, the air smelling of brick

and stone. The courtyard was no longer enclosed. The opposite buildings had been bombed, leaving only the high front façade and remnants of the ground floor. The debris must have been cleared long ago, and some flourishing buddleia had seeded itself in the upper walls.

Gosia noticed her pause on the threshold to stare at the jagged walls. 'From nineteen thirty-nine,' she said. 'Most of the targets were strategic, but some residential areas were hit.'

Feliks looked up at the sky, then positioned them against the broken wall of what had once been a wing of the ruined building so that they were at a slight angle to the harsh sunlight. He flapped his hand to instruct them to move closer to one another and said something in Polish that made Gosia laugh.

'He told me to lift my head or I'll have a double chin,' she translated. 'Cheeky bastard!'

Freya liked being the subject of his flickering glance as he looked them up and down, making sure he was happy with their pose before raising the little camera to his eye. He clicked and wound on several times then moved closer, his eyes already scouting another composition. There was a crack and he fell to his knees. Freya assumed he wanted an unusual viewpoint and waited for him to lift his camera, but then his body keeled sideways and his head hit the dry ground with a thud. Seeing the dark blood pooling around his face, she was about to run forwards but Gosia grabbed her and pulled her back, forcing her down behind the shelter of the low wall.

'Don't move!' she hissed.

Freya struggled, still not taking in what had happened. 'I might be able to help him!'

Gosia held fast, using the weight of her body to pin Freya to the ground. 'If you do, the sniper will kill you, too.'

'I can't just leave him.'

'You must. Your duty is to Bartek.'

'But—'

'Stay down and keep close to me.'

'I can't – I must—'

'Can't you see? It's too late.'

Freya forced her agonized gaze away from Feliks and focused on Gosia's face, inches away from her own. Something warm fell on her neck: Gosia's tears. She gave up the fight.

26

Kirsty, 1989

Managing to penetrate the infrastructure of the very wealthy in order to reach someone like Patty Drexeler, one of those fabled creatures from the society pages of glossy international magazines, turns out to be a far more time-consuming exercise than I'd expected.

'Miss Drexeler has not yet returned from her weekend in Newport.'

'Miss Drexeler does not take personal calls in the morning.'

'Miss Drexeler will be tied up with a charity committee all afternoon. Perhaps you would care to leave a message?'

'Kirsty? Is that you? But this is really something!' Patty's American accent is even more drawlingly exaggerated than I remember. 'Oh, but how is your mother? Don't tell me you're calling with bad news, you poor darling.'

I'd also forgotten how effusive she always was. I hadn't been sure how I'd react to hearing her voice again, or even how clearly I'd remember it, and I certainly hadn't anticipated the instant recall of how her words used to wrap me in a warm fog of approbation and enthusiasm. I have no memory of her ever wanting anything from us as children other than that we had a good time. The pleasure I feel pushes me to realize that casting Patty as the bogeyman in the divorce made it easier to forgive Dad. Or perhaps we let him off so lightly because we were never that invested in him anyway.

Martin has helped me to work out in advance what information I'm prepared to give, and I reply to her question accordingly. 'No, it's not bad news, Patty, although Mum's not been too well, which is why I won't tell her I'm speaking to you.'

'Oh, well, I guess that's understandable.' She sounds disappointed that there's no offer of a rapprochement. 'But I'm sorry to hear her health is bad. If there's anything I can do – you probably won't believe this, but Freya's very, very dear to me.'

I've already decided not to get into past recriminations, and stick to my purpose. 'I was ringing to ask you a question.'

'Fire away.'

'Do you know anything about the work my aunt Shona did during the war? She was in uniform, wasn't she?'

'Sure. We knew a lot of the same people.'

'Was she with the Special Operations Executive?'

'Yes. Polish Section Six.'

I'm taken aback by her prompt reply. 'I thought they weren't supposed to talk about what they did?'

'She didn't.' Patty laughed, her throaty bark eerily familiar. 'She didn't have to. I was what they so gallantly described as an unofficial asset. My house was a neutral zone where people could meet. Discreetly, of course. Any nationality that needed to open a back-door channel of communication only had to ask and I'd send an invitation. It wasn't exactly difficult to work out who did what.'

I think of my visits to Patty's Mayfair home, where her elderly butler would bring us the biggest ice-cream sundaes we'd ever seen. Only much later did I identify the paintings on the walls beside us or realize that the sundaes were served in eighteenth-century Venetian crystal goblets.

'Did Shona go to Poland in the summer of nineteen forty-four?' I ask.

'I very much doubt it. No, in fact, I remember her coming almost every night for a while, looking as if she'd lost a dollar and found a penny.'

My heart thuds. 'Would you remember exactly when that was?'

Her silence travels along the transatlantic line. 'The talk was of the Allied advance into Europe,' she says, after some thought. 'It was definitely before the liberation of Paris. And, of course, the Warsaw Uprising had just begun.'

'And Shona was in London?'

'Yes, I'm certain.'

'How on earth can you be so sure?'

Patty's drawl is stretched even further. 'Honey, I remember every party I've ever given or attended. Ten days ago it was the Met Gala and I can tell you every person who was there *and* what they were wearing.'

I can't help but laugh. 'And my mother? Was she with Shona that month?'

'I was only just getting to know Freya when she disappeared for a while. I think she was ill. She'd certainly lost weight when I saw her again.'

My heart thuds a second time. 'Does the name Wedel mean anything to you?'

'Nothing at all. This is all very intriguing, Kirsty. So what's the story?'

I take a deep breath. This is the first time I've been able to state this as fact. 'I have a photograph of Freya in Warsaw in August nineteen forty-four.' My mind reels: it really *was* Freya. My buttoned-up, old-school 'refrigerator' mother is a derring-do secret agent! 'I wasn't a hundred per cent sure until now that it was Freya and not Shona, but if you're sure that Shona was in London . . .'

I hear a long, low whistle along the line. 'Well I never. She's a sly puss, your mother. I had no idea, no idea at all. And not much gets past me, I can tell you.' There's a sharp pause. 'So why did you have to ask me? Would Freya not tell you?'

'She can't speak. Or write. She has a brain tumour.'

'Oh!' Patty's exclamation carries real sorrow, and I struggle not to cry.

'Her beautiful, elegant mind,' Patty says. 'That's just too cruel. Are you sure there's nothing I can do, nothing she needs?'

'No, we're fine, thank you.'

'But what on earth would she have been doing in Warsaw? She had no link to SOE other than through Shona. And I'm certain Shona was in town.'

'I don't know.' I feel tears coming despite my best efforts. 'I want to understand before she—'

'Don't you worry, honey. Let me think what I can find out. We'll talk again soon, yes?'

'Yes. Thank you.'

Patty hangs up almost immediately, and I'm grateful for her tact.

I've been using the phone on the desk in Martin's study. He and the boys are in the kitchen downstairs where he volunteered to get supper ready and keep them out of the way while I made my call. I seldom sit in this room on my own. With the only light coming from his Anglepoise lamp it's restful to be in someone else's space, especially as he's always been an orderly man. The sight of the chain of paperclips beside the keyboard makes me smile. It's a habit he already had when I first met him. He adds each new one that comes his way to the shiny coil until the length becomes unwieldy and he throws the lot away and starts again. The current chain is reaching that point.

I know these things about my husband that no one else probably notices. But do they add up to knowing *him*? I can close my eyes and feel the touch of my mother's hands, see the fleck of russet in the iris of one eye, or the way she checks that no one is looking before licking a finger to pick up the last crumbs of cake from her plate. Yet I never even registered that a piece of her story was missing, let alone that it might be something so significant. Am I a bad daughter, too self-absorbed and incurious to notice, or has she held her secrets so tight that suspicion was unimaginable?

And, worst of all, is it shallow of me to feel that, had I known, I would have liked her more?

Eric pushes open the door and, seeing I'm no longer on the phone, comes over to where I sit. Not yet old enough to be self-conscious about showing physical affection, he slips his arm around my neck and touches his head to mine. 'Supper's ready,' he says.

I pull him to me, breathing in his boyish smell and thinking how short a time it seems since he would have climbed onto my lap.

'Grandma Freya went on some incredible adventures during the war,' I tell him proudly.

'What sort of adventures?'

'She went on a secret mission to Poland. She had to jump out of a plane with a parachute.'

He laughs with delight. 'Did she have to shoot anyone?'

'No, I don't think so. I hope not. I'm trying to find out more about it.'

'Grandma would make a good secret agent.'

'She would, wouldn't she?'

'Is she going to be OK?'

Eric, my anxious, caring child. 'Not really,' I say. 'But she'll be going home tomorrow and we can go and see her and make her happy.'

He nods. 'Dad says to come for supper.'

'Good. I'm hungry.'

As I get up, the phone rings. I'm tempted to leave it but, worried that it could be the hospital, pick up the receiver. It's Patty again.

'I just thought of someone else you could talk to,' she says breathlessly. 'Shona's fiancé, Leo Tarnowski. He was in Polish Intelligence, so he'd definitely know why Freya went to Warsaw.'

So Shona's fiancé *was* Polish. 'Is he still alive?'

'I don't know, but I can easily get my people to find out.'

I hesitate, aware of Eric beside me. 'He left her on the eve of their wedding. She never recovered.'

'No one ever explained what really happened there. I thought it might be to do with his religion. He was Catholic and she wasn't. I know he loved her.'

'What was he like?'

'One of those romantically patriotic Poles. Quite impossible. The sort that would have felt it their duty to lead a cavalry charge against Nazi tanks. I liked Leo a lot.'

'Maybe he went back to Poland.'

'I doubt it. The fight was over by then and he would never have accepted the Stalinist yoke. Besides, he knew very well that anyone linked to the Government-in-Exile would've been executed on the spot.'

I have to make a decision. Eric is tinkering with Martin's chain of paperclips and pretending he's not drinking in every word. Shona's dead. My mother is alive – just – and this may be the last chance for us all to share her past with her.

'Are you still there?' Patty asks.

'Yes. Would you be able to find him?'

'Sure. The Drexeler name still opens doors. I'll speak to my lawyer. He'll know who to call.'

'Thank you.'

'My pleasure. I'll let you know as soon as I have news.'

'Thanks.'

'How's Archie, by the way? And I haven't asked about you. So many questions!'

'He's fine.' I feel my face go red with shame. 'He's a surgeon, a burns specialist.' Like Dad, except I can't bring myself to say it.

'And you?' Patty asks.

'I'm an academic. Married, two boys. One of them is here with me now, telling me that my supper is ready.'

'Well, I won't keep you. But, Kirsty?'

'Yes?'

'I'm so happy you called.'

27

Freya, 1944

'Are you awake?' whispered Freya, when she heard Gosia roll over once again. It wasn't late, but by silent agreement they'd both sought the privacy of their mattresses rather than attempt to distract themselves from what they'd witnessed.

'Can't sleep,' came the reply.

'Nor me.'

'It'll be dark out there soon. Then they can retrieve his body.'

So, thought Freya, they had both been lying in the dark dwelling on the image of Feliks left to lie alone in the empty sunlit courtyard.

'They'll want the camera back, too. That one was dropped by the RAF. He always said Leica had the best lenses.'

Gosia's voice broke and Freya strained to make out her face in the gloom. She had three hours before changing Bartek's drip again. He had managed to eat some potato soup and was sleeping comfortably. Although Gosia had reported all the news she'd gleaned, she'd said nothing to him of Feliks's death.

'Had you known him long?' Freya asked.

'From before the war.'

'Were you in love with him?'

'No. Yes. I was once. He's been a good friend to me. They'll find a priest and bury him tomorrow.'

'You must be there. It's important to say goodbye.'

'He was so *alive*.'

Hearing Gosia weep, Freya thought of the first time, as a final-year student, she'd sat by the bed of an elderly patient and watched him take his final breath. He'd been given morphine for the pain, and the end, when it came, was almost imperceptible. Death was something that medical students self-protectively joked about until the moment came when each of them was sent to break the news to the relatives. She hadn't yet had to tell a patient their illness was terminal. But none of that limited experience had prepared her for this: Feliks was not a cadaver in a mortuary but a unique smile and glance and spirit, all gone for ever in an instant. It could have been any one of them. It might yet be.

'You saved my life,' she told Gosia.

'I put you in danger. I should never have taken you out there in the first place. I don't know what I was thinking.'

We were only eating cherries, thought Freya. *Stealing a moment to be young and carefree.* 'It wasn't your fault,' she said. 'And I'd have had the next bullet in my head if you hadn't pulled me down.'

'You weren't to know.'

Freya was suddenly sideswiped by the closeness of her brush with extinction. 'Thank you, Gosia. Truly, thank you. I owe you my life.'

'Nonsense.'

Almost automatically she thought of Shona. And then of Leo. Was he going to return safely? How would Shona manage if he didn't?

'You knew Wedel before the war, too?' she asked.

'We worked together. Why do you ask?'

Gosia's tone was sharp, but the ban on an exchange of personal details seemed pointless now. There was no one else to overhear. What did it matter? How could they remain strangers after sharing such an experience?

'He's the man my sister is in love with.'

'He's the reason you're here?' Gosia sounded taken aback.

'Yes.'

'Does he love her?'

Freya hoped that Gosia wasn't about to reveal doubts regarding Leo's character. 'I think so,' she said. 'Yes. Very much.'

'I was in love before the war,' said Gosia. 'We were going to be married.'

'What happened? Was he killed?'

'No, but war changes people. Tell your sister that love is not for ever. She should take love wherever she finds it.'

'She won't believe you,' said Freya, relieved that Gosia's cynicism stemmed from her own romantic experience.

'It's a hard lesson to learn.'

'Wedel means life to her.'

'Does he know that?'

'Probably not. She says his country comes first. I'm only here because she's so afraid of losing him. All the Poles I've met back home seem just as passionately patriotic. Was he always like that?'

'He was one of many men who left so they could continue the fight,' Gosia said. 'What about you? Have you left someone behind?'

'No.' Freya recalled Feliks's smile as he dropped the dark red fruit into her mouth and couldn't stop herself sighing with regret for what she'd never experienced. 'I envy my sister. Even if this war cuts their affair short, she and Wedel should treasure what they have. It's worth fighting for. I'm glad I chose to do what I can to defend that.'

'Bartek seems so much better this evening.'

'Yes. His temperature is down and his wound is looking nice and pink. We caught the infection in the nick of time.'

'I can't tell you who he is, but his recovery will make a great difference to our fight.'

'He needs another two or three days. His treatment can't be rushed.'

'And then you must go.'

'Go where?'

'Home to England. We can send a radio signal for instructions on where you'll be picked up.'

Freya had barely listened when Major P had explained the arrangements for bringing them back. At that point the whole venture had appeared so preposterous that the necessity for a return journey seemed impossibly remote. It still didn't feel real. All that mattered was sharing this moment with Gosia.

'I am so sorry about Feliks,' she said. 'I only met him for a few minutes, but I'll never forget him. Or you, Gosia. Whatever you say, I'm in your debt now, so keep it in your pocket for a rainy day, as my mother would say.'

Gosia's laugh sounded forced but she reached out to clasp Freya's outstretched hand. 'When all this is over you can take me to the Ritz.'

They lay in silence for a while until, hearing descending footsteps, they scrambled to their feet and ran to the bottom of the stairs.

'Wedel!'

'How is he?' Leo asked. 'How's Bartek?'

'Doing well.' Freya was so relieved to see him safe and sound that she hugged him tight. 'And you? You're all right?'

'Yes, of course.' In fact, he looked strained and exhausted. 'So he's going to make it?'

'So long as he completes the course of penicillin.'

'Where is he?' Leo asked, looking around impatiently. 'Can I talk to him?'

She hoped he wasn't going to disrupt Bartek's recovery. 'You can see him when he wakes up. Come and tell us how you are.'

'When did you last eat or drink?' asked Gosia, also trying to distract him.

He rubbed a hand over his face as if coming out of deep sleep. 'Gosia, hello. I've just come from the Old Town. I have messages for Bartek. They want him to join them as soon as he's well enough to move.'

'What's the situation there?'

'We seem to have taken them by surprise. They sent a column of tanks but we threw Molotov cocktails and they turned tail. It's very bad in Wola, though.'

'I heard,' said Gosia. 'We saw some of the bombing.'

'They're burning houses and lining people up to shoot them, even in the hospitals. It's mass slaughter.'

Leo's eyes blazed. His face was thinner, thought Freya, the line of his nose sharper than ever. He rubbed his hand down over his face a second time.

'But we're gaining ground elsewhere,' he continued, making an effort to sound more positive. 'There's heavy street-fighting, but we still have civilian support.'

'There's a piece in the next news bulletin about how people are gathering up all the official portraits of Hitler and sticking them on top of the barricades for the Germans to shoot at,' said Gosia.

'Good! But what about you? How have you been getting on?'

The two women exchanged glances. 'We've hardly been out,' said Freya. 'I have to administer the penicillin every four hours.'

'And I make sure she wakes up in time,' said Gosia.

Freya saw that Leo guessed from the way he looked from her to Gosia and back that they were keeping something from him but he made no comment. She understood why: too many people in this war had stories they didn't want to tell.

'Is there somewhere I can bunk down for the night?'

'I'll show you,' said Gosia.

Freya, suddenly feeling her own exhaustion, was glad to sit down again on her mattress as Gosia found a spare blanket and showed Leo where he could wash. When they returned they stood together at the bottom of the stairs for a few moments. He seemed to be asking her something. She shook her head, not looking at him although she placed a light hand on his forearm. He stepped closer and drew her to him. She remained still, not responding yet accepting his offer of comfort. Freya wondered if perhaps Leo and Feliks had also been friends.

By the end of the week the bombardment had become constant. Even deep in their vault Freya and Gosia could feel the earth shake, and sometimes the lights flickered, making Gosia worry about having enough petrol to keep the generator running. When they ventured out, the sky was a pall of dense smoke, the ground covered with soft white ash, and the sound of gunfire unceasing. With Bartek almost fully recovered, able to dress and take a few steps, although still attached to the drip, Freya volunteered to treat some of the wounded. Day and night AK fighters and civilians were being brought in from the frontline streets where the Germans were trying to break through the barricades. Even though Freya had asked Gosia to teach her a little of the language, her inability to communicate hampered her efforts and in the end she was just getting in the way of those who could offer real help.

But she saw enough for her heart to go out to a city whose inhabitants, often armed only with bricks, hand-made grenades and petrol bombs, were willing to face tanks, planes, heavy artillery and flame throwers to win their freedom.

The weather continued hot and dry. Water was in increasingly short supply and German snipers targeted the women and children queuing at newly dug courtyard wells. Clouds of flies hovered over their makeshift graves. Everyone got used to the smell of open latrines and no one asked what was in the soup served up by the communal canteens. Yet morale remained high. Standing in the open doorway of the bank, Freya heard young voices singing patriotic songs and saw how intent people were on taking action at last.

Leo came and went, gathering information from the high command in the Old Town, relaying it to Bartek and making radio contact with London. After his last perilous journey he returned looking gaunt and ragged, and Freya made him sit still while she cleaned his cuts and grazes.

'This is how Bartek became so ill,' she reminded him. 'You mustn't risk getting an infection.'

He submitted, impatiently at first but then exhaustion caught up with him. He slumped back and closed his eyes.

'There. All done.'

He sat up and mustered a smile. 'Thanks, Olenka.'

He put his head into his hands. Freya looked at him more closely. 'What's the matter?'

'I don't know what to do.'

'Would it help to talk?'

'Is there somewhere private?'

'We can sit on my mattress. Gosia's out and Dr Henryk is with Bartek.'

They settled themselves and she waited for him to speak.

'No one wants to hear the truth,' he said at last.

'About what?'

'Did you know that the Soviets are claiming that all the AK leaders have fled and left the city defenceless?'

'It's only propaganda. People can see for themselves it's not true.'

'But if Churchill won't come out and say that, it might as well be true. That's what I've been trying to get Bartek and the others to understand. They started the Uprising believing that the Allies will help us.'

'Gosia said the RAF made more drops two nights ago,' Freya protested.

'They did, but it's not enough. And if Stalin refuses even to give us air cover, it's all they *can* do. Don't you see? Even if by some miracle we drive the Germans out of Warsaw on our own, and however much Churchill wants to support Polish independence, he and the other Allies aren't in a strong enough position to risk openly defying Stalin.'

'But they must! Once they see the sacrifice that's being made!'

'That's what the AK leaders want to believe. And, now it's started, the Government-in-Exile in London has no choice but to back them up. But they know it's not going to happen.'

'So what *will* happen?'

'We carry on the fight.'

'And us?' she asked. 'Bartek finishes his course of penicillin tonight.'

'I've been in touch with London,' Leo said. 'They've given me a location where an RAF Dakota can land safely and take off again. They'll play a particular Chopin étude on the BBC Polish hour to confirm a next-day rendezvous. I think it may be possible to get out of the city through the new civilian transit camp in Pruszków.'

'When do we leave?'

Instead of answering, he looked down at his hands. A cold dread clutched her stomach. She dared not put her fear into words.

'I'm not going with you.' He said it for her. 'I'm staying here.'

'But you just said the fight is hopeless.'

'All the more reason to stay. I have to do what I can. You'll be able to memorize the messages for London for me, won't you?'

'You can't stay! What about Shona?'

'Tell her I love her, but I can't go back. She'll understand.'

'No,' said Freya, angrily. 'She won't. She never will. The only reason I agreed to come was because it was the only way she could help you. Now you've done your bit. You can't do this to her! Or me!'

He ignored her appeal. 'Gosia will see you safely out of Warsaw.'

'And then what happens to her?'

'Maybe you can persuade her to go with you. I'm sure I can clear it with London.'

'Fine. But you have to come with us.'

He shook his head, not meeting her eye.

'Look, I understand,' she said. 'I do. I feel I'm a part of this now, and I've only been here a week. But surely you can do far more by going back to London. You're the only one who can really brief them properly.'

'I'll tell you everything you need to know.'

'And if I refuse?'

'Then Gosia can do it.'

'What can Gosia do?'

Neither of them had noticed Gosia arrive. Leo shot Freya a meaningful glance and scrambled to his feet. 'Olenka will explain,' he said. 'I have to talk to Bartek.'

Gosia remained silent until Leo was out of earshot. 'What's wrong with him?'

'He wants to stay.'

'What?' Gosia asked, clearly as shocked as Freya had been. 'Why?'

'To join the fight.'

'Is it about finding his mother and sister?'

'I don't know. He didn't mention them. But what can I possibly say to my sister? This will break her heart.'

'It's exactly how he was in nineteen thirty-nine,' said Gosia. 'All he could talk about was honour, patriotism, freedom, so many abstract ideas that mean more to him than any reality he can actually touch and hold.'

'More than love, you mean?'

'Or people as individuals.'

'I think that deep down my sister already knows that,' said Freya. 'It's why she's always so dreadfully afraid that he'll hurt her, however much they love one another.'

'If he's made up his mind, there's nothing you can do.'

'He wants you to come back with me instead.'

'Me?'

'He says you can do his job for him.'

'Oh, can I?'

'And you'll be safe. Please, Gosia, whatever Wedel decides, you could come with me.'

Gosia shook her head decisively. 'It's not possible.'

'So you're the same as him. You choose to stay and fight for your country.'

Gosia smiled. 'No. I'm fighting for a better future, for our children's future.'

Freya heard footsteps and looked around to see Dr Henryk.

He cleared his throat nervously. 'Bartek would like to see you both.'

They found Leo, his face tight with anger, standing beside where Bartek was seated on the edge of his bed.

'I have given my orders that Wedel and Olenka leave tomorrow for their return to England.' Bartek turned to look up at Leo. 'Each of us has our part to play in this struggle. Personal wishes count for nothing. I hope that's clear?'

'Yes, sir,' Leo replied.

Bartek turned to Freya, his expression softening. 'Dr Olenka, you go with my personal thanks and with the gratitude of the Polish people for the courage you have shown in coming to my aid. I owe you my life.'

'I'll pass on your thanks to Professor Florey,' said Freya. 'You owe your life to his discovery.'

'That too. I'm honoured to have received a treatment that I suspect will make a greater difference to this world than all our wars. But, all the same, it's you, my dear, who made it possible.'

Bartek pushed himself to his feet with an effort and stood ramrod straight, every inch the cavalry officer. He clicked his heels and bowed his head as he reached for Freya's hand, hovered his lips half an inch above it. 'I remain your servant,' he said.

'And I, too,' came Henryk's voice behind her.

'Thank you,' said Freya, fighting back tears. 'It's been my privilege to be here. And now you must rest. I'll come back in an hour to dismantle the drip, but you're not to think of leaving here until tomorrow at the earliest. Dr Henryk? You'll make sure of that?'

'Indeed I will.'

Feeling slightly overwhelmed by the attention, Freya was almost glad for once to return to her mattress in its gloomy corner. Gosia followed her.

'It'll be all right now,' she said. 'Wedel will have to follow orders.'

Freya sighed. 'Yes. But I'll always look at him with my sister and know that he would have preferred to stay.'

Gosia seemed to be on the point of speaking, but instead she pulled Freya into a hug. 'It's this war. It places people in impossible situations. You mustn't judge them by the choices they make.'

Freya wasn't sure she agreed but was happy to return Gosia's embrace. 'I'm going to miss you,' she told her.

'They say that the person who saves a life retains an interest in it for ever,' said Gosia. 'I want you to be happy, for my sake.'

'I'll do my best,' Freya promised. 'And if there's ever anything I can do for you, you have only to ask.'

In that moment, she knew with complete certainty that, even if she never saw her again, Gosia would remain one of the most important people she'd ever encountered.

28

Kirsty, 1989

'Olenka,' I whisper.

My mother opens her eyes and looks up at me from where she's dozed off in her chair.

'Olenka?' I'm standing beside her, and this time I say the name as a question, hoping desperately for her confirmation. She's properly awake now but, when her look grows wary, my heart sinks – *please don't let her deny me this* – but then she nods and my spirits soar. For her, too, I sense that it's a gesture of acquiescence and resignation as if, after many years, she's finally prepared to put down a burden.

I pull up a chair beside her and take her hand. 'I'm so proud of you. What you were doing in Warsaw must have taken enormous courage.'

She waves her free hand dismissively and makes a sound in her throat that I interpret as *Don't be ridiculous*. I laugh, mainly with relief although several other emotions are present that I'll have to untangle later.

I'm overjoyed that Chris has volunteered to give up his

Saturday morning to come with me. Although his brother has badgered me with questions since he discovered his grandmother's thrilling past – few of which I can answer – Chris has remained largely content to listen. I'd hoped in the car over here he might have chatted away as he used to but, apart from asking a couple of questions about his grandmother's condition, he spent most of the journey staring moodily out of the passenger window, and I was too scared of provoking another argument about Sydney to break the silence. I should be dealing with this better, but at least he's here now for Freya's sake.

I'd made copies of Tomasz's photograph for each of the boys, and Chris comes over to give one of them to her. She stares at it as he perches on the arm of her chair.

'It's you, isn't it?' I ask.

She nods a second time.

'I'm sorry I didn't ask you before. And sorry that you were never able to tell us.'

She's not listening. She's touching Gosia's face with her forefinger, gently stroking the paper.

She did the same thing when Tomasz handed her the original, and I'd assumed then without a second thought that it was Shona's face she was touching with such sadness. How have I been so blind and stupid that I completely missed seeing the truth when it was right in front of me?

The two young women in the photograph are smiling at the photographer as if sharing a joke. Their shoulders are touching. They're friends.

'You were fond of her?' I ask, for want of anything better to say.

Freya nods, her eyes still on the image.

I realize I haven't passed on the little I know about Gosia because I'd also assumed that Freya had never met her, might not even have heard of her. But her tears that night weren't for her sister, they were for her friend.

'Tomasz would have been about four when that picture was taken,' I tell her. 'Gosia had left him with her older brother and his wife, away from Warsaw. After the war, when the Soviets rounded up all the AK fighters, Gosia was imprisoned and sent to a gulag.'

I wonder how much of this, if any, Freya already knows. 'Gosia had been badly beaten in prison and never fully recovered. She died when Tomasz was thirteen. He went on living with his uncle and aunt.' I try to think what else I can tell her. 'The uncle died a couple of years ago, but his aunt is still alive. And Tomasz has a son, too,' I add. 'Gosia would have had a grandson.'

Freya turns to look up at Chris. She smiles and pats his leg. Although never sentimental she's always had a good rapport with my sons. They tapped effortlessly into a vein of affection that eluded me. Maybe, I think, she finds boys easier. Maybe the closeness of a daughter reminds her too much of her twin.

'Did you fight the Nazis, Grandma?' Chris asks in a serious and respectful tone. 'Did you have to carry a gun?'

She smiles and shakes her head.

'Were you some kind of spy, a secret agent?'

She shrugs, still smiling. I can tell she's actually enjoying this.

'What's the meaning of the chocolate tin?' he asks. 'Mum told us about it. Can I see it? How did you get it?'

I laugh. 'Too many questions. One at a time.'

Freya points across to the teak desk, turns to me and rolls her eyes. It's good to see her back to her old self after the frail figure in the hospital bed. Archie, probably as a peace offering, had taken time off work to bring her home and had stayed a couple of nights to settle her in and assess how well she was going to manage. Last night he and I had a slightly strained but civil conversation in which we agreed that, with a bit more cooking and domestic support in place, she'd be OK for the time being. I didn't mention Patty.

Chris comes back with the tin. 'OK if I open it?'

'It's her sewing kit,' I tell him. 'You've probably seen it before.'

It makes no difference to his eagerness, and his expression as he prises off the lid is heart-warming. For a fleeting moment he looks so like a little boy again that it's impossible to judge whether he can really be old enough to know his own mind with enough maturity to refuse to leave London. I catch Freya watching as he pokes a finger among the buttons and darning wool and wonder what her advice would be.

'Was Wedel a code word?' Chris asks her.

'Or a person?' I ask. 'A fellow resistance fighter?'

She pats my hand.

'A man?'

Pat, pat.

'Did he go to Poland with you?'

Pat, pat.

'Is he someone I know? Would I ever have met him?'

A sharp shake of her head.

I want to ask if he's Tomasz's father, but remember how

furious the question made her when I asked her about that before – although it was afterwards that she first tried to say 'Wedel', and the next time I saw her she gave me the tin. I try a roundabout route.

'Did Gosia know Wedel?'

Freya nods, then rests her head against the back of the chair. She looks drained.

'Might she have met him here in England, before the war?'

No response.

'Do you want me to find him?'

She closes her eyes and turns her head away.

'Let's go and make some lunch,' I say to Chris. 'Leave Grandma to rest.'

In the kitchen Chris heats up a carton of soup while I make sandwiches.

'Why did Grandma never tell us what she did in the war?'

'She probably had to sign the Official Secrets Act. You can be sent to prison for betraying an Official Secret.'

'But it was years ago.'

To him the war is a school history lesson. And yet it's still here, in this house, affecting us, changing who we are, pushing relationships out of kilter, making us angry and happy and sad. My mother's secrets aren't official, they're personal.

I collapse onto the bench seat by the window and try to hide my face from him. I don't want him to see me crying.

'It's all right, Mum. It'll be all right.'

'She's hidden so much of herself. I've never been given a chance to know her. It's not fair.'

'But you're finding out now.'

'Not enough. There are still so many secrets. About her, and Shona, and what happened to Shona, and probably about my father, too. How am I supposed to do the right thing if everything I thought I knew turns out to be wrong?'

Chris sits beside me and puts an arm around me. I turn, grateful to hide my face in his shoulder, noticing as I do how his physique is changing, hardening into young manhood. I mustn't treat him like a child any more.

'Do you want to move to Sydney, Mum? Because if it's not what you want, you should just tell him, tell Dad we're not going.'

I sit up, wiping my face. 'The truth is, I don't know. Part of me thinks it would be an adventure, a fresh start, a new experience. I guess the rest of me is scared of change, frightened of making a terrible mistake. And, if I'm really honest, I don't want to take responsibility, either for going or for making Dad unhappy if we don't go. It's a real honour that the university wants him so much. He deserves this job.'

Chris jumps up as the soup threatens to boil over and takes the pan off the heat. He turns to me. 'Grandma wouldn't have been scared, would she?'

I laugh. 'No, she wouldn't.'

'And your dad wasn't afraid to start again in America.'

'No. He loved it.' I stop myself adding that he was only ever thinking about what was best for him and that I've never really forgiven him for skipping out of our lives like that. I want to hear where Chris's train of thought is leading.

'So what are you afraid of?' he asks.

I'm desperately touched by his insight and concern, but how

can I tell my son that I'm terrified his parents don't love each other enough? Although, in fact, since Martin said he was prepared to turn down the job, that fear has diminished and I've been feeling a little more optimistic that we can find a way through this.

'I don't want to make you unhappy, either,' I tell him, as I go to stand beside him at the kitchen worktop, busying myself with making the sandwiches. 'And I certainly don't want to split up the family.'

'If I came with you, could I come back here for uni if I wanted to?'

'Of course.' I cut the sandwiches in half and put them on three plates as he ladles the soup into bowls, trying not to let him see that I'm holding my breath so that I don't break the spell of us talking like this.

'So I'd be, like, going to Australia for the sixth form. Like going to boarding school.'

'That's a good way to think of it, yes.'

Chris takes spoons out of the cutlery drawer and starts to lay the table. 'OK,' he says. 'No promises, but I'll think about it.'

'That's good,' I say, letting out my breath at last. 'Although Dad will have to let them know very soon what he's going to do.'

'Yes, I guess so.'

'Is that all right?'

'It has to be, doesn't it?' He says it cheerfully, like a joke.

'I'll go and fetch Grandma,' I say.

Freya is sitting so she can look out of the front window. It's a damp, lifeless December day a week before Christmas and there's not much to see, yet she's slow to turn her head and acknowledge me. At some point I'll have to decide whether to tell her about Patty and Leo Tarnowski, but I don't want to upset her for nothing. Patty may not be able to locate him. He may be dead. It may be best to wait and see.

'Lunch is ready.'

I help her up and follow her careful progress to the kitchen. I want to cry out against the necessity of piecing together my mother's past from strangers when she's here beside me. I long for her to tell me her story. But I've left it too late and am wishing for the impossible.

29

Freya, 1944

It was Saturday night and the party was in full swing when Freya arrived. Patty had somehow obtained a magnificent ice sculpture of the Eiffel Tower with which to greet her guests as they stepped into the entrance hall. The elegant staircase was decked out with red, white and blue bunting and, as a maid in a lace cap and apron took Freya's summer coat, she heard a lusty rendition of 'La Marseillaise' being belted out upstairs. Yesterday the German garrison in Paris had surrendered to Allied troops, and, before she'd left the mess, she'd heard the BBC radio news describing General de Gaulle's victory march down the Champs-Élysées to Notre Dame.

Freya had never been to Paris but that didn't stop her sharing the general jubilation that *the* city of art, fashion, food, wine and romance had been liberated. Despite Hitler's threats, the destruction she'd seen in Warsaw could not now happen there. The tide was turning. The war *could* end.

She'd been back in London for a week. After managing their escape from Warsaw, she and Leo had had to wait for several days, hidden in a hot, airless hay barn, until word came that an RAF Dakota was being sent from Brindisi. It would land in a nearby field where they could be picked up. They barely spoke during those days in the barn, both of them traumatized by the sights, sounds and, almost worst of all, smells of the shattered courtyards, streets and underground passages they'd travelled through, often camouflaged among the throng of frightened civilians being herded out of the city at gunpoint. At one point all movement stopped as Gestapo officers dragged out three men, put them up against the nearest wall and shot them dead. Afterwards the German soldiers had yelled at everyone to keep on walking. Their escape from the chaotic but heavily guarded civilian transit camp in Pruszków had been terrifying, and Freya would never forget the bravery of those who had helped them.

After a day and a night waiting in Brindisi for their home-ward flight they had landed at Gibraltar Farm where, exhausted, they found Shona waiting for them excitedly. It was an awk-ward reunion, with neither Freya nor Leo able to share Shona's uncomplicated joy at their safe return.

As Freya took off her stained and grimy Polish garments and put on her own clothes she'd felt as if she was shedding a skin. She would have liked to keep something but had guessed – correctly – that it would not be allowed. The FANY assisting her had seemed to understand, for she'd waited, smiling patiently, as Freya lingered over folding and smoothing the well-worn fab-ric of her final connection with 'Olenka'.

Shona had driven them into London where Freya had been glad to slip away, back into the anonymity of hospital life where all she had to do was fib about the family emergency that had supposedly taken her away for three weeks at such short notice. The city was quiet. All the servicemen had left to join the fighting in Europe, mothers and children had been evacuated away from the flying bombs – and there were rumours among the medical staff that they were to be ready to cope with another new weapon – and, with the hop-picking season about to start, anyone else who could escape from the East End was doing so. Freya welcomed the luxury of streets where, despite the physical damage, people could come and go as they pleased without fear of Stuka dive-bombers or a sniper's bullet.

And she intended that tonight's party, to which Patty had left a telephone message inviting her, would be a cause for unashamed celebration. She was young, she had dared to accept a challenge, and had accomplished something worthwhile. Paris was free, she had survived, and life had to go on.

'Of course, Ernest claims that he personally liberated the bar at the Paris Ritz last night.'

Reaching the top of the stairs, Freya heard Patty's drawl, and her guests' laughter. She took the glass of champagne offered by a manservant and went to stand in the drawing-room doorway, sipping the cold wine and admiring Patty's shimmering gold evening dress, stylishly complemented by bright pink lipstick.

'I wish I'd been there to see it,' Patty continued. 'I had a telegram from him this morning. Frankly I'm surprised he can even remember after drinking fifty-one martinis. It'll be his next short story, you can bet on that. Freya! You came! I'm so glad. There's someone I particularly want you to meet.'

Patty took Freya by the arm and set off across the room, gliding effortlessly through the noisy crowd. She stopped next to a tight group of young men beside one of the tall windows and tapped the nearest lightly on the shoulder. He turned around, smiled at his hostess and then her companion.

'Freya Grant, I'd like to introduce you to Nick Hamlyn. Two such gorgeous young doctors must have plenty in common.'

And she was gone.

Nick Hamlyn was tall with fine red-gold hair, greenish-grey eyes and a sprinkling of freckles over a long, thin nose. His appreciative glance made Freya happy she'd worn the red silk dress Patty had insisted she must keep after her last visit – a dress that had spent the last three weeks in a box at Gibraltar Farm with the rest of her possessions. She was thinner than when she'd last worn it – and was wearing high-heeled shoes this time – and liked the slippery feel of the beautifully cut fabric on her hips as she moved.

'What field are you in?' he asked, politely crediting her with more seniority than she had.

'I'm newly qualified,' she said. 'I'm house physician at Mile End Infirmary.'

'A challenging place to work, I imagine.'

'A bit busy recently, yes.'

She was sure he meant the remark kindly, but she wondered how he'd react if he knew what she'd been up to last week. The knowledge that his assumptions were so wide of the mark boosted her confidence and reminded her of playing the twin trick.

'And you?' she asked.

'I'm resident surgical officer to Archibald McIndoe at the Queen Victoria in East Grinstead.'

She couldn't deny him the pride in his voice: Archibald

McIndoe was a surgical hero, not only for his pioneering work in reconstructing the hands and faces of young fighter pilots who had suffered disfiguring burn injuries but also for his success in rehabilitating their minds and spirits.

'You must be pretty good to get to work with him,' she said.

'I guess I knew what I wanted,' he replied. 'It's always been surgery for me. What about you?'

'Well, to begin with I only took sciences to be different from my sister, and then— But there she is!'

Shona and Leo had just arrived and were greeting people they knew. Freya observed Nick's double-take as he picked Shona out without needing to be told which of the many women in the room she was.

He laughed. 'I see. Although you're obviously the more beautiful twin.'

It was corny but, out of many tired old quips she'd heard over the years, it was not a line that anyone had used before – or not to her, anyway. It was pleasant to be preferred to her sister, and she rewarded him with a warm look.

A maid appeared at her elbow offering a tray of canapés. Nick reached for a circle of smoked salmon and caviar, crammed it into his mouth and took another. Freya, who was also hungry, decided to dispense with good manners and did the same. The maid's smile suggested they weren't the first to tuck into such a ration-free treat.

Nick swallowed and grinned. 'Delicious. Best not to enquire where it all comes from.'

'I'm sure she caught the salmon herself on some family estate.'

'Of course. How very ungallant of me to suggest otherwise.'

She watched his jaw muscles working as he munched his second helping and felt a little ripple of attraction. 'Tell me about McIndoe,' she said. 'What's he like to work for?'

'Less formal than many consultants, maybe because he's a Kiwi – from New Zealand,' he explained. 'It's his way with the patients that's so inspiring. And, of course, it's not just him. He's gathered a team, the best eye surgeon, dentist, gas man, so they can all solve problems together. It's incredibly complex work. Surgery's been revolutionized by this war. The next few years are going to be a real adventure.'

She warmed to his enthusiasm and let him run on, not fully attending to his words but making the most of the opportunity to study him. His hair was straight and silky, his eyes already had laughter lines and, despite the responsibilities he was describing, his freckles gave him a youthful air. He was English, with the athletic confidence of a public-school boy. When another guest pushed past behind him, making him step forward, closing the gap between them, she chose not to move away and kept her eyes on his. He got the message, taking only half a step back.

'Let's get another drink, shall we?' He placed his hand lightly in the small of her back to usher her in front of him and kept it there as they moved through the crowd.

She was not best pleased to be almost immediately hailed by Shona.

'Freya, I need to talk to you.'

'Shona, my sister, this is Nick Hamlyn. We're just going to get a drink,' she added pointedly.

'Hello,' said Shona. 'You won't mind if I borrow her for a moment?'

'Of course not.'

'That was rude,' said Freya, as Shona pulled her away.

'You can find him again later. I have to talk to you.'

'He'll have found someone else by then.'

'Well, you can cut in, can't you?' Shona clearly wasn't in the least interested. 'I'm worried about Leo. Did something happen while you were away that he's not telling me about?'

Freya looked at Shona as if for the first time and saw not a more polished, witty version of herself but someone more wilful and less generous than she'd given her credit for.

'What do you think happened to him?' she asked in disbelief. 'To both of us?'

'But your mission was a success. You're back safely. What has he got to be so bitter about? He's been worse than ever since he got back.'

Freya doubted that Leo had told Shona how desperately he'd wanted to stay and fight, and grasped the impossibility of ever explaining to her why he'd wish to. All Shona could see or feel were her own emotions.

'What's the latest news from Warsaw?' she asked, hoping to deflect her sister's questions.

'Not so good,' Shona admitted. 'They may have to abandon the Old Town. Will you talk to him? Find out what's wrong?'

'It's the war. It's not about you. Those streets are where he grew up, where he was at university. Surely you can imagine what it's like to witness their destruction. It's not like the bombing here. The war there is being fought street by street, building by building.'

'But now Paris has been liberated. The war will end. Why can't he look forward?'

'Why? To make you happy?'

Shona, surprised by the sharpness in Freya's voice, looked at her resentfully. 'I thought you'd understand.'

'You really don't have a clue, do you?' All the fear and tension that for weeks Freya had refused to acknowledge threatened to erupt. She was sorely tempted to let rip, but this was neither the time nor the place. She turned and headed for the staircase, wanting some air.

Someone caught her arm. She turned and was relieved to see Leo, the only person in the room who could possibly understand her feelings without having to utter a word.

'Hello. How are you?' she asked.

He gave a lopsided smile. 'So-so.'

She nodded: there was nothing to say. 'Any word of Bartek?'

His face relaxed. 'Yes, health-wise he's doing fine. I still can't tell you who he is, but we owe you a great debt.'

'And Gosia?'

'Nothing.'

'You'll let me know, won't you, if you hear anything?'

'Of course.'

'At least there's some good news here,' she said, indicating the increasingly raucous party around them.

'Yes, the French have been fortunate. If only they had come to our aid in nineteen thirty-nine, all our stories might have been very different.'

'You still wish you could have stayed?' she asked quietly.

'Of course.' He failed to hide his anger.

'And Shona?'

'I do my best.'

'Be kind to her, Leo. Not everyone sees the world as you do.'

'She knows I love her,' he said. 'The trouble is that I can't seem to believe that love counts for much right now.'

'I know how hard it is,' she said, 'but she thinks the opposite, that if love dies, this war wasn't worth fighting. Perhaps she's right. And don't forget that in a way it was easier for us to go off and make the grand gestures than for her to sit and wait for us to come back safely.'

Freya wasn't entirely convinced by her own words, but she was already regretting her sharpness towards Shona. Hurting her sister was utterly pointless: it was like hurting herself. 'Whatever happens,' she said, 'some good has to come out of it. You and Shona, that's a worthwhile future, isn't it?'

'You're a lot wiser than your sister! And I'll try to do better, I promise.' Leo dug a hand into his jacket pocket. 'I almost forgot. I brought you something. It's worthless, a little memento from my childhood that I've managed to keep hold of, but I want you to have it, as a token of my thanks.' He bowed his head in a formal gesture as, with both hands, he held out a small rectangular object. '*Dziękuję*.'

She saw that it was a decorative tin embossed in lettered script with the name 'E. Wedel'. It weighed nothing in her hand.

30

The following afternoon Nick Hamlyn reached Freya through the hospital switchboard to ask when he could see her again. It wasn't easy to match their rotas and allow for travelling time from opposite ends of London, but over the next few weeks they managed to meet three times. They had a drink in a pub then walked in St James's Park, took in a concert on their second date, and on their third went to the cinema where, in the warm dark, they kissed hungrily in the back row and missed most of the main feature.

On a clear blue weekend in September, Freya took the train to East Grinstead where Nick met her. They caught a bus into nearby countryside where they walked for half a mile along a quiet footpath. He had brought a tartan rug and, without either of them needing to speak, he led her into some trees, spread it on the ground and took her hand. They undressed each other silently, touching, stroking and tasting as they went. Nick was, as she had hoped, experienced enough to guide and excite her, making the anticipated loss of her virginity far more intensely pleasurable than she'd ever imagined.

She lay contentedly in his arms until he sat up, rummaged in his knapsack, and produced a Thermos of tea. She laughed and gratefully accepted the hot drink. After some desultory chat, they made love a second time. Knowing a bit more about what she was doing, she decided, made it even nicer.

After a drink in a pub near the station, during which they said little but shared a happy glow of satisfaction, she returned to London on the train, smiling at her reflection in the darkening carriage window. She wasn't in love with him, and wasn't sure she expected to be, but Nick was a beautiful young animal, and life was far too short to miss out on its greatest attractions.

A week or so later they went to see *Gaslight* in Leicester Square. Freya was exhausted following a twenty-hour shift helping to triage casualties from the new weapon they'd been warned was coming. A kind of rocket, they said, although there had been no official comment, where the first thing anyone knew about it was a huge explosion that left a deep crater and reduced an entire block of dwellings to rubble. A policeman whose arm she stitched up said it would take days to dig everyone out and that hundreds who survived the blast were now homeless.

At the back of the cinema she leant against Nick's shoulder, inhaling the scent of his ancient tweed jacket while watching Ingrid Bergman's beautiful features contort in fear and horror as the lights dimmed and flickered around her. Intent on a long kiss that made her body ache with desire, Freya missed the denouement entirely.

'I've got a surprise,' Nick whispered in her ear, as they stood for the National Anthem. 'I've got the key to a flat near Victoria. It's got a double bed and I don't have to be at work until lunchtime tomorrow.'

She felt a taut nerve deep inside her body turn to liquid. It was the most delicious physical sensation she could remember. 'I'm on at eight,' she whispered back, breathing in the smell of him. 'But that gives us the whole night.'

He held her hand tightly as they filed out of the cinema and headed towards the Underground station. In a dreamlike state in which only her body seemed to have any real existence, she heard the vendor repeating his pitch – *Paper! Extra!* – before she took in the meaning of the headline on his board.

'Wait, I must buy a paper!'

'I don't plan on giving you time to read it!'

'No, wait, I must—' She handed over a penny, took the copy the vendor handed to her and scanned the front page. She had known for weeks how badly the AK's struggle in Warsaw was going but seeing the confirmation of their surrender in print felt leaden. *Gosia!* Had she survived?

She stood still, reading the report from Poland, hardly noticing how she was impeding the stream of people impatient to reach the tube. Nick took her arm and, unable to gain her attention, steered her against the wall of the nearest building.

The Wehrmacht had promised to treat members of the Polish Home Army according to the terms of the Geneva Convention, she read, and to deal humanely with the civilian population; but she knew how empty those promises would be. Hitler had given orders to demolish what remained of the city, and civilians had already been butchered in such numbers that piles of their bodies had had to be burnt in the streets, yet Stalin had continued to refuse all appeals to intervene. A month earlier, when a thousand AK fighters had evacuated the Old Town via the sewers, the

Nazis had gassed them and waited to shoot each defenceless man or woman as they were forced to emerge from the man-holes. Short of water during an unending heat wave with no rain, inhabitants were dying of dysentery and typhoid. And now all that sacrifice had been for nothing.

And Gosia? And Rudzik, Alek, Piotr and all the others who had helped them? What would happen to them?

'Freya?' Nick interrupted her thoughts. 'Shall we go?'

'I can't.' All desire had gone. Nick wasn't yet someone to whom she could turn for comfort, even if she was allowed to explain why she needed it. 'I'm sorry.'

'What is it?' He sounded sympathetic but she could tell that, beneath it, he was annoyed. She couldn't blame him for feeling frustrated. Five minutes ago she'd been equally excited about spending an entire night together, but she wasn't ready to pre-tend to feelings that had completely evaporated.

'Something's upset you. What is it?' he repeated.

She decided to risk a partial truth. 'I have a good friend in Warsaw. I'm afraid for what will happen to her.'

He pulled her to him, wrapped her in a hug, and waited until she heaved a sigh and looked up at him.

'What was she doing there, your friend?' he asked.

'She was Polish.' Too late, Freya saw her mistake: admitting any small part of the truth meant she'd have to cover her tracks with lies. But Nick's sympathetic interest was genuine, and she'd have to tell him something. A pen friend? That Gosia's family used to live in Aberdeen? Each lie would lead only to further complications. She settled on the smallest explanation she could get away with. 'I knew her before the war.'

'Poor darling.' He cupped her face lightly. 'You really are upset.'

She nodded. 'I need to call my sister.'

'Why don't I see you safely home to Mile End? It won't matter if I miss the last train to East Grinstead because I can sleep at the flat. Besides, I'd like to see where you work,' he added, when he saw her hesitation.

'Thank you,' she said, really meaning it. She hadn't expected him to accept her decision so readily and acknowledged that he'd risen in her estimation.

Queuing to buy their tickets, she thought about Leo's grief for his fallen city. Her heart sank as she rehearsed the conversation she'd have to have with Shona, yet there was no one else Shona could turn to. Freya was the only one who had shared Leo's experience, the only one with whom Shona could discuss their secret mission. But surely she'd done all that had been asked of her. She couldn't go on and on being responsible for her sister's feelings.

She and Nick reached the ticket-office window where he requested two singles to Mile End. She nudged him aside and asked instead for two in the opposite direction, to Victoria and the flat with the double bed.

31

Kirsty, 1989

Phyllis says nothing for a while after I tell her that I'm now absolutely certain it was Freya who went to Warsaw. She sits in her comfortable old armchair holding my copy of the photograph in her lap. She can't seem to take her eyes off it. I find it reassuring, especially after Archie's opposition, that she, too, appears to be knocked sideways by this discovery. It *does* matter. I can't explain why, or whether what's most important is that my mother did such a thing or that she kept it secret, but I do know that it changes everything.

Phyllis sighs and looks up. 'You know, in a funny kind of way, I feel as if I finally understand her a little better, as if I can begin to make sense of why I always felt there was an unbreakable pane of glass between us, as if she was afraid that saying too much would shatter it.'

'Me, too,' I say. 'I always thought it was my fault.'

She nods. 'When I first got to know her, I felt that she longed to bridge the distance between us but somehow could never bring herself to do so. And then it became a habit, so much so that maybe she stopped even being aware of it.'

'Do you think she's been lonely?'

'Yes, I do. Especially after Patty went. Patty simply never noticed any barrier placed in her way by anybody.' Phyllis laughs. 'I never worked out if it was sheer narcissism or an amazing knack of getting through to people. Either way, it worked like a charm. So how is she? What was it like speaking to her after all these years?'

'Strange. I was a child the last time I heard her voice. Since then she's been this monster who destroyed our family, yet it was really hard to dislike her. She sounded just the same.'

Phyllis laughs again. 'You can't dislike Patty. I think that's why Freya had to cut her off completely. She was afraid that, if she saw her again, she'd have to forgive her.'

'I don't think Archie will forgive me.'

'He's being silly. Your father's dead. The past is long gone. It's the present that counts. Whatever her many faults, Patty isn't a bad person.'

'He said something about her trying to have Freya struck off. Is that true?'

'It was nothing at all to do with Patty.' Phyllis's cheeks redden and she looks acutely uncomfortable, which is unlike her.

'So there *was* a problem?' I prompt, when she doesn't continue.

'There was a hearing before the General Medical Council,' she admits. 'I promised Freya to keep it to myself.'

'I can always find out from GMC records.'

'That's true. And, in any case, I think the time for secrets is over, don't you? It was to do with Shona. I don't know all the details, but Shona's psychiatrist held Freya responsible for Shona running away from the hospital.'

'You mean when she drowned?'

'Yes.'

'So what happened?'

'No action was taken. Freya was let off with a warning.'

'No, I mean why was Freya blamed for Shona running away?'

It's an effort for Phyllis to push herself up from her chair. It's all I can do not to jump to offer her a hand, but I know she'd hate it.

'I'm going to make some coffee and think this through. If I'm going to break my promise to Freya, then I don't want to end up giving you a garbled version.'

Once she's left the room I get to my feet and stretch my arms and shoulders. I run an eye along her untidy bookshelves, impressed yet again by the breadth of her reading. The mantelpiece and the top of her upright piano are crammed with colourful Christmas cards. I go over to the window where a chill comes off the glass. The view of the recreation ground across the road, where leafless trees drip onto colourless grass, is uninviting at this time of year. For a brief moment I'm far from sure that I can cope with any more revelations.

Archie has made me doubt my motives. Am I really here to help Freya, or just trying to vindicate my own sense of failure? To have the last word now that she can't answer back?

I think of all the times in this room when I was growing up, hanging about while Freya, laughing, opinionated and confident, talked shop with Phyllis, complaining about the politics of the NHS or merely enjoying a good gossip. What made me so instantly assume it had to be Shona in Tomasz's photograph, that it couldn't be Freya who was the interesting one who did exciting things?

I wonder how much Dad knew about any of this. He was never much of a father even before he left. Nick Hamlyn always put Nick Hamlyn first, and we kids were an accessory to the life he wanted to display, like our smiling school photographs on the desk in his private consulting room, there to reassure his mainly female patients. I'm wondering more than ever why she chose to marry him.

And where do the moral niceties lie in his daughter asking his mistress what he did or didn't know about his wife? And what would Freya say if she knew I'd spoken to Patty?

Phyllis returns with a tray bearing two steaming mugs of coffee and a plate of shortbread. I clear some newspapers out of the way so she can put it down and return to my place on the couch. In order to work out what I'm really doing here I need to know as much as possible.

'Right,' she says, lowering herself back into her chair. 'I never knew the whole story, but I'll tell you what I pieced together and hope that Freya forgives me.'

'I feel ambivalent about this, too,' I tell her. 'If you think we're trespassing too far, then don't tell me.'

'No,' she says. 'I visited Freya in hospital last week. I can see that something's preying on her mind. And we don't have the luxury of time to help her find some peace.'

'OK.' I sit back, ready to listen, hoping I won't regret hearing what Phyllis is about to tell me.

'She never explained why Shona's wedding plans were scrapped but, after her sister went home to Scotland, she spoke readily about how worried she was about Shona's mental state. It was pretty clear that she'd had a full psychotic breakdown and that her parents had been absolutely right to have her admitted to the local mental asylum.'

'A psychotic breakdown seems a rather extreme reaction to a broken heart,' I say.

'These episodes often start with fairly normal reactions to stress or trauma,' Phyllis says. 'Like not sleeping or eating, feeling isolated, going over and over what happened and still not being able to make sense of it. But sometimes people begin to lose their grip on reality and experience paranoia and delusions, even full-blown hallucinations. The mind is literally shattered for a while. I've watched it happen in patients. It's like a driver unable to regain control when a car slides on ice.'

'Do they usually recover?'

'Nowadays they do, yes. But we can offer antipsychotic drugs that weren't developed until a few years after your aunt's death. Back then everything was pretty much lumped together under the general umbrella of schizophrenia, and the available treatments, sleep therapy, electroconvulsive therapy or lobotomy, were brutal.'

'Is that what happened to Shona?'

'She certainly had ECT, and her psychiatrist was asking her father for permission to perform a leucotomy – the British term for lobotomy. This was after Shona had tried to run away more than once.'

'I don't blame her!'

'Except that, when she ran away again, she drowned. Some people do need to be taken care of, even against their will.'

'So how was Freya involved?'

'Her father asked her advice about the surgery. He was grief-stricken and blamed himself for not being able to help Shona. So Freya went up to Scotland to see her. She hadn't been for a couple of months. It had been difficult to get time off work, and coal shortages meant that train services could be erratic. She came back a few days later. All she'd say was that she didn't believe surgery was the right course and that she'd had a terrible argument with Shona's psychiatrist, who refused point blank to listen to her. But she must have known that Shona would try to run away again, because she'd sent me a note asking me to help her if she turned up at the infirmary.

'I don't know when she learnt that Shona had gone missing, but about a week later her sister's body was found. I was with your mother when her father telephoned with the news and I've never seen anyone so devastated. I imagine that losing a twin in any circumstances must be soul-destroying, but like that?'

'And the GMC hearing?'

'Shona's psychiatrist claimed Freya had been professionally negligent. The GMC concluded she had been irresponsible but that she had not been acting in a professional capacity. They let her off with a warning.'

'What had she done?'

'I don't know. It never did make sense to me. Encouraged Shona to resist treatment, I suppose. That or perhaps she was merely guilty of being a young female doctor challenging an older male consultant.'

'Then why the mystery? Why did she make you promise not to discuss it?'

'I think it was just too painful. If you'd seen her when she came off the phone to her father . . .'

We both fall silent. I am overcome by a wave of tenderness towards my mother such as I seldom feel. When I raise my head and meet Phyllis's level gaze she gives a small nod, as if she knows exactly how I feel because she feels the same.

'Patty says she's going to track down Shona's fiancé, Leo Tarnowski,' I say. 'What do I do if she finds him? Would Freya want me to speak to him?'

Phyllis smiles. 'You're her daughter, Kirsty. You two are more alike than you give yourself credit for. Use your own judgement and you'll be fine.'

Not so long ago I would have hated to be compared favourably with my mother. Now I feel nothing but pride.

32

Freya, 1945

Freya was finishing in Outpatients when a porter came to let her know that Dr Levenson had arrived and was waiting at the entrance lodge for someone to collect her. Freya had been pleased to hear that a woman had been appointed as the new house physician and hoped she'd turn out to be a friend, so told the porter she'd come herself.

It wasn't that she'd been lonely as the only woman in the mess, but it would be pleasant not always to have to be one of the boys. She got on well with the nursing staff, too, but she wasn't one of them – a division made clearer after Robbie, the anaesthetist, got a student nurse pregnant and she was dismissed while he kept his job.

She emerged into the sunshine at the front entrance and thought how fast her own registration year had flown by. She was now a fully fledged medic, able to decide which speciality she might pursue, and quietly proud that a satellite of a major London teaching hospital had kept her on – even if it was partly because so many men were away doing their national service.

A short, sturdy young woman with a mass of dark curly hair stood outside the lodge. She wore a rather misshapen old tweed skirt with a spotless cotton blouse and held a battered leather grip in front of her with both hands. Her eyes lit up when she saw Freya in her white medical coat.

'Welcome to Mile End, Dr Levenson. I'm Dr Grant.'

'Phyllis, please.' She shook Freya's hand.

'And I'm Freya. Follow me,' she said, leading the way back across the courtyard. 'Good journey?'

'I didn't have too far to come.' She spoke with an unmistakable northern accent.

'Dr Chiltern said you're a Cambridge graduate?'

'Yes. We women were hugely outnumbered and not always welcome, so I'm glad not to be the only one here. I was afraid I might be.'

'Most people got over the shock of my arrival eventually. They're a nice bunch, actually.'

'Well, that's a relief. We had one lecturer at Cambridge who sent us to the library when he taught the men about syphilis!'

Freya laughed as she started up the stairs. 'Well, don't worry, we can offer you plenty of venereal diseases to learn from.'

'What more could a girl want?'

'You've got your room key?'

Phyllis held it up.

'It's just along there, but I'll show you the mess first so you'll know where to go once you've unpacked.'

'Thank you.'

As Freya opened the door she found herself looking at the shabby room through fresh eyes. It wasn't only the furnishings that were more worn and battered than when she'd first set foot there. The war in Europe had been over for two months although they were still fighting in the Far East; the lights were back on in the West End but rationing was tighter than ever; people were exhausted and, while peace could not be far off, the next winter was likely to be as hard as the last.

'It's such good news, isn't it?' Phyllis broke into her reflections.

'What?'

'The election result.'

'Oh, yes.'

'To think that we'll be working in a National Health Service!'

'If Attlee keeps his promises.'

'He will,' Phyllis said confidently. 'He must.'

The recent announcement of a landslide Labour victory had been bittersweet for Freya. One of Attlee's first actions as prime minister had been to withdraw recognition of the Polish Government-in-Exile. Leo's colleagues were already busy moving out of the embassy.

'I wasn't entirely joking about wanting to see lots of VD cases,' Phyllis continued. 'I'm interested in preventive medicine. And once treatment is free for everyone, it can become a real possibility for all kinds of conditions – in fact, an economic necessity. If we can catch symptoms early and educate people so they don't get ill in the first place, there'll be less of an economic burden on the state.'

Freya couldn't help being amused by the eagerness of the newly qualified doctor, even if she agreed with what Phyllis was saying. 'I'm interested in public health, too,' she said, 'although I'm not sure even a Labour government can stop people having sex. In any case . . .'

She was about to tell Phyllis what Bartek had said, about penicillin making a greater difference to the world than any war, but of course she couldn't.

'What were you going to say, Dr Grant?'

'Freya, please. Only that, with the Americans now producing penicillin in such vast quantities, all the new drugs and vaccines that are being developed will do half our work for us.'

'Absolutely! Have you used it yet?'

'I have.' Freya fought down a wave of memory. What was the point when she could never tell anyone? 'The London Hospital's had supplies for more than a year.'

'A couple of years earlier and my brother could have been saved,' said Phyllis, with practised matter-of-factness. 'I only wish I'd been a bit older so I could've gained some experience in a field hospital. Imagine how much you'd learn under battlefield conditions, and how quickly!'

Yes, Freya wanted to say. *You do. I know exactly what it's like.* Instead she smiled and murmured her agreement.

More than anything, at moments like this, she wished she'd envisaged the lingering price she'd have to pay for her impetuous decision to go to Warsaw. She'd believed that its secrecy would ensure that, on her return, the book would be closed and she could simply leave it behind. She'd be protected from having to lie about it because no one would even suspect its existence.

But the experience had changed her in ways that meant not speaking about it had become a kind of lie. Why had no one warned her how the secrecy would become a web – finely spun, but no less of an emotional trap – in which she was caught, perhaps for ever?

It seemed a small complaint when, as she'd witnessed daily here in the infirmary, so many had lost their lives, or limbs, or loved ones, yet she minded badly that it was impossible to explain to Phyllis why she could applaud yet no longer share her uncomplicated sense of adventure.

'If peacetime means an unending parade of hernias and varicose veins,' she said, 'maybe there are worse things to settle for.'

The young woman looked crestfallen. *How dull and pompous I must sound*, Freya thought. 'Look,' she said, 'I've got half an hour free so I can show you around if you like?'

'Oh, yes, please, if you're sure.'

'Ditch your bag over there, and I'll take you down to the wards.'

Forty minutes later, after admiring the new operating theatres and up-to-date pathology lab supplied by the Emergency Medical Service, they returned to the mess. Freya enjoyed Phyllis's enthusiasm and was sure they were going to be friends. She would just have to hide her regret that she couldn't return Phyllis's open-hearted candour.

'Are you avoiding me?' Shona demanded on the telephone the next morning.

'No, of course not.'

'You're fibbing,' said Shona, 'but never mind. You're to meet us for dinner tonight. And bring Nick. Eight o'clock at the Café Royal. Patty's wangled us a table.'

She hung up before Freya had a chance to argue.

Shona was right. Freya had been avoiding her. In the eyes of most Londoners she spoke to, the Red Army had helped to hasten the end of the war in Europe and the new socialist prime minister was right to prefer friendly relations with Moscow. It was almost as if Leo would be exiled all over again. While Freya felt a great deal of sympathy for him, she had no wish to be sucked into his grief or, more accurately, the effect that his inevitable distress would have upon Shona.

Sometimes Freya felt like the little boy in the Hans Christian Andersen story with a sliver of glass in his heart. It wasn't fair to blame Shona for how the Warsaw mission had reshaped her own life in ways that none of them could have foreseen, yet she just wasn't able to rid herself of a little residue of resentment.

Besides, it felt good to think and behave more like a singleton, and it was healthy to encourage Shona not to lean on her so much. Her sister would just have to work out the travails of her love life for herself.

She'd already arranged to meet Nick in town that evening, and now left a message for him with the change of plan. She wondered if Patty would be joining them or had merely used her influence to secure them a table. It would be good to see her – it always was. Freya found the atmosphere of extravagance and exaggeration that Patty created wherever she went strangely restful, for Patty always saw the best in people, making them feel understood without ever having to explain themselves.

Nick liked Patty as much as she did; it was one of the things that bound them together. That and the magnificent sex they enjoyed together. Perhaps it was because, at least to begin with, Freya had never fancied herself in love with Nick – and had assumed he felt the same – that she'd been able to let herself go and be unembarrassed about things that were supposed to be shockingly immoral for a well-brought-up young woman. Almost a year on from the first time they'd made love on a rug in a Sussex wood, their appetite for one another's bodies had only increased.

When, later, she caught sight of him waiting for her outside the Café Royal, her heart skipped a beat. And yet, seeing the closeness between Shona and Leo, who were already seated next to one another on one of the red plush banquettes below the ornately gilded mirrors, she felt a pang. All that she enjoyed with Nick was lovely, yet her feelings still lacked the overwhelming depth of her sister's romance. But, she thought, perhaps that was no bad thing.

The table, Freya saw, was laid for four, which meant that Patty wouldn't be joining them. Leo stood politely, as Freya took her seat, then shook hands with Nick.

'Thanks for coming.' Shona leant across the table to clasp Freya's hand. She looked flushed with excitement.

'What's the occasion?' Freya asked, noticing that her sister wore a corsage.

Shona turned to Leo, her face bright with happiness. When Leo smiled and nodded his encouragement she held out her other hand, showing off the small diamond on her ring finger. 'We're engaged!'

'Oh, Shona, that's wonderful! Congratulations, both of you!'

Freya felt tears rising. Her joy for Shona was entirely

genuine – she and Leo belonged together – but a tiny part of her felt bereft, once again left behind as her sister experienced emotions she couldn't share. She was able to hide her fleeting moment of desolation as Nick pumped Leo's hand, kissed Shona's cheek and called to the waiter to bring champagne. Once they had all sat down again she found Leo smiling at her.

'It's thanks to you,' he said.

'Me? How?'

'The dream of a democratic Poland is shattered. My country's sacrifice was for nothing. I am left stateless. And then I remembered your words: "If love dies, this war wasn't worth fighting." If I'm to keep Poland alive in my heart, then my heart must stay rich and full. Shona has promised to help me with that.'

As Leo and Shona kissed, Freya unintentionally caught Nick's eye. Aware that he was far too much of an Englishman to tolerate such an open display of patriotism, she pretended not to understand his ironic glance. She fully appreciated what a huge renunciation Leo had made and was overjoyed that he had managed to overcome his bitterness. She felt as if an enormous burden she hadn't known she was carrying had slipped from her shoulders. A Shona who no longer feared being hurt or abandoned could now be her very best self.

'I'm glad to do my bit,' she said lightly, as the waiter popped the champagne cork and poured the wine.

Leo raised his glass to her. 'You've done more than your bit, and I thank you.'

She took her own glass and exchanged a silent and private toast in which Shona also joined. Raising her glass higher, she said, 'To you and Shona, and your future happiness together. I couldn't be more delighted for you both.'

They all drank and proposed more toasts and laughed and called for more champagne and ordered some food and finally fell out into the street where, although the empty plinth where Eros should stand was still boarded up, the advertisements were flashing their gaudy lights again in Piccadilly Circus.

Freya and Nick stood at the top of the steps down to the Underground and waved goodnight to Shona and Leo. Then, linking arms, they began to walk towards Charing Cross where Nick would catch his train. Crossing Trafalgar Square, he stopped next to one of the lions and, leaning against the stonework, pulled her to him and kissed her deeply. She felt the familiar thrum deep in her body and wished for the thousandth time that they had a bed they could share. She would have to wait until the weekend when, if the July weather continued fine, they could find a quiet spot in the countryside around East Grinstead.

Nick lifted his lips away from hers and looked down into her eyes. 'We should do the same, you know.'

Her mind had drifted off on a cloud of wine and desire. 'Do what?'

'Get married.'

She laughed. 'Us?'

Nick grinned, not in the least taken aback. 'Yes. Freya Grant, please will you marry me?'

'Oh, Nick, really? Are you sure?'

Marriage – and to Nick – was not something Freya had ever dreamt about, and she was too tipsy to stop herself laughing at the idea. Not that it mattered: she could see from Nick's smile that he'd interpreted her laughter as the delight he'd anticipated.

'I'm sorry I haven't planned this, with a ring and everything, but I do mean it.'

'You're a darling, but we're fine as we are, aren't we?'

'Yes, of course,' he said. 'But I'll get my call-up papers soon. If we're married and I'm posted abroad for my national service, then you can join me. Might be nice to see a bit of the world together.'

'That wouldn't help my career.'

'As soon as I've got my fellowship I might look for jobs in America,' he continued, as if she hadn't spoken. 'Patty says I'd make a fortune as a plastic surgeon in Hollywood! We could have a wonderful life together.'

She took hold of the lapels of his tweed jacket and shook him gently. 'I can't marry you, Nick. I'm very, very fond of you but . . .' She recalled Shona and Leo's kiss and felt a pang of loss. 'But we're not in love, are we? Not really.'

'We don't need all that getting carried away, do we?' He kissed the top of her head. 'We make a great team. Come on, what do you say?'

There'd been many times when Freya had found Nick's lack of genuine interest in her curiously restful. She knew it stemmed from the professionally withheld empathy of the true surgeon. And she was touched by his proposal. But his high-handed dismissal of what she might want was exasperating.

'Look at Shona and Leo,' she said. 'They're in love.'

This time he kissed the tip of her nose. 'Which is why I want to marry you and not her. You've got your head screwed on. You're the sensible one.'

'Sensible enough to question whether we have what it takes to get married.'

'Think it over,' he said cheerfully. 'I don't mind asking you again.'

She looked up into the impassive bronze face of the lion, unsure whether to be pleased or annoyed.

33

The café in South Kensington is busy and I have to wait while the young waitress clears the only vacant table. I'm lucky that it's by the window so I have the last of the afternoon light, a view of families and Christmas shoppers streaming past, and can keep an eye open for Tomasz. I haven't seen him since the day Freya went into hospital, but I told him on the phone yesterday she'd confirmed that she *is* Olenka. He'd seemed unexpectedly calm about it yet had nonetheless been insistent that we try to meet today.

I'm still trying to process what Phyllis told me this morning. My mother is the complete opposite of everything I've grown up believing her to be. She is courageous, bold and committed in ways I never imagined and has also suffered more than I could have known. I think with shame of how often I must have looked at her with the hurtful teenage scorn that Chris has shown me over the past few weeks. She didn't deserve it. If I'd only known the truth about her sister's illness and death, I would never have added to her pain.

I'm so lost in my thoughts and in watching the daylight give way to festive lights that I don't notice Tomasz until he stands beside me.

'Kirsty.' He places a light hand on my shoulder. 'Don't get up.' He pulls out the chair opposite as far as it will go in the tight space and eases himself into it with a cheerful smile. 'Thanks for coming,' he says. 'How is your mother? Is she happy to be home again?'

'She is. She's much frailer, but at least she's still herself.'

'Is she looking forward to Christmas?'

'Yes, although . . .' I force myself to say it '. . . it will be her last.'

'I'm sorry if I brought trouble to her door when she has so little time.'

'Oh, no, not at all. I'm so glad to have found out who she really is. And you should have seen her yesterday with my son, Chris. He was asking questions about spies and guns and she was so happy.'

'Good, I'm glad.'

The waitress returns and we order two Russian teas.

'I'm only sorry you're no nearer to finding your father,' I say.

He gives a wry smile. 'Perhaps if the Berlin Wall had fallen a few years earlier.'

I hadn't wanted to tell him on the phone about my conversation with Patty Drexeler, or her offer to try to track down Leo Tarnowski, and discover that I'm still hesitant to do so. I'm attempting to work out why when he throws me right off track.

'I wanted to see you to say goodbye.'

'What?'

'I'm going home tomorrow.'

'But—'

He laughs. 'It's Christmas. My son will never forgive me if I'm not there.'

'Yes, of course,' I say. 'But you'll be back?'

'No. Perhaps one day you will visit Poland.'

I'm about to say how much I'd like that, then realize how far Poland is from Australia. Martin will be talking to the boys again today while I'm out and then we'll come to a decision so that he can give the university his answer tomorrow. There is no good reason why we shouldn't go and I mustn't let us be held back by fear and indecision. If my mother can jump out of a plane into unknown territory, then so can I.

'This time next year I'll probably be living in Sydney,' I tell him.

'You've decided?'

His expression is grave and I find I'm looking for signs that he's disappointed.

'Yes, pretty much.'

He says nothing but his eyes never leave my face as the waitress brings our order. As she leaves he smiles and reaches out to cover my hand with his. 'You are my friend,' he says, 'just like our mothers were friends. There's a connection I can't explain. You are part of my life now.' He lifts his hand away and places it over his heart for a few seconds.

I'm engulfed by an intense yearning: I want something from this man but have no clear idea what it might be. I feel possessed by emotions I don't understand as if some wind from the past is blowing through me. I look up and he's still studying my face. His eyes are very blue.

'You feel it, too,' he says.

'Don't go,' I say. 'Or not quite yet. There's a chance we may find Shona's fiancé, Leo Tarnowski. He was in Polish Intelligence during the war. If anyone will know about your father, it must be him.'

Tomasz shakes his head and smiles again. 'Tadek will be putting the Wigilia carp in the bathtub any day now.'

He sees my incomprehension.

'We celebrate with dinner on Wigilia, Christmas Eve, before going to Midnight Mass. It's always fish, and carp can taste muddy unless you keep it in fresh water for a few days first.'

'But wouldn't you rather wait if there's a chance of finding out what you came for? You could have Christmas with us. With Freya, your mother's friend.'

'That's very kind, thank you, but no. Tadek will have queued for hours to get that carp so I can't disappoint him.' He sips his tea. 'Meeting you and your mother has made Gosia real to me, made her a part of me again. But my father? Even if I have a name, a face, so what? My life won't change. I think I was carried away by the tearing down of the Wall. It seemed as if the Iron Curtain would be opened to reveal all the secrets that had been kept from us in the Soviet Bloc. But it was a dream and I've woken up now. The family I have is all that truly matters.'

'So I won't see you again?'

He digs into his trouser pocket and brings out a crumpled sheet of paper. 'Here's my address and phone number. You would be very welcome at any time.'

I never expected to feel so bereft. Is this the end of the road for me, too? I've learnt nothing, only piled up more and more questions I can't answer.

Tomasz digs in his pocket again and places some pound coins

on the table next to his glass. 'I must go,' he says. 'I have an early flight and haven't started to pack yet.'

He sees my stricken face and, laughing, reaches across the table to place his fingers against my cheek. 'Don't worry,' he says. 'We're family now, aren't we?'

'Yes,' I say, shaking myself out of my silly mood. 'We are.'

Outside the café he draws me into a bear-hug and then, with just a simple goodbye, he walks away.

I stand back against a bright shop-window display of children's picture books and greetings cards and watch him go. He doesn't look back, and I'm unable to understand how he can bear to leave his father's identity unresolved. Maybe he can be so philosophical because his secret was never a secret. His uncle and aunt never pretended there was no mystery. My mother, on the other hand, had clearly expended a great deal of energy to persuade us all that she had nothing to hide. I see now that her effort of will had sucked some vital air out of our family life. Even if I had suspected her of keeping secrets, I had interpreted it – as, perhaps, she had guided me to do – as the professional habit of medical discretion. Now that I know the truth, it couldn't be more obvious that we have all been bent out of shape by the pressure of this keeping of secrets.

But what were they? Were they even important? Official secrets, or the shame of mental illness or suicide? Merely a promise to a friend not to betray a confidence? Who knows? Perhaps Wedel was her lover. Does any of it matter now?

Do I shrug it off like Tomasz and walk away or is it time to fling open all the doors?

34

Freya, 1945

'It needs tightening on the shoulder, don't you think?'

Shona was in Freya's room at the hospital trying on the wedding dress their mother had sent from Aberdeen. It had already been altered once to accommodate the cousin who had passed it on. Due to rationing it was only knee-length, but was made of rich white figured silk damask, extravagantly cut on the cross, with rows of tiny covered buttons on the bodice and cuffs. A friend had donated a veil and white satin shoes that, miraculously, fitted. With clothing coupons issued when Shona was demobbed early – the new government had little use for the SOE – she'd managed to buy silk stockings and new underwear.

Freya took the pin out of her mouth and, making a small tuck at the shoulder seam, fastened it into the fabric. 'You're going to look beautiful.'

Shona and Leo were to be married at the end of the week in a register office, avoiding any negotiation between her Scots Presbyterianism and his Catholicism, with a lunch party afterwards at the Milroy Club. The weather in the middle of October had been dry and sunny, and they hoped it would continue. Leo's friend Adam and Freya were to be their witnesses, and her parents would travel down from Aberdeen the day before. Leo had wangled a room for them at the hotel that had been the haunt of the now disbanded Government-in-Exile. Freya was sorry that they wouldn't get to meet Nick, who was now serving with the RAMC in Germany, from where he wrote observant and entertaining weekly letters.

The mirror on the inside of the cupboard door was too short and narrow for Shona to get a proper look at herself. She gave up and whirled around so the veil flew up into the air.

'Oh, Freya, I'm so happy!'

'So you should be. Leo's a good man and he adores you.'

'And I love him!'

'So you don't want to play the trick on the day?'

Their laughter was interrupted by a light tap on the door.

'Come in,' Freya called.

'I've found some white thread,' said Phyllis, holding out the wooden reel. She stopped in the doorway and smiled at Shona. 'I don't know that you're going to need it. It could have been made for you.'

Freya took the thread. 'Thanks. Come on in.'

'Oh, no,' Phyllis protested. 'This is a sisterly moment if I ever saw one.'

'Please stay,' said Shona. 'Freya's talked so much about you.'

'If you're sure.' Phyllis sat on the narrow bed and curled her legs under her, leaving the floor to Shona, who did another twirl.

Freya looked from her sister to her friend and felt happy that the circle of twinship that had formed her early life was expanding to encompass new influences that would lessen their need for one another.

'Have you got something borrowed and something blue?' Phyllis asked.

'Most of what I'm wearing is borrowed,' laughed Shona. 'But, blue, no.' She turned to Freya. 'Any ideas?'

'I have a necklace,' she said. 'They're just glass beads but you can try them.' She took them out of the wooden jewellery box she kept in the drawer of her bedside table. 'Here.'

'Borrowed *and* blue.' Shona fastened them around her neck and regarded her reflection in the mirror. 'Actually they go rather well, don't you think?'

'They do,' said Phyllis.

'What about my hair? Up or down?'

'Up,' said Freya. 'Then I can wear mine down.'

'I want everything to be perfect,' said Shona. 'I'm sure it must be bad luck to have anything go wrong on your wedding day!'

'What are your plans for married life?' Phyllis asked, with a smile. 'Any luck with finding a place to live?'

'You're kidding! I'll move into Leo's flat. It's tiny but we'll manage.' She glanced at Freya as if she was about to do something naughty. 'After all, I've been more or less living there for months anyway.'

'Good for you,' said Phyllis, amused that Shona might think she'd be shocked.

'We both need jobs, too. Peace has made an awful lot of us redundant.'

'Are you still thinking of teaching?' Freya asked.

'It seems the easiest option, now they've lifted the marriage bar.'

'I suppose the war has done something for women,' said Phyllis.

'It looks like Leo might have found work, too. Someone at the BBC put in a word for him with a big public-relations firm.'

Freya had a flashback to Leo sitting hunched over beside Bartek's camp bed discussing government strategy for dealing with the Allies, and tried to imagine him with a briefcase and a bowler hat on a commuter-station platform. But then, she thought, it was the same for all servicemen, many of whom had seen far worse horrors and shown more sustained courage than they'd had to do. The return to ordinary life would not be straightforward for anyone.

Shona did one last twirl in front of the mirror. 'I suppose I'd better take this off now.' She shivered with delight and, hugging herself, turned to beam at her sister. 'I don't think I could be more happy. I'm going to be Mrs Tarnowska!'

Four hours later Freya finished the emergency admission of a ten-month-old baby suffering severe dehydration, thanks to acute diarrhoea. His distraught mother in her threadbare coat hadn't stopped apologizing.

'I do wash his bottles, Doctor, only after we was bombed out we had one sink and a privy among four families. I thought I done it properly. He will be all right, won't he, poor little thing?'

Freya had reassured the mother, explaining that they'd put him on a drip to replace his fluids and that she could come and see her baby at visiting time the following afternoon. The poor woman clearly hadn't wanted to leave and stood waving as a nurse carried the child away. She'd probably have a long, cold walk home as it was nearly midnight and the buses would have stopped running by now.

Freya wondered if she could sneak a cup of tea before returning to Casualty. Maybe one of the nurses would manage to bring her one. The mother's plight was another story to tell Patty. After winding up her mobile canteen, Patty was eager to build on her experience in the East End. Since her very first meeting with Phyllis, she'd been trying to persuade the two young medics to band together and use her wealth to put their ideas about preventive healthcare into immediate action. Although Phyllis was full of ideas, she'd have to complete her registration year before she could practise outside the framework of her hospital training. Freya rather thought Patty would have lost interest by then.

She came down the stairs from the children's ward into the main hall and was about to turn right into Outpatients when a familiar figure rose from one of the wooden benches against the wall. 'Leo! What on earth are you doing here at this time of night? You're not hurt, are you? Have you been in an accident?'

'No, no. But I need to speak to you.'

His face was as white as a sheet and he could hardly look at her.

'It's not Shona, is it? Oh, my God, please, tell me. Is she all right? Has something happened?'

'Shona's fine, Freya, I promise. It's not her.' He took a deep breath. 'It's Gosia. She's sent me a message.'

35

Kirsty, 1989

I can't help staring at the massive David Hockney over the wide mantelpiece. The painting's blue sky and palm trees seem even more exotic set against the log fire burning merrily below. Even with the curtains drawn, I can sense the Thames flowing past outside, its chilled winter darkness pressing against the tall windows of Patty's Chelsea Embankment apartment. When she phoned to announce her arrival in London she'd told me that, after the death of her butler, Leighton, she'd sold the Mayfair house I remembered from my childhood. She said she couldn't bear the place without him.

The recollection of Phyllis's sympathy for Patty's lonely childhood, how she'd pretty much been brought up by her grandparents' staff, makes me feel a little less disloyal for accepting her invitation to supper. She'd asked Martin and the boys, too, but that would have felt like taking a step too far into the enemy camp. I dread to imagine how Archie would react if he knew I was here. And yet the past has become such a foreign country that I'm no longer certain which, if any, of the old loyalties remain relevant. I'm hoping that's a kind of healthy liberation and that I won't regret coming tonight.

Patty literally reels backwards when her housekeeper shows me in. 'Oh, honey, you look so like your father,' she exclaims, holding out both hands to me. She's dressed in black slacks and a black roll-neck cashmere sweater, with her signature triple-strand of pearls and a perfectly toned coral lipstick. Her hair colour is just the same and, although she's a little bent with age, she looks as spry as ever.

'I can't believe you're all grown-up,' she says. 'Where have the years gone?'

She sees me looking past her to the Hockney and then to a ceiling-height Christmas tree that must have been profession-ally dressed, below which are piled immaculately wrapped and beribboned presents. Christmas is three days away, and my preparations are nowhere near as accomplished.

'I couldn't resist,' she says. 'You will take them, won't you?'

I don't know what to say, so make a joke instead. 'Can I take the Hockney, too?'

She laughs. 'I'll leave it to you in my will. Oh, Kirsty, it's so wonderful to see you again. After hearing your voice on the phone I simply had to jump on a plane. And Christmas in London – well! Do you think it will snow?'

'More rain, I think.'

'Never mind. Come and sit on the sofa beside me and tell me all about yourself. I hope you've brought photographs of your beauti-ful boys. Do they look like you? I want to know everything.'

I can't help laughing. She's exactly as I remember her and it's impossible not to be beguiled.

The housekeeper serves drinks, leaves a plate of homemade cheese straws on a table beside me, and I answer Patty's shower of questions about my life since I was ten. It's only when she takes me through to an intimate wood-panelled dining room where a table has been set for two that I imagine I might finally succeed in asking some of my own. But I'd forgotten what she's like.

She fusses over making sure I have everything I could conceivably want, insists on watching me cut my first bite of tender lamb to be sure it's not too pink, then puts down her own knife and fork before I can speak.

'I loved them, you know,' she says. '*Them*. Nick and Freya together. I've had three husbands, but they were the love of my life.'

I'm simultaneously appalled and curious. Who wouldn't be if someone offered to lift the lid on their parents' marriage? Especially when my own marriage is carrying me up and away, like a hot-air balloon. On Monday Martin sent the University of Sydney his formal acceptance of the chair they'd offered him. Once Chris agreed to go, I did too, yet I don't really have a clue why. I feel out of control, unable to judge whether to celebrate the decision or be afraid. So why not go for broke, and listen to revelations that may jolt and shock and can't later be un-heard? Let's fling open the doors even if I'm welcoming in the Furies.

'I introduced them, you know,' Patty goes on. 'I told Nick to marry her.'

I take another sip of her superb wine and prepare to hear her version of a story I've never actually been told in full. It strikes me that she's waited a long time to tell it to someone who cares as much as she does.

'What you told me about your mother going to Warsaw in nineteen forty-four,' she says, 'was like one of those safe-crackers opening a fail-safe lock. There was always a part of her that never made sense. And I'm good at making sense of people. But suddenly I heard the tumblers click into place and I understood something that's always bothered me – that was at the heart, really, of what happened later, between us.'

Please don't let her make excuses for what she did, I think. I can't sit here and drink her wine and hate her.

'Freya always withheld a part of herself,' Patty continues. 'I thought she wanted it that way. It's why I was sure that she and your father were right for each other. Neither of them was able ever to be wholly present for another person. Nick because – forgive me – he was ambitious and weak, and Freya, as I believed then, because she simply didn't want to give herself one hundred per cent. I assumed it was because she was a twin. And wasn't it fascinating that a face doctor, as Nick called himself, should choose an identical twin? As if it confirmed his belief there was nothing unique below the surface.'

'And you?' I prompt.

'After Shona died, a part of Freya became even more separate. She and Nick needed some glue to stick together. And goodness knows she needed his support. Losing Shona almost broke her.'

She stops and searches my face for something – understanding, sympathy, forgiveness?

'And you were the glue?' I ask.

'I believed she knew about Nick and me. I believed the arrangement suited her. It pre-existed their marriage, from before they even met. He and I were bits of jigsaw that fitted together but could never be the whole picture. It wasn't what we wanted. But if I'd thought for one single instant that she had no idea, that we were betraying her, I would never – never—'

'You're saying my father lied to you?'

To give her credit, she shakes her head in sorrow. 'No. He never actually told a lie. He didn't have to. Surgeons are good at that, aren't they? He insisted afterwards it had been as plain as day that he wouldn't have told Freya about us. Maybe it was, and I refused to see it. Either way, it was my fault. I assumed something about another woman's marriage that I had no right to assume. The night Nick's father died was the worst night of my life, too.'

'The mistress who is shocked to discover that her adulterous lover is a liar and a cheat?' The words come out of my mouth before I can stop them. I'm taken aback by my own bitterness, and by the clarity of an image I have always resisted, that of my mother's face twisted in pain as she hangs up the phone.

'Exactly that,' she says, with a grim little laugh. 'Though you shouldn't be too hard on your father, honey. He accepted his attractiveness to women as proof that he was a worthy human being.'

Patty's nailed it, I think. No wonder he didn't like it when his sulky teenage daughter failed to fall for his charm.

'So what happened that night?' I ask.

'It was poor Leighton who inadvertently gave us away. When Freya phoned, looking for Nick, and explained why it was so urgent, he became flustered and told her we were not to be disturbed. He didn't want to be the one to break it to Nick that his father was dying, might already be dead. It was just one unholy mess.'

'But you still went with him to Los Angeles.' I may never get another chance to find answers, so I go in for the kill. 'After he betrayed you, too.'

'I couldn't stay in London. Freya wouldn't have anything to do with me, not even with the clinic she cared so much about. I've always hoped that one day out of the blue she'd get in touch and . . .' Patty falls silent. Suddenly her face shows the wear and tear of every day of her seventy-nine years.

'I haven't told Freya you're here,' I say gently. It would be cruel to raise her expectations unfairly. 'Or even that we've been in touch.'

'No, I see that.' Patty picks up her cutlery and moves the baby vegetables around on her plate. 'I felt I owed him something,' she continues. 'I gave him what he wanted, an entrée into the old money in Hollywood so that he could set himself up as a cosmetic surgeon, and made sure he had all the things that carried weight out there, like a nice little Picasso for his consulting room and membership of the right country club. It was a world that could have been made for him.'

'But you didn't stay?'

'No. It didn't work. You see, I loved *them*. Without Freya, Nick was no longer enough. Without you and Archie, too.'

She holds out a hand across the table to me. The knuckles are too swollen for her to wear any rings but the nails are painted an immaculate red. After a moment's hesitation, I take it.

'You were my family, too,' she says.

Patty may be wilful and self-absorbed, driven only by her own needs, but that doesn't mean she lacks deep and genuine feelings. I can't pretend she didn't love us when we were kids, and probably still does, or that the reason I'm here is that, hearing she was in London, a childish part of my heart had leapt with long-forgotten joy.

She lets go of my hand. 'Eat,' she says, gesturing to my plate. 'Or has it gone cold? Shall I ask for a fresh serving?'

'No, really, it's fine.' The food could be a little more piping hot, but I don't want to interrupt the flow. Patty, as usual, won't touch a morsel.

'Anyway,' she ends her story, 'I left him to it and rushed off into a silly marriage that lasted all of five minutes.'

She sits back and watches me eat. 'You look so like him, but I think you're Freya's child. What's Archie like?'

'Pragmatic. A bit bossy.'

'Is he married? Children?'

'He married late. No kids yet. His wife's a doctor, too. They seem happy as they are.'

I brace myself for her to ask if she can see him, but she doesn't, and I'm grateful for her tact. 'Did you really come all this way just to see me?' I ask.

She looks surprised. 'Yes. And to help you find this Wedel, whoever he is.' She claps her hands. 'Columbus! I haven't told you the big news yet. My lawyer thinks he's located Leo Tarnowski. He's alive and living in Switzerland.'

'Oh.'

'I thought you'd be a little more pleased than that, honey. What's wrong?'

'Did you know anything about a General Medical Council hearing? Shona's psychiatrist wanted Freya struck off the medical register for interfering in Shona's treatment. It was just before Shona died.'

'Not a thing.'

'Phyllis never told you?'

'No. I'd never ask Phyllis to discuss your mother with me, not after the break.'

'There's still a secret at the back of all this that I'm afraid could hurt Freya in some way.'

'No,' Patty repeats firmly. 'Freya's already been hurt, by *keeping* her secrets. Secrets my intuition tells me she never wanted to keep. That's the part of her that never made sense until now. Perhaps if she hadn't always chosen silence as her way of dealing with problems, she and I could have worked things out years ago and still been friends.'

She must see the scepticism on my face for she shakes her head adamantly. 'Never mind what's in it for me,' she says. 'My intuition is never wrong. It's time to unlock the safe.'

I stare at the woman who, for most of my life, could not even be named in front of my mother and know that she is right.

36

Freya, 1945

'Gosia's alive?' Freya exclaimed. 'But that's wonderful news!'

'Yes, it is,' said Leo. 'She's been in prison and is being sent to a Soviet labour camp, but at least she's survived the devastation of Warsaw.'

'Then what's the matter?' Freya asked. 'You look terrible.'

'I need to talk to you.'

'I'm on night duty. I have patients waiting.'

'Yes, the porter told me. But please can we talk? It can't wait.'

'Is she under a death sentence or something? Is it because she worked with us? Does she need our help?'

'I'll explain everything. Will you get a break later? I don't mind how long I wait.'

Freya looked at her watch: just after midnight. 'Let me deal with the people already in Outpatients. Unless there's an emergency on the wards, I should be free for a bit. It usually quietens down around now.'

'I'll sit here. You'll come and find me?'

'Yes.'

Freya pushed through the door into Outpatients, anxious to know what on earth could be so urgent as to bring Leo here in the middle of the night and what news Gosia's message contained to upset him so badly. But she had patients to attend to: a young man with a deep gash on the underside of his forearm who gave such an evasive explanation of how it had happened that she suspected it had been while he was committing a break-in. It was a jagged cut and she had to concentrate on keeping an even tension in her stitches while the patient jiggled about nervously, glancing constantly towards the door. He could hardly wait for the nurse to dress it before hurrying off, throwing a brief 'Thanks, Doc,' over his shoulder.

Next up was a shy middle-aged woman with a suppurating varicose ulcer on her leg who kept apologizing for wasting Freya's time. 'After eight kids and on my feet all day,' the woman said, 'what do you expect?'

Freya handed a suspected appendicitis over to the surgical registrar and left the rest for the nurses to triage. She found Leo pacing the worn linoleum of the entrance hall. 'I need to stay near a phone,' she said. 'We can see if there's anyone up in the mess. If not, we can talk there.'

The mess was empty. Freya turned on the lights and decided it was too chilly to take off her white coat. Leo glanced around the room, then threw himself into one of the battered leather armchairs in front of the fire where a few embers still glowed. Freya added the last few lumps from the coal scuttle – they were strictly rationed – and sat down in the opposite chair.

'So what did Gosia say in her message?' she asked.

'She needs my help.' Leo was twisting his hands together and looking at the floor.

'What kind of help?'

'How much did she tell you in Warsaw?'

'About what?'

He licked his dry lips nervously. 'About us.'

'That you were old friends.' A claw of dread grasped at her. 'Why? What should she have told me?'

'We were a couple before the war,' he said, looking at her beseechingly. 'I thought she might have told you. If the Germans hadn't invaded, I suppose we'd have got engaged.'

'So you weren't married?'

'No, no.'

Some of Freya's fear dissipated, but she guessed he had more to reveal. 'Does she want you to marry her now, is that it? Would that help to free her?'

'No, it's not that. It was a complete shock to see her again in Warsaw, but when we spoke about the past she insisted we had no claim on one another.'

'I told her about you and Shona.'

'Yes. She wished me joy. She meant it, Freya. I'm sure she meant it.'

'Then what's the problem? What are you trying to tell me?'

The telephone rang. Freya's mind was back in the bank vault in Warsaw and the sound took a moment to register. She jumped up and went to answer it.

It was the night sister on the Chronic Ward asking if she could come and give a terminal cancer patient another dose of morphine.

'Stay here,' she told Leo. 'I shouldn't be long.'

The sister had everything prepared. Freya signed for the morphine, gave the injection and waited to see the woman's agitation
subside before leaving her in the compassionate hands of the
nursing staff. Walking back along the dimly lit corridors, she
listened to the soothing night noises of the hospital. She felt safe
here, at home, with a confidence in her skill and competence
that had been forged in the fire of her mission to Warsaw.

She recalled sitting on her mattress in the vault and watching
Leo and Gosia as they stood together at the bottom of the stairs
that led up to the banking hall. It was the day that Feliks had
been killed and Leo had drawn Gosia into what she'd been pleased
to see as a comforting hug, assuming that Feliks might have been
a friend of his, too. She didn't think there'd been undercurrents
she'd failed to notice at the time, but what had she missed?

She found Leo in the mess kneeling in front of the dying fire,
holding out his hands to catch the last of its heat. She closed the
door quietly behind her and leant against it.

'What was Gosia's message?'

He turned to look up at her, his face twisted with pain. 'She
has a son,' he said. 'My son. My Polish son.'

Freya felt as if he'd hit her in the face. 'You knew?' she
demanded. 'When we were in Warsaw, you knew and never said
a word?'

'No, Gosia never told me. She said she'd written but I must have
been in France by then and never got the letters. I swear I never
knew. Do you think I would have left without them if I had?'

She knew he was telling the truth: not even Bartek could
have talked him out of staying if he'd known. She went to sit in

the leather armchair. It was late and she was weary. 'You'd better tell me everything.'

Leo came to sit beside her. 'The message came through several hands, so it doesn't say much. But she can't have realized she was pregnant before I left in nineteen thirty-nine. She would have told me. I could have stayed. She could have come with me. We would have done things differently.'

'And if her letters *had* reached you?'

'I suppose I would have gone back and tried to get them both out.'

'You did love her?'

'Yes, of course, at the time.'

'And she knew that?'

'Yes. I don't understand why she didn't tell me about the child when we saw each other again. She had no right not to. He's my son.'

Freya began to have a glimmer of understanding. 'It's my fault.'

'You mean she told you?' Leo's eyes blazed with anger. 'And you said nothing to me?'

'She never breathed a word. I never gave her a chance.'

Leo looked bewildered. 'So why is it your fault?'

'I told her you were in love with my sister.'

'But why would that stop her? Any feelings Gosia had for me belonged to a time and place that no longer existed. There was nothing between us any more. We were no more than friends. It was Feliks she was upset about. You were there, you saw.'

Leo was pleading with her to agree. The flame probably had died for him, but had that been so for Gosia? Had Gosia remained silent only because Freya had told her about Shona? If she could have gone back in time and rubbed out her words, she would have done so in a flash. 'How old is the boy?' she asked.

'He's five.'

Far from protecting Shona, Freya realized she had made everything worse for her. 'What are you going to do?' she asked.

'Gosia is afraid that she may not survive the conditions in the labour camp. If anything happens, she wants me to claim the boy.'

'Where is he now?'

'He's been living with her brother, outside Warsaw. She wants me to get him out of Poland.'

'They'll shoot you on sight!'

'He's my son. I should have talked to Gosia when I had the chance. I should have found out how she really was, what had happened to her after I left. I was too bound up in myself.'

'It's my fault she kept quiet,' said Freya. 'I said I only accepted the mission because Shona was so deeply in love with you. That's what stopped her speaking. She sacrificed herself because of the sacrifice she believed I'd made in coming to save Bartek. She didn't have to. She'd already saved my life, but she did it for us.'

Leo leant forward, his head in his hands. 'If that's true, then she's an extraordinary woman. She joined the AK, even though it meant leaving her baby behind, and fought to the end against the Nazis in Warsaw. I thought I was the great patriot, but I'm nothing compared to her.'

'They may release her,' said Freya. 'She may yet live a long and happy life.'

'I pray she does.' Leo stared into the dying fire for a few moments. 'What do I do, Freya? I have Shona to consider. Do I try to get to Poland? You have to help me.'

'You can't ask me to decide!'

'You know Shona better than anyone. I never understood why she pined for you so much – never her parents, only you – until I discovered that you were twins. Then it all made sense. She'll trust you. What should I do?'

Freya knew what her own answer would be; surely Shona, identical in so many ways, would also find it in herself to live up to Gosia's sacrifice. If any harm came to Leo, Shona would suffer terribly, but Freya would be there to offer all the comfort and support she could. To do nothing in response to Gosia's plea was unthinkable.

'You were willing to parachute into Poland last year,' she said. 'Why not again? Gosia has asked for your help. You have at least to try to do as she asks.'

She was thankful to see the relief in Leo's face, confirmation that she'd said what he wanted to hear, but as he turned away, she also glimpsed an element of foreboding that made her doubt her own words.

Freya found her sister curled up on her bed, facing the wall of the dingy top-floor room in Chelsea where she lodged.

'Shona.' Freya sat on the edge of the single bed and gently tugged her shoulder.

'Go away.'

'I bought some teacakes from that bakery on the corner. Sit up and then I can make us a nice cup of tea.'

Shona shook her head and burrowed further down into the thin eiderdown.

Freya rocked her sister's shoulder gently. 'Come on now. What would you have him do? Abandon the child? Ignore Gosia's plea for help?'

'He lied to me!'

'He didn't know until two days ago. I was there in Warsaw with them both. I saw them together. She didn't tell him. I promise he hasn't lied to you.'

'Then why did he never tell me about her? He's never said a word. Not one. Not even her name. And after you'd met her, he still didn't tell me they'd been together. Why not? What is he hiding?'

'Have you told him about every boyfriend you ever had?'

Shona began to sob in a way that suggested she'd been crying for hours. Freya decided to try a different tack. 'Daddy and Mum will be getting on the sleeper train in a few hours. You don't want them to see you like this.'

'You have to ring them. Tell them the wedding's off.'

'Why?' Freya was taken aback. 'This doesn't stop you getting married. In fact, there's all the more reason to get on with it.'

'No,' she wailed.

'Shona, he loves you. You love him. He can't wait to marry you.'

'I can never marry him now. It's ruined. He's ruined it.'

'Don't be silly. Sit up and dry your eyes and listen to me.'

Shona remained lying where she was but she stopped crying and Freya could tell that she was listening.

'Look, you can't judge people for what happened in the war. They were young, it was the first week of the German invasion, and then Leo went off to fight. They weren't even formally engaged.'

'So he says,' Shona said sarcastically.

'They're good people, and you have to do the right thing here.'

'You marry him, then. He might not even notice the difference.'

'Now you're being childish,' said Freya, beginning to be annoyed. 'There's something you ought to know. I never told you, but Gosia saved my life. We were in a courtyard and a sniper shot dead one of her friends right in front of us. A beautiful young man called Feliks. They might have been lovers once, I don't know. I would have been killed, too, but she saved me. So, you see, you owe her something, too.'

Shona turned her head and stared at her sister with an expression Freya couldn't entirely read. 'Why didn't you tell me that before? Why keep it a secret?'

'I suppose I didn't want to burden you with having been the one who sent me into danger.'

'So you lied, too? You're all in it together.'

'You have to stop this,' Freya said sharply. 'You're being ridiculous.'

Shona pulled herself up, her back against the faded wallpaper and drew her knees to her chin. 'I bet she told *you* about her and Leo.'

'I understand how upset you are, but no one has lied to you. Gosia didn't tell me anything, and neither did Leo. He didn't have a clue that she'd been pregnant or had his child until he received her message the other day. I'm certain the only reason she didn't tell either of us when she had the chance was because she didn't want to come between you and Leo. You ought to be grateful to her.'

'What makes you so keen to stick up for her?'

'It's not a matter of me sticking up for any of you. You and Leo belong together and this is just something that's happened and you have to get over it. You and Leo and Gosia and their son, you're all simply yet more casualties of war.'

'So I'm to be smashed up, like I was when I was bombed out, and then again the second time? Left out in the cold with nowhere to go.'

Her voice rose, and Freya heard a note of hysteria creeping in. Observing her sister more closely, she didn't like what she saw.

'I'm going to make a cup of tea,' she said. 'I think you're in shock.'

She filled a pan with water from the washstand and set it on the gas ring on the floor beside the fire. When the gas failed to light, she scrabbled in her purse for a shilling for the meter while Shona watched her every movement from the bed. Freya had never seen her sister look at her like that before. The fact that Shona's face was a version of her own made it easier to register the change: it was an absence, she realized, an absence of reason, and it filled her with fear.

Her hands trembled as she looked on the shelf for some sugar. Perhaps a cup of hot sweet tea would be enough to do the trick. When had Shona last had any food? The teacakes were fresh and soft enough to be eaten without butter. She probably hadn't slept much, either.

She made the tea and let it brew while she found plates and cut up the teacakes. The milk on the windowsill was on the turn but would have to do. She took the tea and currant bun to Shona on the bed.

'Here. This'll do you good.'

Shona eyed the offering warily but accepted the cup. Freya put the plate down on the bed beside her and withdrew to a chair, wondering what she could say to pull Shona out of this worrying state of mind.

'I've always been on your side, haven't I?' she asked. 'Nothing's changed. Eat some of your teacake.' She waited for Shona to nibble at the spiced bun. 'Leo may not even have to go to Poland,' she went on. 'He's looking into all the diplomatic avenues that may be open to him. He still has contacts that may be useful.'

'If he goes, he'll be killed,' Shona said flatly. 'If he loved me, he wouldn't go.'

'It's his son. Gosia's afraid she might die in the labour camp. The boy's only little.'

'I don't care. He's got his uncle. I'll be left with nothing. Is that what you want?'

'Of course not. What's got into you, Shona? Don't you trust me?'

'The war's over,' Shona said, ignoring the question. 'We've finally made it through to some peace, and he wants to go back and get killed. How can he love me if he thinks like that?'

'Do you want to know why Gosia stayed silent when she saw Leo again in Warsaw?' Freya asked. 'It was for my sake, because she wanted him to be free to come home to you. Can't you be as generous towards her?'

'You'll say anything, won't you? You think I can't see through your lies?'

Shona's eyes had a harsh glitter that bordered on a strange kind of glee, and she shot her sister a look of such deep suspicion that Freya was seriously alarmed.

Although Shona held the lion's share of other gifts – intelligence, wit and flair – she'd always suffered an emotional frailty that sometimes made her weak and selfish. Freya had resisted acknowledging it as a permanent part of her twin's character, preferring to believe that, deep down, they shared a similar stability. But what if that frailty was rooted in something darker? What if the defining difference between them was something that could carry Shona far away from her?

'Please, dear Shona,' she cajoled. 'Eat some of your teacake.' It was the only medicine she had to offer.

The following morning Freya met her parents off the train at King's Cross. She did her best to greet them cheerfully despite having sat up all night with Shona who refused to see Leo and had, wild-eyed, talked incessantly, accusing everyone of conspiring against her.

In the taxi to Chelsea Freya explained to her parents that Shona was unwell and wanted to cancel the wedding. When they entered her room and went to hug her she recoiled as if she didn't know them. They did all they could to comfort, persuade and reassure her but she insisted it was now impossible for her ever to marry Leo.

Three days later, pale and grave-faced, Shona's parents took her home with them to Aberdeen. Freya watched their train steam out of the station and thought that she had never felt more completely alone. If this was what it was like to be a singleton, she thought, she wanted no part of it.

37

Kirsty, 1989

I watch Chris regale my sister-in-law Jo with all he knows about Freya's wartime exploits. He allows Eric to chip in from time to time with his own imaginative enhancements. Freya sits between her grandsons alternately laughing and shaking her head, oblivious of the green paper crown she wears, taken from the Christmas cracker she pulled at lunch.

Archie and Jo came down last night and will go home tomorrow. Mum's been more and more drowsy since the mini-seizure that led to her last hospital stay, so we'd agreed that, not to overtire her, they'd make an early lunch for the three of them and we'd come over afterwards for tea and mince pies.

I'm loving how everyone is listening, marvelling, wishing they knew more, with Freya alert enough to be where she belongs, at the centre of it all. Even my brother is enjoying himself and can see that Freya is happy that her secrets are being shared. I'm not sure, though, that Archie will be ready to hear that Patty gave me dinner the other night.

He catches my eye and leans towards me, nodding towards

the kitchen. 'I might make a start on the washing-up,' he says.

'I'll come and help.'

There's not too much to do. Jo's no great cook and much of their Christmas lunch had come from M&S. Not that Freya has much appetite these days, too often overcome by the increasing nausea that's a symptom of her tumour. As Archie runs the tap and rolls up his sleeves, I wonder how many times we must have stood here as teenagers, squabbling about whose turn it was to dry and put away. Has he forgotten that he hates being the one to wash, or was that never what our arguments were about?

I take a tea-towel off the rail and stand beside him. 'Mum's having fun,' I say.

'Yes. I'm glad we've got this time with her.'

We both know this will be her last Christmas, which is why I'm reluctant to drop another bombshell, but I don't know when I'll see Archie again and I can't keep putting it off.

'Next year will be different in all sorts of ways,' I say, as lightly as I can. 'Did Martin tell you? He's been offered a full chair, back home in Sydney.'

'That's great,' he says. 'Congratulations. How long will you go for?'

'Well, I think the idea is to stay.'

'Permanently?'

'Yes. He wants to be closer to his family. And it's a new professorship, a great accolade.'

'Wow.' He turns to look at me. 'Gosh. I mean, that's wonderful, of course it is, especially for Martin. I know he gets homesick occasionally. But I'm going to miss you.' He moves to hug me, then laughs when he notices his soapy hands. Drying them on a tea-towel, he draws me to him. 'I really will miss you, Kirsty. And I'm sorry if I've been irritable lately. I just get a bit over-protective about Mum, you know?'

'I know.'

Archie lets me go and returns to the job in hand. 'How do you feel about going? Is it what you want?'

'It took me a while to decide,' I say, accepting a wet serving plate from him. 'That's why I didn't tell you before, because I wasn't sure. But now I think it'll be good for us as a family. An adventure, while the boys are still young enough to share it.'

'Good for you!'

'You will come and visit, won't you?'

'You bet! When do you go?'

'Not until after – Martin may have to go on ahead. We'll see what happens.'

'Sure.'

We fall silent, mulling over what we don't want to put into words. I think of what he said about Martin being homesick. How come I never noticed that? And why am I surprised when my kid brother shows more insight than me? Perhaps I should have more faith in him.

What will I do if Patty gives me contact details for Leo Tarnowski? Do I want any kind of contact with the man who caused such misery? And, if so, do I tell Archie?

I look at the dish I'm wiping dry. I remember it from when we first moved to this house after the divorce. It's not even chipped. It's a solid little fact, a piece of our lives, yet neither of us will bother to keep it once Mum goes. Even after everything I've found out about my mother, I'm still standing here doing the same old familiar things. Nothing's really changed. Forty-five years on, can speaking to Leo Tarnowski be any more use in making sense of the past than a teak desk or a serving plate? Does it matter what secrets I learn or what objects I keep hold of?

Three days ago Chancellor Helmut Kohl walked through the Brandenburg Gate in Berlin and shook hands with the East German premier, Hans Modrow. In Romania the Communist dictator Nicolae Ceauşescu has been overthrown. Momentous events, yet, in forty-five years' time, will these men's names still be remembered? It's impossible to tell at the moment they happen which bits of history will come to matter most.

I wish I understood why delving into our shared past feels so much less important to Archie. We had the same childhood yet are very different. Did we just choose to remember or forget different things, tell ourselves separate stories? Even my brother ultimately remains mysterious to me, so how will discovering a few more fragments about my mother's life enable me to feel closer to her?

Archie hands me another dish. 'Thanks,' he says. 'There's room now to leave the rest to dry on the rack. I can put it away later.'

I return to the living room. Someone has switched on the television, allowing Freya to rest while we watch a Christmas special of *Only Fools and Horses*. She's already nodded off, and, asleep, looks so frail that I'm hit with the full force of what's coming. She's going to die soon, and I'm not ready. I can't bear it if all I have left of the mother I never got to know is a copy of a wartime photograph, a codename and a decorative tin box.

38

Freya, 1947

Freya's limbs were so stiff from cold that she could barely climb down from the train once it finally reached Aberdeen after a journey endlessly delayed by snow and flooding. Her father was on the platform to meet her. He looked gaunt and grey and had clearly lost even more weight since she'd last seen him a couple of months before. He insisted on carrying her case, making her glad she'd packed lightly.

'We'll take the tram home,' he said. 'I save the petrol coupons for visiting Shona.'

Freya welcomed the warmth of the crowded carriage, which meant they didn't speak much as the tram wound its route through the wintry city.

Her mother was looking out of the parlour window for them as they walked around the corner, twisting a tea-towel in her hands. Home was one of a row of almost identical low granite houses fronted by small snow-covered gardens. The path had been cleared and the doorstep swept, and as Freya stepped inside, she was met by the delicious smell of her mother's drop scones.

'Come away in and have some tea,' her mother said, as if scolding her for being cold and tired. 'With coal so scarce, we keep in the kitchen where it's warm.'

Freya hung her coat on the familiar peg in the hall, feeling Shona's absence from the house almost too keenly to bear. On her last visit she had been unable to sleep the first night, haunted by the empty bed beside her. Following her father into the scullery kitchen at the back of the house, she saw that the table had been laid with one of her grandmother's lace cloths and a newly opened pot of homemade rhubarb and ginger jam awaited her arrival. The guilt that Freya had now carried for so many months that it was beginning to feel like a natural part of her kicked up a gear: why was she able to have this when Shona, locked away by herself in an asylum for over a year, could not?

'Thank you for coming all this way when you must be so busy with your work, dear.'

Her mother's formality was jarring, as if, no longer a twinnie, she'd become a stranger.

'I'm sorry the train was so delayed,' she replied. 'I hope you weren't waiting all that time at the station, Dad?'

The way her father waved aside her concern meant that he must have been standing around for ages. Her heart went out to them. She *was* busy in London, but the concentration of her work allowed her whole hours of the day in which she could forget about Shona. Although her father was still teaching, her parents had no such luxury.

Once tea had been consumed and cleared away, and they'd caught up on news, including Nick's latest home leave, her mother said she'd let them talk in peace and left the room.

'Thank you for coming, Freya.' Her father repeated her mother's words. 'I'd be glad of your advice. I've made an appointment for you to see Dr Reid, the medical superintendent, in the morning. You'll be able to tell me what we should do.'

'I'll be able to see Shona, too?'

'Yes, if she wants to see you.'

'She was all right about it last time.'

'I don't know what to think. Sometimes she seems better, but then ... Two weeks ago a group of patients were taken for a walk in the grounds and she managed to give them the slip and ran away. They tracked her footsteps easily enough, but when they caught her she fought them every step. They said she was like a wild animal, biting and kicking and screaming all the way back. They had to put her in a padded cell for the night.'

Freya felt a wave of horror and claustrophobia as if it had been her left behind a locked door. 'Where was she trying to go?' she asked. 'Home here to you?'

'If she had turned up here, we'd have had to take her back to the hospital. We don't know how to manage her any more.' He sighed heavily. 'No, she says she has to get to Poland. It's still all this nonsense about secrets she can't talk about because they'd put her in prison, and about Stalin wanting to kill Leo. Dr Reid says this kind of paranoia is a classic symptom of schizophrenia.'

'We don't know what work Shona was doing in London, Daddy,' Freya said gently. 'What she says might be true. She may have had to sign something that said she could be imprisoned if she talked about it. Lots of people in uniform did.'

She longed to tell him everything, but she, too, had signed

the Official Secrets Act in Major P's office and she had no way of knowing how seriously they might view a breach. She daren't risk doing more than hint at the truth and hope her father would read between the lines.

'She'd have told you,' he said simply, cutting her to the heart.

'She wouldn't have been allowed to.'

He smiled sadly, shaking his head. 'I know you two. Thick as thieves.'

'Have you heard anything from Leo?'

'Not since he replied to my letter, agreeing not to contact her again.'

She nodded, her hopes dashed. Leo had come himself to tell her that he would respect their father's wishes. He was applying for jobs abroad and wanted to say goodbye. He'd also told her that he'd managed to exchange messages with Gosia's brother who'd promised that her son was safe with them, and had begged him to leave them alone. Leo was an enemy of the new Polish regime and any further contact would put them all in danger. Freya had wished him luck in finding work, clinging to the increasingly forlorn belief that somehow all would end well. That had been months ago and she'd heard nothing since.

'So what is it that you want me to discuss with the medical superintendent?' she asked her father.

'Dr Reid was very concerned by this latest incident. He sees Shona as still being dangerously suicidal, just like when she first had to go away.'

'That was a year ago.'

'A year in which she's not responded well enough to any of the treatments they've tried so far.'

'Running away isn't necessarily an intention of suicide.'

'In this snow? She showed no care for herself at all.'

'So what does Dr Reid suggest?'

'That she have a surgical procedure called a pre-frontal leuco-tomy. Have you heard of it?'

'Yes.' Freya was horrified. 'The Americans developed it. They call it a lobotomy. Not everyone thinks they're beneficial.'

'He says it would calm her down, lessen her anxiety, stop her acting so impulsively.'

'Yes, by destroying some of the tissue in her frontal lobes!'

'He explained that it's not unlike the effects of the electric shock treatment she's been having. I know she hates the idea of the ECT beforehand but she's always calmer afterwards.'

'He told you that the surgery is irreversible?'

He nods. 'That's why I wanted your advice before I sign the consent form.'

'We can't do that to her, Daddy. There are new drugs being developed all the time. The psychiatrists who are treating men with battle fatigue and the prisoners-of-war from terrible places like the Burma Railway are gaining new insight into all kinds of mental conditions. There must be other ways to help her.'

'Dr Reid says that, if she has this surgery, we might be able to bring her home.'

'But it wouldn't be her.'

'I can't bear to see my little girl in that place.'

'Of course not. Nor can I. But please, Daddy, give her more time.'

He put a hand to his brow, covering his eyes. 'I'd die for her, if it would help. So would your mother.'

'I know. And I'm sure she knows, too. I'm so sorry I haven't been here to help.'

'Don't blame yourself, dear. It was us who told you to stay away. In the beginning seeing you only made her more agitated. She still refuses to see any of her old friends. I only wish I understood why she can't get over what happened and be her old self again. Can you explain?'

'I think it was harder for her in London than she let on.'

'If only she'd told us more, about being bombed out and everything.'

'I still don't understand why she didn't. Maybe it was just the attitude they took in London.'

'And you know her better than any of us.'

'I thought so too,' said Freya. 'But I don't. I only look like her.'

They brought Shona to her in the day room. The other residents of the female villa in which Shona was housed were either confined to their rooms or out at one of the therapeutic industrial workshops on the site. Shona's face lit up when she saw her sister although, as usual, they did not embrace.

'Have you come to take me away from here?' she asked hopefully.

'I came to see how you are.'

'I'm better. They won't believe me, but I am. How are you? How's everyone in London? Have you seen anything of Adam or Jozef? Do they have any word of Leo?'

'Do you want word of Leo?'

'Yes, yes. I'm better now. I can see how ridiculously I behaved. I want to tell him how sorry I am. He'll understand, won't he?'

Freya looked at Shona's eager face: was this a sign of return-ing rationality or merely a new form of mania? 'I haven't spoken to Leo in a long while.'

Shona's face fell. 'Oh, yes, of course. Daddy wrote to him, didn't he? I'd forgotten.'

'It was what you said you wanted,' Freya said gently. 'Daddy thought it was for the best, too.'

'I was out of my mind.'

'And now?'

Shona raised both hands and touched her temples with the tips of her fingers. It seemed an unconscious gesture, but it was the spot where, Freya realized, the electrodes would be placed for electro-convulsive therapy.

'They give me pills to take. They won't let me read any books. They expect me to be happy assembling silly little toys all day, but it drives me mad, and when I complain they take me over to the Medical Section and shock me. It's so frightening, Freya, you can't imagine. Afterwards I can't hold on to my thoughts any more. I can't live like this for much longer. I have to go and find Leo.'

'I don't know where he is.'

Shona stared at her, anger growing in her eyes. 'How could you? How could you let go of him?'

Months of anxiety, compounded by the fear of what her father had told her yesterday about the threat of a leucotomy, made Freya react with anger of her own. 'It wasn't me who let him go!'

She immediately regretted her words. They were mean and cruel, even though a small part of her wanted Shona to recog-nize the suffering she had caused to everyone around her. So life was not perfect – Leo had discovered he had responsibilities elsewhere – but why couldn't Shona have coped with the news and taken hold of herself before she reached the point of spiralling down into insanity?

'I'm sorry,' she said, going to put her arms around her sister. 'I'm so sorry. That wasn't fair.'

To her surprise, Shona laughed and hugged her back. 'That's the first normal thing anyone's said to me in months! Thank you. I'm so tired of being treated like a delinquent toddler.'

Freya stepped back and studied her sister more closely. She was drawn and pale, her hair lank and unwashed, and with shadows under her eyes as if she hadn't slept properly in weeks, but the sly, suspicious creature who'd looked at her sideways with a crazy smile of secret triumph had given up possession.

'You're going to get better,' Freya told her.

'If you help me,' Shona agreed. 'I have to find Leo. I can't be at peace until I put things right.'

'I think he left London a while ago.'

'Did he go to Poland? Is he safe?'

'I'm pretty sure he's not in Poland. But I have no idea where he is. I'm sorry.'

'Have you seen any of his friends? Can they tell you?'

'Everyone's scattered. London's a quite different place these days.'

'But you'll try?'

'You need to concentrate on getting well, on getting out of hospital. You must take one thing at a time.'

'No, no. Only one thing matters. I have no life apart from him.'

'Shona, if you talk like that, they'll think you're still insane.'

'I don't care. It's the truth.'

'You *have* to care.' Freya weighed up how much to tell Shona of her father's discussion with the doctor in charge of her care. 'You ran away two weeks ago.'

'Yes.'

The way Shona stared at her as if puzzled by her reaction made Freya anxious that the new obsession with rejoining Leo was indeed a symptom of a manic illness.

'Dr Reid thinks you may need a different sort of treatment,' she said. 'Has he talked to you about it?'

'I told him I don't want any more treatments.'

'Then what was your plan?' Freya asked. 'After all, we're in the middle of the harshest winter of the century so far. Where did you intend to go? Did you have any money with you?'

'I'd have managed.'

'You could have frozen to death.'

'I don't want to die. That wasn't in my mind. I just want to see Leo again.'

'Then you need a proper plan.'

'I thought you'd know where he is,' Shona admitted. 'But it can't be that difficult to find out where he's gone. His friends will tell me. You're right. If I just take it one step at a time, I can get through this.'

She sounded rational enough; given her present circumstances perhaps, to her, she had taken the only opportunity open to her. She certainly wasn't raving mad or suicidal enough to justify neurosurgery.

She saw that Freya was studying her and reached for her hand.

'Please, Freya. The last thing I need is another doctor. I need you.'

Freya wrapped her coat more tightly around her as she left Shona's villa to walk across the grounds to the hospital administration block where her father was waiting. Surrounded by flat farmland, the snow was deep here, the sky murky and the same grey as the granite buildings around her. In keeping with the rest of the turn-of-the-century complex, the two-storey symmetrical administration building had been designed to look like a country house, with shrubs in front of the tall windows and a clock over the entrance. She hoped that her father's exaggerated respect for Shona's psychiatrist was influenced by how deeply he felt the stigma of his family being afflicted by mental illness, and that the man in charge of the asylum would turn out to be humane and sympathetic.

She found her father sitting in the inner hall. He moved along the polished wooden bench and drew her down beside him.

'How did you find her?'

'Much better than expected. A big improvement on the last time I was here.'

She was glad to see that he took comfort from her words: she might have to persuade him she was right in the face of opposition.

They were called into the medical superintendent's office almost immediately. As Dr Reid came from behind his desk to greet them, she was surprised that he was much younger than she'd imagined. She'd been dreading an inflexible senior consultant who'd qualified before the Great War, but he was barely forty, if that.

'Miss Grant,' he said, holding out his hand with a friendly smile. 'The identical twin!'

'Dr Grant,' she corrected him, certain that her father must have told him her profession.

'Ah, then perhaps you're aware of some of the studies made of identical twins. Such an interesting deformity of birth. You know there's a higher incidence of schizophrenia in identical twins?'

'Yes,' she said, trying not to let her hackles rise. 'Except I don't believe my sister is schizophrenic.'

'Please do sit yourselves down,' he said, indicating two comfortable chairs beside his desk. 'I'm afraid that Shona is not at all well and remains at significant risk of harming herself. Your father has informed you of my recommendation for the next stage of her treatment?'

'Yes, and I am firmly opposed to taking any step that is irreversible.'

'You may be medically qualified, Dr Grant, but in my view it's impossible for a family member to remain objective, especially in such an emotional case.'

'I know my sister. I agree that she's not yet entirely well, but she wants to be, and I believe that, with the peace and quiet of a domestic setting, she can make a full recovery.'

'Would you have her live with you?' Dr Reid sounded amused.

Freya raised her chin. 'Yes, if that's what she wants.' The ramifications of her offer struck her with force: she would have to stop work for a while, and find somewhere for them to live, but it would be worth it. Nick still had several months of his national service left to run so, whatever their future together, the immediate present need not concern him.

'And when she becomes agitated and distressed, or runs away in the middle of the night, or insists that the Soviet secret police want to prevent her marriage?'

'She's not as delusional as you believe.'

'Miss Grant, please try to see that I wish to offer Shona hope for the future. There is no cure for schizophrenia but, after surgery, most patients see a significant improvement in their condition.'

'That's if schizophrenia is the correct diagnosis,' said Freya, as politely as possible, deciding not to bother correcting him on her title a second time. 'Has she been hearing voices?'

'No.'

'Experiencing hallucinations?'

Her father cleared his throat and reached out as if to rein her in.

'No, but she has been paranoid, delusional and on occasion violent.' Dr Reid spoke with genuine concern. 'As well as being a danger to herself.'

'Have you considered that there could be other explanations for each of those separate behaviours?'

'I sympathize with how hard such a decision must be, but you have to put your own feelings to one side and consider the degree to which Shona is actively suffering, and will go on suffering if we don't step in to help her.'

He's not going to listen, she realized. *He thinks he's being kind.* 'Have you asked Shona what she wants?'

'I'd see that rather as abdicating my responsibility as her physician. I'm recommending the best available treatment for your sister's future wellbeing. It's a very safe operation and it may well enable her to resume a fully independent life.'

'But you can't operate without my father's consent, is that correct?'

'That is correct. But your father and I had a long chat the other day. I think you understand the options that remain open to your daughter, don't you, Mr Grant?'

Her father nodded. 'We'll away home and talk it over,' he said. 'I'll let you know in a day or so what's best to do.'

'Of course.'

Dr Reid stood up to show them to the door. He shook Mr Grant's hand first and let him leave the room before keeping hold of Freya's hand long enough to detain her without her father overhearing.

'Don't let him doubt his decision,' he said quietly. 'He and your mother have had a terrible time of it. They need to find some peace, too.'

He smiled consolingly and shut the door behind her.

39

Patty rings me on Boxing Day. 'Have you got a pen, honey? Write this down.'

She reads out an address in a suburb of Zürich and a telephone number. 'That's where Leo Tarnowski lives,' she says.

'Did you speak to him?' I'm scared that Patty has set something in motion that could hurtle out of control.

'No, honey, that's up to you. And I'm going back to New York tomorrow. It was just dandy seeing you again, but I have an important committee meeting coming up, and I don't want you folks thinking I'm barging in on your lives.'

I'm surprised to feel a pang of disappointment, especially as I recognize how her Southern drawl becomes even more exaggerated when she's emotional. 'Don't go because of us,' I exclaim.

'I can always come back another time,' she says, her voice softening. 'And listen, if you want to go to Zürich, my people will help with any travel arrangements. Just ask, OK? And, if Leo remembers, say hi from me.'

'I will.'

'You take good care of your mother, now.'

'I promise. Thank you, Patty, for all your help.'

'Well, goodbye, then.'

'Goodbye.'

I'm about to hang up when I hear her voice again. 'Oh, and, Kirsty, I haven't forgotten about you getting the Hockney.'

The line goes dead. I consider calling her back, but I'm both appalled that she took my awkward joke seriously and overwhelmed by her generosity. Besides, what can you say to a fairy godmother?

I wait until New Year's Day before calling Leo Tarnowski. The unreality of the suspended days between Christmas and New Year somehow makes what I'm about to do appear less outrageous. Besides, it seems appropriate to start the New Year by opening another door and, I hope, blowing out some cobwebs.

The day after Archie and Jo had gone home I'd driven over to spend a day with Freya. I'd noticed she had the silver E. Wedel chocolate tin on the little table beside her chair. She barely tries to speak at all now, and sleeps for much of the day, but when I'd walked back into the room from the kitchen, she'd been stroking it.

'Do you still want me to find Wedel, Mum?' I'd asked.

She'd nodded vigorously, her gaze latched onto mine. I didn't want to risk upsetting her by mentioning Patty and had decided not to say anything about Leo until I'd actually made contact, but I'd reassured her that I was doing all I could to find him.

Martin has offered to take the boys for a walk on Hampstead

Heath this morning, giving me plenty of time to compose my thoughts and make the call. I'm in two minds about wanting to hear Leo's side of the story. Does he even know what happened to Shona after he supposedly all but jilted her at the altar? What do I do if he tries to make excuses? In spite of my dread as I punch the numbers, he's the only person left who might shed light on whatever it is that Freya wants so much.

A woman answers, perhaps Leo's wife, and says something in German.

'I'm sorry, I don't speak German,' I say. 'I'm looking for Leo Tarnowski.'

'Who shall I say is calling?'

'He doesn't know me. My name is Kirsty Hamlyn.'

'Please wait.'

My stomach churns as she transfers the call to another handset.

'Hello, Leo Tarnowski speaking.'

I'm struck by the colossal impertinence and insensitivity of what I'm doing. All my pre-prepared speeches fly out of my head. 'I'm Freya's daughter,' I blurt out. 'Freya Grant.'

There is a horrible silence. I can hear him breathing. What if the shock gives him a heart attack or something?

'How is she?' he asks.

There's no delicate way of telling him. 'She's not well. She has a brain tumour. She can't really speak,' I say in a rush. 'I'm so sorry to ambush you like this, but she has something on her mind that bothers her. Does the word Wedel mean anything to you? Other than being a chocolate manufacturer, I mean.'

He laughs. 'Yes, it was a wartime codename.'

I hold my breath. The Rosebud moment has come. 'Do you know who it was?'

He laughs once more. 'Yes. Me.'

I'm gobsmacked. 'Did you go to Warsaw with her?'

'You know about that?'

'Yes. Well, only that she went. I've seen a photograph of her there taken in nineteen forty-four. But I don't know why she was there.'

'I don't see why you shouldn't be told,' he says. 'The leader of the Uprising had been wounded. An infection had set in and he was dying. She volunteered to go so she could treat him with penicillin. It wasn't just handing out some tablets like it is today. She had to inject him, set up a drip, measure the correct dose, all under Nazi bombardment. She was incredibly brave. He recovered and she never even knew who he was, probably still doesn't, but she did perform a great service for Poland.'

'She never told anyone about it. Not a word.'

'Shona knew.'

The way he speaks her name makes me terrified he's going to tell me something I don't want to hear, that Freya had something to do with Leo abandoning her sister, that Shona went mad because of their betrayal.

But surely, I tell myself in desperation, Freya wouldn't ask me to find him if that was what had happened.

'And now history has come full circle,' he went on. 'The Soviet Union is breaking up. The borders are open. The forces that destroyed our lives – mine and Shona's among so many – are powerless.'

'Is that why you left her?' I ask. I've come this far, there's no point dodging the issue now.

I hear him catch his breath and there's a long pause before he answers.

'Who told you that?'

There's no anger in his voice, but I sense yet another story that I've not been told – or have got wrong.

'Not Freya,' I say. 'She's never mentioned you, not once in all my life. I've been trying to find out about the past.'

'Does Freya know you're doing this?'

'She wanted me to find Wedel. I didn't know it would be you.' I'm flooded with shame that I have barged into this man's life with a tale based on little more than tittle-tattle. 'She has a tin,' I say. 'An E. Wedel chocolate tin. She keeps trying to say "Wedel", and when I ask if she wants me to find Wedel, she's very definite that she does.'

'I gave her that tin,' he says. 'What about the photograph you mentioned, of her in Warsaw, did she give you that, too?'

'No. Someone turned up out of the blue with it. People at the Polish Hearth Club helped him to track Freya down. It's a long story. But the photograph is of Freya with his mother.'

'Not Gosia?' There is an element of shock in his voice.

'Yes. Did you know her? I suppose you must have done if you were in Warsaw with Freya. Do you know anything about—'

He cuts me short. 'I can't tell you any more,' he says abruptly. 'Not without Freya present. She has to hear it. She has to be willing for me to tell you.'

'She can't travel,' I say, rather flustered by this sudden turn.

'Then I will come to her. Where does she live?'

'London. Dulwich.'

'Give me your telephone number and I will make arrangements.'

I tell him and he reads it back to me.

'I'll be in touch,' he says, and hangs up.

I'm left holding the receiver, listening to the drone of a disconnected line. I don't know what to think, or what I've unleashed. All I can do is reassure myself that I have done what Freya wanted and have found Wedel. Yet I'm left with far bigger questions than when I started.

40

Freya, 1947

Freya's father emerged from his study that evening after an hour of silent contemplation and quietly informed her and her mother that he'd come to a decision and had made an appointment for the following day to sign the consent form for Shona's surgery. Freya set about making her preparations carefully. She knew her idea was ludicrous but the alternative had become too desperate to contemplate.

In the car returning from the hospital she hadn't been able to sway her father's faith in Dr Reid. She'd explained what Shona might be like after a leucotomy, how a reduction in her short-term memory could make day-to-day life a challenge and how she'd be left unable ever to feel anything very deeply again. How could she still be Shona without her sensitivity and her passion for life?

'It was an abundance of feeling that led to where she is now,' he'd replied sorrowfully.

'What if you knew for certain that Shona *had* been involved in secret war work?' she'd asked, desperately imagining that she could somehow get hold of Major P and beg him to speak to her father. 'If I could prove that she's not paranoid, would that change your mind?'

But he had shaken his head and looked so ill with grief and the burden of responsibility that she'd respected the medical superintendent's words and stopped pleading, promising to support whatever decision he made.

That night she searched every cupboard and drawer in the bedroom she'd always shared with Shona and made a pile of any item that might be useful. Her most important find was Shona's passport, issued for a school trip to Paris just before the war. Only those taking highers in modern languages had been able to go, and at the time Freya had been bitterly envious. Now she was relieved that it would enable Shona to avoid any delay or red tape if she discovered that Leo had gone abroad.

In the morning Freya took the tram into town, went to the bank and took out nearly all the money in her account, then caught a bus to the village nearest the hospital. Now she was back in the empty day room with Shona, outlining her plan.

'We'll play the trick,' she explained. 'You'll walk out of here and I'll be you for as long as I can get away with it. Only until tomorrow, probably, when Daddy's coming to see Dr Reid. Daddy will know immediately that it's me. But by then with any luck you can be on a train and far away.'

'Yes, yes!'

Wary of how Shona's eyes lit up with feverish excitement, Freya prayed she'd chosen the right course.

'You know the way to the village?' Freya asked. 'Wait there for the bus into town. It'll drop you near the station. Anyone who noticed me coming here will assume it's the same woman going home. You'll find plenty of money in my handbag.'

'Don't worry. I'll manage.'

'I've stuffed all my pockets with toiletries and a change of underwear. I've managed to tuck a clean shirt and a nightdress into my handbag. I know my shoes pinch you a bit but you'll have to manage. I've worn the warmest clothes I could find. If you pin your hair up the way I've done mine, put on some lipstick and pull my hat well down, no one will ever suspect it's not me. I cut a few inches off my hair last night, so we match when it comes to playing my part.'

Freya didn't want to add that she'd rubbed some oil into her hair to make it lank and dirty-looking and also bitten down her fingernails, or that, once they changed clothes, she would rub some mascara under her eyes to give herself dark shadows.

'Oh, I've missed you!' Shona said. 'I never admitted it, but I thought I'd die when I had to leave Aberdeen and go for basic training, then discovered I'd been posted to London, so far away. I need your strength, Freya. I always have.'

'Are you sure you want to do this?' she asked anxiously.

'Yes, whatever happens, yes. I'm losing my soul in here. I can't survive much longer.'

'I'll get back to London as soon as I can,' said Freya. 'You go straight to the infirmary and ask for my friend Phyllis. I sent her a letter this morning. It was too complicated to explain every-thing, so I just told her to expect you. Dr Phyllis Levenson, do you remember meeting her?'

'I think so. So much is hazy. I don't even know how long I've been here or when I arrived or why they brought me. Are Daddy and Mum all right? Have I made them very unhappy?'

'They love you, and want you to be well. That's all that matters. You can't help that you've been ill. Now tell me exactly what you'd do for the rest of the day once your visitor has gone.'

Although answering all of Freya's detailed questions calmed Shona's agitation, her excitement also ebbed away. 'What about you?' she asked finally. 'What if they don't believe you, that you're not me, I mean? What if they keep you here?'

'Don't worry, they won't. They can't. Daddy will sort it out.'

As Shona sat silent, her hands idle in her lap, Freya crossed her fingers, praying that her parents would understand why she'd had to do this.

'Am I chasing a dream?' Shona asked. 'Will I ever be able to find Leo?'

'We can try.'

Shona continued to stare at the floor.

'You can't stay here, Shona.'

'What if Dr Reid is right? He thinks I'm incurable.'

'No,' said Freya, pushing aside her own doubts about her sister's resilience. 'Listen to me. Once you've put on my clothes, you'll feel different. You'll have my strength. All you have to do is be me. You can easily do that.'

'Can I?' Shona looked up with hope in her eyes.

'Yes. You know, I'd have died rather than tell you, but I always loved playing the trick because I got to be you for a little while – to possess your verve, your spirit.'

'Really? I always thought I was a lightweight compared to you, just a social butterfly.'

'Never. You and I together make up one whole person. Take what you need from that.'

'I'll try not to let you down.'

'You won't. Come on, it's time we swapped clothes. Will anyone come in?'

'They might look through the door. Come over here where we can't be seen.'

They stripped right down, exchanging even their underwear. Shona's hand was shaking too much to apply Freya's lipstick so her sister did it for her.

'You'll be fine,' Freya assured her. 'Keep your chin up, Junior Commander Grant, and walk out as if you're back on the parade ground. How do I look?'

'I can't tell. I haven't seen myself properly in ages.'

'Are you ready? Shall we call for a nurse to say you're leaving?'

Shona nodded. 'You're saving my life. Thank you.'

'See you in London!'

The nurse came and, cutting short their goodbyes, escorted Shona to the front door unlocking and locking it again behind her. With efficient authority she immediately shepherded Freya towards the stairs, offering her no opportunity to watch her twin sister walk away.

That night Freya lay awake in her sister's narrow hospital bed hoping that Shona was tucked into the corner of a railway carriage on her way to London. A patient on the other side of the dormitory snored lightly and another mumbled as she rolled over in her sleep. The more distant noises seemed familiar to Freya from her room in the infirmary, except perhaps that the

reasons for the occasional running footsteps, screaming, shout-
ing and banging doors were very different. Her single pillow
was too thin for comfort. As she tried to pull it into shape, she
was hit by the full force of the despair that Shona must have felt
lying here night after night. It suddenly seemed incredible to
Freya how she had managed to continue a normal life while her
sister endured such a hopeless existence.

In the morning Freya followed the women with whom she
had breakfasted across the grounds to the protected work unit
where her ignorance of what she was supposed to do was treated
kindly as if it were evidence of a deteriorating mental state.
After lunch she was given permission to stay behind in the villa
so she could see her father.

He arrived soon after two o'clock, his shoulders hunched and
his face grey with the agony of the paper he had just signed in
Dr Reid's office. He could barely raise his eyes to meet hers but
when he did his expression cleared and his eyes lit up with hope.

'But—'

'Yes, it's me, Daddy. Freya.' She hadn't expected to be so overwhelmed with relief that she *would* be able to leave.

'But where's . . .' He looked around almost fearfully. 'Where is
she?'

'I took her place so she could go to London. I told her to go
straight to my friend Phyllis. She'll be all right now, Daddy, I'm
sure of it.'

'But what about you?'

'Just tell them I'm not Shona. She's had enough time now to
get away.'

The medical superintendent was called. He shook with rage

when he discovered what Freya had done. He couldn't prevent her leaving with her father but said that, as a doctor, she should be ashamed of herself, and promised that he wouldn't rest until he had had her struck off.

Her father was quiet in the car going home. When she tried to explain, he said simply that she knew her sister best.

Her mother, anxiously awaiting her husband's return, was confused when she saw that he wasn't alone. Taking in Shona's clothes and lank hair, it wasn't until Freya spoke that she realized which daughter she was looking at.

Freya's euphoria lasted until she managed to place a trunk call to Phyllis at the infirmary and learnt that Shona had not arrived and had not tried to get in touch.

Freya returned to London the next day on the first available train. She immediately set about contacting anyone to whom Shona might have gone, but no one had heard from her in months. For a week she waited, jumping every time the phone rang or the ward doors opened. Then the call came from her father, telling her that he had been to identify her sister's body, recovered from a river near the hospital, and that she should come home for the funeral.

You knew her best. Her father's words magnified her guilt. Had Shona got lost or perhaps imagined she was taking a shortcut? Had she feared being pursued and taken back? Or had the river always been her intended destination? If she had lost hope, if she was afraid of never finding Leo, or feared she'd be unable to cope even if she did, how had Freya failed to see it? Had she been capable of such cunning? Freya would never know, only that her sister had taken her fate into her own hands.

41

Kirsty, 1990

At the end of the first week in January the arrivals hall at Heathrow airport is busy with bronzed and jet-lagged tourists returning from long-haul holidays in the sun. The weather in London has been mild but I expect they'll feel the cold when they hit the outside air. Leo told me he'd arrive early and fly back the same day, explaining that he was used to shuttling between European cities after working for the Swiss office of an American multi-national since the 1950s. He said there was no need for me to meet him, but I insisted, wanting the time alone that the drive from Heathrow to Dulwich would give us.

I wait nervously as I watch the last stragglers from a Caribbean flight mingle with the first businessmen of the day, and play a guessing game to see if I can recognize him before he notices the sign I'm holding, made for me by Eric.

I worked out that he must be in his seventies at least, and bring to mind how various people described what he'd been like in the 1940s: working for Polish Intelligence, an intellectual, romantically patriotic, and a hot-head. I ask myself for the hundredth time what bond exists between him and my mother to draw him to London today and pray that this meeting is what she wants.

'Kirsty?'

I've failed to spot the slight, upright figure with silver hair and faded but striking blue eyes.

'You must take after your father,' he says, with a warm smile, taking my hand in both of his. 'You don't have their colouring at all.'

He means the twins, and I wonder, somewhat belatedly, what memories my phone call must have revived for him.

'My brother does,' I say awkwardly. 'Thank you for coming. This all feels a bit strange.'

'Yes, it does, but necessary. I've always hoped that one day I might see Freya again. To hear that she was asking for me means a great deal.'

Asking for Wedel, I think, the name on a tin. When Leo phoned to give me his flight times, I did my best to explain the effects of Mum's tumour. She still has short periods of clarity when she's her old self, but I hope Archie isn't proved right, and it *is* Leo she's been asking for. What happens if I'm wrong?

'I haven't told her you're coming,' I tell him. 'It's not good for her to become agitated so, rather than give her too long to antici-pate your arrival, I thought it best just to announce that you're here and bring you straight in.'

'I'm sure you know best.'

We head for the car park, relieved that the surge of anxious people heading into the airport makes conversation difficult. Ignorant of the part he's played in my mother's life, even simple questions, like 'How long is it since you last saw Freya?' feel too loaded to ask. Once we're in the car and I've navigated away from the maze of airport approach roads, it's easier and we exchange information about our present lives.

He tells me that he retired some years ago as head of public affairs for an American pharmaceutical company, after postings in several European cities. He married late and acquired two grown-up stepdaughters, both married with children. His wife is French and a journalist.

Leo is especially interested in my future move to Australia. 'I sympathize with your husband,' he says. 'One's country is a strange part of one's DNA, but it's there, like it or not, sometimes far more deeply embedded than you expect.'

He asks me again about the photograph of Freya and Gosia and how this journey into the past began, so I tell him how Tomasz turned up on Freya's doorstep one evening, looking for someone who might have known his father. I sense him becoming rock still beside me.

'You knew Gosia?' I prompt.

'Yes. Is she still alive?'

'No, she died a long time ago in a Soviet labour camp.'

'Ah,' he says, with a sigh. 'The last news I had of her was when Stalin died and the Polish political prisoners were being released. I thought she'd made it home.'

'That's so sad, after she'd endured so much.'

'She was the most courageous woman I ever knew. Did you know she saved your mother from a sniper's bullet in Warsaw?'

'No! I know nothing about Freya's time there.'

'It was only for a week or so. We flew from Brindisi and dropped by parachute. The AK took care of us. I had political business for the Government-in-Exile in London, and she had her patient to look after.'

'How did you get back?'

'Getting out of the city was the hardest part,' he says, after a pause. 'Then we waited in the countryside for an RAF Dakota to land and pick us up.'

'It's like a movie!'

'Looking back, it was utter madness,' he says. '*Boy's Own Annual* stuff, as you British say. But that's what it was like in those days.'

'I can't believe Mum's kept it to herself all these years. I wish I'd known.'

'A great deal happened in the war that no one ever speaks of.'

I change the subject slightly, well aware that I'm fishing. 'Did you know that Gosia had a son?'

'Yes, I did.'

He turns to stare out of the nearside window as my mind races, trying to fill in the blanks. I'm dying to bombard him with questions.

'What is he like?' he asks finally.

I can't help smiling when I think of Tomasz. 'A lovely man. I like him very much. He's a stonemason. His son works with him.'

'Tomasz has a son!'

My spine starts to tingle. Leo's delight at this piece of information strengthens the suspicion that's been growing since I first mentioned Gosia's name. I glance at him and think of Tomasz's blue eyes. I know I must respect Leo's wish to explain everything when Freya is present, but I curse every red light that prolongs our journey.

I ask Leo to wait in Freya's porch while I let myself in and call out to her. I'm pleased to find her awake, and she greets me with a smile. I try to hide my excitement as I make sure she's comfortable and ask if she needs anything before informing her that she has a visitor. She looks at me quizzically. I pick up the chocolate tin from the table beside her and place it in her hands. She looks from it to me, her eyes widening.

'I've brought Wedel to see you.'

Her mouth opens in shock and she grabs my hand, patting and shaking it repeatedly as she's always done when she's really happy about something.

'Let me go and fetch him. He's just outside.'

When I return, ushering Leo before me, Freya is struggling to rise from her chair. He walks straight up to her, holding her elbow to guide her gently back down and then, taking her free hand, he raises it to his lips. As he kisses it, he clicks his heels together. She laughs and almost playfully waves him away. She points at a place on the sofa opposite. Fascinated by their greeting, I sit to one side, close enough if required to interpret Mum's gestures, but trying not to intrude.

'You'll have to begin,' I tell him. 'She can barely speak.'

'Where do I start? It's been nearly forty-five years!'

'You and Shona,' I say. 'Tell me the story.'

He looks at my mother. 'I loved Shona.'

She nods.

He looks back at me. 'Before the war, in Poland, Gosia and I worked together and we had a relationship. When Hitler invaded, I left with the Polish forces for France. I didn't see or hear from her again until Freya and I went on our mission to Warsaw.' He stops and turns to Freya as if seeking her permission to continue.

She bows her head and, with the flat of her hand, softly beats her chest, an age-old sign of sorrow, regret or repentance.

'After I'd left in nineteen thirty-nine, Gosia discovered she was pregnant with our child.'

'Tomasz.'

Leo smiled with new-found joy. 'Tomasz,' he agreed. 'Apparently she wrote to me but her letters never got through. Even when she saw me again in nineteen forty-four, she chose not to tell me.'

'Why?' I ask.

He looks at my mother again before he answers. 'Freya had done a wonderful thing for our country by risking her life and coming to Warsaw,' he says. 'She told Gosia that she came because of Shona, that we were in love, and that Shona had asked her to do it for my sake. Freya said she believed that was the reason Gosia remained silent.'

'And where was Tomasz?'

'Safe in the countryside with his uncle. When the Uprising failed, Gosia managed to escape through the sewers but later she was picked up and imprisoned by the NKVD. She must already have been weak and malnourished, and they tortured her. Afraid for her life, she got a message through to London to tell me I had a son, asking me to do what I could for him. That was four days before Shona and I were to be married.

'I told Shona that, as soon as we were married, I'd have to try to find my son. She couldn't handle it. I've never understood why she reacted so badly, as if I'd betrayed her in some terrible way. I had no desire to postpone our wedding, quite the opposite, but she called it off and refused to speak to me ever again.'

Freya nods. She looks unbearably sad, but appears composed, making me hope that this meeting is offering some kind of resolution.

Leo addresses her directly. 'You told me that she had a complete emotional breakdown after your parents took her back to Aberdeen,' he says. 'Your father wrote to me, asking me to stay away, not to contact her again. I believed I had to respect his wishes.'

Freya holds out a hand to him. He leans forward far enough to clasp it for a few moments, before sitting back.

'And you never found Tomasz?' I ask.

'No. I tried to make arrangements to go to Poland, and through third parties managed to get a message to Gosia's brother, who was looking after him, that I intended to come. He begged me not to. Any contact with the West was dangerous. I was one of the Cichociemni and if the authorities caught me, his whole family, including Tomasz, would suffer. Gosia, too. He promised to bring the boy up as his own. Everyone I spoke to insisted that he was right and that I must heed his words.'

I wonder if this was why Gosia and her brother had been forced to keep Leo's identity so secret, to protect the family.

'Gosia was sent to a Soviet gulag. When Stalin died, I thought it was safe to try again, but her family had been told she was about to be released. I didn't want to jeopardize her safe return.

I had no idea she died before making it home to her son. She deserved better.'

He turns to me. 'You say Tomasz turned up here to find me. Did I let him down? Does he hate me for abandoning him?'

'No, I don't think he sees it like that at all,' I say. 'In fact, he's remarkably wise and level-headed. I have his telephone number so you can call him later.'

Leo leans back his head and takes a deep, slow breath. He's waited forty-five years for this. I look at Freya and see that she is smiling again.

'But please tell me about Shona,' he asks me. 'Friends told me long ago that she died but they didn't know when or how.'

After speaking to Leo I had decided I was justified in a further invasion of Freya's privacy, and had done a little research in the archives of the General Medical Council. There wasn't much on the hearing into Dr Freya Grant's fitness to practise, but enough to piece together what Freya had done to save her sister.

'Mum, I think I can answer this, but I need to know that's OK with you?'

She looks surprised, but nods assent.

'Shona had been hospitalized,' I say. 'She had tried to run away several times and her psychiatrist wanted to perform a lobotomy. Her father had reluctantly agreed to give his consent.'

'I had no idea she was so ill,' Leo says.

'Freya went to visit her,' I continue, 'and waited until the following day to reveal that they'd swapped places.'

'The twin trick?' Leo exclaims. 'You played that on me the

first time we met. I never told Shona, but it was some time before I could be certain of telling you apart. But if Shona escaped, what happened to her? Where did she go?'

Freya jabs her finger in his direction.

'To me?' he asks. 'She wanted to find me?'

She nods vehemently.

'I wish I'd torn up your father's letter,' he says bitterly. 'I wish I'd stayed. If only I'd been sure she still wanted me . . .'

Mum starts to weep, and I move to kneel at her feet, trying awkwardly to hug her. She pulls at my shoulders, trying to hide in my embrace. I hold her tight, making soothing noises. She and I know how Shona's story ends but Leo is still waiting to be told.

As Mum recovers, she gives me a little push and nods towards him.

'No one knows what happened,' I tell him. 'It was that terrible winter of nineteen forty-seven. Maybe she got lost leaving the hospital, maybe it was an accident, but she fell into a river and drowned.'

Freya points at herself and tries to speak but I can't interpret the sound. She beats her chest again.

'Mum, it wasn't your fault,' I plead. 'You saved her from a lobotomy. She'd tried to get away before. She wanted to be with Leo. That's what was making her ill.'

'Of course it's not your fault,' he tells her. 'How could it be? I'm to blame for not taking the time to speak openly with Gosia in Warsaw when I had the chance. I was a coward. Perhaps if I had, she'd have told me about Tomasz earlier and everything would have been different.'

But Freya shakes her head and jabs at her chest.

'No, Mum, no. You're not responsible for her death. No more than the war or history or an unplanned pregnancy or a psychiatrist who believed that lobotomy was a valuable method of treatment. It was a tragic accident, that's all.'

'Shona always wanted life on her own terms,' Leo tells her quietly. 'I miss her. I will always miss her. But the thought of her having that kind of surgery, it would have been worse than death to her. She'd never have submitted. You have to forgive yourself for what happened.'

The look she gives him is beseeching. I am pierced by my comprehension that *this* is my mother's secret. I feel the full weight of sorrow and waste at how the guilt she has carried for so many years has walled her off from those who try to love her.

'Shona loved you,' Leo reminds her. 'She'd tell you there's nothing to forgive.'

I see the relief dawning in Mum's eyes. Patty was right: it *was* time to unlock the vault.

'Besides,' he says lightly, changing the mood, 'if you want to blame anyone, you must blame my son. The very same person we have to thank for bringing us back together again.'

CODA

Freya, 1990

I sleep most of the time. It's hard to hold on to my thoughts. But I remember that the Berlin Wall is down, and that people are free to come and go. Who could have foreseen that such a cruel regime could collapse like a house of cards?

Leo has spoken to his son. Kirsty tells me that Tomasz will go to stay with his father in Zürich. Gosia would be happy.

Leo says that talking to me was like laying down a heavy burden. I feel the same. I don't know that I can ever forgive myself for Shona's death. My mother never did. It's why, I think, I have always feared tenderness. I don't deserve it. It made me push my children away. But Kirsty says it's easier to love me now that she understands the past.

I wish we'd been warned, when we were young, that secrets and guilt can destroy a life as effectively as wartime bullets and bombs.

I'm tired. I have no words left. If I could speak, what would I say? A whole lifetime of things unsaid.

AUTHOR'S NOTE

Sisterhood was inspired by what I *don't* know about the wartime lives of my mother and her non-identical twin sister.

They were born a century ago. In 1944 my mother left Scotland to work in the East End as a newly qualified doctor. Her sister, with a degree in modern languages, had joined the ATS and already spent a couple of years in London. There she met Jozef, a Polish exile.

After the war, almost on the eve of their wedding, Jozef made some kind of confession, possibly that he had been married in Poland before the war but had since been unable to trace his wife. Whatever the story, my aunt suffered a breakdown. She was hospitalized and later underwent a lobotomy.

I am now the only family member who remembers her. I got to know her well, and loved and admired her wit and spirit, her sarcasm and lack of self-pity.

But I know nothing about what she did while in uniform, how she met Jozef, what happened to him, not even his surname, and my attempts to trace him thirty years ago got nowhere. I wonder how different all our lives would have been if events had not separated him from my aunt.

I created the entirely fictitious characters of Freya and Shona in honour of all that we can never know of the past, and of a life only half lived.

ACKNOWLEDGEMENTS

I began a version of this novel thirty years ago, when I gathered together stories from many people, some of them no longer with us. I owe thanks to all of them for their time and generosity.

My account of the early use of penicillin is based on my late father's experience as a junior doctor at the London Hospital in 1944. I have borrowed several of the extraordinary stories I encouraged him to tell, but all errors are my own.

My understanding of both the SOE and the Warsaw Uprising has been drawn from many conversations and published histories and memoirs. I must particularly thank Elżbieta Moczarska for sharing the story of her courageous parents, Kazimierz Moczarski and Zofia Płoska, both members of the Polish Home Army, as well as Aga Lesiewicz for introducing us, for patiently answering all my questions relating to life in Poland, and for companionable walks on Hampstead Heath. However, all my characters are invented and, again, all errors are my own.

I must also thank the earliest version of this novel for introducing me to Elizabeth Buchan, once my editor and now a very dear friend, and the most supportive fellow author I know.

It was Lizy who introduced me to my present editor, Jane Wood, and I couldn't ask for better. Heartfelt thanks are due to

Jane and her lovely team at Quercus, especially Florence Hare and Ella Patel.

And, as always, very special thanks to my wonderful agent Sheila Crowley at Curtis Brown and her kind and indefatigable assistant Emily Harris.

I finished writing this book during the first pandemic lockdown of 2020, and couldn't have done it without my 'bubble'. You know who you are, my darlings.